THROUGH A

Bakery Window

Romance, mystery, and death in a small New England town

CATHERINE ZEBROWSKI

Catherine Zebrowski

Relax. Read. Repeat.

THROUGH A BAKERY WINDOW
By Catherine Zebrowski
Published by TouchPoint Press
Brookland, AR 72417
www.touchpointpress.com

Copyright © 2021 Catherine Zebrowski
All rights reserved.

ISBN-13: 978-1-952816-78-9

Editor: Kimberly Coghlan
Cover Design: ColbieMyles.com
Cover Image: Watercolor illustration of a small French bakery under a striped marquee, with tables in front of it by Мария Тарасова (Adobe Stock)

First Edition

Printed in the United States of America.

Loosely based on a true story that occurred in a small town outside of Worcester, Massachusetts, I would l like to dedicate the novel to the historians, reporters, storytellers families, and possibly ghosts that have kept this story alive in one form or another for over one hundred years.

Prologue

New Year's Eve, 1898

I

THERE WILL BE A WEDDING in this town soon, and I am one of the few who knows why it must not take place. Before, I thought that if I knew the truth, I could begin to forgive—or at least it would ease my mind. I was wrong. I found answers from an old woman, but she, as it turns out, only knew part of the story, and for a while, I thought I could have peace, until I found myself privy to more information. How I rue that day. Now, I cannot stop. The hysteria grows within while I try to feign calm, and in a year, as the world glides into another century, amid the merry and reckless celebrations, some of us will remain in the shadows, desperate for vengeance, determined to push the past into the future.

II

ALL WAS QUIET FOR WHAT SEEMED like a very long time. Suzanne, who had been wondering why a few empty teacups had been set on the table, lurched forward as one of the cups near her shook slightly. She turned her head and looked toward the door. Mrs. Kaminski made moaning sounds, very softly. Then, in a kind of stuttering voice, she called out a name.

"Mary . . . Mary . . . my baby . . . my baby . . . I feel you near . . . I feel your breath in this room . . . A hand that has touched yours . . ."

Rosanna looked around the table. "Does anyone have a question for the spirit?"

The medium went on moaning and whispering. Her eyes remained closed.

"Mary would like you to know that she is all right. She suffered much when she was on this Earth, but that has now passed. She looks down on all the workers and women and all those who are oppressed and hopes that her death was not in vain."

Then Madame Kaminski collapsed on the table.

Part I
Stonebridge, Massachusetts
Spring 1898

Chapter 1

EVERY MORNING, EXCEPT SUNDAY, Edith Temple left early to open her dress shop at 27 Main Street. She wanted to have time to sit at the bakery for a while and go over the news of the town with Agnes Cunningham. It had started about two years ago when Agnes had lost her husband to a lung disease. Having no children to help, everyone had thought Mrs. Cunningham would sell the business and move away from town after her husband died suddenly, but her resiliency had surprised them all. She walked to the bakery every morning before the sun was up and started baking the breads and sweets that filled the stomachs and warmed the hearts of so many in town.

At first, Mrs. Temple had meant to comfort her and just be a friend by checking in every morning. Now it was a habit, a morning routine she would miss on the few occasions when either of them became sick.

"Yoo-hoo," she called out, opening the door on a brisk spring morning. Her friend was in the back gathering supplies for the day. She came out with a package of napkins, which Mrs. Temple helped her to distribute to all the tables. Though small, it was a very well-run establishment. Maybe not as classy as some of the establishments in nearby Worcester, but it had an ambiance of friendship and warmth that was missing in the large bakeries and sandwich shops opening in the city.

It was a warm place to gather, and since the maids of the two richest families in town were often here either to pick up orders for the families or to have sandwiches on their time off, Mrs. Cunningham was always a bearer of the latest news. She never spread around the crass gossip that she might hear from the workers on their way home from the mills. Like her establishment, Mrs. Cunningham had more class than that, and that's why Mrs. Temple looked forward to their brief morning chit-chats—and Mrs. Cunningham knew all secrets were safe with Mrs. Temple.

When they were finished with the napkins, Mrs. Cunningham came around with coffee from the counter, and the two women sat down at a small table by the window.

"Olive was in here yesterday."

"Oh," Mrs. Temple said.

Mrs. Cunningham sat silently for a few minutes letting her friend wait. She took a sip of coffee. "She had news."

"Oh?" Mrs. Temple said again. "With Old Sawyer, most of the news is bad."

"This concerns Michael, not the old man. She says Lily and Michael went out walking."

Mrs. Temple raised an eyebrow.

"She says the two are a couple and that she heard Michael invite Lily over to the house on Saturday."

"Doesn't he usually work with his father on Saturday morning?"

"He must have asked for the day off. I can't imagine the old man is too happy about that."

• • •

LILY WAS NERVOUS AS MICHAEL led her into the parlor. The dour aspect of this house made her uncomfortable, and though Michael had said it would be fine, she'd expected his mother to be with them in the parlor as a chaperone. She giggled and put her hand over her mouth, which only made it worse. She laughed out loud then snorted.

"Ssshhh." Michael looked at Lily and then up towards the ceiling. "My mother's not feeling well. She's resting upstairs."

Lily flushed and turned toward the window to hide her face. Had her high spirits caused a breach in formality or were they actually sneaking around?

"Don't be shushing her." Olive, the kitchen maid, had come in unnoticed with a tray of muffins and tea. "It's good to hear a cheerful laugh. Lord knows, it can be like living in a coffin around here."

"She thinks I'm about six-years-old," Michael whispered to Lily. "She'd tie my shoes in the morning if I let her."

"If you were six-years-old, I wouldn't be serving you in the parlor with a pretty young miss."

"You're hardly older than I am," Michael said. "And don't think you'll always get the last word."

"I have fifteen or more years on you, young man. There, now I've got the last word, so I'll leave you two alone. I guess that's how they do things now-a-days. Call if you need anything more." Olive left with her hands in her apron pockets and walked through the hall pantry toward the kitchen.

"I really like her," Lily said, smoothing her skirts as she sat on the couch. "I used to think she was formal and stuffy when I came here as a girl." One of the braids around her head was coming loose, and she tried to tuck the stray pieces back as she sat down. Do you think she approves of us being here alone together?"

Michael sat down next to her. "With my father, she is formal; he insists on it. When my father isn't around, even my mother is familiar with her, treats her like one of the family, maybe the daughter she never had. I'm sure she doesn't mind you being here. She's very discrete—more than can be said about the new maid." Michael brushed a curl from Lily's cheek and put his arm around her. She rested her head against his shoulder.

"I'm afraid your father doesn't care for me."

"Don't worry about him. It's just his way; please don't take offence. Anyway, he stays late at the mill on Saturday, often till after sundown. We should have peace here for at least—" He took his pocket watch out and looked at it. "An hour, maybe two, before he barges in."

A few minutes of silence passed between them. He looked at her, kissed her on the forehead, then rested his head on hers. Lily looked in the corner away from Michael. She was not comfortable here, though she wanted so much to be with him.

"What is it?" Michael asked.

"My feet are just really pinched in these narrow walking boots. I wish women were allowed to wear comfortable shoes."

"Are you for the women's rights then?"

"We should have rights—at least to dress as comfortably as men." She sat forward, pouted, crossed her arms, and looked at him with narrowed eyes.

"Are we bickering?" Michael asked

"Just our first lover's quarrel," she said.

He lifted her chin and looked into her face. "It's not a quarrel if I agree with you. Women and workers should have rights."

She pushed away, leaned down, and unlaced her shoes. "You better not let your father hear you say that."

"My father and I don't see eye-to-eye on several things. He doesn't want anything to change. He's afraid of it."

"Afraid of what?"

"Afraid of everything, change."

"How do you mean? Your father seems to have no fear. Everyone is afraid of him."

"Well, he doesn't approve of the trolleys coming through town. He still thinks a covered carriage is the only proper conveyance for people—and even for goods. Business is going to suffer if he doesn't keep up with the times. The other day, Mother wanted to take the trolley into Worcester with her sister just as an adventure, and he wouldn't hear of it. Probably afraid she'd go to a women's meeting behind his back. He won't even let her go to the women's club that helps the needy, afraid he'll lose workers, I suppose, if the masses become too educated. A few years ago, there was a display of electricity at Mechanics Hall, and he wouldn't take me. I had to go with a friend's family."

"My mother wants me to go to those meetings," Lily said. "She says women need more power, need to be educated about finance and politics, but I don't know . . ."

"Really, Lily, you should. There are so many interesting things to do in the city."

She smiled. "Maybe we can take a trolley ride in together."

He hugged her shoulders and kissed her on the cheek. They sat back again in a more comfortable silence.

Lily's day had not started well. Her mother was not happy about her plans to go walking with Michael. First, she'd said Lily was too young for Michael; then she'd been given a lecture on independence. She wanted Lily to be just like her sister Abigail who was going to college. Abigail would have all the opportunities. Abigail wouldn't become too dependent on a man. 'Don't trust men' was all her mother seemed to be saying. Sometimes she thought her mother didn't even trust her father. She noticed that more lately, how couples acted with each other. Of course, her mother and her father had been married for over twenty years, but shouldn't that make them even more intimate together? Maybe love was different with old people. She sighed and leaned forward.

"Penny for your thoughts," he said.

She shrugged, upset at herself for acting so melancholy when she should be enjoying this time with him.

"Want some tea?" He poured her a cup before she answered. She took a sip.

"Thank you. I'm a little tired, I guess, from all the walking. It is harder for women you know."

"I can imagine." He looked down at her longs skirt and pointy boots. "You can take your boots off. Here, I'll help you"

"Don't be fresh," she said. "You won't get a look at my bare ankle." She met his look and laughed.

He took the tea, placed it on the table and kissed her on the lips. The afternoon ticked away as they held each other in silence, so comfortable that they fell asleep and did not hear the carriage pull up into the front yard.

•   •   •

JOHN SAWYER CURSED AS HE jumped down from the carriage and threw down the whip. "These whips could be better used on people than horses," he muttered, stroking the horse as he took off the bridle. "There, girl, good girl." He walked her to the stable, still muttering. His large hands patted the horse once more as the stable boy took the reins. "A dumb horse has more loyalty than a worker. Don't I take care of my workers?" he demanded.

"Yes, Sir," the stable boy said. "Very well, sir. We want for nothing."

"Yeah, well, tell the workers that. They want to sign contracts—let them go up to Lowell, see how they like it there."

The stable boy looked down as he took the reins and lead the horse inside. The new maid, Daisy, looked around from behind the barn as Sawyer turned and walked toward the house, shaking off his suitcoat as he entered.

"Michael, you here?" he shouted up the stairs.

The gruff voice startled Lily and Michael out of their sleep. They looked at each other but, before they could say a word, Sawyer had opened the parlor door and was staring at them.

Michael quickly rose. "Father this is Lily Chapman."

Lily sat with her face down.

"I know who she is. What's she doing here?"

"She's my guest, Father"

"Your guest?" he bellowed "Your guest—that's a good one." He laughed loudly and pounded his fist on the side of the door. "Do her parents know she's here alone with you in the parlor? You sit around doing who knows what while I trudge through my day. Do you care what people think?" He pounded the door again. "Get her a carriage home; then come to my study."

He slammed the door to his study, sat, picked up his pipe, and threw it against the wall. Now even the thought of that small pleasure seemed to have soured in his mouth. "Damn those young people, reckless and foolish . . . know nothing and think they know everything—dammit." He pounded his fist on the desk. "Dammit, I thought all this nonsense was behind me."

• • •

MICHAEL AND LILY HELD hands tightly as they stood together at the door. Lily was trying not to cry; the day was ending worse than it had begun. She looked up at Michael. "We'll never be able to see each other again. Your father hates me."

"He doesn't hate you, Lily; he just gets upset for nothing sometimes. Everything will calm down before you know it, and we'll be able to see each other." He spoke with more confidence than he felt; then he touched her hair lightly and kissed her on the forehead. The sun had just set, and her ride came around. Michael helped her into the carriage. "See that bright star coming up over the horizon? Wish on that," he said, "and we'll be together soon."

Lily smiled and waved goodbye, but as the carriage drove away, she looked at the star. It seemed very faint and far away.

• • •

MICHAEL ENTERED THE STUDY and closed the door. He was hardly in the room when his father got up and came towards him. Daisy crouched in the bushes, listening. She thought it would be hard to hear through the closed window, but old Sawyer was yelling so loud it would wake the dead.

"When are you going to grow up, boy? The horses need tending. There's work to be done at the mill, and you're sitting around the parlor with schoolgirls."

"She was my guest, father. It's perfectly fine now to have a girl as a guest in the parlor. It's nearly a new century."

"Don't get smart with me. You think you know everything—you young people make me sick. It's time to grow up and earn a living. And this is *my* house. You'll have guests when I say you'll have guests."

"But Father, we weren't doing anything wrong."

"You were. You were disobeying me. I want you to think about working. Think about how you would support a woman. I don't want that girl in this house anymore—you hear me? She's too young for you to be courting. I'd have the Chapman's on my back about their daughter as well as everything else."

Michael knew there was nothing to be done when his father was in such a rage and was resigned to hold his tongue. "Yes, father, is there anything else?"

"Isn't that enough? Get out of here." He was walking toward his desk again. Michael stood near the door. "Get out," he shouted. Then he poured a shot of brandy and drank it down as Michael closed the door.

Chapter 2

WHEN MRS. TEMPLE ENTERED the bakery before sunrise, Mrs. Cunningham came right around with the coffee as if she had been waiting for her arrival. The napkins were already out, and she could smell the bread baking. There were already two cups set up at their table by the window. Mrs. Temple sat down while Mrs. Cunningham poured them both a coffee. She put the pot down between them as strands of red and yellow lifted above the horizon.

"There was a big ta-do over at the Sawyer's on Saturday." Mrs. Cunningham said.

"Was Olive in again?"

"No, it was Daisy, late in the day."

"That one's not afraid to say anything; she'd better watch herself if she wants to keep her position."

"I know," Mrs. Cunningham said.

"Well?"

"Seems Sawyer came home, and Michael and Lily were alone together in the parlor. He was furious."

"Were they in a compromising position?" Mrs. Temple asked incredulously.

"No, of course not," Mrs. Cunningham said. "Nothing like that."

"Well, what's it to him, then? Young people are not so restricted now as when we were young."

Mrs. Cunningham shook her head. "Oh, you know he fancies himself better than everyone else. He's afraid of what people will say. There seems to be bad blood between him and the Chapmans. I think he and Mary had a spat, and he'll hold the grudge forever."

Mrs. Temple frowned. "Yes, there was something, some trouble a long time ago, but really I think he's more put off by Edward."

"Probably because Edward's money came from an inheritance, and he's a self-made man. Do you think he could have been interested in Mary, before Edward, I mean?"

"No, nothing of that sort. I forget you didn't grow up here. Mary was the child of a shopkeeper, like us. Her father was not even around. She certainly wasn't the catch of the season."

Mrs. Cunningham poured more coffee in her friend's cup. "Plenty of scandal to be had there, I'm sure."

"Sawyer would have never married her, anyway. He wanted to marry up. I don't know why he cares all these years later. Michael could certainly do worse than falling for the wealthiest young woman in town."

"I don't know, either, but from what Daisy told me, there was hell to pay at the Sawyer's over the weekend."

• • •

MRS. CHAPMAN PACED BACK and forth between the davenport and the fireplace, though she knew it was giving her a headache. Her mind was not easy, and she couldn't stop moving. It seemed like overnight,

Lily had changed. She'd become very defiant. Isn't that what she had wanted—that her daughter would have some backbone? But she worried now—that Lily was too naïve, rather a different creature altogether from her sister, although, oddly enough, in some ways, she seemed to have Edward's personality. But that wasn't quite so either; although Edward didn't like to make waves, he did look at the world with a critical eye. Others might think of him as a pushover but she knew, like most men, he could dig in his heels.

Perhaps she had been too rigid with Lily. Perhaps she should try to be more of a confidant with her; that had worked well with Abagail. But the girls were so different. Whenever she tried that with Lily, it seemed to backfire. She was pacing faster now and getting dizzy but moving always helped her to think. No, she would have to continue to put her foot down and tell Lily she was too young for this romance. Lily must go to college, like Abigail. She stopped and leaned against the fireplace mantle thinking maybe she would take Lily to Europe this summer and show her that a very interesting world exists beyond this town. She looked up at the ceiling and shook her head. Why of all the young men in town, had she set her eyes on Michael? It was so unfair, the kinds of twists that fate would take. She sighed, pushed a stay hair back from her eyes, and looked into the mirror over the mantelpiece.

She had never been very attractive as a child, as her own mother had told her in so many silent ways, but her mother had shown her how to enhance her features, how to make the most of a slightly crooked nose and how to make her eyes look larger. Older now, she'd grown into her face and for a woman in her fifties, her skin was still taut and her hair thick and shiny. Yes, she was actually more attractive now than she'd been when she was younger. She had poise and sophistication, and it was not something she had been born with; most of all, unlike her catty neighbors, she had discretion.

This situation would pass, and she would continue to hold her head high. She regretted now that they had not moved long ago from this small town where everyone knew the family she had come from— and they'd never let her forget it. Jealously, that's all it was, but years ago, the gossip had nearly destroyed her, and she wouldn't let it destroy her daughter. She groped the cold marble shelf and held her body firm against a wave of nausea.

At least, at her age, she didn't have to worry about childbirth, but the thought of those years troubled her too. She worried about what people thought, what they knew. It had been a rough time that she tried to forget—very few knew just how rough. She felt a pang in her womb. Maybe it was women's problems. She thought about calling Dr. Sands but was afraid he would recommend the hysteria cure. She didn't want him examining her insides. He hadn't been there for the second birth. It had all been so troubling and complicated.

It was a wonder Edward hadn't gone and called the doctor when he had seen her hands trembling this morning. Poor Edward was always trying to fix everything, expecting there to be an answer for everything. She supposed she could be stubborn too, but after all, it was her body not his. A knot clenched in her stomach, and suddenly, she was sick again. She made it to the davenport, sat down, and poured a cup of tea. It was cold, and she gagged as it reached her throat. She rang for Suzanne who appeared at once with her head bowed down and her hands clasped in front of a ruffled apron.

"Ma'am?"

Mrs. Chapman looked up and thought how queer the uniform

looked on Suzanne's flat, square body. She didn't want to make the servants wear such uniforms. She had argued with Edward about how it was degrading to women, but he had insisted pushing aside what he called her new-fangled ideas about women, saying she had always been far too friendly with the help.

"The tea's gone cold, dear; please bring me a fresh pot."

Suzanne walked over to the coffee table and picked up the silver tray. "Anything to eat, Ma'am?"

"No, just the tea will be fine. Thank you, Suzanne."

"Ma'am." Suzanne bowed her head and left the room with the silver tray.

Mary's hands trembled. She would have liked to smoke one of her husband's cigarettes; he had left the case open on the mantelpiece. Men had so many more outlets than women. She was glad things were changing. Abigail had been to some Woman Suffrage rallies at college and told her about them. The younger girls did not want to be glorified slaves to their husbands. At the women's club, they stressed educating everyone. They wanted something more, like she always had. She went over and took a cigarette from her husband's case and sat back down. Why did Lily have to show defiance in this way? It couldn't be serious. He was probably the first young man who'd ever paid attention to her. But why Sawyer's son—it was so unfair, so unfair to all of them. Her eyes teared up, and her stomach tightened.

"Are you alright, ma'am?" Suzanne was back with the hot tea. Mrs. Chapman hid the cigarette behind her back.

"I'm fine, dear. That will be all."

Suzanne curtsied and left the room.

The hot tea felt good going down. This was the worst day, and she knew she would have to call for Dr. Sands. It was probably just nerves with all this going on with Lily. She'd have another talk with her. Michael had grown into a nice young man, but that made it even harder—if he'd turned out like his father, Lily would never have even looked at him. She was still quite childish for her seventeen years. It was Edward's fault, always protecting her. She would have to convince Edward that Lily must go to college, like Abigail, and learn to take care of herself, convince him his daughter would not spend her life at the mercy of any man. She would remind Edward that Sawyer had been friendly, or at least cordial, to them at one time, so in a few years, Michael would probably be a tyrant like his father.

She went to the window where a few crows hopped around the back garden. They began to circle and caw and make a fuss. She tapped on the glass, and they disappeared. When she sat again, she noticed the way the light came through the window, and her mind, in a kind of frenzy, followed the dust motes as they moved in tandem, drawn toward the edge of light. In the light, they danced, and she followed their movement. She cocked her head and studied the way they gathered and swept around in the shaft of light until she felt a tremble in her cheeks that rippled—then a tightening in her temples. She gave out a small cry and clutched at her chest. Her head moved from side to side as if saying no to the stirring of dust, no to the slant of sun, and no to the vision of a young girl's face staring through the window.

She dropped the cup she was holding, and tea ran in a muddy puddle across the floor. Running away from the apparition, her skirt caught in the bottom of the door, and she thought how foolish she was. *I didn't do anything wrong. I'm guilty of nothing but trying to right a wrong. I only did the charitable thing.* She put her head down, suddenly feeling old and defeated. She walked slowly up the stairs to her room, grasping the wooden banister. Suzanne watched from the landing then went into the parlor to clean up the mess.

• • •

WHEN EDWARD CHAPMAN came home, he was pleased to find that his wife had taken it upon herself to call the doctor. Dr. Sands was just getting into his carriage when Mr. Chapman arrived and was assured that his wife only needed rest. It surprised him then to hear the front door close with a slam.

Lily bustled into the room and gave him a kiss on the cheek. "Where's mother? I have to talk to her."

"How about talking to your old man or playing me a tune on the piano?" His voice was deep and raspy, a contrast to his pale hair and gray-green eyes. He lit up a cigarette and took a long drag.

"I will later, Father. I promise, but I really must talk to mother now. It's very important. Is she up in her room?"

"Yes, but I'm afraid you can't disturb her right now. Dr. Sands came by to see her and gave her some medicine. She's resting for a while. Her poetry club is meeting here tonight. She'll be resting until then."

"What's the matter with her now? Is she bored already with her latest salons?"

Edward looked at his daughter. Her dark hair made her skin look pale, almost transparent. Her thick eyebrows were drawn together, and her face was down in a pout.

"Lily, don't speak of your mother like that. She loves you, even if you don't agree on everything lately. She had one of her dizzy spells, and I don't want you getting her upset."

"Well, she gets me upset, too. She doesn't allow me to do anything—or even see any boys I wish to be with. She doesn't want me to have a life of my own. She just makes up these dizzy spells to get her own way."

"That's enough, Lily. You'll have to help Suzanne get everything ready for the meeting tonight. Two new members are coming—Mrs. Sawyer and her son Michael. I ran into them on my way home from work."

Lily's face lifted. The color came back to her cheeks. "Oh, father. Thank you for letting me help." She gave him a hug and another kiss on the cheek. "I'd better start getting everything ready."

Edward shook his head, bewildered by the quick changes in mood of the women in the household; although, he was glad to see her excited about something again, the way she'd been moping around lately and arguing with her mother. Maybe they just needed to give her more responsibilities. Lily walked toward the kitchen.

"The meeting isn't until 7:30—how about that piece you promised on the piano?"

"Okay, Father; you're such a dear."

She turned back and went into the parlor. Then she adjusted the piano stool and smiled at him before beginning the tune. Her mind and heart were suddenly so full, it was hard to calm her fingers down and play the quiet, haunting tune that was her father's favorite. The music drifted out an open window to the back yard where Suzanne was out on the lawn shaking out a small throw rug for the entryway.

Suzanne stopped and studied Lily's profile sitting at the piano stool. *Such a sad song for a young girl to be playing*, she thought. *Such a sad sad song.*

Edward Chapman put his feet up, relaxed, and let a long thin cigarette burn down slowly in his hand.

Chapter 3

MRS. TEMPLE STRUGGLED TO OPEN the bakery door and was barely inside when the wind closed it with a thump. Rain splattered down the dark windows.

"Yoo-hoo," she called to her friend, but there was no answer. She shook her umbrella out and rushed into the back.

"Oh, Edith," Mrs. Cunningham said. "I'm running behind this morning, and they'll be coming in for something warm before the sun's up."

"Won't this weather keep them away?" Mrs. Temple asked.

"At this time of year, this is the kind of weather that brings them in. The workers will want something warm to start the day, and the help in the mansions don't bake like they used to."

"How can I help?"

"Put the muffins over there in the oven. Then help me knead some more of this bread."

They worked together for a good half hour, and when everything was out of the oven, they doled out the napkins and sat at their corner table.

"I doubt you'll have anybody just out for errands today."

"You'd be surprised," Mrs. Cunningham said.

"That's true. You can never figure. I may get some buying their Easter hats and dresses, just to make them feel like the season is on us."

"It's April, and the March winds are still with us. The rain is fine, but it's a shame for it to be this cold. I had flowers coming up along the stoop already. They'll be battered down after this."

"Any news from the houses today?"

"I heard that Dr. Sands was at the Chapman's yesterday?"

"For Mary, no doubt."

"They say she has some kind of nervous condition."

Mrs. Temple nodded.

"She wasn't so nervous, once. Not when she and Edward were courting. It was after her children were born. She had a hard time of it with Lily. They had to call in a special doctor, and Miss Parker, the nanny, had to completely take over for a while."

"You'd wonder why she'd be fretting again, after all these years."

"They say sometimes it's hard to see your children grown. Lily will be out of high school soon. Maybe she's afraid of losing her like she almost lost her once."

• • •

MARY CHAPMAN WOKE late and immediately rang for Suzanne.

"Ma'am?"

"Why did you let me sleep till after dark? We're having a salon here tonight." She heard the doorbell ring and hurried from the bed still dizzy from the medicine. "What time is it?"

"Just past seven. Sorry, mam. Mr. Chapman said not to wake you until seven-thirty. He said you needed to rest and had Lily and I take care of the refreshments. Lily is helping with the guests. Everything's okay. I'll help you dress."

"Everything is *not* okay. You should have woken me." She sat down at the night table and wiped her face. She could see in the mirror how Suzanne bristled—the poor thing was probably holding back tears. "I'm sorry" she said. "You were just doing as Edward told you. I'll talk to him." She turned around. "Come, dear; help me fix my hair."

"Yes, Mam. How would you like it? I could maybe put it in braids around the top."

"Hmm, I think that look is more for young people and very old women. Maybe do a French twist and lift it around to the back." Mrs. Chapman noticed her eyes still looked tired and puffy. It must have been from getting out of bed so quickly. She didn't like sleeping in the middle of the day, no matter what Dr. Sands said. She looked up at Suzanne. "Do my face first. See if you can get the puffiness out."

"Yes, Ma'am." Suzanne brought a basin of water and a cloth over to where she was sitting.

"Just a quick facial will be fine, dear."

Suzanne nodded and rubbed cold water around Mrs. Chapman's face and neck.

"Ah, that feels good," Mrs. Chapman said as light creams were rubbed into her forehead and cheekbones.

Next, Suzanne took up the brush on the nightstand and began to twist and lift her hair. When they were done, she went over to the closet, took several dresses out, and laid them across the bed. Mrs. Chapman picked a simple, blue-flowered cotton dress with lace around the sleeves and collar. It was low waisted and had several tiny black buttons down the front. She was a thin woman, and her hair, in a simple elegant fashion on top of her head, brought all the lines of her body up in a stunning, majestic look.

Suzanne could hardly notice the grey in her hair now, or the dark circles under her eyes. She helped put on Mrs. Chapman's shoes, low black suede boots with pointed toes.

"Thank you, Suzanne."

Mrs. Chapman whisked a Japanese fan from the bureau top, held up her dress with the other hand, and walked carefully down the wide staircase to join Mr. Chapman greeting guests at the door.

"Right this way, Grace," he said to the woman entering when he saw his wife coming toward them.

He wore his smoking jacket, but he didn't have a cigarette in his hand. Later, he would retreat to his study for bourbon and a smoke. The woman he'd been talking with was small and thin; she walked with a cane and wore thick glasses. He led her to the parlor, and she sat down chatting with someone else and sipping from a long-stemmed wine glass. Everyone seemed happily involved in conversation. Mr. Chapman stood outside the parlor door and turned to his wife who had sidled up beside him.

"Are you feeling better?"

His eyes looked directly at hers, and she saw the concern but also, what? Distrust? Maybe a little of both. His eyes were a gentle translucent gray that matched the specks of hair starting to show in his mustache. She used to see innocence and a lack of gall in those eyes—but not anymore.

She looked back at him with a cold stare. "I'm not an invalid, Edward. I'm capable of taking care of these gatherings. And don't you dare ever usurp my authority with Suzanne again."

He opened his mouth to defend himself but decided to just move away. He didn't want to start anything. He would have to consult with Dr. Sands again and ask him about her moods.

Mrs. Chapman took a step back out of the parlor to compose herself. Seeing Edward just standing there, acting like he had no idea why she was upset, had taken away her nerve. She stood just outside the entrance and looked inside.

Lily had done a good job of setting up the room. A small wooden table had been placed in the middle of the parlor and covered with an indigo-print tablecloth. Comfortable chairs were set up on both sides of the fireplace, and several spindly wooden ones set against the wall, ready to be put out when the discussion began. Hillary, a maid hired for the evening, looked up from a serving platter and noticed Mrs. Chapman by the door. She smiled and bowed her head. Mrs. Chapman smiled back warmly. One large candelabrum was on a table against the wall, and to one side was a bowl of grapes, on the other a dish of plums, pear halves and orange sections. At the back of the table were several bottles of wine— red, rose, and white with long-stemmed glasses set up in a circle around them. There was a platter of cheese on both sides of the table—and a roaring fire to keep the room cozy and comfortable

Mr. Green took an orange section in his chubby hand, and the juice dripped down from his lips to his chin as he patted Hillary on the backside. Mrs. Chapman threw down the fan, ready to go over and confront him right there, but she knew she'd have to hold her temper. She wouldn't invite him again. Had nothing changed in the last twenty years when the men felt free to have their way with the hired girls? She *would* continue to go the meetings in Worcester, and she *would* encourage the help to go as well. Did some of these men just come because they knew there would be pretty young women here? She shook her head. Maybe she should make it women-only, though the male point of view actually made the evening more interesting. But was it worth putting up with Mr. Green?

Mr. Chapman had come back to the door, seeing his wife's hesitancy, and he put his arm in hers. "Are you quite well?" he asked, which only ruffled her once again.

"Yes, Edward. I'm quite well and capable." She smiled sweetly at Mrs. Bennett who was approaching and said through her teeth, "We'll talk later."

He was running out of patience. "Fine. We'll talk later," he said, as Mrs. Chapman broke away and held out her hand to her guest.

"Lucy, I'm so glad you could come tonight. I didn't know you were back from the continent. I hope you have lots of stories to tell."

Mrs. Bennett was a tall, thin woman in a long, eastern-style dress that wrapped around her like a blanket. Her ear lobes were pulled down by large earrings with an eastern motif, and powder blue makeup covered her eyes from lid to brow. *Never a leg of mutton sleeve for her,* Mrs. Chapman thought. But it was these different types that Mrs. Chapman found interesting as friends—and perfect for literary evenings.

"More important how are you, Mary, my dear? Edward was telling me you had the doctor in? I wasn't sure if you were coming down at all. It's so good to see you." Mrs. Bennet kissed her on both cheeks. "Like the French," she said.

"Edward is a bit of an alarmist." She looked at him then back at Mrs. Bennet. "I'm fine, just tired lately. I haven't been sleeping well, so Dr. Sands gave me some medicine. I think it works rather too well."

"Well, I'm glad you feel better, Mary."

Edward joined them with two glasses of rose and a plate of fruit and cheese. Mrs. Bennet went off to talk with other guests, so Mrs. Chapman sat down and began to pick at the food. It was the first time she'd felt like eating in a while, and she was beginning to relax a little, thinking she may enjoy the evening after all.

She turned to Edward. "I think we should start soon. People are getting a little tired of standing around. Where's Lily?"

"She's showing some new members around outside; they haven't seen all the new gardens we've added."

"I didn't know there were new people tonight. Anyone we know?"

"Yes, matter of fact, Grace Sawyer and her, son, Michael."

She choked down her champagne. Edward, alarmed, gently patted his wife's back. She shooed him away with her napkin.

"Who invited them?" she whispered loudly, glancing around.

"I'm not sure. Lily, I guess, though she seemed surprised when I said they were coming."

Mrs. Chapman fanned herself furiously. Did he have any idea what he had done by holding back this information? She looked at her husband; he seemed perfectly innocent.

"Apparently they've wanted to join for some time," Edward said, "but talking the old man into letting her go was next to impossible." He made a snorting laugh. "Maybe they snuck out."

Mrs. Chapman shook her head. *The things women had to do for a little bit of freedom.* Only now, she had bigger problems and wished at least this time that Sawyer had put his foot down.

"I understand Michael has quite a literary bent, too. He's quite well-read and interested in the arts. Takes after his mother, I guess."

Mrs. Chapman thought she knew where his interests were, but she didn't have much time to think because Lily, Michael, and Mrs. Sawyer were back inside. Lily arm-and-arm in the middle of the threesome. She was flushed as she walked into the room. When she saw her mother, she looked down at the floor.

"Well, I guess we can start now," Edward said above the noise.

Mr. Green, Edward, and Michael, the only three men, maneuvered the chairs and helped the ladies get seated. Lily put her copy of Emily Dickinson's poems on the chair beside her so no one would sit there before Michael. They had all agreed that sitting in the straight wooden chairs was more stimulating for discussion. Later, they would relax and move to the couch and parlor chairs. When everyone was seated, Edward took charge.

"Let's be official about this and take a tally of who is here and who is not. We have two new members who we're pleased to welcome to the group—Grace Sawyer and her son, Michael."

Everyone clapped, and Edward looked their way.

"I hope you can put up with our disorganized and rather bohemian way of doing things. I usually serve as the first master of ceremonies unless someone else wants the job—any takers?" He made a little laugh and looked around. "I thought so."

Everyone laughed.

"Well enough of that. I get an official count of eleven people her tonight: Mrs. Sawyer and Michael, Mr. and Mrs. Henry Green, Mrs. Remington and her daughter Celia, Mrs. Bennet, Miss Taylor, my daughter Lily, and of course my lovely wife and I." Mr. Chapman cleared his throat. "Tonight, we are discussing a contemporary poet of New England. Her death barely a decade ago left a great talent ended. She lived, indeed, as a recluse in her Amherst home. Always dressed in white, seldom leaving her home, they say she wrote of things she had never seen or experienced—purely from imagination."

Lily and Michael looked at each other. Mrs. Chapman watched them, closed her eyes, and swallowed hard. *Edward, what have you done? You should not have let them come without checking with me first.* She took a shallow breath and quietly got up and walked out of the room. Out of sight of the others, she took a deep breath, went to the water closet, closed the door, and cried quietly, putting her hands on the side of the sink, and looking in the mirror. She was already looking disheveled. "Pull yourself together," she said to her image then washed her face and went back to the parlor.

The discussion had already begun. Mrs. Bennet was arguing that a woman with so little experience of the outside world could not understand the concepts of life—Emily Dickinson's poems were all about death.

"Why, look at this poem," she said "A certain slant of light—it's about despair and death. I think she should have spent time out in the world. She wouldn't have been so gloomy. Life is for living." She almost sang the words and looked at Michael and Lily. "Young people, young girls most especially, should look to the future. Live life to the fullest."

Celia and Lily's eyes met. They tried not to laugh. Michael looked down at the book of poems, embarrassed by the wild outburst of emotion. He'd expected the evening to be more formal. He wasn't accustomed to being with a roomful of strangers and didn't like the unexpected.

Beatrice Taylor wasn't at all put off or intimidated by Mrs.

Bennet's theatrics. She spoke in a high-pitched voice, removing her glasses.

"Emily Dickenson was a great fatalist, but she also praised nature and saw the goodness in the tiniest of creatures. She knew that the relationship between life and death was a kind of marriage. She realized the inevitability of everything we mortals try to do to fool ourselves. We plan and strive for what? She wooed death, almost as a lover."

Mrs. Chapman at first thought it was a little brazen for her to speak like that in a mixed group. Then she thought it did make for a more exciting evening and why shouldn't a woman come forward and say how she felt. Again, she thought, maybe they should make it all female and they would all be more open to speaking their minds.

"Her acceptance," Miss Taylor went on, "brought a more peaceful life most could never find in this hectic industrial age. Her poems are a sweet breath of the innocence we have lost in just a few generations as we strive to make life easier."

"But no," Mrs. Bennet said. "Here, in this other poem where she uses the word slant–she uses the word circuit. Isn't that a new word? They use that word talking about all this new engineering of energy."

"That's an old word," Miss. Taylor said. "It comes from the word circuits–you know, like around the perimeter."

"Yes," Mrs. Bennet said. "But she's using it in the new way here."

"Read the poem again," Mrs. Taylor countered. "It could be taken in the original sense of the word, well, and even if not, maybe she's' not so gloomy after all if she can use words in a new industrial way?"

"What page is that poem on?" Mr. Green asked.

Mrs. Bennet ignored him and went on. "Yes, I like what she is saying better in that one, I think; oh dear, her work is such a puzzle."

Mr. Green found the page. "Well, look here," he said. "This is a strange line: *Tell all the truth but tell it slant.* It sounds to me like she's saying to lie."

Mrs. Chapman looked at her husband; shouldn't he try to calm things down?

Miss Taylor looked horrified. "I don't think she's saying to lie. It's just people look at things differently perhaps. We all have our point of view."

"But she says the truth is delightful, but it causes infirmity—what does that mean? It's all full of puzzles" Mr. Green shook his head. "She says it's superb, but it makes you blind—what does that mean? I don't think this is poetry."

"Well, then," Mrs. Chapman said. "As Dickinson is saying, we all have different opinions, different perspectives"

"Maybe she means you can be blindsided by the truth," Lily said.

Mrs. Chapman held tightly to the sides of her chair and stared at her daughter.

"Aha, we've all seen politicians who were brought to ruin by the truth," Edward said with a little laugh.

Mrs. Chapman shook her head. "Let's' not bring politics into this."

"Alright, well," Edward said. "Let's talk about the poetry itself instead of the philosophy behind it." Edward's voice seemed a little too harsh. Mrs. Chapman could see that Miss Taylor had taken offense.

"My dear man," Miss Taylor said. "How can you talk of the poetry and not the meaning behind it? In all literature, we must realize death has more impact than life."

"And lies, apparently, more than the truth," Mr. Green mumbled.

"Yes, yes, yes." Mrs. Bennet stood up waving her hands. "I agree with you Grace, and that is precisely why I feel we should live for the day. Enjoy life while we have it—not be victims of the inevitability of the grim reaper. The ancient Greek plays were mostly tragedies, but, ah, they knew how to live. They built up their bodies with exercise and passion; they ate well and drank well."

When Mrs. Bennet finally sat down, Miss Tayler blurted out her final point. "What I was saying is that all literature deals with tragedy, and there are only pleasant, sometimes comic, interludes to help us forget."

The discussion went on until Mr. Chapman suggested they wrap it up for the evening and decide what house they would meet at next. Mrs. Bennet insisted they all come to her house—she had so many new and interesting things to show them from her trip abroad. When that was settled, Edward, Mr. Green, and Michael put the chairs away and went to Edward's study, leaving the ladies to chat in the parlor.

• • •

LILY AND CELIA SAT together on one end of the couch away from the others. They were about the same age and knew each other from school.

"That Mrs. Bennet is a real card," Celia said. "It was worth being here just to see her and Miss Taylor up-stage each other." They both laughed. Celia took up her fan. "I wish there were some lemonade. It's hot with all these layers of clothes and these shoes. My goodness, no wonder we always want to stay off our feet."

Lily had been admiring Celia's long, navy skirt and jacket over a white linen blouse with ruffles, though she knew it was probably not comfortable. "I'll open the window," she said, "and we can move away from the fire."

Lily took Celia's arm, and they moved toward the door after Lily opened a window. They were now further away from everyone else and whispered together.

"Maybe we should wear bloomers and workman's boots to the next meeting," Lily Whispered. "No one to object since our mothers both think they are becoming liberated now. Is your mother still dragging you to meetings?"

"Oh, goodness, yes" Celia said. "All they talk about is the cause now, but I kind of like to go. They have some good points. You and your mother should join us."

Lily moved closer to her. "I hear even some of the maids go. My father wouldn't like that too much. He thinks my mother doesn't have enough separation with the help."

Celia shook her head. "Why is it the men seem so much more old-fashioned than the women? Although, even some of the women think it's scandalous that Mrs. Bennet travels by herself over-seas."

"Hush," Lily said. "Here she comes."

As Lily's mother descended on her with Mrs. Bennett, Celia excused herself and walked toward the table for cheese and wine.

"Hello, Lily." Mrs. Bennett sat down very close to her. Mrs. Chapman remained standing. "You're such a young lady now and so beautiful. You must have dozens of young men coming around."

Lily blushed and looked down. "There's only one I'm really interested in."

Mrs. Chapman broke in. "What did you think of the meeting,

Lucy?" She looked down at Mrs. Bennet. "Did you know Lily made all the arrangements this time? "

"Oh, the meeting was wonderful, and how about you, my young friend? I suppose you young ones get rather bored with all the talk?"

"Oh no, I found the evening very exciting and entertaining. I do so like reading Emily Dickinson. It's nice to have the male point of view as well. I was especially glad Michael was here."

Mrs. Chapman's eyes narrowed. Mrs. Bennet looked at them both with an exaggerated look of surprise. "Oh, could this be the young man you're so fond of? Young love, so wonderful—he seems very nice."

Mrs. Chapman gave Mrs. Bennet a tight smile and sat down beside her. Actually," she said. "I was hoping you could talk to my daughter about your trip overseas. You know, I may be planning a trip myself soon, and I'd like to take Lily with me."

"That's a wonderful idea. Yes. A well-bred young lady must go to Europe. It's so fascinating. I could advise you on what to see, where to go. Aren't you lucky to have such an opportunity?" She squeezed Lily's hands. "I'm already excited for you."

Lily was alone with Mrs. Bennet. Her mother had gotten up and retreated to the table as soon as she had mentioned the trip.

"It does sound like a wonderful opportunity. I'm just not sure right now if I would want to be away for so long."

Suddenly, Mrs. Chapman was back with a glass of wine for Mrs. Bennett. "What's to think about?" Mrs. Bennett asked. "Oh, yes, your young man. You'll miss each other of course, but he'll be here when you get back."

Mrs. Remington and Celia interrupted to say goodbye.

Mrs. Remington touched Mrs. Chapman on the shoulder. "Thank you for a lovely time. I hope you're feeling better. We'll talk—about the meetings—in Worcester?"

Mrs. Chapman nodded.

Celia and Lily made plans to go walking together on the first nice day of spring. Mrs. Remington said goodbye to Mrs. Bennet, and they headed toward the door.

"Don't forget the next meeting is at my house, 87 Pine view Street" Mrs. Bennet called out as they walked away.

Mrs. Remington half turned around. "Yes, we'll be there."

More people started to leave. Mrs. Green knocked on the smoking-study door, and the men came out smelling of cigarettes and pipe tobacco. The Greens were going out the door, and the rest of the crowd stood around saying their goodbyes. Lily and Michael looked at each other. Michael made his way over to her and took her hands. They broke away from the circle.

"I think your father likes me. There's hope there anyway." Michael looked at Lily. They hadn't been alone together since his father had found them in the parlor.

"Of course. Why shouldn't he like you? I've had enough of being treated like a child. I'm going to see you, whether my mother likes it or not."

Michael smiled at her. "I've missed you, Lily. How about if we go bicycling next Saturday up at Grover's Hill? We can go to the top and look out over all the pastureland; it's beginning to look green and pretty again."

"We can have another picnic," Lily said. "A *real* picnic this time—outdoors. I know it's early, but we can wear heavy sweaters, and there won't be any ants to bother us."

"It gets pretty windy up on the hill, but we can try." When they looked up, most of the group had moved out the door. "I have to go now. Bye, Lily."

"Bye, Michael. See you Saturday."

He wanted to kiss her on the forehead, but instead, they held hands until they were at arms- length and then paused, pulling their eyes away as Michael turned and walked toward the door.

"Lily, Mrs. Bennet is talking to you. Don't be rude."

Lily's eyes darted from the door where Michael had just left. "Oh, I'm sorry. Excuse me, Mrs. Bennet."

"You can call me Lucy now that you're all grown up. I was just telling your mother; you and she should come to tea soon. I'll tell you about my trip and advise you on yours. Keep a date open for that on your calendar." She winked at Lily.

"Thank you, Mrs.—Lucy, that would be really nice."

"Goodbye now." She gave them both a hug at once. "Get some rest, Mary. I'll be in touch very soon."

Mrs. Bennet left, and Suzanne came in to clean up. When she was done, Mr. and Mrs. Chapman sat on the sofa. Suzanne brought in some tea, and Mrs. Chapman poured herself a cup. Her earlier rage at him had tapered, but she did want to discuss the problem of Michael and Lily.

"How are you feeling?" Mr. Chapman lit a cigarette. "I'm sorry I usurped your power. I only wanted you to be rested and enjoy the evening." He turned toward his wife. "Did you enjoy it?"

"It was fine until all this Michael and Lily business. It worries me, Edward. He's the one she's been mooning over these past few weeks."

"Ah." Mr. Chapman suddenly understood Lily's quick change in mood earlier. "You worry too much. He's a nice young man, seems mannered and well bred."

Mrs. Chapman bristled and moved away. "I don't like her getting mixed up in anything with the Sawyers. They're a strange family, especially his father. Could you imagine having to listen to his diatribes every day?"

Mr. Chapman looked at his wife; he moved toward her and took her hand. "Stop worrying, Mary. They're hardly old enough to be serious. The flame will flicker out by itself if we just leave them alone. Lily's barely eighteen."

"Have you forgotten? I was just eighteen when we got married. Young people always think they know what they're doing."

"What's that's supposed to mean?

"Nothing, Edward. I didn't mean it that way. It's just that, you know, that John Sawyer." She leaned forward and crossed her arms. "He always acts like we sort of owe him something. Always goes on about how he made his money with hard work and we inherited ours—as if, as if that is something we are guilty of—as if we don't deserve it."

Mr. Chapman raised his hands in the air. "But, he's like that with everyone. He'll never come here to socialize. It's something he just doesn't do."

Mrs. Chapman sighed. Her nervous stomach was acting up, and she felt dizzy. "I guess it really is Lily I'm worried about. Edward, she's so naive, young for her age. I don't want her to get so involved with any boys. I want her to have opportunities. The world is different now than it was twenty years ago. She needs to learn about the world, learn to fend for herself. I'd like to take her on a trip to Europe this summer."

"Do you think you're up for all that?"

"Stop worrying about me, would you? It would probably be the best thing in the world for me to get out of this town. It would be wonderful for Lily. We could leave in June and be back in the fall before the holidays." Mrs. Chapman rose, and Edward followed.

"It sounds like a splendid idea." He was glad to see his wife excited about something. "I'll miss you though." Mrs. Chapman started to walk away but Mr. Chapman took her hand, held her close, and kissed her.

"Oh, Edward, the servants might see us kissing like this in the parlor. It looks foolish, at our age."

"I don't care. Let them think what they want. I have some papers to straighten out in the study, but I will be up shortly." He kissed her again on the neck before he let her go.

Mrs. Chapman felt good as she got ready for bed. Something had been released with the idea of the trip to Europe. She welcomed the thought of being on her own and breathed more freely. She had been afraid that Edward would not like the idea or that he would insist on coming himself. She needed to build up a tighter bond with her youngest child. Abagail had always been so much easier to understand. She and her youngest daughter were worlds apart. This could be the opportunity to open the barrier between them, and it would pull her away from all this nonsense with Michael Sawyer.

Chapter 4

THE RAIN HAD LET UP FOR THE LAST workday of the week, and Mrs. Temple opened the door of the bakery just as the sun was rising. She was a little later than usual. Mrs. Cunningham was already putting out the napkins.

"It'll be a nice one today," she said, sitting and looking out the window. "Hopefully everyone will be walking out to get their hats and dresses. I just got some new merchandise in."

Mrs. Cunningham went around the back and brought out the coffee. "How are the spring sales?"

"Alright but you know people don't seem to dress up as much as they used to. I'm hoping for the sales in spring coats and shoes as we get closer to Easter. I envy you the bakery. You can keep the same stock all year. You don't have to order new every season."

"You'd be surprised. I have to keep up with what they're serving in the city, and all the rage seems to change often with this generation."

"Did you see Olive this morning?"

"No, but Hilary, the temporary girl at the Chapman's, was in here already. Mrs. Chapman held that party last night, and they were out of everything she said."

"Well, it is good that Mary is up for entertaining. She must be feeling better. What's the new girl like?"

"Seems quiet, nice," Mrs. Cunningham said. "I suppose they need more help now that Miss Parker the nanny is getting on in age. Hillary says she sleeps a lot now but still helps with the kitchen duties. I'm sure they'll keep her in the house though, as she's like one of the family."

"Where else would she go?"

• • •

ON SATURDAY, Lily pushed open the long drapes in her room and saw early-April rain dripping down the ends of pine needles. Her heart fell. It was very early yet, only seven, and they hadn't planned to leave until ten, but even if it stopped, it would ruin the picnic idea. She had decided not to tell her mother anything until Michael showed up at the door. That way, there would be no time for them to argue.

She sat down by a basin of water and washed her face. The water, actually tepid to the touch, seemed very cold on her still sleepy cheeks. She brushed her hair out for a long time in front of the mirror. It fell in dark waves from the braids she often wore. She sat, still in her nightdress, and thought about Michael. What would it be like to be married to him? He was kind and gentle like her father. It was so thrilling when he had kissed her on the lips. She thought about the name . . . Lily Sawyer . . . Lillian Sawyer . . . Lillian Prudence Sawyer . . . she liked the sound of that name.

She put the brush down and looked at the rain dripping down the window. It had gotten heavier in the last few minutes. No matter, she went to the closet to find a walking suit and chose a green wool skirt and a short bolero-style jacket with a lace blouse underneath. The skirt was a few inches above the ankle for walking. It would be warm, maybe a bit too dressy, but she wanted to look her best. It was rather like the suit Celia had worn at the poetry meeting, and Celia had looked so graceful and stylish. Lily looked in the mirror on the inside of the closet door. She was short, and it looked less graceful on her. She wished she were taller. Her best clothes just made her look like a child trying to look like an adult.

She took it off and put on a heavy, red-cotton skirt with a cream-colored blouse on top. It had leg-a-muffin sleeves and a high, stiff collar. She put on some high walking boots that lifted her hem up a few inches from the floor. From her hat boxes, she picked out a wool hat with a wide brim and a thick, red satin ribbon that wound around the brim. It tied underneath. She looked at herself at all different angles in the mirror and was satisfied, so she took everything off and laid them neatly on the bed, slipped on a simple cotton dress, and went downstairs for breakfast.

She walked quietly by her parents' room and was startled by her mother's voice.

"Lily, is that you, up so early on a Saturday morning? Come in. Your father's down in the library. I want to talk to you." Her mother had turned her head from the vanity mirror and was starting to get up as Lily peeked into the doorway. "Abigail is coming home from college for a long weekend today. I was hoping we might go shopping. We could start planning for our trip, keep our minds off the dreadful rain out there." She patted the bench beside her. "Come sit down for a few minutes."

Lily, trapped, obediently moved toward her mother.

"I don't mean to be so heavy with you lately, but really, Lily, you must not go off on such a fancy with the first boy who shows interest."

"I'm sorry too, Mother. I must have breakfast. I'm so hungry, I feel faint. I do have plans for the day. Maybe we can talk when I get back, you, me and Abagail?"

Mrs. Chapman's face turned red. Was Lily openly defying her? "Really?" she asked. "Where are you going?"

Lily moved toward the door, not looking at her mother as she spoke. "Didn't I tell you Michael is coming to pick me up at ten? We made a date at the meeting last Tuesday."

"In the rain?" Mrs. Chapman rose from the chair, the color gone from her face.

"It's letting up a little," Lily said as she stood at the door, her back to her mother.

"Have you lost all your sense? Michael, I know, is a sensible boy. He won't be picking you up on a day like this."

Mrs. Chapman sat down on the bed. Lily turned at the door and looked at her. She walked back and stood in front of the bed. "I don't mean to upset you, Mother, but it's all been arranged."

"Well, I'm your mother, and I forbid you to go out with him. I'm trying hard to get through to you. Why do you taunt me like this?" Mrs. Chapman rubbed her forehead with both hands.

"Now you're starting again, pretending to be ill so you'll get your way. Why can't you understand that I love Michael and he loves me? You won't listen. You just won't listen." Lily picked up the skirt of her cotton dress and hurried from the room and down the wide staircase. She felt dizzy from guilt and hunger and brushed tears away with the back of her hand before entering the kitchen.

The kitchen maid, her nanny when she was younger, stood at the stove. She turned around and looked carefully at Lily's face. "What's wrong, Miss Lily? You look flushed." She spooned hot oatmeal into a bowl and brought it to the table.

"I'm okay. Still half asleep, I guess."

Lily was glad no one else was in the kitchen, especially the new girl Hillary. Her nanny had seen her in tears before; she pulled out a chair for Lily.

"I'll make you a nice strong hot cup of tea. You'll feel better." Lily ate slowly, distractedly. Nanna Parker watched her from the stove, her hands crossed in front of her apron. "Is your mother up? Do you know? I thought I heard you two talking."

"She's up," Lily said looking down into her bowl.

She hardly noticed that nanna Parker had come over to the table and brought her a steaming cup of tea. Her spirits were down after the argument with her mother, and her mother was right—it was doubtful Michael would show up on a day like today. If he did, she certainly couldn't entertain him here—not with her mother glaring at them. She pushed her thick, wavy hair out of her face with one swoop of her right hand and looked up.

"What was it like when you were courting, Nanna? I know you never got married, but you must have had beaus. Were you allowed to hold hands? Go out by yourselves?"

"Oh, everything was a lot stricter then. We could hardly share a few smiles in public." She sat down by Lily. The faint smell of onions and the sweet smell of apples wafted from her thick, red hands. It made Lily feel better, comforted. "But we always managed to sneak away." She paused and pushed Lily's hair that had fallen down away from her forehead and the sticky bowl of oatmeal. "Your mother loves you, but sometimes, it seems, the old are afraid of the young. Maybe they don't remember the restlessness, the intensity, the spirit. Or, it may be they remember it too well. They've felt it all before; they want to protect their children from harm."

Nanna Parker looked very old to Lily. She knew she was much older than her mother. She had grown to an age that many people never lived to, but she was still strong, still working. She didn't work long without getting tired, but she had grown to an age where she could say things openly and truthfully. Lily liked talking with her.

"I remember once when I was about your age, my beau and I snuck off by ourselves. There was a summer party at our house. Mind you, it wasn't a fancy party like you folks have, but a lot of friends gathered. So many people were coming in and out, my ma hardly noticed our disappearance."

Lily stopped moping and looked up. It was hard to imagine Nanny as a young girl with a disapproving mother.

"My beau, Len Cooper, and I walked down a dirt path far in the back of the house that led to a deep pool. I remember everything about the evening. The mountain laurel in over-bloom we passed on the way and the smell of wild teaberry, which we used to pick and chew like gum. Len took my hand and hurried me along. My light, summer cotton dress got caught in the brambles as we raced to the stone wall that we knew marked the end of the path. It was early July, and the blueberries were just ripening. Len picked a handful, and we threw them up in the air and tried to catch them in our mouths. We were laughing loud and shouting to each other until we got to the stone wall. Then Len lifted me up, and we toppled over kissing, and we stayed right on the grass, holding each other until the sun went down."

"Did you get caught?"

"We heard them calling for us, and we both took off in different directions and showed up at the house one before the other. There were lots of people suspicious, but they couldn't prove anything."

"What happened, with the boy, with Len?"

Nana turned her eyes away. Lily felt bad then for going too far. He must have found someone else.

"He had an accident, so they said. I think he was murdered."

Lily was shaken. "How horrible," she said looking down again. Was this all some made up story to keep her from doing as she wished? No, she could see real anguish in Nanna Parker's face.

"It was a long time ago, child—nothing anyone should fret about now. I think of the good times now, try not to mention the darkness. Life goes different ways to sideways from what we think will happen, so I bury what I can't explain and live that night in my memory, knowing I'll never feel that strongly again about another boy or a long summer evening."

"What happens to it? Does everyone bury their memories?"

Miss Parker crossed her arms. "Oh, I guess it gets buried in good ways and bad, maybe in paintings and books and even illnesses that last a long time. It's buried in the stories we tell. The sadness and the goodness, they all wash away into the same stream, then all come back thrown upon the shore to be found by another generation. your mama is afraid for you—afraid of that intensity now. Try to live your own life but also try to understand."

Lily sighed and put the teacup down carefully. "I don't mean to make her angry or sad, but I know I'm in love, and everything seems so special, but no one believes me, especially my mother. She doesn't even try to understand."

"I know, darling, but let me tell you—she understands more than you know. Do what you have to, but think of her, too."

"Thanks, Nana." Lily brought her empty bowl to the sink. Before leaving, she went back to the table. "Nanna," she whispered. "Did they ever find out who murdered Len?"

She shook her head. "I had my suspicions, but they couldn't prove anything."

Lily touched her shoulder. "I'm so sorry," she said. "And thank you for your advice. You are much wiser than my mother."

• • •

SHE WENT BACK UP TO HER room and decided to dress anyway. Then she sat up on the bed with a book. She'd nearly fallen asleep when she heard the clop of horses. She ran to the window as Michael jumped down from a carriage. She watched him walk slowly up the path to the wooden stairs. His gait was slow, and his eyes looked downward. He hesitated before reaching for the brass knocker. Lily pounded on the window, and he smiled. She blew a kiss and ran to the dressing table, pinning up her dark braids. Then she grabbed her hat and ran to the stairs, still holding it in her hand. She stopped at the top of the stairs.

Miss Parker answered the door. "Good morning, young man. What can we do for you today?" Lily knew her mother must be right there too or within hearing distance.

"I'm here to pick up Lily, Ma'am." Michael was dressed in a suit and held his hat in his hand.

Lily's mother rushed between them, her arms crossed firmly in front of her. "Where are you taking my daughter?"

Lily came skipping down the stairs, her cheeks flushed with

excitement. Michael smiled at Lily as he answered her mother's question. "A friend of my father's has an art gallery just to the North of Worcester. It's quite a place with some originals from The Hudson Valley School." He looked at Lily. "I'd like to make a day of it and get something to eat in the city. I know it's not what we planned, but a picnic is out of the question."

"It sounds charming," Lily said. "So cosmopolitan. Mother was just telling me the other day that I should expand my horizons and learn about new things. Weren't you, mother?"

Lily had put her hat on and was tying it under her chin. She went to the coat rack and put on a heavy woolen shawl. Mrs. Chapman stared at Michael as they were alone for a few minutes.

"Exactly where is this gallery you're talking my daughter to? I'll need the address, the name of the owner."

"It's at 226 Salem Street. The owners are McGregor and Winston." He handed her a card.

The name Winston jogged her memory, but she was not sure why. A little troubled, her mind wandered away from the confrontation. When Lily came back, Michael opened the door and took her arm.

"I want her home early," her mother shouted as they walked down the stairs

"Yes, Mam," Michael said. "I'll have your daughter home by nightfall."

Lily stopped at the bottom of the stairs. "Goodbye, Mother. I won't stay out too long."

"Good day," her mother said. "I hope Abagail is not too disappointed that you are out when she comes home to see you." She slammed the door.

Chapter 5

MRS. TEMPLE FELT DREARY EVEN though the weather had turned, and it was a fine spring day. She was not quite feeling herself. She wasn't sure what it was, but sometimes she felt premonitions of a sort. She was trying to untangle the unease of her mind as she pushed the bakery door open and sat down at the table, not even calling out to her friend.

Mrs. Cunningham heard the bell on the door and came out from the back with coffee. "What is it, Edith? Are you alright"?

Mrs. Temple opened her mouth to speak, and then she stopped.

Mrs. Cunningham put a cup of black coffee down in front of her. "Are you alright, Edith?"

She seemed to snap out of it and waved her hand as if sending her thoughts away. "I've just had this funny feeling all morning. I can't explain it. Kind of dreary and uneasy, like something big is going to happen."

"Are you worried about you husband or children?"

Mrs. Temple took a small bite of a muffin. She shook her head. "Not really, just feel like I'm missing something, like something is amiss. I've felt off since I got up this morning."

Mrs. Cunningham touched her hand. "We all have our moods now and then."

"You're quite right. We all have our off days." She shook her head, unable to dispel her sense of doom. "This town is changing," she said.

"That it is," Mrs. Cunningham commiserated. "Be it for better or worse."

"Anything new?" Mrs. Temple asked.

"Well, believe it or not, all the maids were in yesterday—and all at the same time. They were having some kind of meeting. There's a new girl; Kathleen, I think, is her name. She was talking to them all about going to the suffrage meetings in Worcester."

Mrs. Temple looked down into her cup. "Stirring up trouble is what it sounds like. Olive and Daisy better not let Mr. Sawyer get wind of it. Everyone knows how he feels about all that."

"Well Olive didn't say much. Daisy seemed very keen on it all."

"Oh, I'm sure she did."

• • •

LILY HELD ON TO the top of her hat till they reached the carriage; then Michael lifted her up and inside. He was a bit wetter than Lily as he climbed in beside her. The horse and driver were covered in rain blankets.

She was glad they were going to the city. It would give them a sense of freedom that they didn't have here. Her mother was right. The town they lived in was so small. Today, they could be themselves, away from the eyes of their families and neighbors.

"I knew you would come," Lily said, looking up at Michael. "I don't know what I would have done if you hadn't." It felt like they were in a world of their own with the rain dripping on the roof and the steady clomp of the horse's hooves.

Michael took her hands, which were clasped on her lap, into his. "I wouldn't disappoint you like that."

"I had an argument with my mother this morning. She insisted you wouldn't come."

"Let's try to forget about our parents for today. My father's coming down on me, too. Says I'm lazy and childish–says I need to be more of a man. It's funny, really because he's the one who wants me to stay a child." Michael sat up, mocking his father's words. "'I demand obedience.' He's upset because he's losing power over me." He looked down and sighed.

"That's exactly how my mother is. She doesn't want me to grow up."

Michael shook his head. "Here we are, both talking about our parents again. He put his arm around Lily's shoulder, and they kissed. "I'm glad it was raining and we had to take a covered carriage."

They stopped at a bridge to let other vehicles pass. She looked around. Even in April, she still saw a few patches of snow. She watched a few squirrels skittering up trees as she gazed into the deep wood. She couldn't wait until the trees blossomed with the beautiful light green color of new leaves. Wildflowers would cover the grass soon, and the oak and ash trees would be lush and full. It would be a relief to see life again after the barren landscape winter had left. They could have a picnic then.

"A penny." Michael's head cocked to one side.

"I was just thinking what a nice summer we'll have together—picnics in the long grass with buttercups swaying in the warm breeze."

"Sounds romantic, but don't forget the ants and grasshoppers."

"Oh, Michael, stop it."

"It's a long ride. I was afraid you had fallen asleep on me."

It did seem kind of like a dream to Lily, a waking dream. "It would have been faster if we hadn't gotten behind that wagon of hay. Why would they be moving that around in this weather?" she asked.

"It must have been left over from last year."

"We're lucky the horse didn't decide it was his dinner."

As they entered the city, she saw more people walking—people hurrying with long coats pulled up over their heads in the rain. They passed a mill, a long brick building with dozens of small, square windows. It was larger than the ones in Stonebridge. Across the street were mill houses. A few children peered out of windows. Lily saw a little girl with a torn, dirty dress standing, crying in the pouring rain. Someone seemed to be shouting at her through an open window. The mill village seemed to go on for a long time, and Lily was glad the workers in Stonebridge weren't treated like this. Michaels's father was a slave driver, but he saw to it that their families were taken care of.

"I imagine you haven't been here for a while, have you?" Michael asked. "It's changed a lot."

"We used to go shopping here, but now mother usually takes us to a dressmaker in town."

"They might be better off with unions here in the city like up in Lowell. It's a hard choice. If the worker's strike, their families starve so they're caught in a tie that binds both ways. There's talk of organizing at my father's plant. He's all up in arms about it, but I'm not sure it would be a bad thing."

Lily let go of Michael's arm and looked up. "Your father treats his workers fairly. I mean, he yells and complains, but. . . I don't know. Is there really a need for unions if the workers are paid enough and treated fairly?"

"He wields a lot of power over them. He yells and belittles. It takes away their dignity."

They were coming to the shops where traffic was heavier. There were a few horseless carriages and some wagons, but mostly covered horse-drawn like their own. Michael noticed Lily watching two ladies stepping down from a carriage, opening their umbrellas and entering a sweets shop.

He put his hand out the window and tapped the roof, signaling the driver to stop. "Wait here a minute," he said to the driver. Then he went into the shop.

Lily watched people hurrying by with their purchases. Two young girls passed by under one umbrella, walking arm in arm. The hem of one of their dresses was down and trailing on the wet sidewalk, but they didn't seem to notice anything as they chattered and giggled away. Another woman went by with packages piled almost to her nose. A gentleman came along behind her and held an umbrella high over her head and took a few of the packages. Michael came back, kissed her on the lips, and handed her a heart-shaped box with a bow.

"Since we missed Valentine's day," he said.

She undid the bow slowly, embarrassed to have been kissed in such a public place. She was sure the two young girls were watching and giggling. "Thank you, Michael." She lifted the box up and offered him a chocolate. "You know, I'll always be your valentine." He took the chocolate and signaled for the driver to go on.

They rode on for a while, Michael pointing out buildings to her.

"That's the new University of Mr. Clark's. There's some controversy about it, my father said, because he wants it to be for everyone, and they want to keep it only for graduate study. There's the Boston Store."

"I've been there," Lily said. "Mother used to take us there to get our Easter dresses."

They passed the Old City Hall and the new one being built.

"It's so amazing all the building that's going up here," Michael said. "The new city hall was designed by Peabody and Sterns." He moved closer and took Lily's hand. "I hope to work for them someday," he said. "I want to be an architect."

She looked up, startled. "I thought you would take over your father's business. Isn't that why you went to college?"

"Well, I suppose that's what he wants, but really, I want something different." He moved closer and whispered, "The walls have ears—well, in this case, our driver. I've been taking drafting lessons from a team of architects in the city. It's our secret." Then, he said, "My father doesn't even know. It's so exciting. I've wanted to talk about it with you for so long."

"Oh, Michael, won't he be furious when he finds out?"

"I'm thinking of bringing it up to him as a hobby, just so he'll get used to the idea." They passed mechanics hall and then the State Mutual building. "See that, that's the first steel framed skyscraper in this city."

They turned and headed north past another brick building that looked like an auditorium advertising dancers and speakers. It looked deserted this morning, just a few people hanging out on the stairs. Lily supposed it would be very lively come evening. The black smoke from the mills didn't carry this far. They were getting further and further away to a different section of the city.

"I've been to some pretty wild dances here on Saturday nights," Michael said.

"My mother would never let me go there, but I wouldn't mind, as long as I had a chaperone." She took his arm and rested her head against his shoulder. "Will you take me some sometime?"

"I guess I could. Maybe we'll go this summer."

The carriage continued north then turned a corner off the main street to a narrow lane that went up a steep hill.

"We're on Salem Street now," he said. "The art gallery is just over this hill."

The carriage pulled into a narrow driveway surrounded on both sides by tall trees. They passed a sign that said *Macgregor and Winston Fine Art Gallery*. Then they climbed another steep hill, and as they turned a corner, Lily could see the most splendid mansion at the top surrounded by what looked like miles of lawns and gardens going all around and into the back.

"Sometimes they have special exhibits on the lawn on nice days. I used to come here with my father when I was a little boy. Never looked at the paintings—just ran around the lawns."

They were approaching a long row of posts for the horses.

"I didn't know your father was interested in art."

"I think my father might surprise a lot of people, but he doesn't let anyone get close to him. There really is a person there under all that sternness."

Michael jumped down, nodded to the driver, and helped Lily disembark. The rain had almost stopped, but it was still very overcast. They walked arm and arm toward a massive double door with brass knockers on each side.

"Your mother must know what kind of man he really is," Lily said.

"He keeps a distance, even with her. Art is one of his passions. It's funny, though. He doesn't want anyone to know. You know how he is with his rants about working hard for his money and how it wasn't just handed to him. Well, he feels funny, I think, about the arts—as if it's pretentious. Silly really, that he won't admit to the world that he actually is a cultured person. That's why the gallery is special to me; it's one of the few things we really share, besides our love for the horses."

Michael struck the door with the brass knocker. It didn't take long for someone to come to the door, dressed in a formal suit, to usher them in.

"Young Mr. Sawyer, we haven't seen you in quite some time. How's your father keeping these days?"

"My father's doing well, thank you." Michael took Lily's shawl from her shoulders. "I'd like to introduce you to Lily Chapman, Mr. Winston, a very special friend of mine."

"Ah, yes, the young lady. How do you do Miss Chapman? I think I know the name. Your father and I have had some business transactions. Edward Chapman? Oh, are you Mary Chapman's daughter?"

"Yes, Edward is my father." She smiled, pleased that someone from a place like this knew her family. "We live in Stonebridge, quite near the Sawyers."

They were in an entryway with a very high ceiling. Michael brought Lily's hat and shawl to a rack in the corner.

"Hmm, I thought I'd heard the Sawyer and Chapman men were rivals at one time. Your families have crossed before? There were some entanglements?"

Lily was taken aback. Did he mean to make her uncomfortable? "Oh no," she said and laughed as Michael came over to save her. "I mean we've always known each other because we live in the same town, but until recently, when Michael and I started courting, there has really not been a lot of contact."

"Pardon me. I must be mixing up the names. You know how rumors are?"

Lily knit her brow. He seemed a rather peculiar man, questioning her like this.

"Is he boring you with our family history? He and my father have known each other for a long time."

"Yes, indeed. I know everything about your father, though we haven't seen each other in a long time."

Something about the man continued to make Lily uneasy. His pallid skin and the long, formal suit made him look like a funeral director, and his smile, though always there, wasn't a happy or a cheerful one. He looked at her with a curious eye, as if he knew something that she did not.

"Step this way into the main gallery," he said as they walked toward another set of double doors that were open. "You'll find we've acquired a number of new paintings, and please, help yourself to the champagne and cheese on the tables."

It was understood between him and Michael that he would mail out a bill if he did not make a purchase today. They had to have some income to maintain the gallery.

The room they entered was long and wide with a high ceiling. At the other end of the room, Lily saw an archway with a red velvet curtain draped from the top. Smaller, special galleries lay beyond that archway, Michael told her, and they would see it later. Pictures hung everywhere—gilt frames holding landscapes seascapes and portraits.

The portraits were of less interest to lily because *what's the use*, she thought, *of staring at people I don't even know*. The landscapes caught her attention, even from far away. She wondered if they were from the Hudson River School. There were chairs here and there and couches where a few people sat speaking in whispers and viewing the pictures from far away. She was so glad Mr. Winston had finally left them alone. He was greeting more guests so they had a breather from him. People stood here and there for a closer or longer view. One man stood close by a picture with his monocle, examining every last detail and dab of color. Lily stood at the door for a minute not entering, just taking it all in.

Michael pointed to a corner of the room where a table was set up, and a medium-sized balding man chatted with an elderly couple. "That's Mr. McGregor over there by the table pouring champagne," Michael said.

"He so different looking from Mr. Winston," Lily whispered moving closer to Michael. "Are they related or just business partners? Do they live on the premises?"

"They're just business partners and, well, sort-of related. They were married to sisters. They're both widowers now."

"Oh, that's odd."

"Not too odd. The sisters were taking a vacation on a steamship that went down. Most of the passengers drowned."

Lily shivered. "Not too odd, I guess, then." She took Michael's arm, and they walked into the gallery together. He brought her to the landscapes she'd been admiring from far away.

"That one is from the Hudson River School I was telling you about."

Lily stared for a long time at a painting of a waterfall coming down craggy mountains and was fascinated by the wildness and freedom in these scenes. She thought of Nanna Parker, about her falling asleep outside in the grass next to her beloved, and Lily decided she liked the wild, rambling countryside in this land rather than the tame, manicured look of Europe. A trip out west, she thought, might interest her.

"That is the most magnificent priceless piece in the gallery." Mr. Winston was back with two glasses of champagne. He had snuck up from behind and startled them.

"Thank you," she said when he handed her one and gave the other to Michael. "It's my favorite so far."

He looked at Michael. Then back at Lily. "This one," he said, "has a keen eye for beauty." He bowed and left, called over to the table by Mr. MacGregor.

Lily moved closer to Michael. "Does he always sneak up on people like that?"

Michael laughed. "He likes to be melodramatic. I'm used to it, I guess, so it doesn't bother me."

They went over to a table where there were sandwiches, as well as cheese and fruit. This probably meant they wouldn't stop on the way home. Lily was a little disappointed, though she'd rather be home early and not have her mother harping on them again.

They stayed at the gallery for another hour or so and headed back mid-afternoon. The weather had cleared up but was still cold, and the sun was trying to come out. Lily wrapped the woolen shawl around her shoulders. Michael helped her up and into the carriage.

"Let's just go," she said. "Mother will be expecting us at by at least five-thirty or six, and I should spend the evening with Abagail. I do miss her."

So, they didn't stop but rode on quietly, savoring the return journey. Turning the corner onto Lily's street, they heard violin music in the distance.

"That's Abby," she said, and she didn't wait for Michael to help but jumped down from the carriage and followed the music to the backyard where Abagail was playing in the garden. Abagail turned around and smiled at them. "Oh, Abby, I'm so happy to see you." She ran to her sister who had gotten up now and walked toward them with the violin still in one hand.

"Hi," she said and gave Lily a kiss on the cheek. She smiled at Michael, a genuine full smile. "How have you been?" she asked, looking from one to the other.

"We went to an art gallery in the city, Abby. You should have seen some of the landscapes."

Michael interrupted before they got further into conversation. "I have to get home by supper before they send the dogs out searching for me."

"I'll walk with you to the front. Be right back, Abby. I have so much to tell you. Mother is driving me crazy. Where is she anyway? I thought she'd come running out here as soon as she saw Michael."

"I don't know." Abagail picked up the violin and was about to play again. Then she put it down and looked puzzled. "She said she had some business to take care of and left in a hurry. I thought it was kind of strange, but she said she wouldn't be long."

"Oh, well, I'll be right back. We can talk then."

Lily and Michael went around to the front of the house and said their goodbyes. She waved until he was out of sight and walked quickly back. It felt good to be on her feet after sitting in the carriage for so long. She felt a little tired though—and hungry. The afternoon was waning, and she heard the music again before she saw Abagail sitting on the bench surrounded by fruit trees. Lily, struck pensive by the music, stared out into the backwoods. Abigail had not noticed Lily's return, she stopped playing and looked around when she sensed there was a person nearby.

"Lily, you startled me, standing there so quietly."

"I'm sorry. I didn't mean to. I was just listening to the music. I never heard that piece before."

"It's one I just learned, but it's getting cold out here; let's go inside."

"Stay out here for a few more minutes with me, please?" Lily sat down on the bench next to her sister. "Have you ever been in love, Abby? I know Mother is upset about it, but I do love Michael. He's the sweetest person. He reminds me of father. We had so much fun today. I don't mean to put you in the middle. It's just that I'm trying to understand what mother has against him."

"She talked to me already about you and Michael. Something is troubling her, but she's evasive when I ask her why. I do know she thinks you're too young."

"I'm almost eighteen."

"Not until fall."

Lily turned her head away and looked down.

"I'm more concerned about Mother. How is she, Lily? Father says she's taking medicine to help her sleep."

"Everyone's worried about Mother, but I think she's just acting like this to get her own way. She's making life miserable for me. I know she's our mother, and I love her and all, but Abby, you don't have to live with her every day. She's unhappy, and she wants everyone else to be as well."

"She mentioned a trip to Europe. That sounds exciting."

"She just wants to get me away from Michael. I can't believe you're taking her side." Lily got up and started walking toward the house. "Nobody in this family understands. Sometimes it seems like I don't even belong here."

Abagail caught up with her. "Lily, come on. I understand. I have suiters, too. I see what Mother is saying, though. You really haven't seen much of the world yet. You were fascinated by the gallery; think of what it would be like to visit those places, and you must go to college. It really is not like living at home. I have a lot of freedom, and Mother isn't there looking over my shoulder."

"I'd rather be traveling with Michael than with Mother. He's the one who makes it all special. I love him, Abby."

Abagail sighed with the experience of someone barely a year older. "I've felt that way too, but he's the first one, Lily. They'll be others."

Lily stopped and looked right at her sister. "No, Abby, there won't be." They walked through the door in silence, and Lily closed it behind them with a thud.

Mrs. Chapman arrived home as Lily, Abagail, and Mr. Chapman were already eating dinner. Edward looked up as she came into the room. He rose and pulled out a chair for his wife. "What kept you so long? We were beginning to worry."

Mrs. Chapman looked down at the floor and walked to her seat. "I told you I had some business to take care of."

"One doesn't generally do business on a Saturday."

"Just women's business, Edward. You wouldn't really be interested. I'm glad to be home at last to spend the evening alone with my family." She looked over at both her daughters and smiled, put a chicken dumpling on her plate, and tried to follow the conversation as it turned quickly to Abagail and how things were going at College.

She stayed quiet, her mind still on the evening's business, as she looked at Lily across the table. She didn't want to hurt her daughter, but she had spoken today with John Sawyer, had gone to meet him secretly before Michael and Lily got back. He'd assured her he had a plan to get Michael's attention away from Lily. She had told him about the trip to Europe she was planning with her daughter for the summer. yet, she didn't feel entirely reassured about the plan. She'd just have to wait and see what happened.

• • •

JOHN SAWYER CALLED Michael into his study after supper. He offered his son a glass of brandy and poured one for himself.

"We're having a guest in our house for a while, a lovely young lady about your age from Roanoke, a niece of Mr. Winston."

"When did this all come up? I saw Mr. Winston at the gallery today, and I was going to tell you he sends his regards, but he said he hadn't seen you for years."

"I know. We spoke after he saw you. He's in a bit of a dilemma with his sister insisting that his niece come up north for the summer. It wouldn't be proper for her to stay with two middle-aged gentlemen. He's looking for a family for her to stay with."

"Well, that sounds interesting, good, I guess. Are you asking for my permission? What does it have to do with me?"

Sawyer poured himself another brandy. "Most of the burden of entertaining will be on your mother of course, but," he said, looking straight at Michael, "you will be expected to take her, of course, out with the summer crowd to social events and what not."

"That's out of the question. You know Lily and I are going together. I'll introduce her to all my friends, of course. I'm sure she won't be without dates, but I can't be her escort."

Sawyer took a long gulp of brandy and put his empty glass on the table. "I'm sorry Michael, but we all have to do the best we can to make her feel comfortable. It's all been arranged. I've promised Mr. Winston. You may change your mind when you meet her. I'm told she's quite a beauty."

Michael stood and slammed his empty glass on the desk. "I will not be her escort, Father. I will pick her up at the station, but I will fix her up with one of my friends. You knew I was courting Lily when you spoke to Mr. Winston." He walked toward the door.

"Get back here. We're not finished," Sawyer shouted, but Michael was almost to the door. John Sawyer summoned all his control. Hadn't Mary warned him that Michael would have to be convinced—not bullied. He spoke in a softer voice, and Michael turned around, surprised.

"All I ask is that you give it a try."

"I'll pick her up at the station," Michael said and walked out the door.

Strange, Michael thought, that Mr. Winston, who hadn't seen his father in years, suddenly wanted his niece to stay with the Sawyers, but in some ways, he supposed, it made sense. She would be new to the area, of course, and wouldn't know a soul, and those two middle-aged men were only concerned with gallery business and would not be in tune with the social mores of the younger generation. Maybe she and Lily could be friends, but he just couldn't be the one to show her around. His heart was with Lily. He could easily fix her up with one of his friends for double dates. *Maybe Abe Whittier*, he thought. They might make a good couple. He *was* curious to see what she would be like. It might be good too for his mother to have a young woman in the house. His father would allow her to go out more and would be more forthcoming with the money.

He worried about how Lily would take it. He should let her know about this situation right away rather than through gossip—or the papers. If she was that high society, which she might be with Winston for an uncle, her visit north might be a big deal with the local papers. He had to let her know before the weekend.

● ● ●

ON TUESDAY EVENING, Michael's carriage pulled up to the Chapman's door. Lily and Michael had only seen each other briefly for the last few days. He was busy with work and she with her classes. Lily was in the parlor arranging and re-arranging the chairs and the tea things. Michael had said he had something to talk to her about, and this was the first time they arranged a date on a weekday. She hadn't been able to eat much at lunchtime and had no idea why her mother had been glaring at her annoyingly all morning and was now giving her privacy with Michael.

She heard the horses outside and went to the window, pulled the curtains aside just a little, and saw Michael Jump down from the carriage. Then he disappeared, and she heard the brass knocker.

Nana Parker answered the door and escorted Michael into the parlor; then she left the room.

"How are you this evening, Lily?"

"I'm fine, "she said a little taken aback. He was acting very formal. He sat down next to her on the couch, fidgeting with a lace doily and looking down. "Would you like some tea?" Lily began to pour a cup. She tried to catch his eye. *He still has his coat on,* she thought.

He shook his head. "No, thank you. I can't stay long."

It's bad news, she thought. She knew he wouldn't come during the week unless something was wrong.

He turned and put his arm on the back of the couch around her shoulders. She leaned toward him, and he stroked her hair with his fingertips. He was trying to choose his words carefully so she wouldn't misunderstand.

"There's a little hitch in our weekend plans," he said. "We won't be able to see each other on Saturday. Some family obligations I have to attend to." She looked up at him, surprised but not angry. "I'd rather be with you, though," he said and kissed her softly.

She kept an eye out for her mother at the door.

"We're having a house guest for a while," he said. "I'm to pick them up at the station; then we're having a big dinner party Saturday night. I would invite you. I wanted to, but it's just family."

Lily moved away and looked at Michael's face. He avoided her eyes. "Stop being so mysterious," she said. "Who is it, a cousin?"

"I'm not being mysterious," Michael snapped at Lily, instantly regretting it. She started to get up, and he rose too taking her hand. "It's a niece. . . of Mr. Winston's, coming up from the south. I guess my father owes Mr. Winston a favor, so he's letting her stay with us."

"I thought your father and Mr. Winston hadn't spoken in years."

"They hadn't until last weekend. I'm as surprised as you are."

Lily sat down for a few minutes, thinking about what he had said. She hesitated before asking more questions, but she wanted to know. "How old is she?"

"I don't know, really. I didn't ask"

"She must be out of high school if she's coming up at this time of year."

"I think she is out of high school."

"Why is she coming here?"

Michael shrugged "Maybe to look at colleges in New England?"

Or to look for a husband, Lily thought, and suddenly, she couldn't keep up the façade any longer. She walked away, her back to Michael and her head down. He followed her to a window and put his arm around her shoulders.

"They're doing this Michael—your father and my mother, to try to keep us apart."

"No, Lily, nothing is going to keep us apart. Even if that is what they want, it won't work. This girl, she'll just be around, and I already told my father I'm going to fix her up with one of my friends." He turned her around, and they held each other. "Don't be sad," he whispered in her ear. "They can't change the way we feel about each other. No matter how they try. You're the girl for me, forever, Lily, the only one for me."

He could feel her shaking and kissed the top of her head.

"I'm sorry, Michael, I do trust you. I just wish they would accept our love."

"Maybe I can get away this Sunday. We could go for a walk at sunset."

"That sounds wonderful, Michael. I'm sorry for acting so childish. I just didn't know what you meant at first."

Lily saw him to the door, and they kissed goodbye. She watched his carriage drive away. Why did this have to happen now? When everything was going so well between them? She knew she had to trust that Michael's feelings were as strong as hers but, right now, it seemed like one of the hardest things to do. She didn't like Mr. Winston, and she knew she wouldn't like his niece. She went back to the parlor, sat down on the sofa, and took up some needlework but couldn't concentrate. His presence was still in the room, his smell, the feel of his skin, his lips. Her mother came into the parlor with a smug look and two glasses of sherry.

"You look tired." She offered and handed her a sherry. "Take it. It will help you relax."

Lily looked at her mother angry and hurt. "You were listening? You planned this, didn't you? You and old man Sawyer, this was the business you had last weekend."

"For heaven's sake, Lily, calm down. I don't know what you're talking about."

"Please leave me alone." Lily *had* calmed down. She looked at her mother, and in a voice full of anger, but just above a whisper, she said, "Leave me alone, Mother. I want to be alone."

Her mother left.

It doesn't matter what they do, she thought. *Michael has declared his love for me. We've declared our love for each other, and nothing her mother or Sawyer did could change that.*

Lily sat back on the couch for what seemed like hours, sobbing in the darkened room. Her mother looked in from time to time but did not dare disturb her.

Chapter 6

"YOO-HOO," MRS. TEMPLE CALLED as she entered the bakery early Monday morning. Mrs. Cunningham came out with the napkins, and Mrs. Temple set the sugar out on each table. "What a dreadful weekend," Mrs. Temple said. "Thank goodness the weather has turned."

Mrs. Cunningham nodded. She touched Mrs. Temple on the shoulder as she went by to get the coffee. "Daisy was in very early," she said. "You won't believe the news from the Sawyers."

Mrs. Temple sat down at their table when Mrs. Cunningham came around with the coffee. She had brought out special muffins for them.

Mrs. Cunningham put in two sugars and stirred while Mrs. Temple waited as patiently as she could to hear the news. Mrs. Cunningham took a sip of coffee and put her cup down on the table. "The Sawyers are having a visitor."

"Oh?"

"A young lady," she said, "from Virginia."

"A relative?"

"Daisy doesn't think so."

"How old is this young lady?"

"Well," Mrs. Cunningham said, looking down at her coffee and then out the window, savoring the best part. "From what she's heard, just about Michael's age."

Mrs. Temple was taken aback. "Isn't that unusual? Not a relative, you say?"

"Daisy doesn't think so."

"Mr. Sawyer must be fuming. He's so concerned about appearances."

Mrs. Cunningham had saved the best for last. "He's the one who set it up."

● ● ●

ON SATURDAY, Michael loosened his tie as he waited outside the train station. It had turned unusually warm for April, and his suitcoat, which he had already removed, lay beside him on the bench. He started to grab his watch chain to check the time when he heard the train whistle in the distance; the 12:15 was right on schedule. He picked up his suitcoat and squinted in the distance, then looked down at the photograph his father had given him. It was a group picture, probably from school. He hoped he would recognize her; the picture wasn't very clear. He watched the train pull into the station and searched the windows for a face that matched the photograph, loosening his tie again.

The train stopped and people stepped down. He stood among the crowd waiting. Was she lost in the crowd? A mass of passengers hurried out amidst hand waving and shouts in the excitement of re-unions.

Then he spotted her, the last one to get off. She wore a wide skirt with a bustle the girls didn't wear up here anymore, except to formal dances. It must have been impossible to maneuver down the aisle of a small train. She stood still for a minute, opened her parasol, and looked at a photograph in her hand. Then she smiled and waved at Michael. He smiled back, and she waited for him to come to her.

"Louisa Davis?" He held out his hand for her to shake. "Michael Sawyer. How do you do?" He hadn't noticed she held a parasol in her right hand. She quickly moved the parasol to the other hand.

"Pleased to make your acquaintance," she said as she shook his hand very gently, more of a touch than a shake. She deftly moved the parasol back to her right hand.

"I have a carriage waiting to take you to my parent's house. You can rest for a while; then we're having a small family gathering later to introduce you to everyone."

"That sounds lovely. I would like to rest for a while. It seemed I was forever on that train. Traveling makes me tired."

She was tall, just a few inches shorter than Michael, but she seemed, despite the height, more delicate than the girls from the North. Her clothing and manner were different from what Michael was used to. She wore a long, lace-bordered dress, with a pattern of soft blue and yellow flowers that came to a wide hoop at the bottom, and on her feet were high-heeled black boots with pointy toes. Her hair was dark blonde and tied in braided buns on both sides of her head. Her nose was long and slender like her body, and she had a soft shade of blue painted on her eyelids. Her cheeks were colored a pale pink. Her skin, beneath the makeup, was very pale. A few blonde curls fell on her forehead as she looked up at Michael and smiled. He took her gloved hand and escorted her to the carriage. They rode in silence for a long time. Michael tried to think of something, anything, to say.

"I hope you'll like it here. It must be very different from your home."

"I'm sure I will after I have a rest. The journey's taken a lot out of me. I must look just dreadful."

"Oh, no, you look beautiful, really, all dressed up and everything . . ."

"Why, thank you. What a fine gentleman. I'm glad to see they have them up north too." She looked up at Michael from under the brim of her silk hat. Her green eyes met his then looked down.

Michael, embarrassed, retreated into himself again. He was relieved they were turning onto his own street. When they had stopped, he helped Louisa down, and she opened her parasol once more.

Mrs. Sawyer stood at the front door. "Come in, dear. How are you? Welcome to our home." She put one arm around Louisa's shoulders. We have some lunch set up here for you to nibble on, or you might want to just go upstairs and rest. You must be tired. I'll show you your room."

Michael went out for the luggage. He was glad to see his mother so excited about having company. The celebration tonight was the first party his father had allowed in the house for years. There was something odd about his father agreeing to all this, but at least it would make his mother happy for a while. He was back with the suitcases and started up the stairs, but Mrs. Sawyer came out to the landing and waved him back down.

"Leave them at the bottom for now," she whispered. "You can bring them up later. The poor girl's tired. She's going to rest a while." She looked at Michael as he came down the stairs. "I hope everything goes well tonight."

"It'll be fine, mother. I know Father doesn't allow it much, but you've always been a great hostess."

"But it's been such a long time, and you know your father. I hope he doesn't act all put out and gruff."

"He's the one who arranged it all. Stop worrying, Mother; everything will be fine."

Despite Michael's reassurances, he could see his mother was still nervous. They gave the parlor a once-over together. Daisy had spent the entire afternoon cleaning. It was spotless. They had even taken down the heavy winter drapes a little early this year and put up light airy ones for summer.

There were tables on either side of the sofa set with bowls of nuts and raisins. The love seat in the corner had a long, low table in front of it. A large platter was on this table filled with small pieces of meat and cheese with toothpicks in them. There were four matching stuffed chairs in the room, and the sofa was set to the side of the fireplace. Everything looked ready.

Michael assured his mother again and went with her to count table settings. Besides Mr. and Mrs. Sawyer and Michael, there would be his Aunt Mildred, her husband, Cousin Stanley with his new wife, his mother's sister, Rebecca, with her young daughter, Josephine, Louisa, Mr. Winston, and Mr. MacGregor.

"You see, Mother," he said. "An even dozen."

They were both startled when the doorbell rang. Michael looked at his watch. It was twenty minutes early. Olive rushed to answer it, and there at the door, stood Mr. Winston impeccably dressed, as usual; he handed his hat to Olive and straightened his hair in the hallway mirror.

"Welcome to our home," Mrs. Sawyer said. "It's so nice to see you again. Louisa arrived safely, and she's resting upstairs."

Mr. Winston smiled at her. He wanted to see his niece before the party started and also wanted to speak with Sawyer alone. He took her hand, raised it to his lips, and placed on it a small, dry kiss. His long, thin fingers were nearly as dedicate as hers.

"Thank you for opening your home to my niece. Your hospitality is extraordinary. I would like to speak with her before the party. How long will she be resting?"

"She may be up and getting ready. I'll see how she's doing." They walked through the front room, past the stairs and into the parlor. "You wait here. I'll just be a minute."

Mrs. Sawyer went upstairs while Mr. Winston sat alone in the parlor. He sat down on the edge of the sofa, crossed his long legs, and took a handful of nuts and raisins, eating them one at a time. Mrs. Sawyer passed her husband upstairs in the hallway. He was dressed in a suit with a vest and a long dinner jacket. She hadn't seen him look so distinguished in a long time, probably since they were married. "Can you stay with our guest in the parlor, John? I have to help Louisa."

He muttered something at her and flew quickly down the stairs.

Mrs. Sawyer gave a knock on Louisa's door then poked her head in. She was pinning up her hair and looked at Mrs. Chapman in the mirror. "How are you feeling? Rested up, I hope."

She turned around. "Yes, thank you. I feel better now, and I'm almost ready." She waved Mrs. Sawyer in. "I know the guests are arriving, but I still have to put a little color on my face."

"Don't worry, dear. It's stylish for the guest of honor to be a little late. That way, you'll make a grand entrance."

Mrs. Sawyer watched Louisa as she put two fingers into a glass jar and took out a glob of white cream. Not having daughters, she didn't know the fashions of the day. Louisa put a glob into the palm of her left hand, smoothed it with the fingertips of her right hand, finally dotting it onto her forehead, nose, cheeks, and chin. Then she massaged it with both hands into her skin. Mrs. Sawyer realized she was staring at the girl and felt rude. "Is there anything I can help you with?"

"No, thank you. I'm nearly finished."

She took a jar of light brown cream and put some on her eyelids. The effect was stunning in contrast to the lavender dress she wore with lace around the collar. She got up and smiled at Mrs. Sawyer, crinkling up her long, thin nose.

"I'm ready now," she said.

"Oh, I almost forgot why I came up. Your uncle would like to see you alone for a few minutes before the party. I'll send him up."

When she entered the parlor, it looked as if all the guests had arrived. She took a quick count. Mr. MacGregor was the only one missing. He must have been held up at the gallery. She saw Winston in the corner talking to her husband and approached them.

"Excuse me, but Louisa is ready. She's waiting for you upstairs. You could visit with her now then escort her down."

Mr. Sawyer seemed angry with the interruption.

"We'll talk later," Mr. Winston said to Sawyer as he got up and walked toward the stairs.

Most of the guests were still standing around in the middle of the parlor. Mrs. Sawyer went over and broke up the circle. "Please sit down, everyone, and be comfortable. Dinner will be ready in about a half hour, so we have time to relax first."

Michael sat on the corner of the love seat, talking with Cousin Stanley and his new bride. He was clowning around offering them a piece of cheese with toothpicks he had stuck all over it. Mrs. Sawyer looked around to make sure all the bowls were still filled. She spotted her sister on the couch and realized these social occasions must still be hard for Rebecca, who had lost her husband recently. Her daughter Josephine sat beside her. Mrs. Sawyer went over to talk to them. She squeezed onto the couch and hugged her sister.

"I can't believe that is really little Josephine sitting beside you. Before you know it, she'll be a young woman at the cotillions." Josephine looked down, pleased but embarrassed. "How old are you now, dear?"

"Almost thirteen," she said.

Daisy came in with a tray that had brandy glasses as well as champagne. Mrs. Sawyer looked around. Her husband seemed calmer. He stood by the fire talking with his sister and her husband. There was a knock on the door. Mrs. Sawyer went to answer it herself, knowing Olive was busy helping get dinner ready. Mr. MacGregor hurried in, apologizing for being late.

"That's all right," she assured him. "Dinner isn't quite ready, and the guest of honor hasn't even come down yet."

When the guest of honor had not come down, even when dinner was ready, Mrs. Sawyer began to worry. She didn't want to call everyone to the table until Louisa had entered. She was fretting about whether she should go up and hurry them along when Louisa finally made her entrance.

Everyone was struck by her beauty. Mrs. Sawyer actually thought she heard some gasps as Louisa entered the room. She went over immediately, took her arm, and introduced her to everyone. She wore white lace gloves up to her elbows and carried a purple fan in her left hand.

Dinner was ready, so they quickly moved into the dining room.

An elegant white tablecloth covered the table. Fine china marked each place setting, sparkling beneath the chandelier, and candelabras donned each side of the table. Mrs. Sawyer sat at one end and her husband at the other. Mr. Winston escorted his niece to the chair at the right side of Mrs. Sawyer. Michael sat next to his father on the right. Overhead, the glass chandelier lit up the table so the staff could see as they served. The candles had not yet been lit. There was a fire going in the fireplace. Even though the day had been sunny, there was still a chill when the sun went down. The summer curtains were sheer with bluebirds and red roses.

Many of the guests talked as they were served. Michael remained quiet. Louisa knew he was looking at her from the other end of the table. She pretended she didn't see him and continued to talk to Cousin Stanley's wife. He caught her eye for just one second. He hadn't meant to stare, but she was very, very beautiful. A man in a long, dark suit, employed for the evening, came out and lit the candles. They looked right at each other as the chandelier shut off, and the room filled with dim light and flickering shadows.

The table had gotten a little noisy but was subdued now by the sudden darkness. Most of the light shone on Mr. and Mrs. Sawyer at opposite ends of the table. Mr. Sawyer stood up and raised a glass of champagne.

"Before we start," he said. "I would like to propose a toast to our special guest, Louisa Davis. May she have a wonderful visit up North."

"Here, here!" Everyone drank to Louisa and looked down to the other end of the table where her green eyes gleamed in the candlelight. Then everyone settled down to eat and, between sips of wine, to talk to the person beside them.

Michael remained quiet. He looked into the fire and thought of Lily. He wished she could be here; the evening was so romantic, he wanted to share it with her. Someday, maybe she would be sitting in this dining room with him, but he couldn't imagine his father ever drinking to their health and happiness. He watched the flame die down then suddenly catch and come to life on another log. He forced his eyes to move away from the flames that were hypnotizing him along with the wine, adding to his melancholy. He'd see Lily tomorrow anyway despite his father's plans; he'd visit with Abe Whittier too and arrange an escort for Louisa.

It was a leisurely dinner with the guests at the table for well over an hour. The long-coated man and other servers came in and out, refilling dishes, replenishing wine. The clattering of plates and bowls was heard as the main dishes were taken away. The lights came up again as coffee and teas were brought out in large urns.

"We decided to let you see what you would be eating for dessert," Mr. Sawyer shouted across the table in an unusually jovial voice.

A large dessert cart was wheeled out from the kitchen. The choices were many. Thick, chocolate rum cake, pears dipped in chocolate, strawberry shortcake, apple and cherry tarts, and custard. Olive wheeled it around the table and let everyone pick their own. She seemed to be enjoying herself. She couldn't remember when the room had been so full. Her mood of excitement changed when she got to Michael's place at the table. He seemed so sad in contrast to his father's soaring spirits. She knew he was missing his girl, Lily.

After dessert, Mrs. Sawyer suggested they go back to the parlor. One by one, they dabbed their mouths, put their napkins on the table, and followed her. Mr. Sawyer, his brother-in-law, Mr. Winston, and Mr. MacGregor all went into his study for brandy and cigars. The younger men chose to stay in the parlor with the ladies.

In the dining room, the candles were being blown out, and the last of the dishes were being cleared away and brought into the kitchen. Olive was very quiet as she helped dry the large pots and pans. There was a lot of talk among the servants about this new girl, Louisa. Olive kept her mouth shut, but she had her own ideas.

She rubbed the dish towel heavily around the inside of a deep pot, feeling troubled and uneasy. Michael had seemed so unhappy at dinner. She thought of how peculiar the whole evening had been. It was uncanny that the old man had agreed to let Louisa stay here all summer. That meant they would have to do some entertaining for the entire season. Mr. Winston must have been paying Mr. Sawyer a pretty penny for this little arrangement. It must be the money that had lifted Sawyer's spirits. It had to be money. She finished and put it away under the sink.

All the other servants were talking about the evening, but she didn't feel like talking. Besides, the evening was not over yet, and neither was their work. She was tired of all the commotion and went looking for a place to rest for a while peeking into the parlor first to see if the missus needed anything. Everything seemed in order. Mrs. Sawyer and two other women were dealing out cards and doing their best to recruit a fourth partner. None of the young people seemed interested. Olive decided to go upstairs and tidy up Louisa's room. She could be away from everything and rest there but still look busy if anyone came in.

Stanley and his wife sat on the couch with Josephine. Michael sat on the arm of the couch, and Louisa sat in a chair nearby. They were playing a game called mental telepathy. Stanley told them about the game and was explaining it to everyone.

"It's quite simple, really," he said, "but it can be very interesting, especially in a group like this where we all don't know each other too well. Everyone must think of a certain subject, for instance, a color, and then concentrate deeply on one particular color. The first player must go around the group and figure out what color each person is thinking of. The next player would have another subject to guess. Everyone writes down what they are thinking secretly and reveals it later to see if the mind reader was right."

"But it could be just a matter of chance," Michael said. "It doesn't prove anyone is a mind reader."

"That's why the same player tries to reveal everyone's answer. One or two right answers might be coincidence, but if several are correct, it's different."

Michael shrugged. "You go first, then. Let's see if you can read our minds."

"We need something to write our answers on," Stanley said. Michael went to the card table and took out some paper and pencils; then Stanley began. Okay, everyone," he said. "Think of the capitol of a state. Write it down on your paper and turn the paper over immediately." Stanley put his eyes down, and everyone was busy writing.

"Okay, we're ready," Michael said.

Stanley looked up. "Now I'll go around and guess, but you must think deeply about what you have written. Think deeply about that one thing and try to transmit those thoughts to me. I'll start with you, Michael"

There was silence for several minutes.

"I think I've got it—Hartford Connecticut. That's what you were thinking."

Michael had a strange feeling, but despite his doubts, he held up the paper and showed it to everyone. He wondered if Stanley hadn't actually been watching the movement of his hand as he wrote it. Everyone was surprised, and a nervous giggle came from the other end of the couch.

"He's good at this game," Yvonne said. "He's convinced me he has psychic powers."

Michael refused to be spooked by one good guess. Stanly turned to Yvonne. Now it was her turn to transmit her thoughts. She too closed her eyes, and Stanley looked closely at her. No one said a word.

"Boise, Idaho" he said.

'That's it. That's what I have written down."

Josephine took the paper from Yvonne before she could hold it up. "That *is* it," she cried. "His second answer is right, too." She looked in awe at her older cousin.

They could have talked about it ahead of time, Michael thought.

"Will you read my thoughts, now?" Josephine asked and closed her eyes in concentration.

Stanley looked at her forehead. Everyone was looking from Stanley to Josephine. Even the ladies at the table had stopped their card game and were looking in the direction of the couch.

"My goodness, what kind of crazy things are you teaching my daughter?' Josephine's mother asked.

"Shah." Michael sat forward and put his hand up motioning her to be quiet.

Stanley's mother tapped her on the shoulder and whispered, "It's just a harmless game they play where they try to read each other's minds. It can get interesting, really."

Josephine's mother continued to look on, not really convinced that it was harmless.

"It's coming to me," Stanley said. "I think you wrote down Boulder. Boulder Colorado."

She lifted the paper to show everyone the words Boulder, Colorado.

"How do you do that?" Michael asked. "There's got to be a trick."

"No trick, you want to try it? You might be a psychic, too. Why don't you try reading Louisa's mind? See if you can guess her thoughts."

Everyone looked over at Louisa. She looked down at the piece of paper folded neatly on her lap. She was hoping they had forgotten about her answer; she wasn't used to playing parlor games. In her house, the young men and young women would be in two separate groups. She wondered if her eye makeup was smudged or beginning to fade. Michael felt uncomfortable, too. He'd been trying to avoid her eyes since she had caught him staring at her at the dinner table. She raised her eyes, suddenly, and looked directly at him—a flirtatious, challenging look. Caught up in the game, he looked back at her, ready for the challenge.

"I'll give it a try, but I really don't think I'll be able to read her mind. Maybe I'll make a lucky guess."

Michael stared at Louisa's face. The soft, pale skin over high cheekbones, housed a few freckles, showing even through the makeup. A long slender nose trailed down to delicate lips, then a rounded chin, closed tight in concentration.

"Excuse me for interrupting," Stanley said. "I think you are trying too hard. Just relax and let your thoughts flow freely."

Louisa opened her eyes and nodded at him and then closed them again. She took a deep breath and there was silence for several minutes.

"I can't do it," Michael said. "I tried, but I honestly cannot read another person's thoughts. I can make a guess, but that's all it would be. I'll try Austin, Texas."

Louisa shook her head and held up the paper. Augusta, Maine is what it said.

"See, I told you. It's an interesting game, but I'm no good at this psychic thing."

Everyone sat back, a little more relaxed. Josephine was getting tired of the game and decided she wanted to play cards with the ladies. Michael plopped down on the couch where Josephina had been. Stanley and Yvonne were suddenly in close, deep conversation. Louisa leaned toward Michael.

"That was a gallant attempt," she said, "even if you couldn't read my thoughts." Something about her tone of voice made Michael uneasy. There always seemed to be a challenge behind her words. Why couldn't she just say what was on her mind?

"It's just a game," he said. "I don't really care." He sat forward and looked down, rubbing his hands together. Then Louisa said something that surprised him.

"You look as if you're not concentrating on anything tonight. You look sad."

Michael didn't look up. "Well, you see. I have a girl, and I kind of wish that she was here tonight."

"Oh, I see." Louisa said and turned her head away.

• • •

WHEN JOHN SAWYER came out of the study, he saw Michael and Louisa talking, and he was pleased. The other men piled out behind him, smelling of brandy and cigarettes and took the available chairs. Mildred's husband suggested that they stop the card playing and for someone to get up and play the piano for a while. Daisy came in with a tray of coffee and tea for everyone then brought one of the candelabras into the room and placed it on a table near the piano. The other lights were turned off. Josephine was the first to go up and play a few pieces, and when she got tired, Mildred took over. Her fingers sped over the keys in the candlelight. First, she played a loud, dramatic tune, then a slow haunting piece. Josephine fell asleep, her head resting in her mother's lap. Everyone was listening to the music or talking in hushed voices so no one noticed when Sawyer and Mr. Winston quietly left the room and went upstairs.

Olive had fallen asleep in Louisa's room. The piano music woke her, and she crept to the door and peeked out when she heard footsteps. Mr. Sawyer handed Mr. Winston an envelope and swore him to secrecy. Mr. Winston opened the envelope and counted out several bills. Why was Sawyer paying Winston? She shook her head and stood quietly just inside the door, hoping they would not discover her.

Chapter 7

MRS. TEMPLE ENTERED THE BAKERY still looking piqued as Mrs. Cunningham walked briskly out of the back. She was anxious to spread the day's news and wanted her friend to be more enthusiastic. She set down the coffee, ignoring Mrs. Temple's forlorn expression.

"Olive came early Saturday," she said. "Apparently, the guest has arrived at the Sawyer's home, and she put in a huge order for a party they had on Saturday."

"A party . . . at the Sawyer house? That *is* news."

"And the strangest part is that the old man, again, is the one that wanted it—even invited his wife's relatives."

Mrs. Temple looked out the window. "All these parties and salons in town; soon, we'll be no different than the city. It keeps us in business, I suppose. You, anyway."

"Are sales off again?"

Mrs. Temple shook her head. "You know how it is. The more hoity-toity they get, the more they want to go to dress-makers even for everyday outfits. We might have to bring in a boarder."

"Here, let me warm up your coffee," Mrs. Cunningham said. "I'm sure sales will pick up—it's just with Easter being so late this year." She changed the subject abruptly, hoping to perk up her friend.

"The maids were in here again late on Friday. The new girl they hired at the hotel was with them. She was talking about the suffrage meetings in Worcester, trying to get them interested. Then millworkers were in here after work on Saturday talking about some more trouble in Mill Village. One man was beat up and one still missing. Union Organizers is what they think."

Mrs. Temple shook her head. "I've always been wary of all this talk of organizing. Suffrage, uniting, it all seems to bring nothing but trouble. My Jim says unions are wrong. You don't bite the hand that feeds you. I say let them stay in Worcester and Lowell."

"They're already here," Mrs. Cunningham said. "The man that's missing was staying right here, at the hotel. They said the police had all the rooms on lockdown for a while. They even went to the factory and interviewed some of the men."

"Sawyer couldn't have been happy about that. He's said right out if any of the rebel-rousers were found in his place of work, they'd never see the light of day again."

. . .

ON SATURDAY EVENING, Lily walked in the garden, brooding over her loneliness. She wondered what Michael was doing. She was sure her mother had something to do with this and was so angry when her mother had had the nerve to ask her to go to a gathering with her tonight where she said there would be plenty of eligible men. It was so infuriating. Lily walked faster with the crazy thought that she might walk all the way over to the Sawyers' estate and saunter past their house. Michael might see her from a window and rush out and gather her into the midst of the party. She hoped he was not having a good time at all. She sat down on a bench, exhausted, because she had not slept well.

If she could only fall asleep, the next day would be Sunday, and she would see him again. She went upstairs to try to rest, wanting to look in high spirits in the morning though, surely, Michael knew it would be hard for her to think of him with another woman, even if it was a favor for his family. She wanted to be calm when her mother came home—to prove that she was not too young and that hers was a mature love; she didn't want to be swooning and acting all fluttery and silly. She would show them all that her love was patient and enduring like the love in the bible. She picked up Godey's Ladies book and tried to read for a while but could not concentrate, and at 10:30, when her mother came home, the gas lamp still made flickering shadows on her bedroom wall. A knock came on the door, and she quickly moved her eyes from the wall to a book that lay open in front of her.

Her mother entered the room uninvited. "You're still awake?" Her mother sat in a chair next to the fireplace. "It's cold in here. I'll call Suzanne to lay a fire."

"I like it cold; besides, I was concentrating on my studies and didn't notice. I don't have time to talk now. I have reading to do for Monday."

"I do so admire your studiousness, but I wish you had come out to this party. It's important to make connections if want you to have a career. You could have done your studies tomorrow. Everyone asked for you. I'd told them earlier you were coming."

"Michael's coming over tomorrow," Lily said, putting down the book. "I want to have time for him."

"We'll see about that," Mrs. Chapman said as she walked out the door. "I hope he has no more family obligations."

When Mrs. Chapman left, Lily threw her book at the door, got out of bed, and sat in an oak rocker by the window. She drew the long curtains open and looked out at a bright, full moon. Would Michael suddenly have family obligations tomorrow? He said he would come over, at least for a while. He said nothing between them would change. She rocked slowly in the chair, trying to calm herself. If anything had changed, she was sure she would know it right away. If he acted or spoke differently, she was sure she would be able to tell. She walked back to the bed and, with one arm under the feather pillow, fell into a troubled sleep. She clutched the pillow in front of her until one long yawn finally brought her into a more restful sleep until she woke the next morning to a knock on the door. Her mother opened it and called to her.

Lily feigned sleep.

Her mother sat on the bed. "We're getting ready for church. It's after ten," she said.

Lily rolled over and closed her eyes. Her mother seldom went to church. "You go with Father today. I didn't sleep well."

"I thought maybe we could all three go, as a family."

"Maybe next week," she said and covered her head with the pillow.

When Lily heard them leave, she went downstairs for breakfast. She smiled to see Nana Parker in the kitchen. She had been ill for a few weeks, and Lily had not seen much of her.

Good morning," she said. "What would you like? Eggs, oatmeal, both?" She stood against the sink, one hand holding a dish towel on her hip, the other leaning on the counter.

"Just oatmeal today," Lily said.

"I've seldom seen you miss services." She sat down with Lily, poured them both some tea. Lily put her hand on her face, elbow on the table and sighed. "Trouble with your young man?" Nana asked, pushing her long curls out of her face.

"No" she said. "With my mother."

"I was glad at least to see her up and off this morning with your father."

"She's still trying to keep us apart, Nana. She's so impossible. She doesn't understand."

"She will, honey. She will. Give her time."

"He's coming over today, and I hope she doesn't make any trouble."

Lily brought her breakfast into the parlor. It seemed like forever before she could expect Michael to arrive. She sat in the parlor reading until they came back from services then played the piano for her father and tried to avoid her mother, who wouldn't stop glancing at her as if waiting for a breakdown of some kind. She was determined not to spend the day in her room waiting by the window. He hadn't said when he would come; there was still plenty of time in the day.

When he finally arrived, she was sitting on a garden bench sipping tea from a china cup. She heard the horse and carriage and heard her father greet him.

"Well, young man, how are you this evening?" Mr. Chapman asked. "Lily's in the back. I'll get your horse to the stable."

"I'm fine," he said. "Thank you, sir. I hope I'm not interrupting your dinner."

"No, no. We finished our dinner. Just having tea and enjoying the evening."

Lily was using all her self-control to remain seated. She wanted him to come over to her. As he approached her, Lily could feel the intensity radiating between them. Nothing had changed. She was so relieved.

"How are you this evening, Lily?"

"I'm just fine, now," she said.

Mrs. Chapman was watching, trying to see the two from the window. She thought her daughter was silly to be out there with her tea, rushing the season. She sat down, sipping her coffee, leafing through copies of Harpers. Edward stood at the door of the room. She shook her head. "Can you believe that boy is here again with company over at the Sawyer house? You might think he would stay home and help them entertain, but instead, he comes tramping over here when it's barely past dinnertime."

"Calm down, Mary," he said. "Don't get yourself all worked up. What's the harm anyway?"

"I'll tell you what's the harm," she said, her hands trembling. "He's ruining her life, ruining her chances to really be somebody. Do you know she is now saying she doesn't want to go to Europe this summer? She'd rather stay here and go on picnics with him. That's 'the harm.'"

Edward went over to her, put his hands on her shoulders. "Take it easy now. You're getting yourself all upset. I'll get the medicine Dr. Sands left."

Mrs. Chapman shook him off. "I don't want the medicine. I'm not sick."

"It will help you rest."

"Edward, I said I don't want any medicine. Stop treating me like a child or an invalid. Just leave me alone. Please." She turned to him and took his hand. "I'm alright now, really. I just want to be alone."

He left reluctantly and disappeared behind the door of his study.

She went to the window again and watched Michael and Lily walk through the garden until they were out of sight. They looked closer and happier than ever. It broke her heart. She couldn't understand how things had gone so far. Hadn't she talked to John Sawyer and hadn't he assured her that he would no longer be coming around? Apparently, he didn't wield as much power as he thought.

She'd have to talk directly to Michael—and she'd have to do it tonight. She spent the next hour watching out the window and leafing through more magazines as her drink slowly changed from coffee to sherry. She waited with the patience of someone with a purpose until she saw the two figures emerge from the garden path. The sun had set into a bright, clear night with a full moon. They sat on the bench and talked for a while then, finally, stood, and kissed. Mrs. Chapman closed her magazine with quiet determination. The sherry had made her both cautious and bold. She slipped out without a sound, hiding behind the high shrubs in front of the house as Michael and Lily said goodbye a few feet away. She waited several minutes until she heard the door slam and Michael's footsteps moving away.

"Psst."

Michael looked all around, then at the window to see if Lily was waving him a last goodbye. Nothing.

"Michael."

Someone had unmistakably whispered his name that time. He turned around and saw Mrs. Chapman's head around the side of a shrub. She waved for him to come closer. He stared, bewildered at her pale skin and sunken eyes in the moonlight. Her breath smelled like sherry.

"I must talk to you, Michael. It's very important that we talk tonight."

"I'm all ears," Michael said, trying to comprehend what was happening.

"Not *here*," she said, her voice a husky whisper. "Drive off and wait for me at the corner. We can talk there."

"Okay." Michael shrugged and walked toward the carriage.

Mrs. Chapman went into the house and knocked on the door of her husband's study and poked her head in. "I'm going for a little walk," she said. "It's such a beautiful night. I won't be long, but I didn't want you to miss me and worry."

"Why don't I come along then. Keep you company?"

"No, Edward, really. I want to walk by myself for a while. I'm feeling much better. Maybe we can walk together in the garden, later."

"Okay, love. I'm glad you're feeling better. Don't go too far."

But the door was already closed.

Mrs. Chapman walked down the deserted street, clutching a shawl tightly around her. She could have been a wandering gypsy, rather than one of the wealthiest women in town, carrying a bag of old forgotten secrets under her wrap. But gypsies were only known to predict the future. She wondered if she could she change it.

At the end of the road, Michael was waiting. He had pulled the carriage into a small dirt path. Trees overhung both sides. She went to him, and Michael helped her up into the carriage without a word.

"We could go in a little further," Michael said. "I wanted to make sure you could see me."

"Move in for privacy," Mrs. Chapman said, moonlight a burden to her secrecy.

When they were settled again, Michael looked over at her.

"I don't want you to see my daughter anymore," she said staring straight ahead. Her face was rigid. The moon shone on her hollow cheekbones, and an unexpected wind blew around her hair. She turned and looked directly at him.

He felt a shiver, and unable to meet her gaze head on, he looked down at his hands. "With all due respect, Mrs. Chapman, that's just not a fair thing to ask of me or Lily. We care for each other very much. What about me makes you feel so repulsed?"

You're your father's son, she fought the urge to say aloud, and there was a mess of entanglements they all would now pay for one way or another. She tried to push her own deception from her mind. She smiled at Michael. None of this was his fault, but he would pay. Yes, he would pay, too.

"It's not you I object to," she said. "I'm sorry; you must have misunderstood me. I just feel you are holding Lily back. Don't you see that? She's too young for you. She has to grow up first."

Michael looked at her. She looked very calm now—too calm. Her eyes were glassy, her smile too sweet. "Excuse me for being bold again, Mrs. Chapman, but I love your daughter. I could give her the best of everything and make her happy. I have a degree in business and a good future. I'm no gad about or dandy. I think Lily is old enough to make her own decisions. I think your disapproval is what's holding her back."

Mrs. Chapman bristled. "How dare you say such a thing?" she shouted.

Michael looked around and shushed her.

She continued in a loud whisper. "I planned to take her to see all of Europe this summer, but she doesn't want to go, wants to stay here all summer with you. You say you love her, but you're like all men—selfish." She got herself down from the carriage and pointed her finger at Michael. "You won't own my daughter. I won't let you. If you really loved my daughter, you would give her time to grow up. Women are not chattel. We have our own minds. We have our rights. Your love is selfish." She turned and walked briskly away.

"Mrs. Chapman, wait." He watched her disappear around the corner and then sat alone, despondent. Maybe he *was* being selfish, but he couldn't bear the thought of breaking it off with Lily. She *was* young though. She *should* take the opportunity to go to Europe this summer with her mother. She hadn't even told him about that. Maybe he would suggest that they don't see each other, just for a few months. He just didn't know what to do. He could never face Lily in person with that idea. He couldn't bear the look of hurt on her face.

He looked up into the dark sky, suddenly feeling alone and vulnerable. A mantle of darkness covered his thoughts as he pulled on the reins and hurried home. It might be better to write her a letter. It would mean less pain for both of them. They wouldn't run into each other, since she would be away. He didn't want to hold her back. He didn't want to love selfishly. He would buy an engagement ring and present it to her when she came back in the fall, if she still wanted him. He drove the carriage straight home, forgetting to stop at Abe Whittier's.

John Sawyer was sitting in his study when Michael opened the door. Michael hadn't counted on that. He was so preoccupied he hadn't seen the light under the door. The house had seemed empty, and Michael was glad. He needed the privacy.

"Don't you know to knock, boy, before you come in?"

Michael nodded. "Where's everyone else?" he asked, in a flat voice.

"Louisa and your mother are walking in the garden. They're probably lost. Maybe you should go find them." Sawyer looked at Michael and waited several minutes. "Why don't you go find them?" he asked, in a louder voice.

Michael walked over to a window, opened the drapes, and stared into the darkness. He leaned on the windowsill, not turning as he spoke. "Leave me alone tonight, Father. Please, just leave me alone."

"Things didn't go well tonight at the Chapman's?" He stopped there, didn't want to gloat. He could see that Michael's hand trembled, and he was looking down at the floor. He thought he saw a tear on Michael's cheek. The boy was too soft, crying over a woman. He'd been too easy on the boy, but it was too late to change that now. None the less, things were going as he hoped they would, so he tried to be sympathetic. "Sit down," Sawyer said. "Sit and we can talk about it." He poured two brandies.

Michael wiped his eyes and turned around. "I don't wish to talk. I'd really like to be alone right now. I have some thinking to do."

Kicking me out of my own study, Sawyer thought. *The boy has more nerve than I thought*, but things were finally going his way, so he left Michael alone in the room. "I'll see that no one disturbs you," he said and left.

Michael locked the door and sat down at the desk. He took a sheet of ivory writing paper out of the desk drawer. It was embellished with his initials and a picture of a horse in the right-hand corner. He dipped the pen in ink and wrote.

Dear Lily,

I have decided it would be best. . .

He looked at the letter after it was finished. It was all a lie. He hadn't decided anything. He started another letter.

Dear Lily,

I love you. I love you, but it won't work . . ..

He crumpled both letters and threw them in the wastebasket. He put his head down in his hands and sobbed quietly. He would miss her. He would miss Lily.

Chapter 8

MRS. TEMPLE WALKED BRISKLY TO her friend's bakery. She tugged on the door and let it close with a bang. She had news today for Mrs. Cunningham. Her friend came out when she heard the door, and though she knew who it was, she wondered why her friend appeared to be so chipper this morning. She had not seen her yesterday and had been a little worried. She brought the coffee out and sat.

"You're looking well," Mrs. Cunningham said.

"Much better, thank, you."

"Is your mind at ease?"

"Yes, I think it was more of a physical ailment, after all. I was queasy all weekend, just needed some time to recover."

Mrs. Cunningham offered her a muffin. "Funny how the body and the mind work together—at least that's what they claim these days."

"Just tea today. Do you mind? I'm still feeling a little off."

"No bother. It's steeping in the back."

When Mrs. Cunningham came back with the tea, Mrs. Temple took her hands. She looked around before speaking as if there may be someone else in the room.

"Did you hear anything yesterday?" Mrs. Temple asked.

"I didn't. It was a rather quiet day." She took a sip of coffee. "The nice weather coming on and all, I suppose people are sitting in their gardens in the morning rather than coming here."

Mrs. Temple sat back and tapped her index finger on the table. "Well, I'll tell you, there is something odd going on at the Chapman's. My Annie was walking about on Sunday evening, and she saw Michael Sawyer's carriage pulling over into a shady path, just short of Main Street. She thought it might be Lily and Michael wanting some privacy."

"I was wondering what would happen now with that young woman staying with the Sawyers?"

Mrs. Temple moved in closer. "She says she swears she saw Mary Chapman come up afterward and get into his carriage."

"That is peculiar. Maybe she came to bring Lily back home."

"No, but listen. Lily wasn't there at all. Annie said they drove a slowly down the path, and she followed, staying hidden in the trees. She couldn't hear what they were saying, but she said voices were raised, and Mary walked off in a huff."

Mrs. Cunningham put her cup down hard. "I knew Mary was still up to something. I just knew that girl they brought up here wouldn't be the end of it."

● ● ●

IT WAS EARLY AFTERNOON, and Lily walked slowly, turning the corner on her way home from school, thinking about how happy she was to be graduating this year. She was still unsure about college. The seniors had been released early, and most of her classmates were going to a party down at the lake, but she had no interest in going. She turned as she heard a horse and cart pull up behind her.

"Good morning, Miss Chapman," the postman said, reaching into his heavy brown sack. "Let's see. Chapman . . . Chapman . . . Chapman." He shuffled through the envelopes and handed a large pile of them to Lily.

"Thank you." Lily took the letters quickly and walked toward home. The postman lingered and watched her stride as she walked away.

Lily put her books down on the entry table and looked though the pile of mail. Many were typed business letters for her father. There was a letter from Abigail, a colored envelope that looked like a card for her mother, and another letter addressed to Lily. She hurried to the living room and sank down on the sofa. Her mother came in with a questioning look.

"There's a letter from Abby," Lily said, handing it to her mother, "and a card for you."

Mrs. Chapman sat down next to Lily and opened the letter. She didn't notice her daughter beside her carefully examining another one. Lily opened the envelope and realizing it was from Michael, quickly closed it again. How sweet of him to write to her. She took the letter and walked across the room.

"Where are you going? Suzanne is bringing in tea for us."

"Just into father's study. I'll be right back," she said.

The study was uncomfortable for Lily. The furniture dark and heavy, walls covered with pictures of hunting parties. The old family portraits gave off a severe feeling. It was a masculine room. Lily thought she might tell her father about the gallery. Maybe they could pick out some paintings of waterfalls together to brighten up this the room.

Most men didn't like women in their studies, but Mr. Chapman sometimes let the girls in, especially when they were studying for exams. She opened the drapes and let some sun in then stared at the letter on the desk.

Why would Michael send her a letter when they had just seen each other last Sunday? Maybe it was a love letter! She sat down and opened it again, staring at Michael's initials and the horse insignia in the corner.

MS

Dear Lily,

I don't know how to say this without hurting you, so I will just get right to it.

I have dearly loved your company in the past several months, but there is some truth to what our parents say. You are too young to be so involved. It's not right of me to hold you back, to take up all your time. Maybe in a year or so we'll be better at judging our love—or even in several months after you've seen more of the world and gotten to know more people.

You must go with your mother to Europe and be open to new experiences.

Please believe me, I don't want to hurt you for anything in the world, but this is really for the best.

Yours always,
Michael

She read the letter over and over again. She just couldn't

understand. She'd never spoken to Michael about the trip to Europe. She decided she'd go over to his house right now, this afternoon, and talk to him. She wanted to see his face, his eyes. She wanted to know what this was all about. Then, suddenly, her confused thoughts turned to anger. She stared at the closed door in front of her. *This letter is a phony*, she decided, a letter written by her mother, another ploy to break them up.

The anger rose as she looked at the insignia again; it had to be from Michael. Her hands tingled, and she could barely breathe. How could he have written such a letter? She had trusted his love. A sharp pain moved into her stomach. She put her head down on the desk and wept. She felt like a fool. She believed that Michael loved her, but now, he was trying to get her out of the way, probably to make way for that horrible Louisa. It couldn't be a coincidence that he would send her a letter now, right after her arrival.

She tried to cry quietly so her mother would not hear. She reached into her father's desk drawer and took out a shot glass and brandy. By the time Mrs. Chapman called saying tea was served, she had almost finished the bottle. She staggered to the door and collapsed into her mother's arms.

"Oh, Lily, no." Her mother nearly fell backwards under her daughter's weight.

She maneuvered Lily back into the desk chair, and once she was settled, she noticed the letter from Michael. So, this was it. Now she would just have to deal with her daughter's hurt for a while. At least everything was straightening out. Lily would just have a few bad days, maybe a few weeks, and she would do all she could to comfort her. She rang for Suzanne and put the glass and empty bottle away in the drawer.

"Bring the strong, hot tea in here as soon as you can, please." Mrs. Chapman had the words out before Suzanna was even in the room. "Lily isn't well."

Suzanne curtsied. "Some smelling salts, too, ma'am?"

"No, just the tea, and please hurry."

"Yes, ma'am."

From a small basin in the corner of the room, Mrs. Chapman soaked a cloth in water and put it on Lily's forehead.

Lily babbled weakly. "I thought it might help. I felt so awful. I thought it would help. Now, I only feel worse. He doesn't love me. Michael doesn't love me. You were right," she said, and tears fell freely.

"It's okay. I'll take care of you, and you'll be feeling better soon." Mrs. Chapman held Lily in her arms. "I love you, Lily, and so do your father and Abigail. There will be the right young man for you; really Lily, there will be. You're young, so very young."

Suzanna came back with the tea.

"Leave it at the door." Mrs. Chapman gestured impatiently to her. "And please see that no one disturbs us."

• • •

LATER, AS MR. CHAPMAN sat eating silently with his wife, he feared it was a loaded silence. He wondered where Lily was. Because she might be out with Michael, he didn't want to bring it up, as his wife seemed distracted as it was this evening. She gave a long, heavy sigh over her strawberry tart and looked at her husband.

"Lily, again?" he asked.

"She's upstairs sleeping. She's been up there all afternoon." Her voice was low and trembling. "I really don't know how to help her."

"Did you two have another argument? You must stop badgering her." He didn't mean the words to come out so sharply. He picked up his coffee cup and hid from his wife's outraged stare.

"For your information," she said. "It's that young Sawyer who has her so upset. It's just like I told her. He's been deceiving her all along. I feel so bad for the poor child. She's so trusting. I tried to warn her . . ." The sentence trailed off as Mrs. Chapman shook her head and dug into her strawberry dessert with an appetite Mr. Chapman hadn't seen for months.

It seemed strange to him. He put his cup down and stared into space, trying to digest the new information. Michael had seemed so happy and attentive just last Sunday. He was glad all that confusion of youth was behind him.

He looked up as Lily stumbled into the room. Her face looked pale, and dark circles shadowed the space under her eyes. "Lily," Mr. Chapman said, alarmed by how despondent she looked. "Come sit here by me."

She sat down limp and dazed.

He took her hand. "Why don't you have something to eat? I'll have cook make you something special, whatever you want."

"No, thank you, father, I'm not really hungry."

"How about some coffee?"

"I'll get you some," Mrs. Chapman said and went to the kitchen, leaving them alone.

"Oh, Father." Lily cried, and he held her trembling body as tears rolled down his cashmere dinner jacket.

"There, there, my girl. Take my handkerchief and have yourself a good cry."

She pulled away, smiling weakly. "Look at me making quite a mess out of your jacket."

"Don't worry" he said. "You'll always be my little girl, and I'm glad you come to me with your problems."

"It's so confusing, Father. I feel so hurt and so angry." She sobbed into his jacket again.

"I know," he said as Suzanne came in with enough coffee for all of them on a silver platter.

Lily had a few sips and went back upstairs saying she wanted to be alone.

"See now what that young man has done?" Mrs. Chapman asked. "And you said there was no harm in it."

"Do you think we should call Dr. Sands tonight to give her something for melancholia?"

"You're always so quick to call the doctor. Let's wait and see how she is tomorrow."

Mr. Chapman retired to his study and sat down by the desk in his leather chair. Reaching into the drawer for some brandy, he was shocked to find only a little left. He'd better take it easy on the stuff.

Chapter 9

MRS. TEMPLE HURRIED INTO THE BAKERY and slammed the door, putting her umbrella to the side and sitting down without even a hello. Mrs. Cunningham could see she was in a bad way and didn't ask her for help.

"Hello Edith. Let me just get these few napkins placed, and I'll get the coffee."

Mrs. Temple nodded.

Mrs. Cunningham grabbed the coffee from the counter and poured her friend a cup. She felt annoyed that she had to comfort her friend again. Mrs. Temple had become argumentative in the last few weeks.

Mrs. Temple shook her head. "This rain is just unending."

"You know what they say about April showers," Mrs. Cunningham said, trying to be cheerful. She was glad to get off her feet, as she had been feeling somewhat faint.

"Fine for the May flowers, but Easter is a week away, and I don't sell dresses and bonnets in this weather."

Mrs. Cunningham touched her friend's hand. "People always wait until the last minute to do the Easter Shopping. I'm sure everything will turn sunny for the Easter Parade."

"Well, that may be, but I don't expect to make many sales today. It's the bonnets, especially, I'm worried about. The dresses will sell eventually, but this is the time of year, I make most of my money from bonnets"

"I know. I know," Mrs. Cunningham comforted her friend. "Believe me; I know how hard it is to keep a business going, especially now, with all the competition in Worcester. You'll see though, people in this town still like to shop here. Let's hope for the sun tomorrow, and your bonnets with fly off the shelves."

Mrs. Temple smiled. "You're very kind, Agnes."

"Now then, let's have some of my special cupcakes."

They both became pensive for a moment and drank their coffee as rain splashed down the window.

"Dr. Sands was in at the Chapman's again," Mrs. Cunningham said.

"Oh no, Mary again?"

"No, this time for Lily."

"Poor thing. I thought that might happen. I told you I had a bad feeling ever since my Annie saw Michael and her mother together."

• • •

IN LATE APRIL, the weather was warm, and Lily rested in the garden. Before today, spring had been a dreadful, cold and rainy, but it suited her spirit fine. She still missed Michael terribly, especially on the weekends. A great feeling of hopelessness overcame her then left, as quickly. Every time she felt the pain, her thoughts drifted. She could hardly concentrate. *It must be from the medicine Dr. sands prescribed*, she thought.

She looked in front of her at the rock garden her mother planted every year. The delicate green stems of tulips and daffodils appeared through mounds of dirt, the bright colored flowers a mockery of her dark mood. She didn't want to see the pale green buds blossom on the trees. She didn't want to watch any of it—not this year. She swung her feet up on the painted wooden bench and looked up from under a large hat brim, to a cloudless sky.

Mr. Chapman watched her from his study window, flicking the ashes of his cigarette nervously into an ashtray. He didn't like what the medicine was doing to his daughter. She looked so listless. He trusted Dr. Sands, but he couldn't imagine that this numb state was doing his daughter any good. He put his cigarette out and left to have a confidential chat with the doctor.

When Dr. Sands answered the door to Mr. Chapman's firm knock, a look of immense concern came into his eyes, as Edward looked very troubled.

He whisked Mr. Chapman to a chair in front of his desk. "How's Lily coming along?"

"I'm afraid there may be a problem. You know, of course, I've always trusted your judgement completely, and I don't want you to take offence."

"Nonsense," Dr. Sands said. "We've known each other for years. You can tell me anything. Speak truthfully; what's the problem? She's your child, and you know her better than I do. Is she having a reaction to the medicine?"

"I'm not quite sure." Mr. Chapman hesitated then looked up. "She still seems forlorn, and there's a limpness about her and a lack of feeling, even more than before. Can you come see her again, perhaps adjust the medicine?"

Dr. Sands nodded. "Certainly, if you feel it's not helping."

He restrained himself from going into his usual lecture about giving the new medicine time. The Chapmans were very substantial patients of his, and he wanted to keep them pleased. He sometimes had to resign himself to the role of a modern miracle worker.

"I'll be by later this afternoon, see what I can do."

"Thank you. I would appreciate it." Mr. Chapman got up to leave, and they shook hands. "I hope I haven't offended you in any way," he added.

"Of course not, Edward. At the very least you're a bit over concerned for your daughter's welfare. I applaud and respect you for that."

Mr. Chapman left very pleased.

• • •

IT WAS NEARLY four by the time the doctor rapped loudly on the Chapman's door.

Suzanne answered it. "Dr. Sands, back again, so soon?" It was hardly the greeting he had expected.

"Yes, it's me, miss," he said and briskly stepped past her carrying a large black bag. "Could you kindly tell Mr. Chapman that I'm here?"

"Yes sir," she said. "Come right this way." She brought him into the parlor and knocked on the door of the study then opened the door a crack. "Dr. Sands is here to see you."

"Thank you." Mr. Chapman rose quickly and joined them in the parlor. "Ah, my man," he said with a brisk smile and a handshake. "Thank you for coming. I'll take you to Lily. She's been resting upstairs."

Dr. Sands noticed the yellowish stains on Edward's fingertips and the overpowering smell of tobacco on his breath as Edward smiled and led him up the stairs.

Lily, sitting on the bed with a book open on her lap, heard a knock at her door. "Come in," she said, her voice sounding far away.

They both entered and looked at Lily. She hardly reacted to their presence. She wanted to get up, to greet them, but she felt as if they were not really there, as if she saw them through a thin, gray veil.

Dr. Sands pulled a chair up next to the bed. "How are you, Lily. Are you feeling any better?"

"I don't know," she said. "I feel tired, I guess."

Suddenly, her eyes rolled back, and her head rolled forward. Dr. Sands picked up her chin, looked in her eyes, and felt for her pulse. He spoke in a clear, low voice.

"Go to the sink quickly and get me a cold towel."

Mr. Chapman went to the corner of the room and dipped the towel in water. It was tepid, not cold. "Do you want me to go downstairs and get colder water?" he asked as he watched Dr. Sands open his black bag and take out a needle.

"No, tepid is better." He rubbed the water onto Lily's forehead. "If you are squeamish, Edward, it would be better to leave the room. I am giving her something to make her vomit and get rid of most of the medicine. There's too much in her system. I don't know who has been administering it to her, but they obviously have not been following my instructions." He looked directly at Mr. Chapman. "You were right to call me. If she had fallen asleep, it could have been fatal."

Mr. Chapman thought with alarm that they hadn't been watching her very well. Not well enough at all. She knew where the medicine was and had possibly been taking some herself. He left the room and sat in a chair in the hallway with his head down. He was glad his wife wasn't home. She was out on a shopping trip with one of her clubs for most of the day. He lit a cigarette.

"Are you alright, sir. Is Lily alright?" Mrs. Parker asked, by his side.

Mr. Chapman nearly jumped from the chair, his heart pounding. "Lily is going to be alright," he said, trying to reassure himself. "Dr. Sands gave her a milder dose; he says she will be okay now."

"She's had her share of troubles, that one," Miss Parker said shaking her head. She looked at Mr. Chapman's trembling hands. "Is there anything I can do, sir? I'll brew a fresh pot of coffee for you and the doctor. I'll have Suzanne stay with Lily when the doctor is done."

"Thank you," he whispered. "That will be fine."

She looked down at the floor as the long ash of cigarette fell onto the Oriental rug.

Dr. Sands came down and assured Mr. Chapman that Lily would be fine. "She will probably sleep most of the next twenty-four hours," he said. "And after that, I would like you to keep her confined in the room for two weeks. Any stimulation is just too much for her right now." Mr. Chapman nodded and saw the doctor to the door. "It would be best to keep a very close eye on her. Don't let her be alone for a while."

"I'll send Suzanne up there to be with her. She can be with her even at night."

"Don't hesitate to call me if you notice something off again. Light reading is okay but keep her away from the newspapers."

Lily recovered slowly. She was weak at first, but her color and strength came back as the days went by. Suzanne brought trays of food up to her room and sat with her every day. She was only a few years older than Lily, so her task of keeping Lily happy in confinement came easily. They sewed, painted, played checkers, and talked freely. Suzanne was to keep her charge happy and amused, so she evaded the subject of Michael whenever she could.

• • •

SUZANNE CAME INTO Lily's room at 9:30 AM on Wednesday morning, placed a breakfast tray next to Lily's bed, and then opened the long drapes. Lily sat up as sunshine invaded the room. It was nearly two weeks now that she had been confined.

"You look good today," Suzanne said. She watched Lily spread marmalade on the toast, glad to see her appetite had returned.

"I do feel better. Anyway, my body feels better, but I still feel confused." She put the toast down and took a sip of tea. "I still miss Michael. I still care for him, even though he hurt me like he did. Does that seem silly to you?"

"No, I don't think it's silly." She spoke guardedly, staring at a brush on Lily's night table. This was a topic she was told not to discuss. Lily ate the rest of her breakfast silently. When she was done, she went to the mirror, and Suzanne brushed out her hair.

"Why are you spoiling me so much?" Lily laughed. "I can do my own hair."

"Those are my orders, to take care of my Lily. My orders did change a little though this morning."

Lily turned around, frowned, afraid of this change she knew nothing about.

"Do you think you're ready for a walk in the garden today?"

Lily's face brightened. "You mean they're letting me out of prison? Finally, oh, leave my hair; let me get dressed." She stood up and twirled her arms around. "I want to go outside and breathe some fresh air."

"We have to wait until late morning when the sun's a little warmer—doctor's orders."

"I'll put on a heavy sweater over my dress."

Suzanne was firm. "You know I won't go against orders, Miss Lily. I'll open the windows for now to give us both some fresh air."

Later, at eleven, when it was time for their walk, Lily asked if she could go alone. "Please, Suzanne, I love you and I appreciate all you've done for me, but I feel better now. I need some freedom, for my mind, for my spirit. You can watch me from the window. I won't be out of sight. I promise."

So, Lily went out the door alone, and Suzanne sat by the window. She walked around the outside paths of the garden, happy with her own thoughts. She still felt sad but not so despondent. She was sleeping well now and only given a mild sedative if sleep wouldn't come or if she became 'hysterical.' Those fits of worry hadn't happened for several days. She walked toward her mother, who was sitting on a bench near the rock garden.

"Where's Suzanne? Doesn't she know she is supposed to accompany you?"

Lily pointed to the window. "Don't be cross with her. She let me have a few minutes alone. I insisted on it."

"Well, no mind. I can keep you company now." She patted the bench next to her for Lily to sit. Lily was glad to be able to talk to her mother, to find out what was going on around the house. She'd not talked to anyone but Suzanne for so long.

"What have you told the school? Did I miss the exams?" Her voice was a little accusing as if she still held her mother responsible for everything.

"They said don't worry about the exams; you can take them whenever you're ready. Next fall, even, if you want."

"No, I want to get it over with now. I want to graduate this year." She tried to stay calm, but her voice rose.

Fearing hysteria, her mother backed down. "As soon as you're ready, dear. Next week if you want." She wanted to bring up the trip to Europe but was hesitant; she would need to use tact with Lily. "Abagail's coming home this weekend. We're going shopping for the trip overseas. She's decided to come with me. She's very excited about it."

"Abby's going?"

Mrs. Chapman thought she saw Lily's expression lift. "Yes. We're purchasing the tickets this weekend. The ship leaves in two weeks." She moved a little closer and spoke quietly. She stroked Lily's hair. "I don't want to upset you anymore, darling, but I do wish you would reconsider. It would be great fun going on a trip, the three of us. We may never get the chance again."

Lily moved away. After being confined for two weeks, the trip did sound inviting. It would also be a chance to get away from this town, and Lily knew she needed that. She couldn't bear running into Michael with another woman. She looked up at her mother.

"Um, I'm not sure. Would we be expected to go on Mrs. Bennet's tour, ten countries in half as many weeks?"

"Heavens, no," her mother said. "We can take our time. We could even stay until late September."

"I'll think about it a little more, but I would want to take the exams before we go."

Mrs. Chapman looked down at her daughter, pleased. Lily was a survivor, too. Suzanne came out with a tray of sandwiches for lunch, and they stayed outside until the pesky mayflies sent them in the house for relief.

• • •

THREE TICKETS WERE ordered for the trip the next weekend, and Mrs. Chapman and her two daughters got ready to go shopping.

"See that you don't wear Lily out," Mr. Chapman ordered.

Mrs. Chapman whispered, "Really, Edward. It's the best thing in the world for her; even Dr. Sands says so. I promise we won't do too much walking."

"I'll see my girls tonight, then," he said. Then he kissed his wife on the cheek and waved to his daughters, already in the carriage.

A man in a dark uniform took Mrs. Chapman's hand and helped her into the rounded velvet seats next to her daughters. Then he climbed into the high seat and steered the horses into the city. Mrs. Chapman felt proud and happy riding with her daughters beside her. She hadn't felt so happy in a long time. They would be in Europe this summer. Everything would be okay after all. She looked at her daughters across from her, listened to them talking and laughing. They had grown into strong, graceful women. She would open the world to them and provide them with what she had never had: a sense of freedom. She sighed and took her gloves off, one finger at a time, placing them neatly on her lap. She looked around at the green buds on the trees. A look of worry crossed her face as if spring reminded her of an old wound felt but not shared. She looked down at her gloves.

"Why so quiet, mother?" Abigail leaned over and put one hand on her mother's shoulder.

"Oh, don't worry about me. I like listening to you two talking and planning." She looked at her daughters with a tight smile holding onto the bitterness that her memories had triggered. Then she touched Abagail's cheek with her thin fingers. "It's nice for us all to be together again. I'm glad you and Lily are both coming."

"I'm glad too, mother," Abigail said. Then she turned around to Lily.

Lily had to talk to keep her thoughts from wandering. She was trying not to think about Michael and how, a few weeks ago, they had ridden these very streets together. At last, they pulled up in front of Chamberlain's, an exclusive women's store. Lily and Abagail jumped down from the carriage while the driver helped their mother.

Lily hadn't been in this shop since she was a little girl, as her clothes were generally made by a seamstress in town. They walked up a few carpeted steps that lead to a glass door. The inside was very spacious with large windows and an open staircase leading to the second level.

Mrs. Chapman walked toward the staircase and didn't notice that her daughters were no longer behind her. At the top, she looked over a wide balcony to the bottom floor where she saw them trying on hats.

Lily adjusted a large straw one with a velvet ribbon. She stood and watched them for a while until Lily noticed her in the mirror. They waved to each other; then she turned and walked toward the dresses, satisfied that the girls would find her.

She stopped at a small café, partially enclosed, with windows that looked over the balcony. It must have been recently built because she didn't remember it. *What a lovely place*, she thought. Eight or nine small round tables painted white with spindly legs. They almost looked like garden furniture. That's where they would have lunch, she decided, and walked on to the dress area.

Lily and Abagail had gone from the hats to the shoe department. They tried on several pairs, but nothing was right.

Lily was beginning to feel tired. "Let's sit for a minute," she said. "Let's sit on the bench right near the fountain."

"We might get a little wet from the spray."

"I don't mind. Do you?" Lily asked.

"I guess not—we could close our eyes and pretend we are sitting by a waterfall," Abigail said with a bright smile.

Lily thought of the pictures she'd seen in the galleries and thought of Michael again. Abagail sat down on the outside of the enclosure and watched people walking by; Lily went inside and stared at all the coins in the clear water. She threw a penny in and watched it fall to the bottom then looked up noticing how the water in the middle of the spray sometimes picked up the colors of dresses and bright parasols as people walked by. She and Abigail laughed at people with parasols—they were so old-fashioned.

The bright noontime sun shone through the huge glass windows, and beads of water evaporated or fell with a tiny splash back into the pool. She watched it all, and her mind formed an image of she and Michael having a picnic in the tall grass. The wind swept softly over the ground as they opened a basket of sandwiches and fruit. Michael put his head in Lily's lap, and then it began to rain in large soft drops, but she didn't feel cold or chilled. She looked down into Michael's face, and it turned into a bead of water bursting, and suddenly, she was looking at the fountain again.

She felt Abagail poking her. "Lily, there's Mother. I think she wants us to come up."

Mrs. Chapman took them to the small café she'd seen earlier. Most of the tables were full, so they had to wait in line at the door with menus to peruse while they waited. The choices were omelets and sandwiches and pastries. The smell of coffee was strong, and Lily noticed the pastries inside a glass counter. She watched people sipping cold lemonade and ices as the three of them were whisked to a table right near the edge of the balcony by the large window. Mrs. Chapman ordered tea, the girl's cold lemonade. There was champagne too. Mrs. Chapman said they could all have a glass for dessert.

"I love it here," Lily said. "This is better than going to a dressmaker. It's so tiresome waiting to be fitted."

Mrs. Chapman touched Lily's hand. "You'll love the outdoor cafes in Paris." She took a sip of her tea. "Have you girls found anything you like?"

"They have some nice hats," Lily said. "But we didn't put any aside. We couldn't make up our minds."

"You'll need several for the weather in different countries, not to mention the trip over. The sun can get very hot above the salt water, never mind the wind. Buy as many as you like."

"That would be about a hundred," Abagail said looking at Lily and giggling.

The girls talked about the shoes they'd seen and the kind of dresses they were looking for while Mrs. Chapman sipped the champagne that they now had for dessert. They raised their glasses in a toast to all the adventures they would have in the summer when suddenly Lily pounded her glass, much too hard, down on the table.

Mrs. Chapman followed her daughter's troubled expression to the floor below where Mrs. Sawyer stood with a tall, young woman, picking out hats and scarves. Lily got up from her chair quickly and walked out of the café. Mrs. Chapman and Abagail exchanged glances, left money for the bill, and joined Lily, leaning sulkily against the wall.

"She's a bit overdressed," Mrs. Chapman said. "No one dresses like that to go shopping. Did you notice how everyone was looking at her oddly?"

Lily remained leaning against the wall for support. Abagail took her arm. "Come on. Forget about her. Let's go look at dresses," Abigail said.

Lily shook her head and stood frozen for several minutes. After a while, she followed her sister to the dresses. Her mother stayed behind to be a lookout and let Abagail know if they started coming up the stairs. They didn't want Lily to have the misfortune to have to actually talk with Mrs. Sawyer and Louisa. Fortunately, they only purchased a few hats and left the store quickly.

● ● ●

As Suzanne walked through the door of the bakery the smell alone raised her spirits; she had been thinking of skipping the meeting because she was so tired, but Mrs. Chapman had encouraged her to go, even said she could have the evening off, as she and her daughters would be out shopping for the day.

She looked around, and Daisy waved her over. She saw steaming pots of coffee and tea on the table.

"What took you?" Daisy asked. "We've been waiting to have our pie."

"The walk itself today nearly killed me," Suzanne said pulling off her bonnet and rubbing her chapped, red hands together. "Pour me some tea, would you?"

"Tell us about the meetings in Worcester. That's what we came for," Olive said, excitedly to Kathleen.

"Yes. Well, I've been to several of the meetings and know they would very much like women in service to attend. They told me to encourage everyone and to let you know that they have a lot of legal and practical information." Then, she added in more hushed voice, "They even talk about how women in service can avoid conflicts with the men of the house." Her face flushed in anxiety—or perhaps anger. The women looked around at each other. Eyes went to the floor. "They can help with situations." Then, louder, she added," If you don't have transportation, they will send a carriage to pick up a group in town if you can make your way to this bakery."

"Is there a meeting this evening?" Suzanne asked

"Not tonight," Kathleen said. "I'm here today to gage interest. I've already met with some other women, and there's a crowd of at least 5 or 6 so far that want to attend the next meeting. If you put your name down on this sheet, I can show them the interest, and I'm quite sure they will send a carriage out this way. I'll be letting you know soon when the next meeting will be held."

Suzanne noticed all the names and added hers to the list. She and Daisy exchanged glances.

"There's something else," Kathleen said. She leaned in toward the group and spoke in a whisper. "I have also found a group in Worcester, somewhat related to the women's issues, who call themselves spiritualists."

"Is that a religion?" Daisy asked.

"No, it's kind of for fun but also kind of interesting," Kathleen said. "They're holding a séance this evening."

"A lot of nonsense," Olive said, sitting back and crossing her arms.

"I've heard of séances," Daisy said. "Is that where dead people come alive"

Olive shook her head.

"No nothing like that," Kathleen said. "They might have a medium there—someone who claims to reach the spirits of those who've passed on."

Suzanne looked at Daisy. "Gives me the heebie-jeebies."

"Well, there is room in a carriage if anyone wants to go with me this evening. I can bring you back home later." She looked at Daisy and Suzanne who had both pushed their chairs away from the table.

"I'm going to have a powder," Daisy said. "And I'm taking Suzanne with me." She took Suzanne by the arm and pulled her toward the other side of the room.

As soon as they were gone, Olive looked wearily at Kathleen. "They're only young girls. Why would you get them mixed up in that nonsense?"

"It's part of the movement. You heard them talk of the power of spiritualism for women. You should come with us. How would you know anything about it if you've never been?"

"It's all tricks."

Kathleen started to get up from the table. "Well then, come," she said, "and you can enlighten us all about the tricks afterward."

Olive regretted that she had encouraged the girls to come here. She didn't like Kathleen inviting the girls to go off to Worcester.

Daisy and Suzanne stood outside the water closet. "You're not really thinking of going, are you?" Suzanne asked. "It sounds creepy."

"It might be fun," Daisy argued "We never go out anywhere. If we don't go out, we'll never meet a husband."

"Yes, well, I don't want to meet a dead one."

Daisy laughed. "Come on. It'll just be fun. Afterwards, maybe we can go out somewhere that they serve liberated women and have that sherry."

"I don't know," Suzanne said.

"She assured us she could give us a ride back, and Olive knows her. She wouldn't introduce us to someone who is disreputable. Please, I want to go, and I won't go without you. Well, I might, but I feel I shouldn't."

"Do you have any money so we could get our own carriage back if we have to?"

"I have enough to cover both of us. It will be so much fun going to Worcester."

Suzanne looked at her skeptically. "Okay, but we will not leave each other's side all night. If one goes to take a powder, the other will too, and if either of us gets scared, we'll leave together."

"I swear I have enough to cover us both," Daisy said.

"Well, be careful with taking out that purse, since we'll be in the city. You might want to hide that money in your shoe."

"Good idea."

The three went off together to Olive's disapproval. Kathleen's covered carriage provided them shelter from the wind. Suzanne, still reluctant, looked at Daisy. One of the reasons she had agreed to come was to keep an eye on her.

They sat in the carriage as it plodded along into the city, Daisy and Kathleen doing most of the talking. Though Kathleen was closer to Olive's age, she had a youthful way to her. She and Daisy talked about how excited they were about the séance and though Kathleen kept insisting it would be great fun, Suzanne had a feeling of dread when she watched Kathleen—as if fun was not really the reason she was attending. No matter, she had made Daisy show her the money so she knew they had the means to get back by themselves if things went awry.

Kathleen pointed out the Quaker Meeting House where the suffrage meetings were held as they passed a large stone building with many windows and decks on the lower and upper levels. It was an unusual place that Suzanne thought looked more like a fancy dance hall than a place of spirituality or religion. She stared at the building as they passed, even craning her head to look at it until it was out of sight.

"That's quite an interesting building," Suzanne said. "Simple but grand. Why don't they have the séances there?" She would have been more comfortable in a more public building and was somehow drawn to going inside. After they had passed and turned a corner, her feeling of unease returned. They were in a narrow ally now with smaller houses.

"The family we will see tonight does go there," Kathleen said. "But they prefer to have the séances in their home. It's a smaller, more intimate atmosphere."

The driver halted the horses, and the three women stepped down with his help. Dusk was falling, and Suzanne was glad when she noticed the house was not as dark as she thought it would be. As they walked up a short hill toward the house, Suzanne turned around to gage how long it would take to walk or run back to the road. She had hoped the house would be on the main street. There were lanterns lit around the house, and she saw a face at the window.

Quickly, the door opened, and a short, thin man, dressed in a suit, welcomed them. "Kathleen," he said, "you brought some friends."

"I hope you don't mind. I was spreading the word of the women's meetings in Stonebridge today, and they seemed interested."

"Oh, that's splendid," he said. "I'll take a few more chairs out."

"Can we sit away from the table and just watch?" Suzanne asked, already apprehensive.

The man looked askance at Kathleen, and she laughed. "Oh, Sam, don't look so worried. They're not here to catch you in any trickery. They've never been to a séance, so they're nervous; that's all. It's better if we all sit at the table," Kathleen said to Suzanne, "but you will not have to be a controller if there is any levitation. You only need to sit. That's all that will be required of you."

Suzanne swallowed hard and looked at the door.

About half a dozen others came out of a side room. Kathleen began the introductions, and they all sat down at a large, round dining room table that had been pushed toward the far wall of the room.

Mrs. Kaminski, the woman who had been introduced as the medium tonight, sat in front of a curtain that had been hung from the ceiling. They were in a drawing room that was rather plain and devoid of furniture. Besides the table and chairs, there was a love seat and few stuffed chairs pushed up against the walls away from the table. There was a fireplace and a few large pictures on the wall, but the room's wallpaper and hangings were quite plain. Suzanne took a seat furthest from the wall and the medium. After they were all seated, Sam's wife, Rosanna, began to speak.

"We welcome you all here to our session tonight, and we are grateful to have Mrs. Kaminski here to uncover the knowledge of the spirit world. We sit at the spirit table as Elizabeth Cady Stanton sat in Senaca so many years ago when, with the help and faith of our sisters, she penned the Declaration of Sentiments, bringing organization to the great suffrage movement. In that spirit, knowing the guidance we receive from the spirits will free us and all those who labor and are oppressed and wronged. We now will be silent, and Madam Kaminski will try to intervene on our behalf."

Suzanne looked over at Daisy who, unbelievably, seemed to be trying to stifle a giggle. Then she glanced over at Kathleen, who looked serious, almost trance-like.

Suzanne, who had been wondering why a few empty teacups had been set on the table, lurched forward as one near her shook. She turned her head and looked toward the door. Madam Kaminski made moaning noises, very softly. Then, in a kind of stuttering voice, she called out a name.

"Mary. . . Mary, my baby. . . Mary my baby's baby. I feel you near . . . feel your breath in this room . . . a hand that has touched yours . . . touched by a presence in this room . . ."

The teacups clattered. Rosanna looked around the table. "Does anyone have a question to ask of the spirit Mary?"

They all looked around at each other. Suzanne wanted to leave but knew she couldn't; Kathleen looked down at the table, trembling.

The medium moaned and whispered. "Mary would like you to

know that she is all right. She suffered much when she was on this Earth, but that has now passed. She looks down on all the workers and women and all those who are oppressed and hopes that her death was not in vain."

Then Madame Kaminski collapsed on the table.

Suzanne looked at Rosanna, alarmed.

"She'll be fine. Don't worry, dear. It takes a lot of energy to transmit messages from the spirits. She needs a deep rest for a few minutes."

After several minutes, Madam Kaminski raised her head and took a deep breath.

"Should we go on? Rosanna asked her. "Would you like to try again?"

Madame Kaminski shook her head, and Sam, who sat next to her, took her hand. Sam said, "I think maybe that was quite enough, it was a quick burst but quite powerful."

Madame Kaminski nodded, and Sam got up and put on the gas lamps over the fireplace. They had no electric lighting in this room. It was considered bad for séances, an interference to the spirits. The chairs were brought away, and the table was moved to the middle of the room as the guests scattered around to the more comfortable chairs. Cups filled with actual tea were brought in along with a fresh apple tart. Suzanne and Daisy sat together on the love seat. Sam stood by the fireplace talking with Madame Kaminski, and Kathleen sat in a chair next to the girls.

Rosanna came over and brought them tea and apple tart. "Are you treated well by your families?" Rosanna asked, looking from one to the other.

"We've got no complaints," Daisy said, looking at Suzanne.

"None at all," Suzanne said. "We're very lucky, really. I've been with the same family for several years now."

"You're very young, though," Rosanna said. "What age were you when they took you out of school to work in service?"

"Oh, we were both able to finish our schooling," Suzanne said feeling a little uneasy.

"Well, I'm very glad you came, and I hope you come to the next meeting. Sam and I are the ones who have arranged rides for the domestic help to be able to attend. You'll find kindred voices there. I'm glad you are settled with good families. Some of the things we hear from these girls are just terrible. We fight for justice for all our sisters."

Suzanne nodded.

Kathleen, who had been listening, stood and paced the room. Suzanne watched her agitated pacing while Daisy talked with their hostess. Then Kathleen moved to a chair across the room and looked up at the ceiling, lost in thought.

It seemed there was more to this evening than a bit of fun for her. Maybe she fancied herself a medium, too? Suzanne stood and went over to Kathleen, bringing her a cup of tea. She touched her on the shoulder

Kathleen didn't respond at first. She was looking down at the floor and then up at the ceiling. Suzanne thought this had been all too much for the poor woman, and she worried that they might have to find their own way home after all.

"Kathleen. *Kathleen.*" She called out a few times, and finally, Kathleen looked toward her but, she stared absently as if she was looking right through her.

Suzanne held out the cup again. "Some tea?" she asked. "You look very tired. We should all be getting home soon."

Kathleen looked up. "Yes, of course, I'm sure you need to get up early." She took a sip of the tea. "I'll have Sam get the coach. I feel ready to retire, myself."

Kathleen put her tea down and went over and spoke to Sam at the fireplace, and a carriage was brought round to the front.

"Thank you for coming." They shouted and waved. "I do hope you make it to the next women's meeting."

Daisy and Suzanne waved back then stepped up into the carriage. Daisy was still waving out the window as the horses began to move. "That was so much fun," Daisy said. "I'm so glad we came."

"It was interesting."

"Could you even believe when she started moaning and whispering a name? I almost fell over in my chair, but then they would have just thought that I was channeling the spirit."

Suzanne poked Daisy and nodded toward Kathleen who rested with her head against the side of the coach. Daisy, clueless, went on.

"And she chose the name Mary to be the spirit. I think it is safe to say there is always at least one person in a room that has a deceased relative named Mary."

Suzanne sighed and gave up trying to get Daisy not to offend their friend. It seemed Kathleen had fallen asleep anyway.

Chapter 10

MAY HAD DESCENDED WARM AND sunny on the town of Stoneridge. Mrs. Temple entered the bakery with a quick step and called to her friend.

"Yoo-hoo. Agnes?" She sat down at their table gazing at a line of daffodils that were in over-bloom along the walkway. "Agnes, do you need my help, dear?" When there was no reply, she was on her feet again, going round to the back.

The coffee was on, but Agnes was slumped down in a chair, with a dozen cookies on her lap and on the floor.

Mrs. Temple screamed and ran over to the sink to get water. She gently splashed the water onto Agnes' face. "Agnes, Agnes," she said as she gently tapped her friend's. cheeks

Mrs. Cunningham moaned. Mrs. Temple gently moved her to the floor and made her way to the telephone in the corner. where she called the police. Then she went back to her friend, comforting and holding her until the doctor came.

• • •

THE NEXT FEW WEEKS were extremely busy for Lily. She was determined to finish her exams and be done with them before she left. Suzanne helped her pack a large trunk, but she still had a lot of organizing to do herself. Their ship was leaving Boston Harbor May 30th, and the trunks had to be there ahead of time to be loaded onto the ship. She had only been in Boston once before, and she didn't remember much except the smell of salt and sand that stayed in her hair and her clothes for days.

The morning they were coming to pick up the trunks, she was still packing. Feeling overwhelmed, she sat in front of the vanity and combed her hair out in front of a large oval mirror where she could see almost everything in the room because the mirror was so big. She saw clothes still draped on chairs, all cosmetics and necessities lined up on the bureau, her carrier bag opened near her pillow, and the bed itself.

She was frightened suddenly at the thought of sleeping in hotels with strange beds, and she thought of something Michael had told her the day they went to the gallery—Mr. Winston and Mr. MacGregor's wives had both drowned while traveling on a ship. She felt homesick already, and they hadn't even left yet. She thought of the warmth of home, and she thought of Michael as she wound her hair into long, thick braids around her head.

It would be good for her to get away, she told herself. She'd be older and more sophisticated when she got back. Maybe she and Michael could be together then. She would prove to them all that she was old enough for love. She could already feel herself growing older and struggling to become stronger. She could feel herself becoming more independent. This trip would change her—she was sure of it. It already had.

She pinned her braids up and looked up at the window where she heard a peculiar noise. A large blackbird flapped its wings wildly trying to land on the narrow window ledge. Another came and flew directly at the window glass, then another. She held her breath. Then she heard squawking and looked out to see several of them circling above the roof. She supposed she would have to get used to it—she'd heard that seagulls could be very noisy, but it was unsettling. She let her breath out and got up from the vanity, dressing quickly for breakfast.

Lily had hardly slept that night because of the excitement. She and Abagail had stayed up much too late talking and playing music. Their father had sat in the parlor enjoying the violin and piano duets. He knew he wouldn't be hearing them again for several months. Lily wished he could come too, but he said there was too much work for him to be away that long, and he cheerfully said that his wife and daughters were independent women now and did not need a man to tag along.

Part II
Summer

Chapter 11

BOSTON HARBOR LAY IN FRONT OF THEM like the gaping mouth of a giant swallowing up small sails in its rough waves. Lily blinked. It was cool by the ocean, even with the sun out; she wrapped a woolen shawl around her shoulders. Her mother had given her stomach bitters because she had felt sick in the carriage and was afraid it might forebode sea sickness. Now, with her stomach calmed, she watched the steamship crew open the gates to the walkways. The crowds pushed their way forward. Large, red stacks gave out puffs of black, and soon, people were already congregating and leaning against the railing of the deck. Lily's father stood beside her and asked how she was feeling, his voice almost drowned out by the splashing waves and the blasts of the ship.

"Okay," she said and looked at his eyes, which were the color of the ocean.

"You better run along with the others, now. You don't want to miss the boat."

She looked down, and her chin trembled. "Oh, Father, I wish you were coming. Can't you come too?"

"I wish I could, but it's too long to leave my business."

"I'm going to miss you," she said, embracing him, burying her head in his woolen sweater.

"No tears now." He pulled her from him, wagged his finger, and kissed her on the forehead. "I'll miss you too, so be sure and send me postcards."

"Every day," she said, and she turned around, rushing toward the crowd where Abagail and her mother were waiting.

Lily took her mother's right arm, Abagail the left, and they battled the crowds together. She felt a little sick again as she was jostled between hoops, parasols, and travel cases. The captain welcomed them, and a steward told them their room number. Then they took their places at the ships railing and searched the crowds for Mr. Chapman. Lily spotted him first and waved furiously. They heard a loud whistle.

"Get ready girls, "Mrs. Chapman said, holding firmly to the railing.

The long whistle ended, and the ship moved. Lily was thrown back with the sudden movement. She laughed, clutched the railing, and squinted, trying to see her father through the sun and waves and saltwater spraying on her face.

Mr. Chapman watched the vessel till he could see only brightly colored hats and dresses on board, hands waving and heads bobbing in the distance. He needed a cigarette and turned to walk toward the waiting carriage. He'd have the driver take him to a smoking lounge in Boston. He turned around for one last look, but the ship was out of sight. The harbor was empty except for a few small sails, and the rugged sea air slapped him in the face.

• • •

LILY AND ABAGAIL sat on the ship's sturdy wooden benches as they had come to do every afternoon except when it was raining. Lily wasn't even sure what day it was. There were few clocks on board, and one day was pretty much like the rest. So far, the trip was boring, though it was relaxing on the ship. She hoped they would soon reach England.

She looked over at Abigail, who was reading. "I hope we get to land soon," she said, but her sister had not even heard her, as she was so enrapt in her book. Lily put her head back and closed her eyes. She hadn't gotten seasick as she had feared, and the crew did everything to make guests feel at home; even the portholes in the rooms had dainty floral curtains on them.

The dining room was beautiful and spacious. It had two levels and a large, carpeted staircase. They ate there every night. Afterwards, a band played, and people danced on the lower level while those at the tables watched from the upper balcony. It was a good place to meet people, but Lily was not really interested in making friends. She and Abby watched night after night and commented on the closed society forming in front of them. They knew they were lucky to have each other; some other girls sat alone looking uncomfortable and lost.

Some mothers had great expectations for their daughters on these cruises. It was a different society on the ship. You could meet a young man in the afternoon and dance with him that evening. Social mores fell away, which brought a sort of freedom, but it was all a fantasy, Lily thought—people thrown together. The shallowness made her lonely for Michael. Abagail nudged her arm suddenly and looked up from under a white straw hat. Two young men were approaching them.

"Don't make eye contact," Abagail whispered. Lily looked down.

One of the two came up to Abigail, his hair parted in the middle and slicked down. He wore a bright colored shirt, knickers, and high socks.

"My friend and I were wondering if you and your friend might want to go for a stroll around the deck?"

"No thank you," Abigail said. Lily could tell he was full of himself, as he was shocked at her refusal.

"Well, perhaps I'll see you at the dance tonight at the fancy dress ball?"

"Perhaps," Abagail said and gave him a sidelong glance as he walked away. "Dandies," Abagail said as soon as they were out of sight. "And he was so sure we would jump at the chance."

They looked at each other and laughed. Then Lily looked at her sister. "The ball is tonight?"

"Why do you think Mother wants us back to the cabin early?" Abigail asked.

"That means we land in England sometime tomorrow."

"Aren't you ready for something different?"

"More than ready," Lily said.

The fancy ball was the grand finale of the ship's passage. A bar was set up early in the dining room for socializing, but mostly men were there. The women were busy getting their daughters ready for what would be their last chance to meet eligible men on board—or to form a lasting bond with someone they had met earlier. Mrs. Chapman hoped her daughters would meet someone, maybe not a real love but, especially for Lily, someone who would keep her mind off Michael. She ordered a bottle of sherry to be brought to the room.

Lily and Abagail had just come back and started the long process of dressing. The sherry came promptly, and she offered the girls a glass.

"No, thanks, Mother," Abagail said as she tightened the laces of a corset. I need all my facilities for this maneuver."

"Let me help you," Mrs. Chapman said, putting down her own glass. "How are you doing, Lily?" She turned around to see her other daughter struggling with laces.

"I'm not sure. I don't know how people dance in these."

"Very slowly," Abagail said.

Mrs. Chapman shook her head. "What am I going to do with you two?"

Lily dug into her trunk and pulled out a series of petticoats in a flurry of white silk. She put them on one by one. "Oh, I hope they don't have a fire going in that room," she said. "I hope they keep all the portholes open."

Mrs. Chapman's eyes gleamed as she looked at her daughters fully dressed. "If there's royalty on this ship," she said, "you'll surely meet them tonight."

She stared for a moment at Abagail who wore a low-waist, green silk gown. It had a thick blue sash at the waist the same color as her eyes and featured a high-neck and long sleeves both bordered in pale blue lace. Her thick, straight hair was pushed back and up with a few strands falling over her cheeks and forehead, framing her face. Mrs. Chapman got up and arranged these stray hairs into curls with a round iron, to make them look softer. She placed a decorative comb with blue and white flowers into her oldest daughter's hair and put an ivory cameo onto the collar of her gown. She put some pale pink color on Abagail's cheeks and a hint of blue on her eyelids.

"There," she said and opened the closet door so Abagail could see herself in the full-length mirror.

Now it was time for Lily's 'finishing touches.'

Lily's dark hair contrasted with a light rose-colored dress, and around her waist was a sash of the same color bordered in dark, red roses. The same pattern of roses bordered the collar and sleeves with gathered white lace around them. It was simple and stunning. Mrs. Chapman placed a comb bearing red and pink roses into the top of her braided hair and added red blush to her cheeks and a soft brown color to her eyelids. Lily took her turn in front of the mirror; then they were ready to go.

The ball had already started. Mrs. Chapman walked in, fanning herself nervously with a small, round-handled Japanese fan. The room had been transformed with rich velvet curtains and couches set up around the dance floor. A chandelier hung from the high ceiling. Girls here and there sat on couches, and young men lingered with their arms on the backs of chairs. The dance floor was large, and at this time, only a few were dancing.

Mrs. Chapman was so glad she could offer her girls this glimpse of real society. She wanted them to be strong and independent, oh yes, but she also wanted them to have all the opportunities in life. Isn't that what it meant to be all a woman could be, to have choices? They could do important charitable work and still fight for suffrage, make a real difference from a place of power and wealth.

She walked up to the balcony. Tables were set up for dining, simple and elegant, with white linen table clothes and a vase of colorful fresh flowers on each one. She sat down in front of the balcony, and it seemed as if she could almost touch the chandelier. It threw its soft light over the dance floor and over her daughters, the most beautiful women here. A waltz started, and Lily and Abagail, who had been seated on a velvet couch, were led to the dance floor by two young men. She watched her daughters for a while and then lost them in the crowd.

Mrs. Chapman stretched her legs out and repressed a yawn. She wanted to order a glass of champagne but wondered if it would look strange, a woman drinking by herself. The evening would be boring for her, but it was worth it, having her two beautiful daughters with her in Europe. She'd have to devise a plan to keep them busy, especially Lily, to keep her mind off Michael. She thought of the time she'd secretly spoken to Michael; she'd felt so foolish, so desperate but it had turned out for the best.

Lily came up and drooped on the chair beside her.

"What's the matter, dear? Are you alright?"

"Just tired, I want to sit out a few."

"I'm glad you're having fun."

When the dance ended, they spotted Abagail and waved at her. She made it up the stairs, holding her dress so she would not trip. "Thanks for rescuing me," she said. "I'm bushed."

Mrs. Chapman called a waiter, who approached in a formal black suit with a white cloth over his arm. "May I help you, ladies?"

"Yes, could you bring us a menu and three glasses of champagne please?"

The champagne came quickly, and they held up their glasses in a toast. They were watching the dancers whirl around and the reflections from the chandelier in front of them when the music stopped abruptly. The dancers all looked up. Several of the staff including the captain stepped onto the stage. Mrs. Chapman thought such an interruption was in poor taste; Lily held her breath, remembering the shipwreck she'd heard about.

The captain spoke. "I don't want to alarm you, but I hear there are already rumors going around about a cable I received today. As you know, President McKinley recently declared war with Spain over affairs with Cuba and Puerto Rico. This will influence our itinerary more than we had first thought. For you who are staying on this excursion through the summer, we just want to let you know we will only go as far as Paris. The war seems to be drawing out rather longer than we had expected, and we will avoid all the countries in that area. The date of return will remain the same; we will simply spend more time in France and the Netherlands and then return to England before sailing for home.

"Again, we hope we didn't alarm you, but certain waterways may not be as friendly as we had hoped at this time. If there are any special accommodations that must be made, it will be done at our guests' convenience. Again, please go on with the celebrations. I assure you there are no concerns in the waterways here, and we will land in England safely tomorrow."

When the band started again, a different feeling hung over the room. Everyone stood as they played the national anthem, and then the waltzing resumed. Mrs. Chapman and her daughters talked about England and what they would do there. They drank the rest of the champagne and tried to forget the news of the world, but the ship no longer felt as safe. A kind of silence pervaded the merriment, knowing their country was at war—and no amount of glittering decorations could take that away. It seemed worse, somehow, and more shocking because they had left their homeland and were out at sea.

Chapter 12

THE NEXT DAY, THEY EMBARKED IN A small coastal town, and Lily was exhausted with all the unloading. It took most of the day to settle in. She went to bed early, still feeling like the sea was right beneath her head.

She woke up before the others and opened her window, breathing in the cool ocean air. She had been so tired she had hardly noticed anything the day before. It was only now that she noticed the quaint village with long, narrow streets and red brick buildings. All the yards were square and geometrical with thick grass and surrounded by low brick walls. Sheep grazed on nearby pastures.

A woman walked with a shawl wrapped around her and a kerchief tied under her chin. Her hair fell out in unruly curls in the damp sea air. She carried a pail of milk. A young man went by on a bicycle dressed warm in tweed and corduroy. He spotted Lily watching him and beeped his horn as he went below the window. She nodded to him and blushed then closed the shutters.

Lily wished she could spend more time in this seaport town, but she knew it was just a stopover as her mother had said. They'd be heading for London and some grand hotel later this morning. She dressed quietly and went downstairs for breakfast. The sun had come out, and the sea air felt good, so she took a walk along the narrow streets after breakfast.

There were shops a few blocks down, and she pushed one of the door handles, hoping to find some special gift or keepsake. It was locked. She heard church bells and realized it was Sunday, so she turned and walked back to the inn. Abagail and her mother were waiting there, and everything was ready for the train to London. A coach picked them up and brought them to the station where they were reunited with many people they'd met on the ship.

The train ride to London was more comfortable than Lily had expected. She sat by a window, daydreaming and looking out at fields of long grass and grazing sheep. They passed through small villages and towns, but the streets were mostly deserted. When they stopped, it was usually at rickety old platforms that served as train stations.

She was glad when they announced teatime and came around with scones and scalding tea. It was a diversion. Although she wasn't very hungry, Lily buttered a scone and bit into the warm pastry while she let the tea cool for a while. She looked at the scenery again and drank the tea in sips, feeling homesick.

She'd write her father a long note tonight she decided, tell him every detail of their adventures. So far, she'd only sent him small post cards. There may be letters for her at the royal hotel in London. She hoped so. She ate another scone, pushing some crumbs off her lap and licking butter from her lips. She looked closely at the wildflowers in the fields, trying to identify them. She saw a bridge coming up over a river and moved away from the window; going over the rickety bridges gave her the willies.

The first thing she would unpack when they got to the hotel would be her notebook and pen. She had so much to tell her father. She wished she could write to Michael and share her thoughts with him too. If he could only see her now, traveling all over Europe. She was becoming an independent woman, and when she got back in the fall, she would be older and mature enough to be with him. Her mother would say it was foolish to think this way—that Michael didn't love her.

She unzipped her small carrier bag. Michael's letter was inside. She'd brought it to Europe, thinking in some way, he would be with her. It also had his address if she decided to write, but she knew that would be foolish. She closed the bag again but didn't stop thinking about how he'd still said he loved her.

Mrs. Chapman saw signs of melancholia clouding Lily's face and took her daughter's hand. "We're almost there. It will be more interesting in London. You'll see; we'll be much busier."

"What will we do there?"

"We'll go to the theatre and have dinner out every night. During the day, we'll go to museums, and the shops in London are exquisite. You'll be surprised. Lily, you won't have a minute to be bored."

"Is it debutante season in London?" Lily asked.

"It's just starting. Those are private parties, so we won't be invited to any of those, but I didn't know you were interested in any of that."

"I'm not, really. It's just fun to watch everyone all dressed up. They say some of the debutantes in London are from royalty. Do you think we'll see royalty?"

"Maybe," Mrs. Chapman said.

They settled back again and had a small meal before arriving in London in early evening. The Chapman women walked into a lobby of richly upholstered chairs and gleaming marble tabletops. Mrs.

Chapman marched to the desk for the key to their room. The lobby was crowded with people smoking and talking. They passed a man smoking a cigar, his head hidden behind a newspaper. Several people stood at the bottom of the stairs.

They had a whole suite, and Mrs. Chapman was pleased by what she saw. The front room had a fireplace with a pair of high back rockers on either side. Their trunks had been sent ahead of time and were placed in the corner of the room on a thick rug. There was also a sofa in this room and a wooden writing desk in the corner. In the middle of the room, a small wooden dining table held a vase of freshly cut flowers.

Lily sat down on the sofa. She was tired from all the traveling and just listened as her mother and Abagail inspected the rest of the rooms.

"Lily, you won't believe this," Abagail shouted. "It's so quaint. There's a bowl filled with fruit on each nightstand and antique brass candlesticks."

Mrs. Chapman came back to the front room and started to unpack a trunk.

Lily got up, opened her trunk, and took out several items. She went to her room, closed the door, and opened her travel bag. The first thing she took out was the letter from Michael. She held it to her heart for a few minutes; then, she put it into the draw of her night table. She put her diary and books on top of the table and hung some clothes in the closet. Then she put her nightgowns and undergarments in the high chest of drawers. She put her brush and comb on a marble washstand beneath a small mirror. With all her possessions around, it was beginning to feel like home. She sat back and yawned. The shades were pulled down in the room, but a little sunlight filtered through. She knew that sunshine was rare in London so she didn't mind this little bit of light interrupting her dark solitude.

Mrs. Chapman gave a soft knock on Lily's door. She opened it a crack, and seeing Lily asleep, she closed it again very quietly. She went to the front room where Abagail was sitting at the writing desk. "She's already asleep. Can you believe it?"

"It's good she's sleeping, though, isn't it? Didn't the doctor say she shouldn't overdo it because exhaustion had brought on her breakdown?"

"Yes, that's true. I'm glad she's finally able to rest."

Mrs. Chapman walked to the center table and rearranged the flowers in the vase, thinking now that the danger seemed to be over, maybe she herself could finally get some rest.

Abagail put her pen down and folded the letter to put in an envelope. "Do you have any letters to post, mother?"

"I have a few postcards. We can just take them down to the lobby, but let's wait until after Lily wakes up. We have dinner reservations downstairs tonight, so I'm not going to let her sleep too long."

Lily slept for over an hour, but her dreams were not restful. Her body thrashed from side to side as her mind produced jumbled images of daytime thoughts. She saw a waterfall like the one she'd seen in the Winslow Homer Painting, which at first gave her a great feeling of peace and contentment, but something was off. She heard its roar and saw the clear water rushing into smaller and smaller falls. She saw someone in a boat at the top of the falls.

It was her father waving to her, not watching at all where he was going. Michael was in the boat. They both waved and waved, smiling at her. She was trying to shout, trying to warn them about the falls, but nothing came out. She tried to scream, but they just kept smiling and waving, even as the boat went over the falls. She could see and feel them falling and falling. She lurched forward, grabbing for them as she opened her eyes to the strange, darkened room.

Everything came back slowly as she stared at the ceiling. She lit the candle, walked to the window, and lifted the curtain. It was drizzling, and gaslight reflected in puddles below, as people roamed the streets. Even at this hour, walkers and livery drivers, carriages and horses streamed through the streets as if it were daytime. She shivered thinking about what went on here after dark. Walking slowly to the vanity, she brushed out her hair, washed her face in the basin, and blew out the candle. When she went to the front room, Abagail was reading by the fireplace and didn't see her come in.

"Where's mother? Is she sleeping?" Lily asked.

Abagail, startled looked up. "No, she's getting ready for dinner. We were going to wake you soon. We have a reservation for seven-thirty." She noticed the dark circles under Lilies eyes. "Did you sleep?"

"Pretty well," Lily said. She didn't want to talk about her homesickness right now. "Where are we going to eat?"

"Downstairs, right here in the hotel."

"Will it be formal?"

"Probably. It seems everything here is."

"I guess I better get ready, then, I had wanted to write a letter to father, but I suppose that would make us late." She looked at Abigail. "You know how mother is—if she said seven-thirty, then she'll be dragging us out of here very soon."

Lily left to dress, wishing she could just go into the kitchen of her own home and have something to eat, dressed in everyday clothes.

"Letters can be posted right downstairs," Abagail said as she left, "so you can write it when we get back."

•   •   •

THEY STAYED AT THE hotel for dinner that night, but soon, Mrs. Chapman had them going out all over London. They went to theatres, concerts, and museums where Mrs. Chapman wasn't afraid to chat with everyone while the girls held back. On the way to the theatre one night, she made acquaintance with an American woman who said if they were around for a while, she would try to get a seat for them in her opera box. The next morning, they found the woman's calling card for them at the hotel lobby. She'd invited them to a small, private party that afternoon.

Mrs. Chapman was overjoyed. It was unusual to get such an invitation so soon; however, she had told her they were only in London for a few more days. The woman had told her she had grown up in Boston and wanted to talk with someone from home. It would be such a good opportunity, and who knew what contacts might come out of it. There was a lot of packing and organizing still to be done, but she was determined to fit in this afternoon garden party. She stopped Lily, who was packing her trunk.

"Wait. Don't put everything away. We haven't left London yet."

"I'm leaving out just the things I'll need for traveling."

"You better leave out one more visiting suit. Look at this. An invitation to a private party from the woman I spoke to last night." She held up the card. "Isn't it wonderful, Lily? Aren't we lucky? We've been invited to someone's home in another country."

Lily frowned. "I still have a lot of packing to do. Isn't the train leaving early tomorrow? I don't think I'm up for it."

"Lily, honey, this is quite an honor for us." It was ridiculous to have to convince her daughter. "Don't be silly. If it goes on too long, we'll bow out early."

Lily raised her eyes to the ceiling.

"Have you seen Abagail? Mrs. Chapman asked. "I thought she was in her room."

"She went down to the lobby, I think, to read the paper."

"I'll have to go fetch her so she can get ready." She turned around. "You pick out something nice to wear. This really is an honor. We'll have plenty of time for packing later."

Lily heard her mother's hurried steps down the hallway; then she heard the door shut firmly.

• • •

MRS. WENTWORTH SAUNTERED out the front door when their carriage pulled up to the house. "My new American friends," she said. "I'm so glad you could make it."

They looked around, hearing music and laughter coming from the back yard.

"We'll go out back there in a minute. Come this this way. I'll show you my house. Get the lay of the land, as they say, back home."

She took a cigarette out of a case and offered one to Mrs. Chapman. Shocked that she could openly indulge, Mrs. Chapman shook her head. Her hostess shrugged and led them all upstairs.

"I love this room," she said. "The boys used to do their studies here where it was quiet, but now that they're older, I get it all to myself. I love sitting at my desk and writing in my diary, watching out the back window."

Lily stood in front of the huge upstairs window, looking out to the back yard curious about the voices and music. It looked like at least a quarter acre of lawn and gardens out back surrounding the paths that led into a thicket of bushes beyond. There were low bushes that were well groomed, and beyond them, she saw fruit trees with a dirt path leading through the middle. Lily missed the large trees and forests of America. Everything was low bushes and shrubs, very green and leafy.

Tables and benches were set up all around, and there were also small square canopied houses here and there on the lawn in case of rain. Lily saw two young men coming out of one of the canopies. One was tall and had to duck coming out. He resembled Mrs. Wentworth. His hair was parted directly in the middle, emphasizing a slightly pointy nose and a round, jutting chin. He looked very British. Mrs. Wentworth had mentioned she had sons. She watched another young man picking flowers. He handed them to a woman nearby with a mock bow. They laughed. She put some flowers in her hair and one in his lapel. Lily looked away from the window, thinking of Michael, and she noticed her mother frowning.

"I'm sorry," Mrs. Wentworth said. "I'm sure you girls would rather be outside with the young people."

Lily's mother narrowed her eyes at Lily.

"Come, I'll take you down now and introduce you around." She looked at Mrs. Chapman. "Then you and I can come back in and talk."

"Nonsense," Mrs. Chapman said. "You are a very gracious hostess."

"No, No. You can't fault them for being young and wanting to be in the middle of everything." She smiled at Lily. "I don't have any daughters, but I have three sons. They're all the same, can't stay cooped up too long in a stuffy house." She motioned for her guests to go through the door before her.

They walked downstairs to the back of the house and through a large sitting room. This was much different from their home where only the kitchen and cooking rooms were in the back of the house. It had high ceilings like the rooms upstairs and seemed much larger because there was not much furniture. There was a plush red carpet on the floor and cream-colored walls hung with oil paintings. There was a piano, a cello, and a violin in one corner, and a long, polished wooden desk sat along one wall. Two love seats sat kitty corner, and several wooden chairs with velvet seats leaned against a wall.

Large glass doors led to the back yard, where a canvas tent was set up, which Lily had not seen from the window. The musicians played under this, and to the side, two long tables were filled with pastries, fruit, scones, plates of fish and meat, salads, and pitchers of cold lemonade. There were also pots of tea and coffee and bottles of champagne.

"This is our music room," Mrs. Wentworth said as they passed through. "It's very open and airy. In this country, we're all getting sick of the heavy Victorian gloom in our houses."

Lily wanted to say something about the new architecture in Worcester and that she knew someone who wanted to be an architect, but she feared making her mother angry.

"It's so wonderful to have a room like this during the winter; we do all of our holiday entertaining in here, but I'm so glad the sun is shining today." She hurried them through and opened the glass doors once again, letting her guests step out first. "Let's move away from the music so I can introduce you. Then you can come back to the tables and help yourself."

As they entered the back yard, Mrs. Chapman stayed abreast with her hostess, while Abagail and Lily moved behind them, using them as a shield. The introductions were awkward, and Lily felt shy, but when they were finally done, they made their way back to the tables. Then, Mrs. Wentworth and Mrs. Chapman went back into the house leaving Lily and Abagail to fend for themselves. They were speaking to each other, but their eyes were on everything else in the yard as they nibbled fruit and sipped champagne.

"Which are your boys?" Mrs. Chapman asked. "I've been trying to pick them out. Are they very much like you?"

"Point out the ones you think are mine, and we'll see how well you do."

Mrs. Chapman took a sip of tea, and her eyes scanned the yard. "I think the blonde haired one standing by the musicians looks quite like you."

"Pick out the other two now before I tell you if you'd make a good snoop for Scotland Yard.

Mrs. Chapman put her cup down and sat forward. "The tall, stout one on the right walking through the fruit trees with a lady on his arm. That's my second guess."

Mrs. Wentworth looked at her and smiled. "And?"

"And that charming young man with the slender nose and rounded chin talking with my daughters, making them feel at home."

"Right on two counts. I might consider hiring you as a detective.

The one by the musicians, I cannot claim as mine, though he is a good friend of the family. The stout man in the garden is my oldest, and the two over by your daughters are indeed my boys."

Mrs. Chapman leaned back and took a sip of tea. "I would never have taken them for brothers, those two. The smaller one looks so different, and he's quite younger than the others."

Mrs. Wentworth laughed. "Yes. He is quite younger than the others, and I'm afraid he hero-worships that older brother, follows him everywhere. Neil doesn't mind most of the time, but it can get tiring. As far as looking different, I'm afraid that Jonathan will never quite look like his older brothers, as he has a different father."

Mrs. Chapman froze, nearly dropping the teacup.

"You see I was widowed young and remarried, continuing my family." She gave Mrs. Chapman a sly smile as if she were somehow enjoying the awkwardness. "So, you see, nothing untoward. Things are not always as they seem."

There were several minutes of silence between the two women. Mrs. Chapman stared up at the ceiling, a little jarred by the phrase 'Things are not always what they seem.'

"No doubt, though, my youngest will be as handsome as his brothers in a few years. His father is handsome enough," Mrs. Wentworth finally said.

Mrs. Chapman pulled herself back to the present and looked at her hostess. "Forgive me. I'm sorry, I didn't hear the last thing you said."

"Oh, it wasn't important anyway." Mrs. Wentworth gently patted Mrs. Chapman's small hands, noticing, for the first time, how delicate she was. "Please tell me about Boston now. Please. I miss it so much.

You left from the harbor, was it, three weeks ago? I used to love walking down by the harbor as a little girl. I had to have a chaperone, and even still, my mother didn't like me going, but I just couldn't resist the invigorating cool air. I was a bit too independent for her. That's why my parents brought me here for my 'coming out.' I ended up marrying and staying here, but my heart is still in Boston. What is it like now?" She took a cigarette from a case and handed one to Mrs. Chapman, who accepted it.

She described the people she knew in Boston. They talked of politics and the latest fads, often comparing one country to the other. Mrs. Chapman told her about the strength of the women's suffrage movement even as nearby to her as Worcester.

When they left the party late that afternoon, Mrs. Chapman felt good. Mrs. Wentworth kissed her on the cheek before helping her into the carriage.

The next day was taken up with traveling. They took the train to a seaport town, then a ferry to the Hook of Holland. There, they embarked on yet another train that took them to Amsterdam and another grand hotel.

Lily was tired when they finally reached the hotel lobby. She sat down in a rounded leather chair and put her carrier bag down next to her. Eventually, they got their key and went to the room. After a light supper, they hired a carriage and rode through the main streets of the city. It was just after dusk, and they couldn't see much but very old buildings with white lace curtains pulled everywhere. Mrs. Chapman said there were a lot of nice museums in this city. Lily yawned.

At the end of June, they headed from Amsterdam to France. At least this time they didn't have to take a boat; they were on the continent now so all the traveling could be done on trains. The railroads seemed to go through the middle of nowhere. What a contrast, Lily thought, to the bustling cities. She was losing track of time being on holiday so long and was hardly aware of the motion of the train as its rocking lulled her into a half sleep. Her head became fuzzy and her breathing longer and relaxed. She leaned her head against the window and closed her eyes, imagining she was at home riding in a carriage and that Michael was sitting next to her. She could almost feel his hand on hers as she fell asleep.

Chapter 13

MICHAEL CLOSED THE GATE BEHIND HIM with his head down. He hardly noticed Abe Whittier jump down from the carriage, hitch up the horses, and come over to meet him. Abe gave his friend a hearty pat on the back, but Michael's eyes still looked to the ground.

"How'd you get the old man to give you a day away from the lovely Louisa? He's letting you out with the outcasts of society tonight?"

"Hey, keep your voice down before he grabs me by the throat and pushes me back in. He knows things aren't working out, and he's madder than a fighting cock. I don't understand why he cares. What's it to him?"

"Well, then, let's haste to the alehouse. Christopher is meeting us there. You can complain to us both about your woman problems and your father who's trying to get you by the throat." Abe pushed his head back, crossed his eyes, and let his tongue hang out.

Michael laughed a little. "He is, you know. He's choking me to death with this stupid Louisa business."

They were in the carriage, and Abe picked up the reins. "Well, you can forget about it tonight. Tonight, we celebrate. The pubs will be crowded, and everyone will be too sick to come forth on the fourth."

"The way I remember it, tomorrow is the day for celebrations."

"That's the old-fashioned way," Abe said. "Christopher always starts celebrating on the eve. There's a party at midnight. They had kegs of beer shipped in from Boston. We decided to start, Christopher and I, just a little earlier than that. Wanted to take you out and cheer you up. Look at all the people on the road, even tonight. I can't even imagine these streets tomorrow."

The streets were jammed with carriages and crowds of children parading. Firecrackers were already going off.

"I'll do my celebrating at home tomorrow," Michael said. "With all the noise, the horses will be spooked."

"Where's your sense of adventure?" Abe asked as the two jumped down from the carriage.

Christopher was waiting for them outside the alehouse door. His gloved hands cupped a walking stick, and his thick glasses made his blue eyes look distorted and large. His red hair was slicked down to prevent curling, and his eyes swam behind the glasses. Michael thought he was quite a dandy.

"I thought I'd *drop dead* waiting for the two of you," he said. "I was beginning to think I had been stood up." He narrowed his eyes and leaned forward on his walking stick in a pretense of anger.

Abe blamed it on Michael. "Our friend here is a little slow tonight; seems he has women troubles."

"Oh, gad, the worst kind. We must get down to the business of drinking at once." Christopher said as he walked over to Michael, clicking his cane on the sidewalk with each step. "Is it unrequited love, poor fellow? We'll get the brutish girl for you." He used his cane for a fencing weapon, striking the air.

"Worse than that," Abe said. "He has *too* many women. One his father is throwing down his throat and one away in Europe because her family deems him unworthy."

"Poor chap, two women, what trouble." Christopher exclaimed, "This calls for some serious drinking." He shook his head and led them inside to a corner table.

Michael sat on a bench that jutted out from the corner. Abe sat next to him, and Christopher occupied a rounded chair on the other side of the table. Michael felt relieved sitting in this dark, hidden corner, as it matched his mood. The sun sank, and the windows clouded over with smoke and dusk. They finished the first round of beers, talking about their plans for the rest of the summer.

After another beer, Abe and Christopher got into a discussion about philosophy and religion. Michael couldn't concentrate, and he looked around the bar. It was getting crowded, and the talk was getting louder. He felt himself falling into a world of feelings and impressions as he tried to think out his immediate problems. He swallowed half a glass of beer at once and wiped the cold foam from his mouth.

"How are you doing there, old boy?" Christopher asked, looking at him, his eyes swimming behind his thick-rimmed glasses.

Michael thought he must be on some drugs. "Don't worry about me. I'm fine," Michael said and went back to his brooding uninterrupted.

He stared at another full glass of beer in front of him. He was so sick of his father hounding him about Louisa—asking what was wrong with her. Isn't she rich, beautiful, and well bred, he would say. *Yes, she's all that,* he wanted to say to his father. *She's all that, but I don't love her. She isn't Lily.*

He looked around and suddenly wanted to see Lily more than ever, just as a man hopped off his bar stool and raised his glass, singing *Yankee Doodle Dandy*. Others joined in. Abe and Christopher raised their glasses and downed their beers after the last chorus.

"If our fathers could only see us in this den of inequity, they'd disown us," Abe said and filled their glasses again from the pitcher on the table.

"Here's to our fathers disowning us," Christopher shouted, and Michael joined in the toast with them.

Michael bowed out of the midnight party. He decided to write Lily another letter. He closed the front door quietly and crept into the study before going up to bed, leaving the door open a crack to make sure he could hear if anyone was wandering about. He sat down on the overstuffed chair behind the desk and tried to write, but his hands shook. He put the paper away after a few illegible tries and went up to his room for the night. He was woken by his mother at 8:30 AM, saying it was time for services.

"I'm not up for it this morning," he told his mother. "I have a bad stomach." Michael turned over, moving his eyes away from the window curtain she opened.

"Do you want some bitters?"

"No, I'll be fine. I just need to rest."

"Okay, then. I'll have Olive come check on you later."

Michael heard her footsteps retreating down the stairs. He kept imagining the clattering and talking in the breakfast room and couldn't get back to sleep. He decided he would get up and write the letter after they left. It seemed like forever before he heard the front door close. Then he went to the window and watched the carriage pull away. After it had disappeared, he threw cold water on his face and looked in the mirror. His eyes were bloodshot but not too bad considering how late he had gotten home. He'd shave this morning and try to make himself presentable as possible. As soon as he finished the letter, he would pay a visit to Mr. Chapman to get an address.

He dressed slowly and stretched out his muscles, trying to get rid of the pain in his back and head. In the breakfast room, he had a cup of hot tea and toast. His head felt a little better after the tea, and Olive, who had served him, sat down in a chair nearby.

"You had a very late night," she said.

"Were you up all night spying on me?"

"I didn't have to be. I can see the effects this morning."

"Well," Michael said. "What's wrong with celebrating the country's birthday?"

"Nothing wrong with that; only, I think you're trying to forget someone rather than trying to celebrate."

"You know me well."

"I've known you for a long time. You miss Lily," Olive said.

Michael looked at her a little suspiciously, wondered if she was talking with his father about the Louisa situation.

"I can see you're troubled, Michael. You don't want to disappoint your father, but Louisa is not the one for you."

Michael looked up at her. He wondered how she could be so perceptive. "I'm going to do something about it," Michael said. "I have to. I'm going to write a letter and go over to the Chapman's to get an address. I might need your help. He might be angry with me and refuse to give it out. Everything is such a mess. I just don't know what to expect."

She poured the rest of the tea into his cup and patted his shoulder. "You know I don't like to go against your father, but I'll see what I can do if you need my help."

They looked at each other.

"How's your stomach now?" Olive asked.

"Much better," he said and took off in the direction of the study.

Olive stared into his empty teacup, wishing she knew how to read tealeaves.

Michael found the desk area in disarray. Three notes, rolled up in balls lay on the floor near the wastebasket. His notepaper was upside down, sticking out of the top of the desk drawer. The round, decorated cylinder holding pencils was on its side, and the cover had not been put on the inkwell. He was alarmed at first. Had his father read one of the unfinished letters? Probably not. His father didn't usually come in here on Sunday. Besides, his father would eventually be finding out anyway, but it was better that he didn't find out yet. He dipped his pen in the inkwell.

MS

July 4, 1898
M. Sawyer
81 Granite Road
Stonebridge, Mass.

Dear Lily,

I'm writing because there is something you must know. I regretted the last letter I wrote to you as soon as it was mailed, even before, but I wrote it under extreme pressure from my father and your mother.

My feelings for you never changed. I love you as much as ever and miss you terribly. I hope you come to see me again when you return from overseas. Everyday gets more difficult not hearing from you or knowing where you are.

I wouldn't blame you if you found someone else, but please write and let me know how you are. I've been very unhappy since you left. Please answer my letter and let me know if things can be the same when you return.

I'll be waiting every day to hear from you. There's so much I want to tell you that I just can't say in a letter.

I love you, Lily, I really do. Please come back, I'm truly miserable without you.

Yours Always,
Michael

He quickly folded the letter, put it in an envelope, and sealed it. He looked at the blank front. The next hurdle would be to get Mr. Chapman to give him the address. He arrived at the Chapman house wearing his best suit. He rang the doorbell, and Mr. Chapman answered it himself, dressed in a formal suit and holding a cigarette.

"Lily's in Europe right now with her mother and sister," he said. "I thought you knew."

"Yes, I know." Michael tried to make his voice sound even and strong. "It's you I want to talk to. May I come in?"

"Of course," Mr. Chapman said. He led Michael to his study where they sat down in two round-backed leather chairs. Mr. Chapman sat forward and flicked his cigarette ash into the ash tray. "What's this about? I just got home from church services. Saw your father and the women—they said you were ill. Isn't there a picnic this afternoon put on by the church?"

Michael sat on the edge of his chair, leaning towards Mr. Chapman. He took the letter from inside his pocket without saying a word. His hand trembled.

"Let me get you a brandy?" Mr. Chapman asked.

"No, thank you." Michael took a deep breath.

"How is it you're not at that picnic with the young people today? If it's business you must discuss, it can certainly wait until tomorrow," Mr. Chapman said.

"No, it's not business, sir. It's a letter. . . for Lily. I don't know where to send it." He looked down at the rug, not ready to see Mr. Chapman's reaction.

"A letter for Lily. I see." Mr. Chapman cleared his throat and was silent for a minute. "I'd like to give you the address, Michael. You seem very sincere and somewhat distraught, but you see, Lily was ill just before she left for Europe. I don't want to do anything to upset her. I trust you must feel the same."

Michael looked up in a panic. "Lily is ill? What's wrong with her? Why did no one tell me?"

"It was just a bout with melancholia. Calm down, my boy. Have a little brandy. She was fine again before she left, and the doctor said the change of scenery would make her better than ever."

"Was it from the letter she received from me?" Michael's hands shook. He clung to the new letter. His face was red.

"There was something about a letter, yes, but that's . . ."

"I didn't want to write that letter. It was your wife that made me write it," Michael shouted.

Mr. Chapman looked at Michael confused. He got up, patted him on the back, and poured them both brandies.

Michael sat back with his head in his hands. "I'm sorry, sir. I didn't mean to say that. I didn't mean to shout."

He handed a drink to Michael. "Well? Is it true? Did she make you break things off?"

"Yes, sir, "Michael said. "She disapproved of us from the beginning."

"I was aware of that, but I didn't think she would go that far. Why would she?"

"That's what I don't understand," Michael said." I've never done anything to offend your wife, and Lily sincerely cares for me, too."

"I know she thinks Lily is a bit young for you."

"But I'm not trying to rush Lily. All I want is a chance to show her how I really feel. Please give me an address so I can communicate with her again."

Mr. Chapman leaned back in thought. He was angry that his wife would interfere in such a way. They had spoken about it, but she had not really told him the whole story. As usual, she had gone to the extreme and indirectly caused Lily all that pain.

"Give me the letter," Mr. Chapman said. "I'll post it in the morning."

Michael held onto the letter protectively, as he wanted to post it himself. "Can't you give me the address?"

"I'd rather not," Mr. Chapman said, preferring to maintain some control over the situation.

Michael shrugged and handed over the letter, thanking Mr. Chapman graciously. He felt he'd made quite a fool of himself, but at least the letter would be on its way, so it was worth it.

"She may not get it for a few weeks," Mr. Chapman said as they parted at the door. "The mail is forwarded to their next hotel address if they are en-route."

Michael looked skeptical.

"Don't worry; she'll get it. I just didn't want you to be expecting a reply soon."

"Thank you, again," Michael said, and he walked away relieved. The letter would be on its way, and he was partially free of the burden he had carried since he sent the first one.

Chapter 14

HE HITCHED UP THE HORSES AND JUMPED back in the buggy, but he didn't feel like going home. He was thinking of telling his father about the letter now that it was on its way. He wanted everything to finally be out in the open. But first, he needed some time alone.

He looked up at the sky as he steered the horses down Main Street. The sun was bright, and he squinted at the carriages around him. Some were horseless now. They were noisy and took a lot of work. Many of his friends were thinking of getting horseless ones, but he liked horses. Caring for them in the stables gave him peace and solitude. He and his father had only one stable boy because they both liked getting up early to brush and groom them, even on cold winter mornings.

The horses clomped past Granite Road, and Michael kept them from turning. Instead, he turned a mile and a half down the street onto a dirt path that led to Grover's Hill, where he and Lily had planned to have a picnic, back in spring. The horses obeyed his gentle tugging as they went down the path that had become overgrown; it widened at the end and opened to a meadow of low grass. High grasses and reeds grew at the bottom of the hill as there was a pond to the right of the meadow with trees behind it. Michael led the horses there. He tied them to a tree where there was shade and gave them water. It was so peaceful now, but later, there would likely be fireworks here. He looked at the hill and wiped sweat from his forehead. Taking his canteen of water, he walked towards a hill.

The sun beat down on his forehead as he climbed, making him feel dizzy, but it did feel good reaching the top. It would never have done to have gone right home after talking to Mr. Chapman. He was too excited. They would have insisted he go to the picnic, and he just wanted to be alone with his thoughts of Lily. He sat down on the grass, took off his shoes, and rubbed his feet. Then he took his socks off too—something he hadn't done outside since he was a boy. He thought how silly he must look with a suit and no shoes and laughed aloud, leaned back on his elbows, and stretched out. There were no large trees on top of the hill, only shrubs and stones and grass. He squinted up at the cloudless sky. There was something special about this hill, just the quietness of it all. He took a deep breath and sat up, crossing his legs and looking over the surrounding countryside.

With his back to the horses, he gazed down the other side of the hill. It was even steeper on this side, and at the bottom, he saw a thick pine grove then a small cluster of houses. The village was far away but looked closer from where he sat. He put his hand up to shade his eyes, looking beyond and thinking of Lily traveling all the way across the ocean. Suddenly, he heard a noise behind him, but when he turned around, he saw nothing. He listened again. It was the horses complaining. It was so foolish of him to have left them there unattended, today of all days. He fumbled with his shoes and socks and ran quickly to the other side of the hill.

"Hey," he shouted as he ran, but his heart pounded, and he was too out of breath to get any more words out. As he slowed to a walk and got closer, he saw his father. He took out his watch fob and realized it was mid- afternoon.

As Michael approached, his father took his jacket out of the carriage and threw it at him. "You could dress yourself decent on a Sunday, at least. What's wrong with you? Your mother's worried half to death about you. She said you were too sick to go anywhere today."

"Didn't Olive tell you I was feeling better and I went out?"

"Olive is good for nuthin." Sawyer's voice broke off, and he looked at Michael. "Sometimes I think you enjoy making trouble. You have your mother all worried, and Louisa's all upset because she didn't have an escort to the picnic."

Michael threw his suit jacket back into the carriage. "I don't know what to say, Father. Let's go home and talk about it. You can take the carriage."

"I'd rather walk," Sawyer said and turned down the path before Michael could stop him.

Michael waited in the carriage until he knew his father would be home; he didn't want to pass him walking. Then he started the horses off in a slow trot, feeling sweaty and uncomfortable in his suit and very hungry. He didn't go into the house right away. He took the horses to the stable and gave them a cool rubdown; then he walked into the kitchen through the back door.

Olive was in the kitchen mixing something in a bowl. "Well, there was a big ta-do here this afternoon when they came home and you weren't here. They asked me where you had gone. I just said I didn't know."

"Sorry, I didn't mean to get you in the middle." He stood by her at the counter. "Anyway, Mr. Chapman took the letter. He's posting it tomorrow, and I'm going to tell Father what I did. He can't stop anything now."

"Oh, I'm happy for you, Michael." She wiped her hands on her apron. "But I don't think it's such a good idea to confront your father. Wait a little, at least until you hear from her."

"I want it all out in the open. Even if she doesn't answer, I'm going to keep trying. I'm tired of this charade with Louisa."

Olive removed a tray of sandwiches from the icebox and a pitcher of lemonade. Michael grabbed for a sandwich, but Olive slapped at his hand and put it back on the tray. "You have to come into the parlor with everyone and eat properly and wash your hands first. They smell like the horses."

"They're all in there?" Michael asked. He had thought only his father was home.

"Of course, they're home." Olive put her nose in the air and strutted with the tray. "She simply could not go to the picnic without an escort." Olive reneged and handed Michael a sandwich then left the room, balancing the tray as she opened the door.

Michael sat in a wooden kitchen chair. His muscles ached from the walk, and his mind raced trying to figure out what to do. He'd go upstairs and change as soon as he ate and avoid the confrontation with his father until tonight. He didn't expect Louisa to be here and have missed the picnic, but it wasn't his fault. Plenty of the girls went on their own these days. He couldn't even go for a walk in peace on a Sunday afternoon. He heard the door behind him open with a bang, and he thought it was Olive bringing back the tray, but it was his father.

"Come into the parlor," he said, and he went back through the door before Michael could answer.

"Dammit," Michael said. He wanted to talk to his father alone, but if his father insisted on keeping up pretense, he'd speak his mind in front of everyone. He got up grudgingly, walked into the parlor, and slouched down in a chair in the corner. He gave his mother and Louisa a dismal smile and muttered a greeting. Louisa looked dismayed and his mother confused.

"Why are your clothes all a mess? I thought you were ill?" his mother asked.

"I felt better, mother," he said "and decided to go for an afternoon walk. I thought the air would do me good." He walked over to the table and hoarded several small sandwiches to take back to the corner, enjoying his status as an outcast.

"Well, your stomach seems to be cleared up," Mrs. Sawyer commented as he wolfed down the sandwiches. She offered Louisa some lemonade, and they talked about the picnic, completely ignoring Michael while his father stood like a pillar of stone by the fireplace staring at him.

Why did his father want him in here anyway? If it was just to make him feel uncomfortable, it wouldn't work. He was sick of the pretense and needed to leave the room, so when he finished eating, he excused himself and went upstairs to change. Then he grabbed a book on the nightstand and stretched out to read, glad to be alone.

There was a knock on the door.

"Come in. Come in." He sighed, put the book down, and sat up as his mother entered. He waved her to sit down. "So now you're here to remind me of what a lout I am."

She sat in a chair near the fireplace. "You lied to me this morning," she said "and your rude behavior in the parlor just now was inexcusable. You're acting like a stubborn little boy. What's wrong with you?"

"I didn't lie to you. I *was* sick." He put his head down. "I stayed out too late last night, had a little too much to drink."

"Michael, I don't understand what's happening to you." Her voice was less harsh. "You're not acting like a gentleman where Louisa is concerned at all. It's not like you."

"I don't want to be with her, and Father is throwing her down my throat. I really don't care for her, Mother. I played along for a while just to please you and Father, and I thought maybe even. . . well, I thought, it might work out, but it won't. I still love Lily."

Mrs. Sawyer shook her head. "You still feel that strongly. Well, you mustn't be rude to Louisa, Michael. You'll just upset her more. Of course, you *will* have to let her know."

"I don't mean to be rude. I don't like acting that way, but I feel trapped when I'm with her. I don't know why Father went and brought her up here like he was trying to push us together. It's really his fault. None of this would have happened if he stayed out of my business. Now I'm going to hurt someone else, and I don't like to hurt people."

Mrs. Sawyer put her hand on Michael's shoulder. "You can't blame your father for everything, you know. You have to take some responsibility."

"He's always trying to run our lives. The last thing he wants is for me to take responsibility. If he and Mrs. Chapman hadn't interfered, Lily would still be here, and we would still be going together."

"I don't know what his objections were. She's a very nice young woman, but if you're sure you don't want to escort Louisa anymore, then you should tell her right away. That is, if you're sure."

"I'm sure," Michael said.

Supper was a sullen meal in the Sawyer dining room. Olive stood by the door for a moment before she brought in dessert. Michael was eating ravenously again and Louisa was pouting. Mrs. Sawyer looked from one to the other, and Mr. Sawyer's face was like stone. Once in a while, Mrs. Sawyer made a stab at conversation, but for the most part, the whole table was silent. Olive left and brought in tray of fresh peach shortcakes. Everyone refused them.

After supper, old man Sawyer retired to his study. Mrs. Sawyer, Michael, and Louisa moved into the parlor. Mrs. Sawyer asked Olive to bring in a decanter of sherry and then joined the young people on the couch. She poured them all a glass of sherry and looked at Michael. He would have to begin the conversation.

Michael looked at Louisa. "I apologize for the way I've been acting. I was very rude in here earlier. I understand that you expected me to escort you to the picnic today." His throat was very dry, and he took a sip of sherry. "Up here, I don't know if you realize it, but many of the girls go to daytime activities unescorted. You could have gone without me. I'm sure you would have had a good time."

She looked down into her sherry glass, smiled, and opened her mouth to speak, but Michael cut her off. "The problem is that sometimes, I have other things to do. I did mention when you arrived that I would introduce you to some of my friends. I think it's time I do that now. There are several guys who would love to take you out."

"What about Christopher? Could he be my escort for the rest of the summer?" she asked.

"Christopher, why sure. He would love to take you around." *Wow,*

Christopher, he thought and let out a little laugh of relief. "You should have said something earlier."

She leaned in toward him and took his hand. "I didn't want to hurt your feelings. Your father said a girl had taken off on you and that you were feeling despondent."

Michael didn't know if he was angry at his father or happy with Louisa. He had been feeling despondent so he could see how she had misunderstood.

"No, I mean, yes, Lily did go off to Europe for the summer, but she'll be coming back, and I know Christopher would be happy to be with you. It's too late now, but I'll ring him first thing in the morning. The truth is, I felt a little selfish keeping you all to myself."

Louisa sat back and took a sip of sherry. Michael took some sherry himself, and they sat together enjoying some small talk into the evening.

• • •

WHEN SAWYER REALIZED that Michael and Louisa were no longer a couple, he called up Winston, furious. "There's no point in her staying here now," he said. "You'll have to make other arrangements for her if you want her stay the rest of the summer."

After he hung up, he thought perhaps he should have been more cautious in complaining to Winston. He had been just so damn angry that their plan had not worked. It wasn't Winston's fault; young people these days were so full of whimsy.

Michael could tell his father was furious the next morning. They both ate breakfast in silence. He ignored Michael's morning greeting and was silent as they walked out to the stables.

He threw himself into work and ignored the parties and picnics that went on in July. It was August first, and it had been several weeks since he had given the letter to Mr. Chapman. He rushed into the house every afternoon to see if there was any word from Lily. Each time, he was disappointed.

Michael slouched down in his chair more despondent than ever. He would check with Mr. Chapman tomorrow. If Lily did send a letter, she'd probably send it there. It was a last resort, but he had to do something. Maybe Mrs. Chapman had seen it and confiscated it.

The letter had gone out with the other mail on Monday July 5th. It had been put in a brown sack and carried to Stonebridge Country Store. It was picked up late in the afternoon and went to the main office in Worcester. Then it went on a train to Boston Harbor with all the other overseas mail. One of the Stewards was piling mail into a compartment on the ship handfuls at a time. One letter slipped out unnoticed and fell into the water. He closed the compartment and started to turn around, but someone nearby noticed the envelope and retrieved it, dripping in his hand.

"Better put this one in there, too."

The steward took the dripping letter shaking his head. "Probably can't even read the address now." But he could still read it through the smeared ink

Miss Lily Chapman
Grand View Hotel
Rome, Italy

He shrugged, opened the compartment, and threw it in.

Chapter 15

THE CHAPMAN WOMEN WERE IN THE outskirts of Paris watching a celebration of Bastille Day. Lily and Abagail leaned over the railing of a terrace and watched as a small child let go of a red balloon. It floated over the roof of their hotel. Mrs. Chapman sat on the patio in a white lounge chair with an umbrella attached, trying to relax. They had just arrived at the hotel, and there was still a lot to unpack. They were to stay here several weeks because of the cancellation in Italy. She took a cool drink of lemonade and fanned herself, watching her daughters.

"This celebration kind of makes me homesick," Abagail said as a confused horse reared up when a firecracker went off not too far away. "We missed all that at home this summer."

"It's interesting seeing Independence Day in another country, though," Lily said. "I mean, seeing how they celebrate and socialize. I'm finding that people are pretty much the same all over the world, only they speak different languages."

"It's more than that, Lily. I think you're simplifying things."

"Maybe," Lily said, and they both looked beyond the parade to watch sheep grazing in a field. "I suppose they have different customs, too."

"And the language is more of a barrier than you think. We better stick close to Mother. She knows more French than either of us."

"I speak quite fluently," Lily said. "I took two years in high school." She was still getting used to speaking of high school as the past. Her life had changed so much this year. It was all both exciting and unnerving.

Their attention was suddenly drawn to the parade again as a band played the French National Anthem and a row of coaches with men dressed in seventeenth century attire followed. Lily thought they looked handsome in their three-cornered hats and ruffles at the collar and wrist, but it all went by so fast. The music was soon far off in the distance, and a few stray buggies that followed the parade were all that was left to see. Some had colored crepe paper hanging from them and bells attached to the horses' feet. As the last of them went by, the sheep looked up, bleated, and then went back to their grazing. Lily and Abigail watched as everything disappeared in the distance; then they joined their mother at a small, round table.

Mrs. Chapman was tired. It was early afternoon, but she was weary from all the traveling. The patio they were on also served as one of the hotel's dining rooms.

"I know it's early, girls, but I am going to order something and then go for a nap. You can do as you please."

Lily and Abagail ate a full meal, and while Mrs. Chapman slept, they made plans for the next day. The girls were sharing a room in this hotel, and they spread out travel brochures on Lily's bed. Most were in both English and French, and Lily tried to read the French. There was a street not far away with nothing but shops. Abagail pointed it out to Lily on the map.

"I think we went by there in the coach on our way here. Isn't that where the curio shops were?"

"Yes," Lily said "and the dress shop mother wants to take us to. It looks like we could almost walk there."

Abagail took up the brochure and looked more closely. "It does look close. Maybe we could go there tomorrow."

"Why not today?" Lily frowned.

"Not without Mother on our first day here."

Lily's trunk lay open on the other side of the room.

"Are you all unpacked?" Abagail asked.

Lily nodded

"Me too," Abagail said. "I'm going to check on Mother." Abagail opened the door to her mother's room quietly, and seeing that she was still asleep, she went back to where Lily was sitting on the bed.

"I can hear fireworks," Lily said as she got up and went to the window. "I'd love to go for a walk in the park across the street."

"We can't go out alone today, Lily. People are drinking to celebrate, and it's almost dusk."

"But I'm bored," Lily said. "It's tiresome being cooped up in rooms all the time."

Abagail looked around. "I suppose we could go as far as the terrace without Mother. We'd have each other for protection, and our room's not far away."

"We could leave a note for Mother. Maybe she'll join us later. And let's get all dressed up," Lily said. "As if we we're going out fancy. I wonder if it's too warm for shawls."

"We could wear the silk shawls we got in England," Abagail said.

"They look fancy, but they're not too warm." She wrote a quick note to her their mother.

The terrace was much more crowded than it had been earlier. It was about eight, and people were eating dinner and finishing off bottles of wine. The people here seemed to eat dinners with many courses and to linger at the table afterwards. They weren't so rushed to be done and washed and off to something else. Lily and Abagail were seated at a table near the railing. They weren't very hungry and decided just to order desert.

Over strawberry pie with whipped crème, the girls talked about all they had done so far and how it seemed so long since they had left home. A candle on the table was lit as the night grew darker, and the girls both ordered a sherry.

"It's hard to believe we're in another county so far away from home," Lily said. "Though it could be home except for all the people around us speaking another language. I don't understand as much as I thought I would. They talk very fast." It made Lily uncomfortable. She leaned in close to her sister. "Do you think they're talking about us . . . because we're foreigners?"

"Don't worry," she said. "They're probably wondering what we're talking about too."

A waiter was suddenly standing beside them. "Anything else, Mademoiselles?"

"Oh, two more sherries, please," Abagail said and giggled as he walked away.

They sipped the sherry as the night wore on. The candles on the table were the only light tonight because fireworks were going off in the distance, creating long beads of yellow dropping from the sky. It was getting hard to see to the other side of the terrace, but they could still hear lots of voices and glasses clinking.

"Are you glad you came after all?" Abagail asked after several minutes of silence.

"Yes, I guess so," Lily said. "It's kept me busy and given me some new dreams. I miss home though. Don't you?"

Abigail didn't answer at first. She could hardly see Lily's face in the darkness. Lily was sitting with her head down. "Are you still thinking about Michael?" Abagail asked softly.

"Yes."

"It gets better with time, though, doesn't it?"

"I guess, a little."

"Let's order some more pie and teas to finish off our evening."

"Just tea, maybe," Lily said.

"Are you okay?"

Lily turned towards the table again a little more composed. "Yes, I'm fine."

They drank their tea and sat for a while in silence.

Fireworks lit the sky one final time, and when the noise was over, Lily's voice broke the silence. Abagail could not see her through the darkness. "I'm going to get in touch with him again when we get home," Lily said. "I have to talk to him. There had to be a reason for him to change his mind so abruptly. Do you think that would be foolish?"

Abagail shook her head. "I don't know. You must do what you feel in your heart. It seems clear to me, but you know him better than I do. Try to enjoy yourself here, though. Save your thoughts for Michael till we get back."

"I think I'm going to like France," Lily said, feeling better after talking with Abby.

Mrs. Chapman was awake when they got back, leafing through magazines on an armless divan. She couldn't read French very well but liked to look at the fashions and hairstyles, so much more elegant than those in the U. S.

"Tomorrow we go shopping at the best stores in Paris," she said. She had gotten up and was placing the magazines in a neat stack on the table. She was ready to talk now, wanted to know all about the people they had seen, what they'd eaten, wanted to know if the celebrations continued, but Lily and Abagail were tired, and after a few minutes of drowsy conversation, they kissed their mother on the cheek and went to bed.

Mrs. Chapman lay awake for a long time. She wasn't tired now but also wasn't fully awake. Her drowsiness was irritating. She got up and brought the magazines into her bedroom. Her eyes looked at the pictures, but her mind wandered. She remembered when she was a girl of about twelve, skinny with wispy hair. Her mother had tried to train the thin strands into thick baloney curls like the girls in the magazines.

"I'll take you to the best shops in Paris someday," her mother would say as they stood in front of a large mirror. Her little girl eyes pled for acceptance as her mother pulled the thin strands to the top of her head. "A little silk here, a bustle there, you'll be dazzling in rich brocade," but Mrs. Chapman had always felt the burden of her plainness, and she knew they didn't have the means for her 'coming out.' Her mother was very pretty, and she was a Plain Jane at twelve. Everyone said she looked like her father—and had his courage, too.

They had money once, but he had lost it in a bank failure and had died when she was a baby, before she had gotten to know him at all. Her skinny shoulders drooped, and her hair fell as her mother sighed and looked disapprovingly in the mirror. "Paris will help you. Someday, it will be Paris."

But she'd done well for herself just the same marrying Edward. She wondered sometime what had attracted him: her forbearance, her persistence, the very stubbornness that drove him crazy now. She'd never had many courters like the beauties of the town, but she had one loyal man, and that was everything. And she did love him, even with the cruel talk that went around town at the time of their engagement that she just wanted to marry above her station. It had been hard at first with all the gossip. Edward had been considered a good catch, and many wealthy debutantes had still smiled at him flirtatiously even after their official engagement. She heard the talk saying the marriage would never be happy, but Edward still adored her, and that had just made everyone more set against them, especially his parents. They'd wanted him to marry someone prettier, wealthier. She tolerated them, and they tolerated her, just to keep up appearances during the courtship, even while accusing her of being deceitful to their son. When they used to come to visit, they would always act gracious but would never invite her to their home. She supposed that since Edward was their only son, they were protective, but they were so stuffy and hypercritical, even his sisters. She didn't care if she was never invited to their home on holidays, though she'd felt bad at first; because of her, Edward seldom saw his family.

In their years of marriage, she had only been deceitful to Edward once—only once, many years ago, and it was hardly the way everyone thought. She closed the magazine and went to the window. Everything would be fine now. She was in Paris with her two beautiful daughters, and it appeared everything would be as she always dreamed it would be. She opened the curtains and looked out into the dark night.

Chapter 16

PARIS WAS A DAZZLING ESCAPE FOR THE Chapman women. A week then two went by, and they were never at a loss for a new café or shop to visit. Mrs. Chapman wanted them each to have one tailor-made dress, a Paris original. They went for long fittings together and walked off their restlessness in the parks and down the wide boulevards. It was called promenading, and when you worked up an appetite, there was always a café nearby where you could sit for hours and watch others. No one hurried you from the table or thought you were rude to watch.

Mrs. Chapman and the girls sat at an outdoor café drinking coffee and eating heavily buttered croissants. They watched people in the park across the street, bright parasols bobbing in the sun. A woman took off her long, lace gloves and put them in a small clutch purse. It was almost the end of July, and the sun was very strong this time of day. A man strolled by them with a lady on each arm. He smiled at one then the other, engaged in light pleasant conversation. What they called in France a ménage à trois.

Abagail finished her croissant and licked her fingertips. She patted her stomach. "By the time our gowns are done, we won't be able to fit into them. I feel like I need to move around after all this eating and drinking."

"Don't do that in public," Mrs. Chapman said, horrified. "People will get the wrong idea."

Lily and Abagail both laughed.

"Anyway," she went on. "We do a lot of walking here. I think we walk most of the food off."

"I'd love to go bicycling," Abagail said, looking at her mother guardedly.

"Oh, could we, Mother?" Lily asked. "That sounds like so much fun."

Now they both looked at her.

Mrs. Chapman shook her head.

"I don't like the idea. You hardly know how to ride as well as these people who are bumping about here. This isn't the countryside you know. These aren't country roads. You don't even have the proper clothes."

"Oh, please, Mother. We'll go very slowly, and we'll go back and change first," Abagail said, as she crossed her arms and frowned. "We've only been doing what you want to do."

"Yes," Lily said. "Standing all that time for those terrible boring fittings."

"Oh, all right, but I feel like I have two twelve-year-olds with me instead of two grown, young women. We'll have to buy you sporting outfits, and I'll have to find some way to amuse myself."

They bought the new outfits that day, but it was too late in the afternoon to start riding. The next morning, after a light breakfast, Abagail and Lily changed into their new clothes. They wore bloomers made of light cotton and large sleeved blouses that ballooned out and caught in a thick belt around the waist. Their hair was tied back, and each had on round-toed sturdy shoes.

"You'll never win a beauty contest," Mrs. Chapman said as they strode out of their room.

"What are you going to do while we ride?" Lily asked.

"I'm not sure," she said, "but I'm sure I'll find something to do in this large city. I may sit in the park for a while."

"Unattended?" Abagail raised her eyes in mock surprise.

"It doesn't matter with an old woman like me."

"Don't be silly, Mother—you're not old, only liberated," Lily said with a smile.

They both kissed her on the cheek and walked out the door.

"We'll be careful. We really will," Lily said.

"You make sure you stick together." It was the last reprimand before the door closed.

Mrs. Chapman watched them from the window. The hotel supplied bicycles. Most beginners took lessons at the Velodrome and rode around sheltered from the sun and the rain, but of course, her daughters insisted they didn't need lessons, and they would bicycle down the wide sidewalks.

She went down to the hotel lobby to be in the company of others, and sat in a velvet chair, reading an English newspaper. Soon, a forgotten cup of coffee cooled on the table beside her. She wished she could buy an American Newspaper, but the N. Y. *Times* was only available here on Sundays. She was getting bored when she saw the mail delivery coming and watched the desk clerk put envelopes into all the little wooden compartments. She put down the paper and went over to the desk.

"Madame?" the desk clerk asked.

"Chapman," she said, pointing to one of the boxes.

The desk clerk turned around and pulled out several envelopes. That was good; she'd have something to do for a while.

"Chapman" he said and smiled graciously as he handed her the missives.

"Thank you." Mrs. Chapman went back to the chair but did not sit down. She folded the paper under her arm and looked down at the cold, thick coffee. "Ugh," she said. She left it on the end table and walked through the front door. Squinting into the bright sunshine, she decided she needed a parasol. She went back up to the room to get one, but she couldn't find one to match her outfit and decided she didn't care. Maybe she was getting liberated after all. She went out once again to sit in the park, her letters and paper in hand, grabbing a few magazines on the way out.

There was a bench available in the shade, so she folded up the parasol and set it down beside her then put the rest of the magazines and letters down too and looked around for a few minutes. It was a beautiful park with narrow, rounded walkways bordered by lush flowers on both sides. There were some high trees with swings hanging between thick branches several feet away. A young man pushed a very fashionable girl on one of them. They were talking and laughing; a diamond ring gleamed on her left hand.

To Mrs. Chapman's left were some well-manicured shrubs about four feet high. She could hear children's voices on the other side. Occasionally, a head bobbed up over the top or around the corner. *They must be playing a hiding game*, she thought, when she saw a child come to the other side of the shrubs and crouch down.

Mrs. Chapman picked up the mail and thumbed through it. She hoped there was something for her. A letter from Edward, ah, that was good. She hadn't gotten one for a while. It had been addressed to a hotel in Italy. Then she remembered she had forgotten to tell Edward all the details of their changed plans. He knew they wouldn't be going to Spain because of the war, but she had not told him they had also decided against Italy, that they would make up the time by staying in France longer, then go back to Holland.

So, she'd get old news but news all the same. She was thankful that the hotel had tracked them down; others on the trip were having problems with their mail. One letter for Lily looked like it had been through the mill, with smeary ink and no return address. It was probably from one of her schoolgirl friends. The younger ones were not all that concerned about neatness or appearances for that matter. They didn't realize the importance of impressions. Anyway, it had made it here. She put it aside and read her own.

Much later, the girls rode up to Mrs. Chapman on the bench, slowing down and putting one foot on the ground to stop their stride. Full of energy and sweat, they leant their bikes against the bench and talked with their mother.

"Well, how was your ride? Mrs. Chapman asked.

"It was great fun," Abagail said. "We want to go again tomorrow."

"If you don't mind," Lily said.

"We'll see about that tomorrow."

The three of them walked back toward the hotel, the girls holding their bikes, Mrs. Chapman the letters and newspaper.

"We're starving," Lily said.

"Bring your bikes back then and change out of those sweaty

clothes. We can dine out on the veranda like the first evening we spent here. We got our mail today, too. A letter came from father, and a rather damp letter came for you, Lily, though I'm afraid it's all old news. It was sent to Italy and forwarded here." She started to hand the letter to Lily.

"I'll read it when I get back to the room," Lily said and handed it back to her mother while they went to return the bikes.

They washed and dressed for dinner, feeing hungry and tired. Lily could already feel the muscles in her legs stiffen. The water from the basin felt good, and she massaged her calves with cotton towels. They both wanted to wash their hair, but it would take some time to dry, so they decided to leave that for tomorrow.

The letter lay forgotten on Lily's nightstand. Her mother had brought it in earlier. Her eye caught it as she washed up, making her curious. She dried off, quickly dressed, and put her hair up. Then she took the letter to a comfortable chair by the fireplace, where she turned it over and broke the seal with thumb and forefinger. When she saw Michael's insignia at the top, she held her breath until she felt dizzy. Her hands trembled. She tried to concentrate on what she was reading, but she was still dizzy. She took a deep breath. Panic, happiness, surprise—everything mingled within her at once, and only phrases were lifted by her eyes from the words on paper.

Reading the phrases, she whispered them aloud. "I regretted the last letter I wrote you." Her breath caught in her throat. "My feelings for you never changed." A small sigh escaped her lips. "I still love you and miss you terribly." Her hand flew to her mouth in joyful surprise. "Please come back."

She held the letter so tightly it almost tore the paper. Then she sat back and let her breath out. Then tears came. But why had he done it in the first place? Why had he put her through all this? She forced herself to read the letter over again, this time more carefully.

"I wrote it under pressure from my father and your mother," she read. The muscles in her back tensed, and her legs ached. Blood rushed to her face. She swallowed hard and tried to breathe slowly.

Her mother came to the door and knocked lightly. There was no answer so Mrs. Chapman opened the door.

"Are you ready?" Mrs. Chapman asked. She looked at her daughter's face and at the letter she held tightly. "What's wrong? Honey, is it something in the letter?" She reached her hand out, wanting to read the letter that her daughter clung to. She walked toward her daughter. "Show me the letter, Please."

Lily stared at her and screamed something unintelligible. Mrs. Chapman moved closer to comfort her.

"Get out of here," Lily said in a low guttural voice, almost a growl. "Get out of my room."

"What is it, Lily? What's wrong?"

"Get out." Lily's scream shook her whole body.

Mrs. Chapman left the room apprehensively to get Lily's nerve tonic, and then she listened by the door as Abagail approached Lily with the medicine.

Abigail opened the bottle. "Why don't you take some of this? You'll feel better."

"I suppose you knew about this too," Lily shouted at her. "I suppose you too thought it was for my own good."

"What are you talking about?"

She thrust the letter in front of Abagail's face, and the medicine almost spilled on the carpet. Abagail started to read keeping an eye on Lily.

"How could you do this to me, Abby? You're my sister. I trusted you. You never said a thing to me about all this—never told me what was really going on."

Mrs. Chapman stepped through the cracked door.

Lily looked at her mother and sister. "I hate you both. You lied to me. Michael never stopped loving me, and I'm going back on the next steamer that leaves for the United States. I can't stand being here with you two another day."

"Lily, I was not the one who wrote that letter, if that's what you're thinking," Mrs. Chapman said. "I did talk with Michael once and told him I thought you were too young for him. That's all."

Mrs. Chapman put her head down. She couldn't bring herself to look at Lily. *That foolish boy,* she thought. *That foolish, foolish boy.* She knew there was no stopping Lily when she made up her mind about something. In the last year, she'd become completely headstrong and would not listen to any advice.

"I should have known it was you and Mr. Sawyer all along. Especially when he brought that girl up from the Virginia, but it didn't work. Michael loves me. You didn't care. You just didn't care."

Lily sobbed.

Abagail held her. "I didn't know about it, honest," she whispered in Lily's ear. Abagail picked up the medicine bottle and offered some to Lily.

Lily shook her head. "I just want to be back with Michael. I don't need any medicine."

"Then give me some," Mrs. Chapman said. She swallowed a few teaspoons full, pushed her head back, and let out a long sigh.

There was silence for a few minutes. Then Lily got up, brushed herself off, and walked toward the door. "I'm going down to make arrangements for passage on the next liner going home."

Mrs. Chapman could not contain herself. "Lily, don't be foolish. We only have a few more weeks on the continent; surely you can wait. Write him a letter if you want. Tell him you will see him soon. Don't just pack up and run home with one word from him."

Lily didn't even break a stride. Mrs. Chapman's answer was the door slamming as Lily left the room.

Abagail shook her head. "Mother, I can't believe you interfered like that. Did you arrange all this with Mr. Sawyer? You can't really blame Lily for feeling betrayed."

Abagail continued to look at her mother in a curious and unbelieving way but Mrs. Chapman was caught up in her own thoughts stuck on something Mrs. Wentworth in London had said— "Things are not always as they seem." The phrase went round and round in Mrs. Chapman's head, but she couldn't explain any of the past to Abagail, as she'd never even been able to explain it to her husband.

Lily was distressed when she returned and looked at her mother pleadingly. She spoke calmly, but her hands trembled. "There is a liner leaving in a few days for home, and I even told them it was an emergency, but you have to sign for the ticket, Mother. Please let me go. I need to see Michael. I will forgive everything. I promise, if you let me go back to him now."

She went to her mother, rested her head against her knee, and began to cry again.

Mrs. Chapman stroked her hair. "Lily, can you just wait a day or two to make up your mind? Write back to him if you must, but don't cut our trip short. At least, think about it. We'll be leaving France in a few days for Holland. Make up your mind then."

Lily got up and sat on the bed with Abagail. "Maybe I'll think about it overnight."

Mrs. Chapman got up and left the room.

"More than anything in the world, I want to see Michael," Lily said, kicking her shoes off, "but you know, Abby, I'm not sure if it will ever be quite the same. I must find out the truth of it all. He *did* write the letter, and it *did* hurt me. I'm going to be more careful this time."

"Good," Abagail said. "It's better to be careful—not so ruled by your heart."

"Easy to say."

Abagail nodded. "I really didn't know what Mother was up to, I hope you believe me. I knew she didn't want you two together, but I can't believe she would be so underhanded."

"I know. I'm not surprised old man Sawyer would object. He's so gloomy about everything, a tyrant to Michael, but I don't know why Mother thinks our love is somehow doomed."

They could hear their mother moving around again. She opened the door, looking groggy. "I'm getting hungry, but I don't feel like going out anymore. I'll ring for room service. You two can go out if you want."

They all stayed in and ate. The three of them sat around a wooden table in the small front room eating a light supper of finger sandwiches and talking about all the sights they had seen on the bike ride that day; no-one mentioned Michael.

It was raining the next day, and the girls decided they didn't want to ride in the velodrome in Paris where all the beginners were learning. After breakfast, they went back up to the rooms and sat on Lily's bed looking at travel brochures.

Mrs. Chapman came in to join them and sat in a chair with a stack of her own. "Lily, I don't want to upset you, but you have to make up your mind soon."

Lily sighed and nodded. She stared at the wall next to where her mother was sitting, as if seeing her mother's face would weaken her resolve. "I need to go back, Mother. I need to see him."

"So, you're not going back to Holland with us? I have brochures here about a new museum that just opened—and a very chic café. We'll be back in England after that and then heading home; it's only a few more weeks."

"Mother, please. I've made up my mind."

"Then we shall *all* go back now."

Lily looked back and forth at her mother and Abagail. "No, I don't want to ruin *your* trip."

"I don't want you traveling by yourself. If *you* go, we *all* go, and that's the end of it."

Mrs. Chapman's mind was racing. She had taken more of Lily's tonic for nerves this morning. Sometimes it put her to sleep, but other times, it was like she was jumping out of her own skin. Suddenly everything was confusing again, and she didn't know how to protect her own daughter.

"How about if you send him a cable, right now, today and tell him how you feel and that you will be home in a few weeks? Tell him anything you want—just stay with Abagail and me for the rest of the journey."

Lily looked down.

"Well, I don't want to end the trip for you and Abby. I suppose if I could tell him right away how I feel."

Mrs. Chapman and Abagail looked at each other.

"We'll go down right now if you want and send a cable," Mrs. Chapman said. However, when they were in England again, she decided to talk to her friend Mrs. Wentworth and fix Lily up with her handsome, charming, and eligible son.

Chapter 17

THE FIRST WEEK IN AUGUST, MICHAEL WAS just getting out of work and planning to cool down the horses and maybe take one out for a ride to the hill. Some of his friends were going swimming, but lately, he was not very good company. Riding made him relax, but he still worried and wondered if his letter had made it to Lily.

Before he could go out to the stables, there was a knock on the door. Olive answered it.

A man stood at the door and handed her an envelope. "Telegram for Mr. Sawyer."

She hardly had a change to say "Which Mr. Sawyer" before the messenger was gone. She looked at the envelope. "It's for you, Michael."

He jumped down the last two stairs and pulled it from her hand.

"Michael!" she yelled.

"Sorry," he said and patted her shoulder.

He ripped open the envelope and read.

Dear Michael,

*I'm sorry I did not respond to the second letter **stop** We never made it to Italy because of the war **stop** It was eventually forwarded to* *our hotel in France **stop** We are leaving for Amsterdam then back to London for the farewell leg of our tour **stop** I miss you terribly and I will see you again in a few weeks **stop** I love you, Lily*

Michael held the note to his breast and quickly into the study so no one would see him. There, he put his head down on the desk and wept in happiness and relief.

Later, he went to the stable and cooled down the horses but decided he didn't want to be alone. He wanted to celebrate. He rode one of the horses to the swimming hole where he knew Abe and Christopher would be, and afterwards, they went all the way to a tavern in Worcester. He didn't tell them about the telegram.

Abe and Christopher watched the women, but Michael watched the clock and listened for its chimes. Time now was an ally, not an enemy. It was just a matter of waiting, and they would be together again.

At first, he didn't want to tell them, but then, after they tried to get him to join them in talking with a group of young women, he felt compelled to explain his reticence. One of the girls had been so bold as to walk into the tavern and shout, "There is a beautiful sunset out there. You wouldn't want to miss it."

Most of the men had shaken their heads and went on drinking, but Abe and Christopher dragged Michael out—not to see the sunset but to talk with the woman and her friends. Michael *did* watch the sunset and only half-listened to the others banter until Christopher stabbed his foot with the cane to get his attention. Michael frowned at him and kicked him lightly in the shin.

"Listen up, my good man. We were just telling the girls here how you have recently suffered not one but two broken hearts. The poor chap, he's sworn off love altogether."

Michael laughed a little and looked down, but they were all staring at him. "Everything is good on that count now," Michael said.

"Oh, gad," Christopher said. "He's got a third—one for each of us. Why, I'm sorry girls; we may not need your company after all." He leaned on his walking stick as they all continued to look at Michael, who was clearly embarrassed.

The women laughed. "We'll be off then," the one who had come into the tavern said.

"Oh, no, no." Abe gave Christopher a look. "He didn't mean anything. He's just a joker. You're a cad," he whispered to Christopher. "We'll never find women with you around."

"What about Mr. Gloom over there, or whatever his mood is now, saying that he doesn't need anyone?" Christopher replied.

Abe and Christopher started to walk back into the tavern, and Michael stared at the last of the sunset then followed them in. When a pitcher of beer was brought to the table, Michael poured them each a glass. Then, he raised it and said, "Look, my friends, here's what's happened. I wrote a letter to Lily in Europe, and she sent me a telegram just today. Tomorrow, I will be sending her back my confession of love. Things are on again. We love each other, and by this time next year, I hope she will be my bride."

"Here, Here, good fellow," Abe said, and they all drank a toast to Michael and Lily.

Chapter 18

NOW THAT IT WAS DECIDED THAT THEY would continue their trip, Mrs. Chapman and her daughters determined they would make the most out of their last day in Paris.

Lily insisted they go to an art exhibit, and Mrs. Chapman, wanting to mollify her daughter, used one of her contacts from Mrs. Bennett to get them into an afternoon salon. It was not a traditional gallery but instead featured works by new artists like Gauguin, Degas, and Van Gogh. Very modern artists, Mrs. Bennet had told them, a school that had started with the impressionists and now was branching out into new forms. Lily marveled at the paintings, especially the bright colors of the Van Gogh. She had been hoping to meet the artists, but Gauguin lived in Tahiti now, and Van Gogh had tragically killed himself. Degas, she found out was not very sociable, and though he had been invited, had not come.

She thought of Michael and the gallery he had taken her to, ever since he had sent her the letter. Maybe, maybe they would go on a honeymoon in France, she thought.

In the morning, it was time to pack. Lily would be glad when it was over, when they weren't living like gypsies anymore, though she had to admit she was enjoying the adventures. The packing and unpacking were just so tedious, and everywhere they went, they bought new items and had more to pack. Thank goodness the special gowns were not ready and would be shipped later. When everything was packed but the carrier bags, they finally went to lunch on the terrace where they had dined their first night in Paris.

"I have a brochure here for a new museum in Amsterdam. It just opened a few years ago," Mrs. Chapman said taking out papers from her traveling bag as she ate a cranberry salad.

She handed it to Lily, and she and Abagail looked at it together.

"We had so little time there earlier," Mrs. Chapman said. "This time, we'll have nearly a week to relax and see the sights."

"That's all the time we'll have," Lily complained. "We might as well not even unpack."

"We'll have more time in London that way. The end of summer should be wonderful there. It will be the tail of end of high season for balls and parties."

"But we won't be invited to any," Lily said.

"Yes, but it will be very exciting to watch it all, and well, you never know."

Lily looked at her, uneasy.

"Anyway," Mrs. Chapman said, "we have to get down to business now and get our packing done. Let's finish up here. They'll be coming soon to collect our trunks. The train leaves just before five."

The Chapman women were taken to the train station in a coach with red and gold brocade seats. Lily stared at the Eiffel tower as it disappeared in the distance. "They do things big here. It's a grand city but also has a lovely stillness about it. I'll miss the artists that are everywhere and the quaint shops all mixed in with the more sophisticated ones. I can see why people come here to paint."

"If you lived on the continent, you could come here all the time," Mrs. Chapman said.

"Perhaps we will all live here, someday," Abagail said. "Ah, but father would never go for that."

Mrs. Chapman sat straight up as if she had a wonderful new idea. "One of us could move here, and the others could come and visit."

Lily thought of herself and Michael coming here for their honeymoon and staying forever. "Maybe, Mother. Maybe that will happen."

Mrs. Chapman felt cheered. Her mother had always said Paris would save her. She would miss Lily an ocean away, but since Mrs. Wentworth was from Boston, if Lily ended up with her son, they could come visit often.

When they finally boarded the train, they were weary, and after eating a light supper, the girls dozed off in their seats while Mrs. Chapman was busy writing a letter, telling Mrs. Wentworth when they would be in London again and that one of her daughters was very interested in spending time with her handsome son. It was too late to post it when they got to their hotel in Amsterdam, so she stuffed it into her traveling bag until morning.

The hotel in Amsterdam was old with very high ceilings. They all shared one large sleeping quarter with a smaller room for sitting. Lily had not been too happy about that arrangement, as she liked to wake up early.

In the morning, she tiptoed out to the sitting room while the others were still sleeping and opened the shutters to a large window. Standing to the side, she peeked out not to be seen in her nightdress.

You had to be careful in a different country. She had heard about the red-light district and didn't want someone to see her like this, but it was hard to look away. Their hotel was close to the quays, and already, there was lots of activity.

There were street vendors, couples walking, and children playing. With all their traveling yesterday, they had been quite worn out and slept very late. It looked so quaint from the window. She wanted to dress quickly and walk over the bridges and purchase flowers from a vendor. Were there artists here too? Maybe she would see someone working on an oil painting. She went back to the room and got dressed, trying to make noise now, trying to wake the others.

Her mother sat up. "Is it morning already?"

"Nearly afternoon," Lily said. "They'll be serving lunch when we get downstairs." Lily washed her face and started to brush out her hair. "Can I go down on my own? Please, Mother? You and Abagail can rest. I'm bored up here and can't wait to go out in the sunshine."

Mrs. Chapman wanted to remind her that she would have missed all this if she had left, but she held her tongue, glad Lily's mood had lifted. "Give us a few minutes. We'll all go down together."

Lily dressed and left the room. It seemed forever before Abagail and her mother were ready. She heard them in the room slowly washing up and dressing, and she leaned her head out the window and took in the smell of the seas mixed with spices and fish. The sun was hot already, and she could hear peddlers, shouting, bicycles bells ringing, and the ocean splashing onto the dock. It was like Boston Harbor, only much quainter.

I've already improved on my sophistication, she thought. *Here I am just a town girl, and a big city looks quaint to me.* Her mother had said they would be going to a new museum while they were here, and she hoped it had some French Impressionist paintings.

"I'm famished. Can we please go down and have something?" she called to her mother.

"Just let me grab my bag, and we'll go," Mrs. Chapman said.

They had tea and omelets in the small dining room off the lobby. Lily said she didn't want to eat too much. She wanted them to go out onto the streets and bridges as soon as possible to find some of the wonderful fresh fish she smelled all morning while they slept.

"What happened to famished?" her mother asked.

"I just wanted to get you down here," Lily admitted "because I want to go outside."

"Well, you two finish up here while I take care of some business at the desk."

"Do you think there might be letters waiting?" Lily asked, wanting to go with her mother. Maybe there was a response from Michael, but she knew it was too quick for that yet.

"Perhaps," her mother said. "If you're finished and really just must go out, I will meet you outside the door. Don't go far." She walked quickly, not wanting her daughters to follow her to the desk and see her business. She turned around as she left the enclosed breakfast area and called to them. "We'll need parasols; it's very sunny out."

Lily and Abagail looked at each other. Mrs. Chapman had insisted they all use them on this trip, and they had agreed, sullenly.

"We'll go get them," Abagail said, "and meet you out front."

They had a long walk with their parasols along the wharfs and bridges. Lily was looking through all the wares. She had to find something special—something to bring home to Michael—something she would not be able to find anywhere else in the world. She had thought maybe she would find a replica of one of the impressionist paintings, but most of the items being sold here were clothing and food—practical things. She bought herself a new shawl. It was light and fringed, and when she caught up with her mother and Abagail, she put it on and twirled around for them.

"Even that's too hot for today," Abagail said. "Though there's a bit of a breeze right by the water."

"Exactly," Lily said. "That's why I bought it. Would you like me to buy one for you?"

"No, thanks," Abagail said, giving her an amused look. "Not my style."

Mrs. Chapman felt the material between her thumb and forefinger. "Not much heat in that. You look like a gypsy."

"I'd love to be a gypsy," Lily said. "Now that I'm out of high school, maybe that's what I'll do. Mother, show me your hand. I'll read your palm."

"Don't be silly," Mrs. Chapman said, but she let her daughter take her hand and turn it over.

"I see travel in your future. Lots of Romance and a man waiting and waiting for you on another shore." She put her mouth down in a pout. "But I see sadness, too. Something mysterious is going to happen." Then her eyes opened wide. "No, it can't be. I see doom." She clutched her hand to her chest.

Mrs. Chapman was taken aback. She felt dizzy and she hadn't even taken Lily's medicine for sleeping last night.

"She missed her calling," Abagail said. "She could have been another Sarah Bernhardt."

Lily released Mrs. Chapman's hand and took a bow.

"I'm hungry now," Abagail said.

They walked toward a café while lily lagged, still searching out a gift for Michael. Abagail called for her to catch up.

"I don't know about these places by the water," Mrs. Chapman said. "I don't know if we should be seen in them."

Abagail rushed her mother through the door. "Oh, Mother. What are you afraid of? Someone will see us? We don't know anyone here."

"At least the fish will be fresh here," Lily said. "We can eat fancy tomorrow."

They lingered in the café and talked about plans for the next day. Lily was suddenly feeling sad. As her mother spoke about their plans to go to the museum district, she stared out the window at all the activity on the bridges and boats, and she felt like she just wanted to be home. If she could just hop on one of those boats, anything, even a rowboat, that would take her across the ocean to Michael, she would have done it just then, right there. She knew they would go on one of the touring boats this afternoon. Her mother had insisted on it, but if she had her way, she would have them stay on the tour boat across the miles and miles of Atlantic waves all the way to America. She looked back at her mother who was busy making their plans for the next day.

"We'll go to the Rijksmuseum first, then to the new Stedelijk Museum, and we will eat somewhere special, somewhere elegant."

It all sounded very far away to Lily, the strange sounding words, the thought of spending another day walking. It made her drowsy, along with heat and the glass of sherry they had with dessert. Abagail and Mrs. Chapman almost had to pull her up from the table.

"Guess you should not have gotten up so early," Abagail said. "And woken us up."

"Do we *have* to go on the sight-seeing tour *today?*" Lily whined.

"Yes, Lily. It's been all scheduled for us. You can rest on the boat, but you must come with us. I don't want you going back alone."

Lily raised her eyes toward the ceiling. "Okay, okay. I'm coming. No need to drag me."

Mrs. Chapman and Abagail let her walk out on her own but, once they were out in the air, they each took one of her arms and walked toward the dock where the sight-seeing boat waited. They sat on the top tier of seats through the late afternoon, Mrs. Chapman and Abagail taking in the history and the sights while Lily, her head pushed against a pillow and her new gypsy shawl wrapped around her, slept peacefully to the water lapping and the smell of brine.

The next day was overcast in Amsterdam. Lily, again, woke before the others. The bridges and wharfs were covered in fog and rain. She heard the fog horns blaring over the jingle of bells on horses. The peddlers tried to protect their wares from dampness, and some had set themselves up in little lean-tos for the day. Mist hung around the lamppost lights. They were still lit, so it must have been quite early. Lily tried to rest on the divan in the front room, knowing they had a long day, but she was restless. She had left the window sash open, so she watched the rain drip down in long beads. A dampness lingered in these old brick buildings, and a deep, haunted feeling trembled up her arms. She shivered and put on the wrap she had bought. It still smelled like the sea. Maybe they would go to an actual gypsy fortune teller today if they could convince Mother. It would be fun. Maybe just she and Abby would go. As soon as she heard some stirring, she went into the bedroom and began to wash and dress.

"Just put on something simple for now," Mrs. Chapman said. "After breakfast, we'll get dressed properly and do our hair for a day of culture."

"I can see why there are so many painters in Europe," Abagail said as she dressed. "The scenery, the sky, the ocean. It's all so moving. I can't wait to see the paintings today. We'll have to go on the water tour again. Lily, really, you missed so much."

"Maybe just you and I tomorrow," Lily whispered into Abagail's ear. "I want to visit a fortune teller, but we best not tell Mother."

Abagail nodded.

After breakfast, Lily dressed quickly in a long, sleek skirt of navy blue and a tailored jacket with leg of mutton sleeves over a white pleated blouse. "I'm kind of glad it's raining today," she said as she put her hair up in sausage curls. "It will keep us all from getting too hot. I'll meet you down in the lobby," she said when she was dressed.

"Don't forget your parasol," Mrs. Chapman shouted from the bedroom.

Abagail was helping their mother with her hair. "Keep your head still," she said.

Lily didn't know why her mother thought they needed parasols when it was raining, as they would be in carriages for most of the day, but she took it anyway and went down to the desk in the lobby, asking about mail. She hoped that there would be a return correspondence from Michael, but there were just a few missives. She sat in the lobby and put them in her lap, waiting for her mother and sister.

· · ·

AS THE CARRIAGE jostled along, the rain seemed to be letting up. Lily was glad. Maybe after the 'culture' of the day, they would be able to walk along the quays later and mull through the peddler's wares. It had become her new hobby in this city. In the excitement of not knowing what you might find, the hours slipped away. When she got home, she thought antiquing might become one of her new hobbies. It wouldn't be the same back in America, though. Here, everything was so old.

When they got to the museum district, the rain had nearly ended, and sunlight fought with cloud. Mother had been right about the parasols, Lily thought. The first museum they went to was the Stedelijk. Built only in the last few years, it looked very impressive from the outside with spires and many windows. Lily felt dwarfed by its high ceilings. She and Abigail followed their mother around at first, unsure of protocol.

Her mother sat down after a while in a long divan in the corner of the room, gazing at paintings from a distance. She told her daughters she liked to look at pictures and artifacts that way; it was more relaxing and gave you a better perspective, but Lily was worried about her mother. At certain times of day, she lacked vigor, and she wasn't herself. Abby and she had talked about it and had checked to see if she was still taking Lily's nerve medicine. Some was gone, but there was also some left. She was just older than they were, Abagail had said, and as they came to the end of this long trip, she was bound to get tired.

"We'll insist that she rest, and we'll go off without her tomorrow," Lily said.

Abigail nodded.

They went off on their own then, according to their interests. Lily was not interested in the militia equipment and artifacts, but she was interested in the room with the chronometry and medical pharmaceutical items.

After looking around, they all met back together in the front room and sat on the divan. Lily was getting bored and was happy to move on. They were getting up to take a coach to the Rijksmuseum, but Mrs. Chapman said she wanted to walk.

"Are you sure you're up for it?" Abagail asked

"I'm not an old lady. I 've just had a rest, and after this stuffy building, the walk will do us good."

So, they walked out into the sunshine and breathed fresh air.

"I do love the paintings and artifacts," Mrs. Chapman said "but, you know, being in a building with all these old treasures kind of gives me the willies sometimes."

Lily and Abagail agreed as they walked up a wide staircase in this much older museum. Mrs. Chapman kept up with them for a while then found a comfortable chair next to a small window. There was a lack of windows here, which made her feel like the air was too close. She understood though that they had to keep the paintings from direct sunlight while enhancing the room with the proper lighting to make the paintings appear as the artist had intended. Still, did it have to be so dim and dusky? She felt like she was suffocating.

She waved to her daughters as they exited into another room, hoping they weren't worrying about her. They had talked of going off by themselves the next day, giving her a day of rest. *That might not be a bad idea*, she thought and took of sip of water from a pitcher on a nearby table. No food or drink was regularly allowed in here, but they did keep water in because they didn't want any ladies fainting.

Lily and Abagail stayed close together, marveling at the paintings.

It was so impressive to see the Old Dutch Masters. They stood a long while by the paintings of Vermeer. Lily, who was used to the Hudson River Landscapes, was amazed by the interior scenes. She was taken in by the intimacy of Vermeer's *Woman Writing a Letter* while Abigail thought Vermeer's masterpiece was *The Love Letter*. To Lily, *The love Letter* was disturbing, so dark and gloomy, it didn't seem to express any of the happiness of love. They both laughed at the painting of the milk maid.

"That's what I shall do," Lily said. "Now that I am out of school, I will be a milk maid."

"Mother would never agree to that, Lily, and neither would I."

"I don't need anyone's approval," Lily said. "I am a liberated woman. Besides, she is very pretty, and someone might come along and paint a masterpiece of me."

Abagail nearly fell over laughing.

"I know, not very likely," Lily said

They stayed in this room for a long time. Lily was drawn again to paintings of the sea, showing how the ocean can be both beautiful and destructive, and she suddenly became fearful of traveling by water again, but they would have to if they were ever to see home. She supposed that's what great art did, roiled up your emotions of what was beautiful and awe-inspiring and fearful all at once. She shivered and looked around for her sister but found she was alone in the room and went off to find Abby back in the front room with her mother. She sat down in a chair next to them.

"I'm glad you're back. Have you seen everything?" Mrs. Chapman asked. "Abagail and I were just talking about dinner. Are you hungry?"

"Starved," she said. "Where shall we go?"

"I've been looking at some brochures, and it is hard to choose when you're not familiar with the area. Abagail just suggested going to ask for a recommendation from one of the curators, who are likely to be natives of the area."

"I'll go over now," Abagail said. "you can stay here with Mother."

"I want to go somewhere nice. A bit fancier than where we have been eating," Mrs. Chapman said a bit too loudly for a museum. She didn't seem to notice the attention she drew. "Make sure you say you want somewhere nice, clean, and fancy."

Lily bristled. Her mother still looked a bit piqued and probably didn't realize how her voice carried. She took her mother's hand.

Mrs. Chapman smiled and looked at her. "Did you enjoy the museum?"

"Yes, Abby and I had fun. I like this one better than the other one. How are you feeling?"

"Just a little tired, dear; don't worry about me. I think it is the stuffiness in these old buildings. Once out in the fresh air again, I know I will be better, and I do have an appetite. I hope we can dine close by."

"I'll get you some more water," Lily said. When she came back, Abagail was walking back to them.

"There are a few places suggested," Abagail said. "The closest is a place called the Schippers Café."

"Is it fancy?" Mrs. Chapman asked.

"Well, I don't think it's like a ballroom, but I was told it has a lot of charm. They said the food there is magnificent."

Mrs. Chapman looked a little skeptical.

"They also said many famous people go there when they don't want to be noticed. It's kind of like a special, hidden treasure only the locals and the stars of the stage and artists frequent."

"It would be nice to go somewhere small but exclusive. I just hope the food is good," Mrs. Chapman said.

"Mama," Lily said, a word she only used when she felt a sudden intimacy with her mother. "I'm sure the food is fine."

So, the three Chapman women went out to get a carriage to the Schippers Café, but first, Lily looked out the window as they rode along and thought of Michael; she wished he was here with her and they could talk about the differences in American and European Paintings.

When they entered the Café, Mrs. Chapman was taken a back. The main dining area was one long narrow room with round arches every few feet, giving the feeling of being in a large room but also enclosed, almost like a tunnel with many open terraces. She felt suffocation again and was not sure if she could stay, but as she walked inside, the abundance of mirrors and lighting made it seem larger, and she relaxed. There were also some small rooms behind closed doors that were opened occasionally for the waiters to go in, carrying trays laden with food hidden under covered dishes. She wondered what famous people were in those rooms and what delicacies they had ordered. Each arched area had a small table surrounded by spindly chairs, not rugged, but quite elegant. Mrs. Chapman put her parasol down and sat, enjoying the moment so glad that her appetite had returned, happy to be with her daughters, and happy to be in a foreign land away from the troubles at home.

She felt more hopeful than she had in a while. She had a plan for

Lily when they got to England, and she believed it was a good one. She believed it would get Lily's mind off Michael for good. Everything would work out fine, and neither she nor Lily would need the nerve medicine once they were home. She smiled at her daughters and took a few sips of sherry. Dusk was falling over the windows; she looked around at the sparkling lights, the reflections of the sparkling in the many mirrors behind the long bar, and the teardrops of cut glass that sparkled in the mirror from the chandelier that hung above their table.

When they got back that evening Lily hurried in and went to the desk to see about messages. There was a telegram for her.

> *Dear Lily,*
>
> *I received your telegram stop Thank you so much for answering and letting me know that you are safe stop It sounds like you are well stop Have a wonderful time for the rest of the summer stop I will see you when you get back stop I am counting the days Love, Michael*

Chapter 19

LILY RESTED IN BED WITH HER EYES OPEN wrapped in a cocoon of dreams, listening to the quiet snoring of her mother and the deep breathing of her sister. Such a grand day she had spent with her sister and mother—and then, the cable from Michael. How could she be so lucky? Giddy, she put her head on the pillow and closed her eyes, hoping her mother and Abby would again sleep late, and drifted off to sleep.

"Lily, it's nearly noon." A whispering voice interrupted her dreams. Abagail tugged gently on a wisp of Lily's hair then stroked her forehead. "Wake up, sleepy head. Mother said to let you rest that you're just catching up, but I know you wouldn't want to spend the whole day asleep."

"You're right," she said. "I wouldn't."

"Do you still want to go out today, just the two of us? Mother said she is going to stay in and rest."

"I would," she said. "I mean, I will. Yes, I want to." She laughed. "Abby, it was so late last night, I didn't tell you, but I got a cable back from Michael." She got out of bed quickly and danced around in her nightgown. "He said he misses me and will be waiting for me when I get back. Oh, Abby, I'm so happy. I feel better about staying on the voyage now. I don't think I'm going to tell Mother, though. She'll just get all riled up."

Abagail agreed, and they left the room and found their mother sitting by the fireplace reading. "I already went down and had some breakfast and checked for mail, so you two can be completely on your own today. I don't think I will even set one foot outside. It is tiring touring all around the continent, trying to keep up with you two."

"Mother," Lily said. "This is what you wanted."

"Oh, being here with you girls is my dream come true, but I am travel weary and ready for a day all alone."

"I love you, Mother," Lily said, kissing her on the forehead.

Abagail kissed her mother too and followed Lily out the door.

They hurried down the stairs. "She forgot to make us bring parasols," Lily said. "She must be really tired."

The day was sunny, and they decided to find a café outside the hotel for lunch. "Not fish today, though," Lily said, "my stomach is a little delicate."

"We should go somewhere Mother would never go." Abigail said, "Let's buy food from one of the street peddlers and sit in the park.

They followed their noses to a stand that had Dutch food heaped on platters. It was part of an open-air market with a few tables nearby. They looked at the Noodles and meat and what looked like nuts in sauce. A server behind a window looked at them.

"What is it?" Lily asked, but the woman did not seem to understand. She looked at Abigail. "Should we eat something if we don't know what it is?"

Abagail shrugged. "It smells good."

Lily gave the woman some coins, and the noodle sauce was heaped on two plates and handed to them.

"This is delicious," Abagail said after slurping the last of the noodles and nearly spilling the sauce on her dress. She laughed. "I like this not eating fancy."

They roamed along the quays afterwards and among the peddlers in search of inexpensive treasures. After a while, they went back to the paths and rested on a bench, watching and commenting on everyone walking by.

Abagail took Lily's hand. "I'm so glad we're on this trip together. It would have been so boring if you hadn't come." They got up and walked arm in arm. "Let's see if the tour boat is leaving soon. Lily, you missed a lot when you slept through that a few days ago."

Lily rolled her eyes. "I suppose we *must* do everything *you* want. You were always the bossy one."

"That's not true," Abagail said. "Who says I'm bossy?"

Lily laughed. She hadn't expected Abby to be so indignant at her teasing. "*I* do," she said, "as your younger sister who always had to play what *you* wanted."

"Okay, then, so what do *you* want to do?"

"Well, actually I do want to go on the boat tour, but, first, I'd like to find a gypsy woman who reads palms."

Abagail stopped and stepped back a little. "You were serious about that?"

"Why not?"

"Mother would kill us."

"She'd never know." Lily reached for her sister's hand again and pulled her along. "Let's do it. It will be fun."

"You just want to see who you're going to marry."

"Don't you? And she could tell us how many children we'll have."

"What if she tells you something you don't want to hear?" Abagail asked.

"Then . . . I guess I won't believe her. I guess I'll agree with Mother—that it's all foolishness."

A path led from the dock down a long alley that led to the fortune-teller's hut. They poked their faces in and saw that she was busy. She put a finger up when she saw the girls, gesturing them to wait a few minutes. They stood outside the door and looked at each other.

"You're really going to do this?" Abagail asked.

"Yes, aren't you?"

"It looks a little strange in there."

"Do you think she looks scary?" Lily asked.

"No, just odd, and I thought she would be older, kind of like a witch."

"She's older than us, anyway," Lily said.

The client came out of the hut, and Lily and Abagail watched them leave, trying to read their face. "Was it good news or bad news?" Lily whispered.

Abagail shrugged.

The fortune-teller came out and led them to her small table. She sat behind it, and Lily and Abagail sat on a bench on the other side. They hadn't noticed when they peeked in before that there were two small children wrapped in blankets sleeping in the corner.

The fortune-teller, a woman with a long, thin face wore a kerchief wrapped around dark curls. Her lips and cheeks were painted red. She spoke in broken English.

"Palm or Crystal?" she asked pointing to the crystal ball that was in front of them on the table. "Palm, two coins, crystal, four."

The girls looked at each other; they didn't feel like laughing anymore. They shared a brief look of apprehension, but Lily didn't feel that they could leave now. She took out two coins, feeling more comfortable handing over her palm to be read than leaving her fate to the round reflective sphere in front of them.

The woman took the coins then took her hand. She had planned on telling the woman what she wanted to know about, to ask her specific questions about marriage, or perhaps about money, but once she was in the hut, she was in another domain. This was the place of the gypsy, and the woman cast a mood around her clients. This did not feel like a parlor game. The gypsy cradled her hand, held it firmly but not tight. The woman's fingers felt warm. She pointed to some lines on Lily's palm.

"A long lifeline," she said. "That's good." She looked more deeply. "There is another strong line here, though, a branching off. That one is shorter." She looked up at Lily. "Your life could go two ways." Looking down again, she pointed out many small, short lines. "These are your choices, chances that can be taken or not." Next, she pointed to several lines branching out from the bottom of Lily's thumb. "I see children in your future, and they will bring you happiness, but first, there is pain."

Lily smiled, looked at Abagail, and began to relax a little.

She let go of Lily's hand. "The lines in your palm hold much promise," she said. "Promise for a long happy life, but there is also much crisscrossing of the smaller lines. Those lines, it is hard to say—they are your choices. Some may be sorrows, but you will overcome them. You may make some choices and then regret them."

Finally, the fortune-teller smiled.

"You are young and you will have a good life," she continued. "I see good health and many children. Use your strength to overcome your sorrows." The fortune teller then looked at Abagail.

"No, thank you," she said.

Lily thanked the woman and shook her hand, and they left quickly as another client waited by the door. They walked in silence until they came to a bench.

"Let's sit," Lily said

The sun was still hot but the day was waning, and a breeze from the ocean swept through the park. It was high tide, and Lily could hear the waves slapping the docks not far away, mixed with the screech of gulls and the whistle of tugboats. They would rest a while before going sight-seeing, she thought, until the ocean calmed down.

"It wasn't quite what I thought it would be," she said.

"Me either."

Lily looked down at her hands. "It was kind of off-putting."

"It was," Abagail said. "Being in that tent was kind of frightening." She looked at Lily. "I wouldn't have let her take my hand."

"We were already inside; I couldn't exactly say no thank you. I suppose I could have given her a coin and said never mind. I guess sometimes Mother is right. It wasn't like the Ouija boards that we use for parlor games."

"We don't have to go on the ferry, if you just want to go back now."

"No, No. I'm fine. Actually, I'm glad I did it." Abigail stopped playing when she sensed someone was nearby. "I've always wanted to have a gypsy read my palm, and now I know I'm having many children. Can you believe that?"

"She said 'maybe,'" Abigail answered.

Lily pushed her arm. "Don't be such a spoil sport."

They were walking toward the dock.

"Okay, well, how many will you have?" Lily asked.

"I don't know," Abagail said. "I may never marry and never have children."

"Don't say such a thing."

"Lily, I'm not complaining, I'm only saying it's my choice."

"To be an old maid?"

"To be independent my whole life."

"Well, I know you will be a wonderful aunt to all my children," Lily said.

"Do you really think what she says will come true?"

"Don't doubt her, Abby, or she may put a curse on us."

"Really, Lily, from this point on, I forbid you, as your older sister, to go to any gypsies, play with Ouija boards, or go to any séances. You're much too superstitious."

They paid their fee and were helped onto the sightseeing boat. Abagail took Lily's hand and scurried up to the top for seating. "I want to be in the middle because last time we were all the way at the back, and the water sprayed up as it moved, and near the front, people were stretching their necks to see because the driver blocked their view."

• • •

MRS. CHAPMAN HAD not stayed in bed all day but snoozed in a chair by the fire. She was looking through some new poetry books that she had brought, trying to pick one for their next poetry evening, which would be in the fall. Of course, it wouldn't be held at their house this time, but she wanted to have a say about who they would discuss. There would be so much to talk about with her friends when she returned. She would probably join some new clubs, with more confidence now that she was more traveled.

Her head felt a little off today, and even her mouth felt a little sticky. She was thinking of taking some of the nerve tonic but decided she could get through without it. She felt anxious to be back in London.

She was still waiting for a letter from Mrs. Wentworth, hoping there would be invitations waiting for them. Debutante Season was almost over, and she hoped Neil had not been scooped up already by some young lady. The cotillions were over, but there would still be parties. She knew sometimes Londoners left town in August and went to their country homes. Maybe they would get an invitation by her to a lovey place in the countryside.

In the late afternoon, she went downstairs for an early supper, and the girls came in just as she was finishing up. She saw them in the lobby from a window in the dining room and hurried out motioning them to come join her.

"Are you hungry?" she asked.

They looked at each other. "We could eat," Abagail said.

They told their mother all about their day, leaving out the part about the gypsy, and she sat back and enjoyed their stories. They were ravenous; she could tell, and they seemed to have had fun. She ordered them all sherry, and they lingered in the dining room while the sun set into a pink arc across the sky.

Red sky at night, sailors delight, she thought, and reminded them they would all be getting ready to sail again in the morning.

The Chapman women were getting good at packing. What had been such a chore seemed more relaxing, as mother and daughters had established a routine in this roving lifestyle. They also knew that this was the beginning of the return trip. It made them all less anxious to be starting the leg of the journey towards home. They traveled in a coach to the Hook of Holland then boarded a ferry to a seaport on England's western shore.

Lily hoped they would land at the same town they had been in before. It was midweek, and the shops would be open this time. She wanted to explore a place outside of London.

"Do you think we might be able to go somewhere away from the city this time?" Lily asked her mother as they sat on deck watching the waves.

"Maybe," she said. "If we're lucky." She thought this would be a good time to remind Lily of Neil. "I've written to Mrs. Wentworth, you know, the lady from Boston with the three sons."

Lily nodded.

"I got a telegram from her last night. The season is over in London, and I'm hoping we get an invitation to her countryside home. They'll all be there. Her son did not put in a pledge with anyone this year."

Lily nodded, only half listening. She wasn't sure what a pledge was but wasn't really interested enough to ask.

"She said she was looking forward to seeing us again, all of us. She said her sons thought we were all very charming."

"Well, if we can get out of London and see the countryside, I'll be happy," Lily said and got up to join her sister who was above deck watching the waves. She was wearing the gypsy shawl she had gotten and wrapped it tightly around her. "Mother said we may be invited to the countryside. She's been touch with Mrs. Wentworth and said their family goes away from the city for two weeks in late summer."

"I hope her son Neil is there. I'm looking forward to seeing him again," Abagail said.

"Mother said something about him. He didn't take a pledge or a vow or something."

"Good," Abagail said. "He's still available."

Chapter 20

Lily's Travel Log
August 10, 1898

I HAVE DECIDED TO WRITE IN MY TRAVEL journal every single day while we are in London this time. I want to be able to describe to Michael all the sounds and smells and tastes that we encounter on this last part of our voyage. It also gives me time to just be alone. We're staying in a hotel not far from the Wentworth's for a week or so, and then we will go with them to their country home. It is very noisy in the city with people riding and walking the streets all hours of the day and night. We only arrived today, and after a long coach ride from the coast, we dined quickly and came to our rooms, nearly fainting with exhaustion.

Mother has all kinds of plans for us already. Plays, operas, museums—it all sounds very cultured but I do hope Abby and I can manage to have some fun.

August 11, 1898

Today, after breakfast, we walked around the city because it was actually sunny early, so everyone said that later in would be raining.

After lunch, we went on a quick visit to the Wentworth's, and Mother was giddy. She seems to have perked up since we have arrived. It is hard to describe everything in this bustling ever-changing city. I poked into a few shops that looked interesting, but Mother kept pulling me along, saying we didn't have all day. The smell of the horse dung is terrible in the streets, and the Thames water is very dirty. No one would want to swim there—no one would want to swim here anyways because the constant rain makes it feel cold, even in the summer.

I wonder if Michael is jumping in the swimming holes at home. I do wish I was spending the summer with him. It would be warmer in so many ways.

Mother seems a little put off now because she wanted to be invited to a dinner party at the Wentworth's, but we have not received an invitation. She spent the afternoon up in the rooms while Abby and I went out seeking more shops and sights. We needed the umbrellas in the afternoon, and we weren't disappointed in the sights. Even in the rain, there are organ-grinders and fish sellers; we went by a circus being set up and watched as animals were herded into pens and tents pulled up high. We decided it looked like an interesting adventure for tomorrow, but Abby said we must not tell Mother and, this time, absolutely no palm readers.

August 12th

We are invited to high tea at the Wentworth's house tomorrow, and I am so glad because mother has not been acting herself as if somehow that family was supposed to be in charge of all our entertainment from the time we arrived. Abby and I tried to get her to go on a sightseeing tour with us today, but she would not leave the rooms. I'm worried about her and think she has started taking my nerve tonic for sleeping again, but it does not seem to be helping her nerves at all. It put a damper on my enjoyment of the day, but now she has perked up because of this invitation.

We are to dine out tonight and go to the theatre. I was wishing we could see something contemporary by Oscar Wilde, but mother insisted on Shakespeare. I was so hoping he and Mr. Yeats would be in London now that I've read their works. Mr. Yeats is very handsome so it's just as well. I might swoon if I saw him in person.

I mustn't show this page to Michael, although I'm sure there are a few stage actresses he would go silly over. I'm glad that Mother finally wants to go out. We'll be getting ready soon.

August 13

Last night and today were so busy. I am feeling rather exhausted, but I did want to write down my thoughts as quickly as possible while they are fresh. The theatre was wonderful with huge high ceilings and chandeliers that shook sometimes when things got riotous on stage. We saw a Shakespeare Comedy, and it even had a dog in it—a man playing a dog. It was hilariously funny especially the play within a play with a group of men and the one playing the dog tromping around. It fit my spirits well rather than something tragic like *King Lear*.

Mother had been hoping there might be something playing that was a little deeper and more tragic, but I think a laugh was just what she needed. Her spirits are much better today.

The gathering at the Wentworth's was more of a literary salon than a tea, and it was very interesting indeed. It is exciting that the Wentworths know so many literary people. Her husband has a boring job at a bank, but he is a big supporter of the arts, so there was music and poetry and, of course, some political discussions. It is just as well that I don't know the politics of this country very well because some of those discussions became very heated. I wouldn't have wanted to take a side.

The men and the women, at least at the Wentworth parties, don't seem to retire into different rooms. We were one group for the entire party. If one wanted privacy, they had to get umbrellas and go walking in the rain. The large room in the back is perfect for music and poetry recitals. It was all very fun and relaxed. There were small children running around amongst the grown-ups, as Mrs. Wentworth said she didn't want any of the young mothers to miss out. We don't all have nannies, she said, and she also loves to have the different ages gather.

There were indeed some very old couples who mostly sat watching and listening. Mrs. Wentworth is a very gracious host, and her sons were a lot of fun. Frederick, the oldest, is quiet and reserved. He spent most of his time with his fiancé, but I noticed his voice became louder when he got pulled into discussions of politics. That's when he came alive. I heard Ms. Wentworth tell Mother that they were quite sure he would have a career in politics, perhaps even in Parliament.

Neil is very fun-loving with a literary bent and has been going to salons since he was quite young. He said his brother Frederick would take him to some of the more interesting ones, though their mother didn't know. Neil also gave me a book of poems called *The Book of the Rhymer's Club* to borrow. My favorite is of course by the Poet W. B. Yeats. His poems touch my heart, and he is also very handsome. Neil told Abby and I that this party was not where the real literary scene gathered. The real literary scene was something that his mother and our mother probably would not invite to their doors. He promised he would take us out tomorrow on a tour of the pubs where the real drama was lived as well as written.

Jonathan, the youngest, is very sweet and barely fifteen. He mostly played games and conversed with his cousins, though I did notice he managed to follow Neil around whenever possible.

Abby and I played a piece on Piano and violin; a young friend of Neil's disrupted things a bit by playing one of the new fast pieces instead of a waltz, and some couples found partners for a country dance. Mrs. Wentworth seemed more amused than upset, and I heard her telling my mother it's just the way it is with boys.

Abby was taken up in the country dance by Neil, but I left the room and watched from outside the door. I was feeling shy and didn't want to dance around so wildly. I think Abby and Neil are rather hitting it off, and Mother seems a little upset about that. Maybe she thinks I'll feel left out. It's more like we're the three musketeers I told her to lighten things up when we spoke before bed, but I can see those two are gravitating toward each other. We mentioned to her that Neil was taking us out sight-seeing tomorrow, but we didn't tell her where we were going. We just hope she'll let us go on our own with him and not feel she has to be there to chaperone.

August 14

We had the most exciting, fabulous day today. Abby and I are both in high spirits. We went to dinner by ourselves because mother was sleeping when we got back, and we didn't want to wake her. I don't know whether to be worried or relieved at how much she has been resting today. She certainly needed to catch up on her rest, but I hope she is not taking too much of my medicine.

Today, Neil took us out on 'his private tour of London.' When I told him how much I enjoyed the poetry book, he took us to Fleet Street where the Rhymers would sit around drinking from tankards and smoking pipes and sharing their poetry. It's all so romantic. I said I wanted to peek in because maybe we would see Mr. Yeats or Mr. Wilde, but Neil said neither of them is in London right now. We had come here about five years too late for that.

He also took us by St. James Theatre where Wilde's play *The Importance of Being Ernest* had first been staged. He told us Mr. Wilde sometimes even joined the Rhymers, but that was when they had met in private homes and how Frederick had once gotten him into one of the home salons because he had a friend who was a poet. Oh, if we had only been here a few years ago!

Of course, his little brother Jonathan just had to come along with us, and since he and Abby were again preoccupied with each other, they teased Jonathan that I was his date. He didn't seem to mind, except for the embarrassment, and I made it clear that I was practically engaged to a man back home.

Mother was right that having friends in a city abroad makes all the difference. Neil took us to a lunch spot we never would have found on our own. This last week has been the most fun part of the trip, and soon, we will be going to the countryside with the Wentworths, which will be another nice change.

August 20th

I have not been writing as I said I would, the last several days being such whirlwind. Everyday Neil takes us out—I'm sure he just wants to be with Abby but feels he must include me. Sometimes Jonathan is with us and sometimes not.

We try to get Mother to come now but she stays behind. She has visited with Mrs. Wentworth a few times but mostly stays at the hotel. I told Abby today I would stay with Mother and try to get her to go out while she and Neil went off, but she seemed insistent that I join them—as if she wants but does not want to be a couple. I asked her to tell me about them, but she insists they are just the best of friends. I have told her I thought one of us should try to pull Mother out of the stupor she's been in, but Abby does not seem to notice. She says we should get all we can out of being here since probably neither of us will ever be here again.

Unless you and Neil marry, I wanted to say, but she does not seem to want to talk about that. She doesn't seem to notice Mother's decline, and I feel like I am the older sister right now, and I go with her to make sure she is safe and that she and Neil are not doing anything too wild. I don't know if Mother is worried that she may get into trouble with him.

It seems I can't talk to either of them at the moment. I'm glad we are going out to the countryside soon. I hope it will temper Abby's giddiness and lift mother's spirits. Two weeks of London is enough for me. At first it was exciting, but everything is just too much too fast for my nerves, and it's raining all the time.

August 24

We finally leave for the countryside tomorrow. I have had quite enough of London. although we've had some wonderful sunny days and went to another outdoor party at the Wentworth's yesterday. It broke up quite early as we all were concerned about packing. We are going to leave the heavy trunks here at the hotel because they will be taken to the harbor town the last day of August; we will have to procure our own coach to get us there because we will still be in the countryside, and the transportation for this trip is set up from London. I am a little anxious about these arrangements because I don't want to miss the steamer home.

Mrs. Wentworth travels often between countries and insists we shouldn't worry because she has made these kinds of special arrangements several times. It is making packing a little difficult because we can only take what we absolutely need in our valises, but again, they say not to worry because the countryside is much more casual. We will not have to dress for shows, opera, or fancy dinners. I hope the weather stays good.

It was so nice to be outside yesterday where we were able to stroll through the paths in the back garden. You can get lost back there. I took a path by myself and marveled at the size that the roses grow in this country. They say it's the rain. It's very peaceful back there, and with all those large bushes and flowers, I thought at first I might have fallen down the rabbit hole. I watched for a smoking caterpillar and stopped a few times to see if the roses spoke to me.

So sad that Mr. Dodson died this year—if he were still alive maybe I would have run into him in London. I should ask Neil if he ever met him.

The only ones I ran into on the path were couples looking for privacy, including Abby and Neil. It may take some doing to get my beloved sister out of this country when it's time to go. At least

Mother got out again, and her gloom seems to have lifted, but she continues to fret about Abby and Neil. Maybe she is afraid Abby will leave college and stay here. She does seem to think Abby is the silly one now, which takes some of the attention off of me, thank goodness.

Neil insisted again that one of his friends wants to speak and take me out, but I told him I am not interested. I think it may be at the urging of my mother that he is so insistent.

August 25

Today was very long. It rained throughout our long coach ride. I hope this is not a harbinger of what is to come. The horses go slower, trying to traverse on a day like this, so we did not make good time at all. Picnic baskets had been made up with the thought that we could stop and enjoy them in a lovely meadow on the way, but as it was, we had to eat as we rode.

Mother and Abby and I were in one coach, Mrs. Wentworth and her boys in another. Abby was a little put off because she had wanted Neil to ride with us, but Mother insisted just the three of us, and I was glad because it would have made Mother uncomfortable, and we wouldn't be able to talk as freely with another person sitting so close.

For once I agreed with Mother, but I didn't want to say it out loud and upset Abby. I am actually missing her company now, and I want to spend as much time with her as I can while we are still here. I rather wished Neil wasn't coming, though I know that is selfish. He and Frederick may stay only a few days because they have business to attend to in London.

August 26

I slept well after all the traveling yesterday. It's a very charming place we have come to, and I feel more relaxed already. I've woken early and decided to write. I am hungry, though breakfast is not for another half hour. Abby and I have a room together, and Mother has a separate one. I can see sunlight shining around the shutters, but I don't want to open them and wake Abby. I'm glad we share a room; that means I'll have some time with her, though there certainly will not be as much privacy in this rambling cottage as there was at the hotel.

The boys are staying in another wing altogether, but there is not much separation from what I could see last night. It was late and already dark when we got here.

I would like to go out for a walk, but I am not sure if that would be acceptable. I'll wait a few more minutes and wake up Abby so we can go down together and have breakfast.

I hope it stays sunny. I'm sure there are lovely places for walking here.

August 26

I think I will very much enjoy our time here. It's much more relaxing than the city. The day remained sunny, and the sun stays out until quite late. Even Mother was persuaded to take a walk after breakfast, and the air is doing us all some good.

Some neighbors came over in the afternoon, and Abby and I put on our comfortable bicycle outfits to join in on a game of catch me if you can. The grounds are spacious, and since we are not in the city, it seems to be acceptable to wander as you will. The freedom feels wonderful after all the cities and hotels.

The house is a bit smaller than the one in London, so it feels crowded, but as long as it's not raining, I have my private time outside. Besides the two wings of bedrooms upstairs, there is a large kitchen and dining room downstairs as well as a parlor and kind of conservatory at the back of the house. They do have parties and gatherings here, so the conservatory looks quite like the music room at their house in London. Large and rather empty except for a piano and chairs pushed up against the walls. Sometimes I go in there and play piano in the afternoon. Then I think of father and miss him. I will be glad to see him again. It's a good room for music; the sound reverberates but not too much. The piano is well-tuned giving off a rich sound, and I love that it is situated kitty-corner to the glass doors that open to the back yard. I can stare out at a wide meadow as I play.

The wildflowers and grasses are just beginning to have a weathered look to them, and a breeze pushes them to one side or another. The summers don't get as hot here as at home, and with all the rain, the meadows stay in bloom long after ours have withered.

August 28th

I have been too little disciplined and too tired to write the last few days. We went for a tour around the countryside yesterday, visiting shops and local pubs, and friends of the Wentworths from the local villages. They have been coming here for many years. It was fun but a little tiresome to meet so many new people.

Everyone wanted to serve us food and drink, of course, so I rather ate too much and tried to drink nothing stronger than sherry. I was happy to find we were not far from Liverpool, as we will be leaving from at the end of the week.

Mother seems tired; I think she is still using the tonic. It does help her sleep, but the next day, she is so groggy, it is somewhat worrisome. Abby continues to spend all her time with Neil; I don't know what they are going to do when the time comes for parting.

The weather is turning colder here. It's hard to believe that summer is ending, and we will be going home to the smell of apple orchards and the sight of leaves turning.

August 30^{*th*}

We have had a lively day here. The Wentworths are having a house party tomorrow, and it took all day to prepare for the celebration. Although there is a maid here who cleans and tidies the house, we all helped with organizing, cooking, and baking.

Mrs. Wentworth is somewhat unconventional in that she does not keep much help. Every time the men came into the kitchen, Mrs. Wentworth shooed them out, especially Neil who wanted to be with Abby. They had their chores.

Abby and I watched out the kitchen window as the boys slaughtered the chickens. I had never seen chickens running around headless before, and I daresay I will have nightmares tonight. There was also wood to be chopped, as it is getting damp in the evenings. Mother and Abby and I feel it most, being unaccustomed to the damp climate.

The boys laugh at how Abby and I are always bundled up in shawls. Mrs. Wentworth says her parties are casual, so we don't need to fuss over dress and hair. They are expecting a lot of people, many from the city. Musicians, poets, politicians—I do wish Mr. Yeats or Mr. Wilde were in the county right now, as they may have been invited, though Neil says they would have been too controversial for his mother's taste. Yeats, he says, is very much into spiritualism, and Wilde has spent time in prison. A great travesty of justice that, he said.

He says his father, being a businessman, has to avoid every impropriety, which can be very tiresome for the family, but he said he told his parents long ago he would let his opinion be known, whether it was fashionable, politically or not. I can see how Abby is attracted to him. They both have very strong ideals and spirit. I'm sure she has given him an earful about the woman suffrage many times by now.

Mr. Wentworth has spent most of his time doing business in London, only coming to stay over and go back in the morning. Tonight, he has come and will stay for the weekend.

August 31

I am so tired. I will only just crawl into bed in a few minutes. The day was wonderfully fun. I hope to remember it enough to describe it in these pages in the morning.

September 1

We all slept quite late, and I can see between the shutters that the sun is already shining. I am trying to write, but there is scarcely light in this dark room. Abby just opened her eyes and then just laid her head back down on the pillow, so she is awake. I am going to open the shutters just a little, I told her, so I can see to write. She nodded with her eyes closed then turned over and buried her face in the pillow.

I can tell she is getting sad about the end of our journey. Soon, she'll be begging Mother to let her stay on all the way to the English

Holiday Michaelmis. She's already hinted about staying on for a while, but Mother is having none of it. Neil will have to come to America, it seems, if he wants to keep seeing Abby.

The party was so much fun yesterday. If only Michael were here, it would have been perfect. Local guests started arriving soon after breakfast, and croquet and cricket games were going on outside. We were blessed with a sunny day. Lunch was like a picnic with tables set up outside. It was charming, elegant, and casual all at the same time.

In the afternoon, chairs were set up inside and out. Piano and cello music drifted through the audience seated in the chairs to the backyard where guests gathered to play crochet and catch the ball.

I had a lovely time for a while just swinging on a large wooden swing hoisted up on two large elms. I had my bloomer outfit on, which gave me the freedom to go as high as I wanted. It was a good vantage point from which to watch all the activity.

Some of the games ended up rather comical, as there were some run-away balls that rolled down the grassy hills of the back yard. Watching it all and listening to the music drifting into the backyard made me think of home, and Father and Michael.

I watched couples in the paths trying to get away from the crowd. If only my love had been there to walk the paths with me. Maybe someday Michael and I will have a home here with lush green gardens and giant roses. Then again, it rains here a lot so I'm not so sure, but it is magnificent when the sun shines. I guess we will just have to come and visit Abby and Neil. Abby doesn't appear to be hampered by the frequent rain.

Several young men came over and offered to give me a push during the day, no doubt sent by my mother. She seems to have misread me, thinking perhaps that I feel anxious or isolated, when I just want to be by myself. I always made small talk and took a few of their pushes, but as none could convince me to get off and wander around with them, they quickly gave up. It was rather annoying that I knew Mother had sent them over, but I don't want to confront her about it because she seems to be getting more anxious as our time comes to leave.

I'm sure she is concerned about Abby. She is old enough to stay on if she really puts her foot down, but I don't think she would defy Mother like that. I hope she will come home with us and think things over before making any rash decisions about her future.

The boys put all the tables together outside, and about 30 of us sat at one long table. Servers came out with platters heaped with roasted chicken and potatoes, poached pears, and spiced apples. Many of the flavors were unfamiliar but quite delicious. We sat for hours passing around dishes, listening to Neil's jokes, where he holds back nothing about society and politics. He is quite the wit.

All the young people were gathered at one end of the table and the older and children were seated together. Sometimes it was necessary for someone to yell down the table, and at one point, Mr. Wentworth said they needed to move the bottles of champagne down the table because all the fun seemed to be coming from our end.

By the end of that long dinner, I was ready to retire, but everyone insisted the party was just getting started. We moved back into the music room and took seats for the recitations. Poems were read that were original and some that were old favorites. Pantomimes were acted out, and jugglers performed. As the sun set and the candles were lit, the chairs were moved to the sides, and young children were put to bed. Some, who would not be staying overnight, were bundled up in the corner on blankets, though I don't know how they were expected to sleep, as the music was lively.

Everyone partnered up and insisted that I take part. We were taught the steps to a country dance, and we sashayed around each other, up and down the long room; then, the top couple formed an arch with their arms that we had to duck beneath. Sometimes we would change partners, so I was never sure who I was supposed to be with, but someone would take my arm, and we would go stepping down the hall again. It really was great fun, though at this point, I was so tired that my partners were holding me up.

When that was finished, a slower waltz played, and I was asked to dance but said I was frightfully sorry, but I was just too tired. The sun had set, candles were lit around the room, the children in the corners had fallen asleep, and a fire blazed in the fireplace. I was persuaded to go up and play a duet on piano with Abby on violin, and thankfully, it was an old eerie tune I knew well, or I would have made many mistakes. It was Father's favorite tune, and I imagined he could hear the notes all the way across the ocean, reminding him that we would soon be home.

Today will be another busy day because we will be packing for Liverpool. Our trunks are already there. I'm glad the sun is out because I want to take one last constitutional, as they call it here, along these paths and hills. I want to go do it early in the day before packing because I have learned the rain can come on very quickly.

September 2

It has been a long and somewhat disturbing morning. Abby seems so lost and confused, and Mother worries me with her nerves. It is rather strange; in a way, this entire trip was planned because of my problems, and now, I am the one fretting over Mother and Abby.

The day started off rather eerily. After breakfast, I went for a walk by myself in the hills behind the cottage. I was really enjoying myself, taking in all the smells and sights for the last time. I had had to kind of sneak away because Mrs. Wentworth had told Mother that I shouldn't be going off alone like I had been. I didn't understand the concern because I took a walking stick, wore comfortable shoes, and felt I wouldn't run into any animals out there larger than a hedgehog. Besides, it did not at all look like rain, and I was getting to know the countryside.

I wasn't too long on the path when I heard a rustling in the bushes around the corner, expecting a bird or small animal edging along near where I walked. I stopped and tried to see into the high brush, but there was nothing, so I went on. As I turned the next corner, I was startled by a man walking toward me. He was quite far away, but I could see that he walked with a limp and had a white rag wrapped around his head with what looked like blood, as if he had suffered some kind of head wound.

I stopped, frozen in place, my heart pounding, trying to turn and run. When I looked up, just seconds later, there was no one there. I turned and fled as fast as possible back to the yard, all the time wondering with his limp and his wound how he had been able to disappear so fast.

Was he really there at all? Was it all the food and drink from the night before causing me to imagine something so frightful through my waking eyes?

Neil was out in the yard and came to me when he saw me running. He said I looked pale, and he held me as I trembled, even in the sun. I told him of the person or the vision. He said sometimes there were soldiers that had not done well in the war or other odd types roaming around the country paths. He said I shouldn't be walking alone and took me into the house, sat me down, and gave me some tea. After I had calmed down, I went upstairs to finish packing.

September 3

I only have time for a few scribbles this morning because the train will be here soon to take us to Liverpool. I am quite exhausted, as Abby was very restless and sad. We talked about how hard it was to be away from someone you loved which we both know about. She finally cried herself to sleep, so we both got a few hours of rest. This is the last time I will be writing in the journal unless I take it up again at home. I can't say I'm looking forward to a week on a ship again, though it will bring me back home and to Michael. I wonder if Neil will make any promises to Abby before we leave for America. She didn't say it aloud, but I think that is what she is hoping.

Chapter 21

The Chapman women sat in the train as it rumbled through the countryside, the girls opposite their mother. Lily stared out the window, and Abigail, exhausted, had fallen asleep on her sister's shoulder. Mrs. Chapman stared at Lily who tried to avoid her mother's eyes. She looked so troubled, and Lily had expected her to be relieved because Abby hadn't insisted on staying. Never mind that they would be home soon and her mother would be a celebrity in their small town; with the contacts she had made, new invitations and social engagements would await her.

Instead, she stared wistfully at Lily; her face looked firm, and she held her body rigid as if she were steeling herself against some catastrophe. It wasn't a long ride, so they were not to have a meal on board, but they were served tea and scones. Mrs. Chapman thanked them and put the tray on the seat beside her. Abagail awoke, and Lily leaned forward to pour the tea.

"We need to keep our strength up," Lily said. "You know the tea onboard is not going to be anywhere near the quality we get here."

"I'll miss the delicious tea here," Abigail said with a sigh as Lily handed her a cup. Then she put it down on her lap and began to cry softly.

Their mother's face softened, and she put her arms out toward her oldest daughter. "Abagail, dear, you need to pull yourself together." Lily quickly grabbed the tray so that Abigail could sit next to their mother who gathered her into her arms and dried her tears with a handkerchief "I've never seen you quite like this."

"I know," Abagail said. "I'm being silly. I'm actually crying because I had such a good time these last few weeks. I just don't want it to end."

"Oh, Abby, I'm sure you'll see him again, and you can write."

"We talked this morning," Abigail said, looking out the window smiling. "He's so romantic. He says that his father has business in New York in a few months, and he will talk his father into letting him come along." She looked up. "Could he come visit and stay with us?"

Her mother smiled but seemed somehow unhappy.

"Or I could go to New York and stay with him. His mother will probably come and visit Boston where she grew up."

"It's something we'll talk about when we get home," Mrs. Chapman said.

"He also wants me to come to London next year, a little earlier in the summer."

Mrs. Chapman didn't answer but got up and poured herself tea. Lily buttered a scone and offered it, but her mother shook her head.

"You're invited too, of course, and Lily."

Lily had poured herself another cup and was eating the buttered scone. She brushed the crumbs off her dress. "Oh, no, I'm not going anywhere next summer unless Michael is invited too."

"You were so good, Lily, to stay on this trip after the misunderstanding with Michael was cleared up. You must have wanted to just flee home."

"I almost did. Don't you remember? You're the one who talked me out of it."

Mrs. Chapman looked away at the mention of Michael. Her mouth once again set tightly in a grim frown. She fingered the bottle of nerve tonic in her travel bag.

"I did, that's right. It seems I had more sense a mere month ago than I have now," Abagail said.

"Now you're in love. It has nothing to do with sense," Lily said with a sympathetic smile.

They laughed and chattered away. Mrs. Chapman fingered the travel bag again and excused herself to use the toilet.

It was windy and cold when they got off the train and moved in a group to the dock where the steamer awaited. It was certainly colder than it had been in Boston in June. Lily and Abagail each took one of their mother's arms and held their hats on with the other hand. Even tied under their chin, there was a risk of them spiraling off their heads in such a wind. When they got very close to the water, the brine slapped up into their faces.

By the time they were on board, their clothes were wet from the heavy mist. With no one to wave to from the deck, they went down to their berths and changed into dry clothes. Lily and Abagail went back on deck as the ship pulled away.

"In case you're wondering," Abigail said, "Neil wanted to come to the ship, but I told him not to. It would be too hard for me to say goodbye here."

• • •

THE SEA WAS ROUGHER on their journey back to America. Mrs. Chapman seemed to be the one with sea sickness this time. Between bouts, Abagail and Lily tried to coax her into eating more. She had become quite thin. Still, she did accompany them to the dining room most days, and she seemed to rally on the last day with the fancy dress ball. She helped her daughters dress and fussed over their hair. Then she took a nap before the party while the girls whispered together.

"She's still trying to find us good husbands," Abagail whispered.

Lily touched her piled up hair. "Maybe she hasn't noticed we've both found our own. Apparently, she doesn't approve of either of our choices." She looked over at her mother sleeping. "She's gotten so thin. I'll be glad when we get home and she can see Doctor Sands."

"I think she'll be alright. She's getting accustomed to us growing up; that's all. It must be hard to let children go."

Lily sighed, thinking of Michael and his father. "Especially when they don't go the way that you want them to."

"She needs something to do. I hope she starts going to the suffrage meetings in Worcester. We should all go together."

"Maybe" Lily said. "We could try to get her to become a spiritualist. Maybe take her to a séance."

Abagail laughed, and they sat together making plans for a double wedding in London the next summer.

"Let's not let Mother in on it right now. Let her have this evening to try to snag us husbands of her choice," Abagail said.

"I'm glad we have our wedding plans all set," Lily said. "I suppose eventually we will have to let our future husbands in on it."

Abagail got up and took Lily's hand. They danced a waltz around the room together while their mother slept.

They awakened their mother long enough after the start of the ball to be fashionably late. She dressed quickly and ushered them into the makeshift ballroom. This ship's rooms were not as grand as the one they had sailed on earlier. The dining room was one level only, but it was decorated lavishly. Many of the tables had been removed, and plush chairs and loveseats surrounded the dance floor. The band was just beginning a waltz when they entered, and the girls were approached for a dance right away. Mrs. Chapman sat in a chair in the corner with a small table beside her. She sat and watched her daughters whirl around wishing the dance could go on forever—with her and her girls protected in this room on this sea, away from the problems and complexities that awaited them on land.

She tried to forget the urgency she felt of doubling down her efforts to keep Lily from heartbreak. She should have told them all long ago, but it seemed Lily was just a child until this year. How would a child understand there are certain gains and losses as a woman becomes an adult? After the rigors of childbirth, a woman longs for a tiny hand in hers. How can a kind act become such an injustice to nature? Something would happen, she decided. She had faith that something would unravel to cause a turnabout in plans. It had to; she was too weary to stand her ground anymore.

The next day, preparing to land in New York harbor, Mrs. Chapman was finishing up her packing while Lily and Abigail stood on the deck, holding tight to the railing. They both wanted to be the first to spot the statue of liberty through a dense fog.

"There it is," Lily said as the fog horns blew. "We're home." She hugged her sister and pointed in the westerly direction.

"It won't be long now until we get to wait for our train in that smelly grand central depot," Abagail said. "I hope it's not raining so we can sit out on a bench while the arrangements are being made."

"Hopefully, Father will have made the arrangements ahead for us. Mother sent him a telegram with our time of arrival."

"Those are rarely exact," Abigail said.

Abby seemed put-off this morning, and Lily supposed she was missing Neil. She wondered who else might be waiting at the harbor and hardly dared to hope that Michael would be there. They went down, knowing it would be very soon, picked up their travel bags, and accompanied their mother back up to the ship's railing.

"Don't forget to hold on tight," Lily said, remembering the last jolt when the ship had stopped in Liverpool and nearly sent them flying.

The fog was dense so they couldn't make out anyone on shore yet. The whistle blew one long blast up to the sky, and the ship stopped. They disembarked in a crowd of restless passengers, still unable to make very much sense of the land. It was much clearer than this when they had left Boston in June.

Mrs. Chapman and her daughters clutched each other's hands, struggling to stay together as they were swept down the wooden walkway that met up with the land. At the bottom, the crowd dispersed, and Edward, father and husband, approached them with his open arms. A little behind him and to the side, Michael stepped quickly, searching faces.

Lily, searching as well, found his eyes smiling back at hers in joy. Mother, father, and daughters all held each other for a long time until Lily turned and buried her head into Michael's overcoat. They stood embracing for a few minutes, and then Michael, not heeding who was watching, lifted up her up off the ground and whirled her around. He kissed her on the forehead, and then they followed the others walking toward the station. The fog was burning off, and though still quite cold, the sun was breaking out, taking away the chill.

Michael and Lily walked behind the other three holding hands as they walked over the Brooklyn Bridge and to the station. Michael had never seen it before and told Lily how impressed he was with the size.

"But not the smell," she said. "I hope it doesn't make Mother sick. She's been somewhat delicate the last few weeks."

"Listen to you," Michael said. "Fussing over your mother. You've grown closer to her, I hope, on the trip."

"I have, in some ways."

Michael spoke in a lowered voice. "I worried a little when I sent you that letter that she would be unnerved and somehow blame you."

"I think it may have been a turning point," she whispered back, not mentioning that she had decided to immediately head back home to him at first. She liked that he seemed to perceive her as more grown up now, able to take care of her mother. She had seen many things that he had never even seen now. This was the first time he'd been in the grand central station, and she had been in it once before when her family visited New York. She was glad she had kept the travel journal up for at least part of the trip. There was so much to share.

Arrangements had been made for the train, so they didn't have to linger in the smells and racket of trains coming and going. They walked quickly past several trains to be seated on their own. The train rumbled through the Berkshires to their home in central Massachusetts. Lily sat with Michael, looking out the window at forests.

"I missed the trees," Lily said.

"They have no trees in Europe?"

"Well, no forests, like this, not where we were anyways. We were mostly in the cities, and the countryside in England only has, what look to me, like shrubs. No thick forests like these but they have lots of flowers in London and in the countryside. You wouldn't believe how large the roses grow."

Michael looked at her, smiling. "I so missed you, my flower, my love, my Lily of the valley."

She rested her head on his shoulder, and they were both silent as they looked out the window at the leaves that were beginning to turn.

Abigail had fallen asleep sitting between her mother and father. Mrs. Chapman looked out the window at the colorful leaves. *This is the just the beginning*, she thought, *the beginning of the dark season.*

Part III
The Dark Season

Chapter 22

FALL HAD DESCENDED ON STONEBRIDGE, Massachusetts with the smell of apples and with the giddy sound of children jumping into piles of leaves. Most of October was unusually warm, but as Halloween and all Saints Day approached, cold breezes blew around the overcoats, and men and women held onto their hats as they made their way down Main Street. Hairdos refused to stay put, horses got agitated and, even those lucky enough to be inside a covered buggy, were slapped in the face by brutal wind as soon as the doors were opened. It seemed as if overnight the trees had let go of all their leaves, and though not a snowflake had yet fallen, everyone in town was preparing for the time of year when people would stay inside in the light and warmth of the fire.

As October wound its way into November, most small towns in New England, where the fine weather and merriment of summer had faded, began to prepare for cold, snow and dark evenings. These darker seasons were both good and bad for the shopkeepers. November, especially, seemed dreary. The foot traffic on the main streets was sparse, as the thoughts of Christmas gifts were not yet compelling shoppers to go out.

In Stonebridge though, the merchants were excited with not only

Christmas this year but a marriage of two very prominent families that would bring both business to the dressmakers, to the gift shops, and to the only hotel in town where the wedding was to take place. The engagement had been announced right after the Chapman women had gotten back from Europe, and the wedding was to take place in early January.

Mrs. Temple was already seeing business pick up, and Mrs. Cunningham, who had recovered from a bout with heart trouble, was back at the bakery ready to serve the town.

"It's Amazing," Mrs. Temple said to Mrs. Cunningham as they sat in the bakery with their coffee. "I know I won't get the business of the Chapmans or the Sawyers, but I'm seeing so many more people coming in thinking about a new dress or new hat this year. They say it's for Christmas, but it seems like even people who are not invited to the wedding want to have new clothes just to watch outside the hotel."

"I know," Mrs. Cunningham said as she filled a box with eclairs. "Since they decided to have the wedding cake made here, it seems like everyone wants to come and buy their own little cakes. Who would have guessed that grouchy Sawyer would have done something to help all the businesses in town?"

"As well he should, "Mrs. Temple said. "Practically the entire town works for him." They both looked up to see Suzanne hurry by across the street. "She's probably on her way to the dressmakers, picking up a scrap of material or something else."

"I see her go by every morning," Mrs. Cunningham said, "but usually not this early. You might think they would have waited until the summer rather than having this poor girl run ragged down these winter streets to get everything arranged."

"It is a bit peculiar," Mrs. Templeton agreed, "the hurriedness of it all.

. . .

LILY SHOOK HER HEAD as she descended the stairs and looked at Suzanne

"She hasn't picked anything yet?" Suzanne said.

Lily shrugged. "I don't know why she's being so difficult."

"Lily," Suzanne whispered. "We both know your mother has always had her difficulties."

"I know, but there's so much to manage now. I want everything to go perfectly, and I'm doing it all myself. Indeed, rather than helping me, she is adding to the tasks by refusing to make up her mind about something as trivial as material for a dress."

"I'm sure she'll pick something in this next pile."

"If not, I will pick it for her." Lily took the last basket of scraps and tromped up the stairs.

Suzanne went to the kitchen to make tea for everyone and brace herself for crying or an argument. She would be glad when it was over and done. Mrs. Chapman hardly ever came out of her room until afternoon. She had no idea how that woman would hold up through a wedding. She couldn't let herself even stop to talk in the shops because everyone wanted to gossip about the hurriedness of it all and what was going on with the missus.

Lily came back rather quickly, put the basket down, and held up a swatch of rosy silk and lace. "She picked one."

"Oh, that color will look so nice on her."

"I'm afraid you know what this means, though."

"Yes, I'm quite ready to take another walk down to the dressmakers."

"Thank you. You're such a dear. I would, but I have someone coming over about the invitations in a few minutes." Lily smiled and added, "And then Michael is picking me up in the carriage. We're going to talk with the priest."

Suzanne took Lily's hands and squeezed them both, sharing the excitement of two young women preparing for a wedding. She then went for the door. "At least she's made a choice so I won't be trudging down there after scraps any longer."

"That's true, though I dread trying to get her down there for the fittings."

Suzanne headed back to town with the good news for the dressmaker, and on the way back, she ran into Daisy. She hadn't had time to sit and talk with the other maids for some time because everything had gotten so busy.

"Come have tea at the bakery," Daisy begged. "It's been so long since we've just sat and talked."

"Who's we?" She had not spent much time with the other maids since the séance. She was wary of Kathleen since they'd gone, and to make things more complicated, Miss Parker was sick again, and she didn't want everyone asking about that.

"Olive will be there."

"Not Kathleen?"

"No, but I don't know what you have against her."

She finally agreed to sit with them for a few minutes, and Daisy waited for her to return the swatches; then they walked into the bakery together.

"Look who I found," Daisy said as they approached a table in the corner where Olive sat waiting for her tea. She pulled out a chair next to her for Suzanne. Olive waited for Suzanne to be seated to speak, aware everyone in the room wanted to hear their conversations right now. They had become celebrities because of the upcoming wedding, and Olive did not want to let one bit of information or rumor go around because of something she said.

"So, they gave you a minute or two off to sit with us?" Olive said to Suzanne. "I see you running around ragged."

"There's so much more to be done in the house of the bride."

"And how's Miss Parker?"

Suzanne shook her head. "Not well. I do hope she hangs on through the wedding."

"And through Christmas," Daisy said. "It's so sad when someone dies at Christmastime."

"I'm trying to keep her condition from Lily and her mother as much as possible."

"They will be a great comfort to her at the last. She's like family to them," Olive said

Suzanne picked up her tea, which Olive had just poured. "One good thing is that Mrs. Chapman has finally picked out the material for her dress."

"That's a relief for you," Olive said, "but she's getting very thin, isn't she?"

Suzanne nodded. "There will have to be some fittings before it's done."

Olive cut a muffin into four pieces and buttered it. She looked at Suzanne, whispering. "Do they know what's ailing her?"

"A nervous condition of some kind is what I've heard."

"I hope it's not women's trouble. She is of an age. Be terrible if she had to have surgery, now, right before the wedding."

"Let's talk about something else," Suzanne said. "I barely get out anymore, and I know it will be like this until after the wedding. Let's just sit and enjoy our tea."

"Amen," Olive said.

"Speaking of which . . ." Suzanne gestured that they move their heads closer together in a huddle, and she whispered, "Lily and Michael are going to set everything up with the priest today."

"That's so exciting," Olive whispered

Daisy crossed her arms and hugged her shoulders "and so romantic."

· · ·

MR. CHAPMAN GOT up from his desk when he heard the bell ring. He was answering the door quite often lately, as Suzanne was so busy with the wedding plans. He really didn't mind, but he did wish that Mary wasn't spending her days upstairs. Normally she would have answered in Suzanne's absence. And where was Lily? Probably upstairs too. She'd just had a meeting with someone, and as soon as they left, she had hurried up to her room. The house was as busy as a train station lately.

Mr. Chapman opened the door to Michael. "Morning, young chap. Lily just finished a meeting. I think she's upstairs. Come in, come in."

Michael nodded and entered the front hall.

"I'm sure she'll be down shortly. Come, have a brandy with me while you wait. Lily," he shouted up the stairs. "Michael is here."

They entered the study, and Mr. Chapman waved Michael over to a stuffed chair in the corner. He took out a bottle and poured two glasses. "No decanters for us men. Not for me anyway. Straight from the bottle is how I like it."

He sat down on a stuffed chair beside Michael and could see that Michael was nervous. He handed him a glass trying to put him at ease.

"Thank you," Michael said.

"It will certainly be nice to have another man around here. I have been quite outnumbered for so many years. Where are you and Lily off to today?"

"We have a meeting with the priest, and then we're going for a drive into the city."

"Oh, I daresay, you don't want the brandy then."

Michael smiled. "Yes, probably best that I wait until after we've seen Father Mackay." Michael glanced over at the desk. "I didn't mean to interrupt your work this morning. You look quite busy."

"Oh no. It's nothing at all. I'm glad to spend some time with my almost son-in -law, and I'm glad you're taking Lily out of the house. This wedding business, very hectic, as I'm sure you know; she needs to get away."

"It hasn't been too bad over at our house. I guess the bride has the brunt of it— with dresses, hairdos, flowers. I am hoping to pull her away from all that just for the afternoon."

"Ah, splendid, "Mr. Chapman said. "I couldn't have picked a better man for my Lily." He smiled again at Michael.

He wished he could get his wife out of the house. Wouldn't it be wonderful if he and Mary could just get a carriage and go out for the afternoon? It would do her a world of good. Maybe he would ask Mary to go out with him as if they were young again. The doctor had said anything he could do to get Mary out of bed never mind out of the house would be the best medicine for her.

Michael's face brightened as Lily entered the room. He stood, went over to her, and took both her hands.

Lily looked over at where her father sat. "I see he's trying to ply you with brandy, and it's barely noon yet."

"We thought better of it when I told him we were to see the priest."

"Good," Lily said.

Mr. Chapman got up and gave his daughter a kiss on the forehead then he headed back to the desk piled with papers. "You two have fun this afternoon."

Lily looked at Michael, puzzled.

"Surprise" he said. "I have the afternoon off so we can go into the city and get away from all the madness here. No appointment for you, no lists, no dressmakers—just you and I, going to shops and dining afterwards."

"But Suzanne and I were going to write out the invitations today."

"Today is *our* day, Lily. We haven't had a day to ourselves in a while. Tomorrow, you can write out the invitations. I'll help."

Lily smiled. It would be nice to get away from the house. They hadn't done that for ages. Michael was so romantic. He took her hand, and they kissed on the lips. Mr. Chapman, at his desk, pretended not to notice.

Michael had done it right. He had hired a man to drive so he and Lily could be together in the covered buggy. He pulled the window curtain closed, put his arm around Lily's waist, and pulled her onto his lap. They tried to kiss as the seat shook one way then another. A recent storm had rutted the road so they could hardly get a decent kiss until they turned on to the main road. As they approached downtown, they kissed once more in a deep tangle of lips and mouth, lily on Michael's lap and his hand behind her hips.

Then Michael put his nose right up to Lily's ear and whispered, "It won't be long now when we can sleep together every night." Michael's breathy whisper tickled Lily's ear, and she smiled.

He pulled open the curtain as they approached the church, not wanting any rumors of impropriety. Their meeting with the priest was satisfactory and quick. They had already hinted at a date in early January and decided it would be on Saturday, January 7th—the first marriage of the New Year. First the ceremony, then the mass, and then they would leave for the hall in the hotel. A fee was arranged, and Lily was told she would have to speak with the town florist for any arrangements they might want at the altar. Father MacKay blessed them and their upcoming marriage, and as they went down the church stairs back to the waiting carriage, they saw Olive, Daisy, and Suzanne.

Suzanne ran up to them. "Oh, Lily, I hope you don't mind. I ran into these two, and they wanted me to go to the bakery for tea. I'll hurry back now so we can do the invitations."

Lily touched Suzanne's shoulder with a gloved hand. "No need to hurry. Michael and I are going out for the afternoon." She looked over at him. "He's taking me to the city for dinner and shopping. We do have the date set, though after talking to Father MacKay. We'll get them done tomorrow."

Olive and Daisy were standing a little bit ahead waiting.

"I'm glad you and Olive and Daisy are going about together. It's almost like the three of you will be family too."

Michael helped Lily up into the carriage, and she waved to Olive and Daisy as Suzanne walked back to them. They kept the curtain open on the way into Worcester. Lily rested her head on Michael's shoulder.

"We finally have the date set," Lily said. "It feels more real and not just a dream." She looked up at Michael. "And Mother even picked out material for her dress today."

"I'm glad," he said. "But let's forget about dresses and hairdos."

As the carriage jostled along, he thought about what he had had to do to get the afternoon off and spend some time alone with Lily. His father and he had argued again, even though he had kept the plan to himself until the last minute, just so his father wouldn't have time to object. He had gotten up very early and gone into work so his father wouldn't complain when he left at noon, but still, he'd ranted at Michael when it was time for him to leave. His father had known about the meeting with the priest but had expected him back in the afternoon. Michael had claimed to have business in Worcester, and when his father asked what kind of business, he had just walked out the door.

He heard his father yelling as he left, complaining he was not ready for marriage if he could not manage to put in even a full day's work. He frowned and looked straight ahead.

"Michael," Lily called rather loudly to him. "What's wrong?"

He turned to her and smiled. "It's nothing."

"No, tell, me what's the matter?"

He gave a long sigh and held Lily to him. "The usual,' he said. "An argument with my father."

"Oh, Michael, will they ever stop?"

"I imagine once we're married and there is nothing they can do about it."

"I don't understand," Lily said, "how something so important to us can cause them such unease."

"It's not just that. He knows my heart is just not in the factory. I wouldn't labor in one nor do I want to own one. There will be a reckoning, Lily. I can feel it coming when I tell him I don't plan to stay there. He has no one else to take over. I want to be an architect, map out the angles of skyscrapers. The future is steel not leather. It may make it hard for us though; he may disown me."

"I don't care," Lily said. "As long as we're together."

He closed the curtain and kissed her. "My father and your mother are just stuck in the past. They'll never be modern." He put his hand under her chin and raised her face to his. "My opinion is, they are simply too old." He kissed her lips.

"They are quite old, but I just wish they could share in our joy."

Michael and Lily kissed again; then he opened the curtain as their carriage moved up the main street. He pointed out a building to her. "Someone my father knows bought this entire block and had this built just a few years ago. He used to be a carriage maker in the area; now he's built a university. Besides physics and math, it has studies in the new field of psychology."

"It certainly is a new world blossoming before our eyes."

"Maybe our children will go there some day," Michael said.

Lily who had been staring at the building turned around to Michael. "It is a new field isn't it, the study of the mind? Some people think it's all a hoax. Did you know that Daisy and Suzanne went to a séance in Worcester?"

"A séance? Mother is under the impression that they go to woman suffrage meetings. She has been encouraging it and has promised them she will not say a word to the old man. She thinks they are all wrapped up with the unions, but séances? I don't know if she would be too pleased about that."

"I think they were going to the suffrage meetings at first, but there is a group that also holds séances. It might be fun to go sometime."

"Pah—not for me. I'm a man of science. Besides, these spiritualists have nothing to do with psychology. It's actually the study of the human mind, why people act the way they do. My father thinks it's hogwash, but I think it's all just a new way of looking at behavior. Some police are even using these psychological techniques in New York to solve crimes."

"'I've heard of Freud," Lily said. "Father has his books. That's something they don't teach in school. They say it can be too troubling for women to read."

"Well, when you are my wife, I would want you to read anything that you want and make up your own mind if it is troubling or not"

"Well then, when I am your wife, I think I shall go to the women's meetings and take you with me."

"Your mother has taught you well" he said, and to Lily's surprise, they pulled up in front of the Worcester Hotel.

"Oh my. I didn't know you could dine here if you weren't a guest."

"They'll sell their wares to anyone," Michael said. "Like all good businesses—anyone that can pay."

As they entered the foyer Lily, who had never been inside, was struck by the graceful yet modern furnishings. The couches, the chairs, even the chandeliers were missing the ornateness she expected in these pricey hotels, and when they were taken into the dining room, it was very expansive yet simple. Along one side of the room was a bar, and along another, a bank of high windows presented a view of what seemed to be the entire city.

"The seven hills of Worcester," Michael said as they were seated and Lily stared out the window. "Did you know Worcester was built on seven hills?"

"It's breathtaking," she said. "I had no idea we would be dining in such style today."

"So, what were you expecting from your husband-to-be, club sandwiches and lemonade? If you prefer, we could wait a while and eat from the night wagons."

"Night wagons." Lily gave him a look. "What's that? It sounds suspicious, like something that someone would disappear in and never come back."

Michael laughed. "They're only the wagons that come around for the workers doing the night shift. You wouldn't like the food. Believe me; I've eaten from them. As well as sending me to college here, the old man used to have me work shifts in the factories before he gave me a position. He called it an apprenticeship."

Lily stared at Michael. He had so much knowledge. The champagne had come, so the waiter poured, and they drank a toast.

"To our wedding," Michael said.

"And to our children, who will be so smart and knowledgeable with a father like you. A palm reader in Holland told me I might have five."

"Oh, my, I guess we better get started right away."

"After the wedding," Lily said.

Michael winked at her.

"Well, she said, the lines on my palm are rather crossed. It mightn't be five."

"You see, she's given herself an out, in case her guess is wrong."

"So, you don't hold much faith in palm readers or séances?"

"Amusement only, though I hope they are not all girls," he said. "I would be dreadfully outnumbered."

"Whatever they are, boys or girls, they will all go to university."

"Everyone," Michael said. "We shall be modern parents of the new century."

Chapter 23

THANKSGIVING WAS QUIET IN NEW ENGLAND at the turn of the century. The shopkeepers closed their doors early on Wednesday, knowing there would be no business except at the bakery where those who were unable to bake would buy pies, if they could afford it.

Sawyer gave turkeys to all his employees so that no matter their circumstances, they would at least have a hearty meal like the rest of the town. Mrs. Temple always invited Mrs. Cunningham over for holidays, and like all other families and friends gathering in this small town, they took time out from talk of the general problems around them and concentrated on the people gathered at the table and the wonderful feast.

• • •

LILY AND MICHAEL had spent the week before Thanksgiving trying unsuccessfully to convince their parents that they should all eat together this year, as they would soon be one family.

On Wednesday they took a walk through the deserted town and embraced at the doorstep in front of Lily's house. "I just can't bear to have to wait all the way till next year to share this special day with you. I'll be thinking of you every minute."

"I know," Michael said, "I'll get away as soon as I can. We're having my cousin and my aunts and uncles. Everyone usually falls asleep soon after dinner."

"My mother will probably retreat to her room before dessert is even put out. At least Abby will be here; she has a long weekend off from university."

"How is Abby, and how was her trip to New York?"

"Oh, she's great. I haven't had much of a chance to talk with her about New York and Neil because she's been away at school, but when you come tomorrow, we'll have a great chat, the three of us."

"I can't wait," Michael said and kissed Lily, reluctantly letting her go prepare for the celebration with her family.

Thanksgiving was always a quiet family time, and Lily held on to the thought that next year she and Michael would be a family. They had decided already that this year they would spend Christmas together no matter what their parents said about it.

Lily walked into the entry and the wonderful smells of the baking pies. She hurried downstairs hoping she was not too late to help. She loved to help Suzanne with the baking on Thanksgiving Eve.

"Am I late? Have I missed all the fun?"

"The mince is done." Suzanne wiped her hands on a sticky, spotted apron "But you can help with the apple."

"What do you need me to do?"

"First, go put on an apron; then you can cut up these apples. I was just mixing the spices together. I don't like to cut them up beforehand because the edges might brown."

Lily hurried to a cupboard and put on an apron then started peeling the apples.

"Leave some for the stuffing," Suzanne reminded her. "Put a few aside by the bowl over there with the nuts and cranberries."

"Yes, Ma'am." Lily put aside a few apples and cut the others in quarters then eighths.

Suzanne, busy with crushing spices in a pestle, turned around suddenly, covered her face, and sneezed. She rushed to the sink and washed her hands. "Did you have a nice outing with Michael today?" she asked.

"We didn't go far, but we had a good evening. We walked out by the hill even though it was starting to snow." There were several bowls set about with spices that Suzanne was labeling. Some were for the turkey and vegetables. "You'll have a big job tomorrow getting the turkey in," Lily said.

"I figure it's just as well. I'll be up very early to put the turkey in so I'd rather have everything cut up and crushed and ready."

"Except the apples," Lily teased her. "Or they'd go brown."

Suzanne looked at her with a sideways smile. "That's right. Now bring the slices over here so I can mix them in with the spices."

Lily cupped the apples in her apron and brought then down the long wooden table to Suzanne. The dough was already laid out. She had missed that part, the kneading when you got covered with flour. It had been her favorite part when she was a child. She was sure she had rather hampered than helped at that time. Back then, she would have been helping Nana Parker.

"How's Nana?" Lily asked.

Suzanne swished each piece around in the bowl of spices before putting it into the crust. When it was piled quite high, she added the top layer of dough; then she trimmed some of the crust along the top and finally crisscrossed a few pieces over it all.

"About the same," she said. "Rebecca is looking after her."

"It makes it hard for you with all the holiday baking."

"I'll manage." She patted some extra butter on the top and sprinkled some sugar over it. "There," she said. "These should brown up nicely." Lily rushed to the oven and opened it for her. With the pies baking, Suzanne sat down and put her hand on the table. Her hair was falling out of a kerchief, and her apron was stickier and more stained than before. She filled her cheeks with air then let out a breath. "At least that's done."

"I'm sorry I got in so late. I should have been here earlier to help you."

"Not at all. This is my job—not yours. It's better for you to spend time with your fiancé."

"You are so good to me, Suzanne, so good to all of us. I feel bad that we don't have more help. How will you manage with the turkey tomorrow? Abby and I could get up early just to get it in then go back to rest again."

"Don't you worry about that. Josephine will be here early tomorrow to help for the day. She'll be quite happy for the wages."

"Is that your little sister?"

"Not so little anymore. She'll be finishing school next year and looking for a placement herself."

Lily got up and ate a piece of apple that had been rejected for the final pie. She turned around then and looked at Suzanne. "Are you and Daisy going to the women's meetings in Worcester?"

Suzanne took off her apron and walked over to the stove. "Daisy has been. I haven't."

"But you went to a séance with her."

"I did."

"What was it like? Was it scary?"

"Silly, I should say. It did make me uneasy though. That's why I haven't been back for a meeting. I find the set up peculiar. The couple who hosted the séance is very interested in the girls in service, and they pay for a carriage to come pick up everyone in the small towns who want to attend."

"I don't find that peculiar."

"I guess not in itself, but this woman who works at the Stonebridge asks about the families, says her sister was in service at the Sawyers and maybe here years ago, I would imagine before you were born."

"She's not a young woman then?"

"Not as young as we are, but not that much older—younger than Olive, anyway.

"What's her name?

"Kathleen, Kathleen Murphy, I think."

"I'll have to ask my mother about her."

"Oh, please don't. Your mother may take offense. She may think I've been indiscrete in giving out information."

Lily sat down again. "Suzanne, she would never think such a thing, but you are right; Mother can be unpredictable lately. I'll ask Father if he knows the name."

They heard the front door open and rushed into the entry as Abagail was closing the door.

"Welcome home," Lily said, taking off her apron. "I'm so happy to see you."

"I'm glad you've made it safely," Suzanne said.

"It smells so good in here. Can we sneak a piece of that pie tonight?" Abagail asked.

"Of course. I made a small pie just for the three of us," Susanne said.

"Hurrah," Abagail said and followed the other two down the hall into the kitchen.

Suzanne put the kettle on to boil as the girls sat down for their Thanksgiving eve ritual of eating the first pie.

• • •

THANKSGIVING DAY dragged by for Lily. It was just the four of them. Mrs. Chapman had no living relatives, and Mr. Chapman was estranged from his. She wished they were at Michael's house. She knew there were aunts and cousins and friends there to share the feast.

In comparison, their celebration seemed dull, though the turkey and stuffing were delicious. Besides the apple, Suzanne had filled it with raisins and nuts. There were Johnny cakes and jam cakes and it should have all been wonderful, but there were just not many people, or at least not the right person to share the day.

By late afternoon, when her mother had gone up to rest and her father had gone to his study, she had given up on Michael showing up. She and Abigail sat in the parlor, eating more pie and reminiscing about Europe. It was nearly dark when Michael rang the doorbell. Suzanne had been given the afternoon off to be with her family.

Lily ran to answer it. "I didn't hear your carriage?"

"I rode over, easier to just slip out that way."

Abigail stood by the door of the parlor. "Are you going to invite him in or what?"

Lily took Michael's hand and led him into the room. "It's been so dull around here," Lily said. "Hasn't it?" She looked at Abigail.

"No duller than usual."

"We just don't have enough family to gather. Next year, maybe we'll have thanksgiving at our own house." She looked at Michael. They sat down together on the couch. "We'll invite both families and all of our friends."

"We better find a big house then," Michael said.

"Especially with those five children," Abagail added

Michael laughed. "Oh, yes. Lily told me all about that. She's told me a bit about your adventures this summer, but I understand you have had your own adventures more recently in New York City with Neil, your Englishman,"

"I was so nervous, at first, seeing him again. You know how it is when you're on vacation and you get caught up, and everything seems so grand. You are just not sure if you remember everything correctly."

"Was it the same?" Michael asked.

"Not the same, I'd say, but just as wonderful. He was such a good sport about everything. We wanted to spend all our time together, but his father was there for business, and his mother had come to see relatives, so she insisted we accompany her with all her visiting. Most of her family has moved from Boston to New York."

They all looked up as Mr. Chapman came into the room. Abigail ran to her father and hugged him.

"Why don't I get us all a bit of brandy," he said, going back into his study and coming out with a decanter and four glasses. "This is the part of the holiday that I like," he said. "All the preparations and feasts are over, and we can all sit back and relax."

"Next year," Lily said, "we'll have our own house and invite everyone over. We'll take Suzanne away from you for the day because she is the only one who can make such pies."

Mr. Chapman looked at Michael. "Your plan is to take our help with you when you marry?" He made a snorting chuckle. "Just how many girls are you taking from this household?"

Michael swirled his brandy in the glass and took a swig. "This is the first I've heard of the Suzanne business."

"Well, you don't expect me to do the Thanksgiving preparations by myself," Lily said.

"I don't expect you to do them at all. We will have help, Lily."

"But I like helping Suzanne with the pies and the stuffing." She looked at her father. "You will let us steal her, right, just for one day?"

"Well, I suppose, if it's just for the one day."

The fire was warm, and the brandy was warming their insides. They sat chatting for a while until Michael said he must get going or he would fall asleep altogether. He hadn't brought a carriage, just the horse.

"That's right," Lily said. "Maybe you'd better stay the night after the brandy."

Michael shook his head. "With the way everything is going, I'm afraid that might look a bit untoward."

"I could have our stable boy drive you home in a carriage," Mr. Chapman said.

Michael sat forward. "That may look even more untoward. I'm fine, I'll take Molly back. She knows the way if I have forgotten."

"I'll have some tea brought in," Mr. Chapman said. "Hot tea should get you sober." He got up to find Suzanne, and Lily followed him into the kitchen.

"We gave Suzanne the evening off, Father, to be with her family. I'll get the tea," Lily said.

"I think I'm about ready to retire. I'll just say goodnight to your young man," Mr. Chapman said.

She filled the kettle with water and looked over at her father. "Suzanne has met someone who says her sister used to work here. Her name is Kathleen Murphy. I don't know her sister's name. Does the name ring a bell? It might have been the Sawyers she worked for—she would have been in help here before I was born."

Her father looked down, as if he were looking for words. "There may have been someone by that name. I don't remember exactly. I know for a while we had a frequent turnover of help."

"I guess I wouldn't want to ask Mother about it—the way she's been acting lately."

"No," he said. "I wouldn't."

Lily steeped a pot of tea as her father quickly left and closed the kitchen door.

Chapter 24

ALL OVER THE VILLAGES AND CITIES of New England, December came in mild that year. The merchants were overjoyed to have carriages and walkers downtown every day. It proved to be the best season in many years. The horses were not overburdened with piles of snow filling their hooves. Only children complained that the ponds and rivers were not frozen enough for skating, and the hills were not covered well enough for the sleds and toboggans. The grown-ups pushed away these complaints and told the children the fine, mild weather would save them money on wood and coal, so they might get something extra in their stockings this year.

The town of Stonebridge was twice blessed with the marriage of Lily and Michael to keep the coffers full well into the New Year. It was a spectacle and a boon for the town and would bring more work to the butlers, the maids, the shopkeepers, and the hotel owner.

Usually, as soon as the trees came down and were hauled out of the houses, everyone sank into a winter slump. This year, they would have a few more weeks of celebrations. There was a rumor that the millworkers would be getting some extra days off, with pay. Some other rumors were going around that the town was not so lucky, that the families still had problems, that poor Mrs. Chapman's health was deteriorating, and there were whispers that they should put the wedding off until summer.

Mrs. Temple entered the bakery just after six. She sat at their regular table, and Mrs. Cunningham came around from the counter to join her with two cups of coffee.

"I don't understand why they don't wait a few months," Mrs. Temple said. "I don't know what to make of it."

Mrs. Cunningham took a sip of coffee and put the cup down. "Gladys told me that she has already missed two fittings. They have to keep taking the dress in. She's gotten awful thin."

"Why doesn't she just go to the house for the fittings?" Mrs. Temple asked.

"I heard Mrs. Chapman doesn't want her there."

"And why isn't the doctor doing more? I haven't seen him there lately," Mrs. Cunningham said.

"In those homes, they have him in at night. Don't want anyone to know their business." Mrs. Temple drank her coffee, looked out the window. "It's a shame, though. Must put a damper on everything for Lily."

"Mary has gone downhill since they came back from their trip. Maybe it was too much for her."

"It's peculiar, how those people can have everything and still be so troubled."

"Money doesn't buy happiness," Mrs. Cunningham said.

"No, it surely doesn't," Mrs. Temple said. She stared out the window. The streets were empty. She wondered why her friend even bothered to open up this early in the winter. Of course, she was probably here baking anyway, so she supposed if opening the doors might bring anyone in at all, it would be worth it.

"I wonder if something happened on the trip," Mrs. Cunningham said, "to make her ill?"

"They didn't go anywhere exotic, that I know of."

"No, I don't think they did."

"Maybe she's worried about her other daughter, the one off at college. I heard she met a young man overseas."

"I didn't hear of that," Mrs. Cunningham said, putting her cup down and crossing her legs. "She met a foreign man?"

"Not exactly foreign. He's English, but his mother is from New York or Boston. He grew up over there, of course. His father works as a businessman in London and New York. Maybe she's afraid of losing Abigail to the other side of the pond."

"It seems they should have enough money to travel back and forth, if that's what's she worried about."

Mrs. Temple shrugged. "I suppose I should go and open. I'll take a package of the johnny cakes today."

Mrs. Cunningham went behind the counter and put together a box of fresh cakes. Mrs. Temple retrieved them from the counter, paid, and left through the glass door.

• • •

LILY DIDN'T KNOW if she was more agitated about Christmas or the upcoming wedding. There was so much to do, and everyone had an opinion. It should be such a joyous time, and yet, she felt weary and exhausted. Abagail wouldn't be coming back from college until the day before Christmas Eve, so she had to make up the Christmas menu. Nana Parker was very ill, and her mother continued to spend her days upstairs—or sometimes up in an attic room. She called it her study. Dr. Sands had given her drops similar to what Lily had taken in the spring, but it made her mother lose her apatite. She complained that food had a funny taste. Lily tried to coax her to eat and spoke to Father about getting the doctor in again to change the dosage.

So now she was taking care of her mother with everything else and worried her mother might collapse on the way to her special room, although it was only a few steps above the second-floor landing. Her father watched her mother when he was home, but lately, he seemed to be working more than ever, and now she had the Christmas arrangements to worry about as well.

She and Michael had vowed they would spend Christmas together this year, and now, it looked like they would have to wait until after the Christmas Dinner. She sat at the dining room table, staring out at a gentle snowfall, and didn't notice Suzanne come in from the side door.

Suzanne touched Lily's shoulder not wanting to startle her. Lily jumped.

"I have the list from The Stonebridge," she said, "to choose the menu for the wedding."

"Yes, well, now we have to do a Christmas Dinner too." She looked at Suzanne and shook her head. "Mother is no better. We won't be going to the Sawyer's for dinner, after all." Her lower lip trembled, and Suzanne went over and kissed her on the cheek. Lily cried, and she held Suzanne's arm. "I'm so sorry. I thought we could give you the whole day off this year."

"Don't you fuss. I wasn't expecting the whole day."

Lily composed herself and looked up. "It will just be the four of us, so you shouldn't be here long. Abby and I will help."

"Don't you worry about that. Josephine will come to help again and be glad of the money she'll be making."

"I'm sorry. It's just there's so much to organize with Mother the way she is now, and I've never really run a household before."

"You are doing fine, you can depend on me, Lily. I'm going to make us some tea, and when I come back, we will make out the wedding menu and the Christmas menu."

"We have to finalize the bouquets, as well," Lily shouted as Suzanne was leaving the room.

"Okay," Suzanne said, poking her head in again. "I think the list of flowers is in the drawer in there. You look for that while I get the tea."

They spent the afternoon going over lists. Lily felt less anxious when her mother came down the stairs, dressed and ready for a late lunch. She beamed at Suzanne.

"You two look busy," Mrs. Chapman said.

Suzanne went quickly into the kitchen; she and Lily had been so busy they had forgotten about lunch, and she hadn't expected the missus to come down. She would warm soup and put together sandwiches for them.

"We're setting up the menu for Christmas," Lily said as she took up all the papers and quickly put them back in the drawer. She didn't want her mother to see they were also organizing for the wedding. She went over and kissed her mother. "Now you can help us."

Suzanne stuck her head in. "Soup and sandwiches are being prepared."

"That sounds like a delightful meal for a snowy day," Mrs. Chapman said.

Mother and daughter sat in silence for a few minutes, and their eyes met. They both wished they could bring back some of the easy banter from the trip last summer when Lily had thought her mother was so full of life and able to take on the world. Now Lily saw her mother's eyes as sunken and glassy, and Mrs. Chapman saw Lily's eyes too bright with false hope.

Mrs. Chapman's gaze moved to the papers still on the table. "What have you decided," she asked, "for Christmas?"

"Oh," Lily moved the papers in front of her. "We're thinking of goose this year, rather than turkey, kind of an English thing that Neil had mentioned once. I think Abby would like that. Also, we might try plum pudding to fit in with the theme. Have you ever had it? Suzanne says there is a recipe in her family they've made for years."

"That sounds very nice," Mrs. Chapman said

Suzanne came in with soup and bread and sandwiches.

"She approves of goose and plum pudding," Lily announced.

"It's set then."

They ate, quietly content. Mrs. Chapman had insisted that Suzanne sit and join them. Mrs. Chapman's presence in the kitchen lifted Suzanne and Lily's spirits. It made them feel she may have turned a corner. When they were done, Suzanne brought out a platter of cheese and grapes for them to have with the bread.

"Why don't you open a sherry for us?" Mrs. Chapman asked Suzanne. "Let's all three of us women sit and share a sherry as the men do."

Suzanne and Lily looked at each other, unsure if this was good idea.

"We are all liberated now, aren't we? Are you not going to the meetings with Olive and Daisy? I think it's wonderful that you all go." Suzanne got up to fetch the sherry.

"I have been meaning to go again, but I'm just trying to get my strength back first," Mrs. Chapman said. "Mrs. Bennet told me the girl that works over at the hotel is the one who has organized you. Says she's quite the ringleader." She looked at Lily. "I may hire her to help with Miss. Parker—so Hillary can have a day off now and then."

Suzanne caught Lily's eye then left. She came back and poured them all a glass of sherry. Mrs. Chapman raised her glass, and Lily wondered what they would be toasting. She would be shocked if her mother raised a glass for her and Michael. She had been carefully keeping the conversation away from that topic.

"To the Christmas Holidays," Mrs. Chapman said.

"Here, here," responded both girls.

"It's been so warm," Suzanne said. "I'm glad we're getting a little snow to make it pretty with the decorations." She looked at Mrs. Chapman. "You should take a trip into town. It's so pretty with every shop decorated."

"Perhaps," Mrs. Chapman said, and she indicted to Suzanne she wanted another glass of sherry.

At first Mrs. Chapman became very talkative, asking Suzanne more about her family traditions at Christmas. She asked her about the women's meetings and assured her that Josephine could have employment here, helping early Christmas morning. Mrs. Chapman even told some stories about Christmases when Lily and Abagail were little girls. How they decorated even the stairs and newel posts with holly and the girls would steal candy canes from the tree. It was hard for Suzanne to imagine such a cheerful holiday in this house. In the four years she had been here in service, it had been a formal affair, the girls leaving with friends as soon as the dinner was served and Mr. and Mrs. Chapman left on their own to sit quietly by the fireside. She wondered why Mrs. Chapman wouldn't want a wedding to bring grandchildren in a few years. She seemed to be nostalgic for a house with children.

Lily watched her mother. Maybe the sherry had done her some good. She spoke of everything but the obvious, and Lily wondered if the medicine was affecting her clarity. Had she forgotten entirely about the wedding? She wouldn't bring it up anyway. It was such a relief to see her mother eating again. Maybe she would gain a few pounds back, and they wouldn't have to bother her with another fitting.

Mrs. Chapman suddenly stopped talking and stared down at the table. Suzanne and Lily looked at each other. "I think I'll go up now," she said.

Suzanne and Lily each took an arm and brought her up the stairs and got her settled in the bed.

"I'll just have a nap," she said. "We'll go look at the lights later."

Back in the dining room, Suzanne cleared the dishes, and Lily took the lists from the desk drawer again.

"We still have work to do," Lily said. "You're coming back, I hope."

"I'll be right back."

They seated themselves again in front of the lists.

"That was a good interruption," Suzanne said.

"Oh, the best. It's been days since she had lunch down here. Tell me you think she's improving."

"Today was certainly an indication."

"I feel so much better that everything will move along well now."

"Be at ease, Lily; she is improving, and you have me to help you with the details. I forgot to tell you we received more rsvp cards back today." She took a packet out of her apron pocket. "I put them all in this envelope. We've heard from almost everyone that was invited now. This will help us with planning the menu."

"Suzanne, you're such a dear. Mother will probably sleep for the rest of the afternoon. I wasn't sure if she should have sherry with her medicine, but I couldn't very well tell my mother she couldn't drink."

"Nor could I say such a thing to her."

"It is awkward, isn't it? I'm so glad you're with me to help and see what's going on. I don't think Abby understands because she's here for such a short time, and Mother acts differently when she's here. Sometimes I still think its's all an act because she wants to get her way. Do you think it's an act, Suzanne?"

"It's gone pretty far for that, and you know your mother has always had a nervous disposition. I heard that women get more anxious at her time of life. There is something else, though. Maybe she's afraid of losing you and now Abagail too. Who knows what they'll do if they decide on marriage?"

"I'm just glad you're here to help," Lily said. again.

That evening, as the sun was setting, Lily and her father were having an early supper. Mrs. Chapman seldom joined them for meals now. Lily told her father about the lunch with Suzanne and her mother, how her mother seemed to be getting her appetite back. "Maybe we should wake her to be with us," Lily said.

"No," her father said. "Let's let her rest. Dr. Sands said she might have what are called episodes of euphoria. He said sometimes these things come in spurts."

Lily looked somewhat downcast.

"It's a very good sign that your mother joined you today but it does take a lot out of her. She needs to rest."

"Should we wait, Father?" Her voice trembled. "Perhaps until summer?"

Her father sat back and brushed his mustache with his hand. "No," he said. "I don't think so."

"Because everything has been put in motion now?"

"Well, there's that, but also, your mother seems to feel this doom about everything, and I think that would just extend her feeling."

"So, you think she'll be better when the wedding is over."

"I think so."

As Darkness entered the room, the light of the fireplace and the new dim, electric lights gave the room a shadowy eeriness.

Mr. Chapman got up to pull the curtains and saw a carriage. "I think your young man is here."

Lily ran to the window. "This is a surprise. I'm going to get the door before he even knocks," she said. "Surprise him back."

Mr. Chapman took his daughter's hand. "Go out and have fun with Michael tonight and try not to worry about your mother's gloom."

She kissed her father on the cheek and ran to the door. Michael was just stepping down from the carriage. It was the one with curtains, she noticed. They called it their courting carriage. It would be an evening of romance.

Michael ran to her, picked her up, and carried her to the carriage.

"My," she said. "You're carrying me over the threshold a little early."

"Let's pretend we are married already, and this is our gypsy caravan."

As he plopped her down on the seat, Lily looked around, miming surprise. "But there's no stove for me to cook?"

"You never have to cook," Michael said. "We will eat berries."

"Do you think berries grow under the snow?"

"For winter, we will knock on doors and give blessings to the houses that provide for us, or, if you prefer, I will go into a cave and wrestle a bear."

"But they will all be sleeping, though I do hear that bear meat is very good this time of year."

The carriage had started up and was still on the rough back roads. Michael fell onto Lily, shaking his hair wildly. Then he growled.

"You're my big loveable bear," she said, laughing.

Michael looked at her and growled.

"By the way," she said. "Where are you taking me? I'm not dressed for anything fancy."

"I thought we might go to Worcester to see the lights and displays."

As they drove through the town, Lily felt a little sad. She and Suzanne had talked about taking their mother to see the lights. She wished her mother was here with them. Her presence sat like a ghostly thought across from her and Michael.

Michael lifted her chin up. "Why so gloomy?"

"Just thinking," she said. She wanted to tell Michael about her mother's breakthrough today, but she kept it to herself determined that at least Michael would have the evening not thinking about their parents.

"The lights here in town are quite beautiful. I like how they've lit up the trees and tinseled doorways, and that little bit of snow has added to the sparkle," he said.

She turned and looked at Michael. "There is a lot to do before the wedding."

"I know. That's why I'm taking you away this evening."

"Things are falling into place, anyway," Lily said, "with Suzanne's help."

They rattled on quietly along the road to Worcester. Lily put her head on Michael's shoulder, and he pushed aside the window curtain. The quietness of the landscape seemed to fall upon the carriage as if the horse plodded through a dream landscape. The carriage driver's lantern cast streams of light along the sides of the road that stretched out in an arc, making the new snow sparkle. Above, the sky had cleared, and stars appeared, draping the dark with a mantle of brightness.

"This will be our best Christmas," Michael said.

Lily didn't answer. She had fallen asleep beside him.

Chapter 25

DAYS BEFORE CHRISTMAS, A BLEAK RAIN fell over most of New England, driving everyone inside by the fire. Mrs. Temple entered the streets a little later than usual and headed for the bakery. Surely very few would be out in this miserable weather, but she knew Agnes would open the bakery. Certain specialties had to be picked up today. This could go on for days, and no one would want to take the chance of waiting until the last minute. Still, she was relieved to see the light inside. It was early morning and very dark. The only ones out right now were the factory workers who could not miss a day at this time of the year.

She entered the bakery, and Mrs. Cunningham came from behind the counter and put a coffee pot on their table. Mrs. Temple closed the door on the driving rain and wind. There was barely a fire set, so she hurried to the table and put her hands around the warm coffee cup.

Mrs. Cunningham drank her coffee and looked at her friend. "I didn't know if you'd come today. Not this early."

"Well, surely, I can't miss any chance of business at this time of year."

Mrs. Cunningham put her hand on her friend's arm. She hadn't meant it as a rebuke. She was truly happy for the company. "I'm really glad you came. I just got here this morning, myself. The coffee's a little weak; it's barely brewed."

"Agnes, don't be silly. Your coffee is delicious, as always, and it's warm. You'll probably have more customers than ever today."

"I hope so. It's dreadful in the winter to run a shop, isn't it, on a day like this?"

Mrs. Temple sat back. "Yes, but we have been lucky this season up until now. I'll help you get the fire up in a minute."

Rain and sleet streamed down the front window as they both silently watched a hooded woman carrying a basket hurry past.

"Is that Suzanne? My goodness, what do they have her about now?" Mrs. Temple asked.

"Would you recognize her all bundled up like that?"

"I know the coat, surely. She bought it at my store just last year."

"Do you think she's off to the dressmaker?"

"I don't think so. Gladys told me that the dress is done. She said Mrs. Chapman is awfully thin, though, said she hardly used any material at all."

Mrs. Temple shook her head. "So where would they be sending Suzanne off this early in the morning?"

"Maybe to the hotel to check on seating or the meal. There's a lot goes into organizing for a big wedding."

"Well, I know, but would it have to be done this morning, in this weather?"

"It's coming up soon. The holidays will barely be over. I know it's a big job for me, and I'm only doing the cake. I don't want to start on it until I finish the Christmas and New Year's orders. I can imagine the caterers at the hotel want the menus set by now, and you know the way Mary Chapman is with making up her mind."

"They say she's doing better. I heard she was out shopping one of the warm days last week. I didn't see her in my shop, though."

"They say she sleeps till afternoon now, so we'd probably be closing our shops before she even got out of bed."

"Days like this, I wish I had such a life."

Mrs. Temple got up from the table. "Could I get some of your seedcake today? I don't know how many will show up, but on a day like today, I like something to offer the customers."

Mrs. Cunningham went behind the counter and fixed a box for her friend, wrapping it in wax paper to repel the rain.

• • •

LILY SAT IN THE PARLOR. She had tended the fire this morning because she knew that Suzanne had errands to do early in town. Cold sleet hit the windows as she sat among the lists and papers that constituted the preparation for a wedding. Suzanne had been somewhat reticent with her this morning, when Lily had given her permission to go on a personal errand. She supposed they all had too much to do but, still, Lily was put off. She always told Suzanne everything. At least Abby would be home soon, and she hoped her sister's arrival would lift a gloom that was falling again on the household.

Her father had told her that she and Michael could live here if they wanted, but she and Michael were anxious to find their own home. It made her feel better to think about the future and the changes the new century would bring. Michael and she had talked about how they would decorate in a modern style. They wanted to get rid of this heavy feeling of the stuffed chairs and wallpaper they had grown up around. Their house would have to have plenty of light and thinner curtains. They were still discussing whether they even needed to have help. Lily told Michael it may not be necessary at first. When they had children, they would hire a nanny. Before that, she could cook and clean.

She looked up and saw Suzanne's hooded-drenched figure running by the window, and she hurried to the door to let her in. Then, she helped her take her coat off and grabbed a towel from the kitchen to dry her hair.

"You'll catch your death," Lily said, "going out on a day like this."

They moved into the parlor. Suzanne stood by the fire and began to cry. "It's Josephine. She's sick."

"Has the doctor been in?"

"He was, two days ago. He gave her medicine, but she's not getting any better."

Lily took her hand, led her to a chair.

"I went to check on her this morning, and she's gotten worse overnight," Suzanne said. "With this weather and so many sick, he could not come again today, and he had the chemist make a stronger vial, but no one could bring it over. I had to fetch it."

"You should have told me," Lily said. "If there is anything we can do."

"I didn't want to bother you, and I thought she would be better today. It was such a shock to see her still sweating with fever on this dreary day. I don't think she'll be working here Christmas."

"Suzanne, don't worry about that. Abby and I can Manage Christmas. Everything is ordered, and there's only the four of us."

"I did not want to burden you with this, but Nana Parker is still not well. Hillary will be busy tending to her through the Holidays."

"I must go up and see Nana Parker," Lily said.

"She usually sleeps in the morning. I'll tell Hillary to come down later and tell you when a good time is for visitors."

"Is Daisy's friend Kathleen still helping her too?"

"Yes, she's up with them today. It takes two sometimes to move and bathe her now."

"Shouldn't we be paying her, then? I hope she hasn't put her hotel job at risk."

"Hillary brought it up to her, but she says she wants no money."

"I must get up this afternoon or maybe see Nana before her bedtime. I feel so terrible that I have been neglecting her."

"You've been very busy with your own worries. The girls are nursing her fine."

"I will get up there before the end of the day and read to her. I miss the stories she used to tell. I suppose she has no strength for that anymore."

"Hillary says she does ramble on sometimes, often about things that happened years ago."

"Those are the best stories."

"Thank you for getting the fire going," Suzanne said, drying her hair with the towel.

"I'm glad you're alright. You looked a fright when you came in just now. I couldn't imagine what had happened."

Suzanne smiled. "I'm sure I still look a fright. I'm going to change, put my hair back up, and put together a tea for you and your mother. I was going to stop by the bakery this morning and pick up something special for you to make up for going out so early, but I was drenched by then."

"Don't worry about us; take your time." When Suzanne got up to leave for her quarters, Lily took her hand. "Try not to worry," she said. "I'm sure your sister will be better soon."

"Ah, Lily, I hope so with the help of God and the new medicine."

After she left, Lily sat and watched sleet drip and tumble down the window and felt the warmth of the fire behind her. The days were so busy, she hardly had time to see Michael. He had promised to stop by on Christmas Eve, and after dinner on Christmas Day, he was going to send a carriage over for her and Abigail. *God willing,* she thought, *we won't all catch what Josephine has,* bringing illness and misfortune to the door at Christmas, or worse, on her wedding day.

Later in the day, Hillary came down and told her Nana Parker was awake and that Lily could see her. Lily walked gingerly up the back stairs, holding her dress up each narrow, winding step. She had forgotten how low the ceilings were in this area of the house. She wasn't so tall herself, but still the narrow corridors and lack of ceiling height made her feel a distortion that nearly made her dizzy. Her stomach lurched with the smells as she was led into the sick room. She sat in a chair by the bedside, smiled at Nana, and took her hand that was limp and warm. Her eyes were glassy. She was afraid she had come too late to have any last words. Then she felt her hand squeezed, and eyes focused on her.

"I won't see the new year," the old lady said.

Lily lifted her hand up and kissed it. "Don't say such a thing."

"I've seen my share of years, and it's been good—such a privilege raising you and Abigail." Her eyes went to the window, and her mind wandered off again.

Suzanne had warned her that she fell into rambles. Her tongue moved, and she said words but none made any sense to Lily. She tried to pull her back. "Abagail is coming," she said, "for Christmas. We'll both come up and see you then."

Lily looked up as Hillary came near. "At least she recognized you for a few minutes," Hillary said. "She mostly talks gibberish, hardly notices anyone or anything these days."

Before she left, Lily placed Nana's hand back on the blanket and kissed her forehead.

•   •   •

ABIGAIL CAME home early on Christmas Eve Day. Lily whisked her immediately into the kitchen where they were already beginning to bake and prepare for Christmas.

To Lily's relief, Suzanne had made it back. Josephine's fever had broken with the new medicine, and now she was again taking charge in the kitchen. Lily was chopping nuts while Abagail and Suzanne peeled and parboiled carrots and potatoes. Their faces flushed in the hot kitchen. The weather had turned mild for the holiday.

Suzanne went down to fetch some fresh herbs, and while she was gone Lily turned to Abagail. "Didn't know I'd pull you into kitchen duty."

"It is quite a surprise," Abagail said "but a pleasant one. It smells so good in here."

"I'm relieved that Suzanne is here. I know the two of us couldn't have put together a decent pie."

"Has she been away?" Abagail asked.

"Her sister's been sick, poor thing, and Suzanne has been run ragged with her duties here and helping her family."

"Is it serious?"

"Josephine was supposed to work here today and help her with the Christmas meal but was burning up with fever up until yesterday."

Suzanne came back carrying a bag of leeks, garlic, cinnamon sticks, and spices. She gave the greens to Abigail to cut up, and she chopped the garlic. She began to cough and turned away.

"Let me do that," Lily said.

"No," Suzanne said. "It's good for me. The strong smell will remove a cold I might have picked up from my sister."

"How is Josephine?" Abigail asked.

"Much better." Suzanne turned away from the saucer of garlic, tears welling up. "But everyone in the house is afraid of getting it now."

"A lot of the girls at college left earlier this week because of illness going around there," Abagail said.

"Michael told me the factories are running with a skeleton crew," Lily said. "So many are home sick."

"Is it true" Abigail asked, "that Mr. Sawyer gives a turkey to each of his workers for Christmas?"

"A turkey plus a bonus," Suzanne said.

"Well, it's nice to know," Lily said, "that my soon to be father-in-law has *some* kindness in his heart."

Suzanne put aside the garlic and washed her hands before taking the pies from the oven. "He's really not a bad man, at all," she said. "He's good to his workers."

Lily put the parboiled potatoes into water to keep them from turning brown.

Suzanne put the pies on the counter, wiped her hands on her apron, and wiped her brow with a towel. "My father says the unions will only make it harder for the workers. They could be let go. He says the unions bring a lot of trouble, but I don't know. He wants to get my brother in there now."

"I'll talk with Michael. I'm sure he'll get your brother a job," Lily said.

"That's just it. He's arguing with my father that he would rather have a union job. He'd rather travel all the way to Worcester every day. My father says they have dues and actually take your money, but my brother says they fight with the owners to get a better wage."

Lily wiped her hand on a towel. "Mr. Sawyer is strictly against unions. He and Michael argue about it all the time."

"That doesn't surprise me," Abagail said. "I've been to meetings at school that are very pro-union. They say women have come as far as they have because they stick together. Maybe Mr. Sawyer is good to his workers, but not all bosses are so generous."

"Just as, sometimes girls don't end up with a good family," Suzanne said. "I've heard some terrible stories from the other girls who attend the meetings. That's why I hope my sister gets settled with a family around here."

They were starting to put everything away and to organize the pies; the potatoes and the carrots at the end of the counter were to be stored downstairs until the morning.

"So, then, we're done here," Suzanne said. "I'll do the washing up. Thank you for helping. I work for the best family in the world."

Lily and Abigail both embraced Suzanne. Then they took off their aprons, which were a sticky mess and left them on the table. They had grown up helping in the kitchen since they were young children and hardly realized how unusual it was. Mrs. Chapman had always insisted they mingle with the help. It was one of the things that her in-laws held against her—that she didn't know how to run a proper household—that she had not come from money.

"We are going to start on the pie tonight," Abagail said. "We know where you hide it."

They left the door open to let the smells of Christmas waft through the pantry and permeate the house and went into the parlor where their mother was sitting reading a magazine.

Mrs. Chapman got up and embraced her daughter. "Abagail, I didn't even know you were here."

"I was on kitchen duty," she said.

"Now it's time for decorating," Lily said, looking around at the tree and the ivy hanging near the fireplace.

Abagail shook her head. "I'm going upstairs to unpack."

Lily headed back to the kitchen, intent on popping corn to string on the tree.

• • •

TOWARD EVENING, Suzanne brought out turkey soup and fresh bread, which was the Chapman tradition of Christmas Eve. They ate by candlelight; then Mr. and Mrs. Chapman both retreated to his office to share cocktails and a cigarette, which was also their tradition while their daughters wrapped presents and put them under the tree.

Suzanne came into the parlor carrying bowls of nuts and cranberries along with an apple pie and put them on a small table away from the fireplace. Lily was hanging strings of popcorn on the tree when the doorbell rang, and Suzanne went to answer it.

Michael came into the room as Lily stepped down from a chair. The new guest entering and Lily's descent from the chair must have created a stir in the air. The candles flickered, and the dying fire made shadowy figures of them all. Lily felt a chill and turned toward Michael who came over and took her hands in the darkness. Suzanne quickly re-lit the candles and stoked up the fire while Michael and Lily hid behind the Christmas tree, kissing.

"You smell like cinnamon," he whispered in her ear.

"You smell like the outdoors."

There was another smell, one Lily could not put her finger on, a smell of dirt or maybe just the pine that had been so recently cut. They were standing behind the tree and moved out when the candles were relit. Everyone looked puzzled a moment then laughed as Michael took the popcorn string and put it across his upper lip, pretending it was a mustache then around his neck as if it were a string of pearls before he pushed the chair aside and finished the task of gathering the end and encircling the tree.

"My, oh my." Abagail laughed. "Some things require a man's touch."

"It only takes a bit of height," he said as they all sat down and looked at the tree.

"Perfect," Lily said, moving closer to Michael.

Abagail cocked her head. "Does look rather picture perfect, I would say."

"I see a woman's touch, as well," Michael said, pointing out the pine wreaths on the windows and the holly berry and leaves flowing down the sides of the fireplace. "It's surely as impressive as anything we saw in the display windows at the city."

"It's missing something though," Suzanne said. "Isn't it?"

"It's missing a child's touch," Lily said. "Teddy bears, dolls, toy soldiers, and rocking horses. We're too old for all that now."

Michael put his arm around Lily. "I suppose we can change that before next Christmas."

Lily blushed.

"I was only thinking that it was missing food," Suzanne said, laughing. She went into the kitchen and came back with the apple pie.

"Splendid," Michael said. "We can start on the pie tonight."

"Let me get the tea ready, or maybe coffee this evening?" Suzanne said, as she looked at Abagail and Lily.

"Could you do both?" Lily asked.

"As you wish, madam." Suzanne bowed.

Lily and she both laughed, and she left the room. Abagail had gone over to the tree and was placing candles-holders in the branches.

"What were you laughing about?" Michael asked.

"Suzanne and I were pretending to be very formal."

"My father would never let there be joking around with the servants like that."

"She's not really a servant; she's just help," Lily replied. "That's what Mother has always said."

"I noticed that your whole family seems to be close with the house staff," Michael remarked.

"Does it bother you?" Lily asked.

"No, not at all. It's just that in our house they are treated differently," Michael said.

"I suppose we all became like friends. Abagail and I even help with preparing the Christmas meal. We used to do that with our Nana when we were small." Lily's visage changed, thinking of Nana. She frowned. She and Abagail would go up later tonight, even if she was sleeping. She would have to prepare Abagail first.

Suzanne came back with tea and coffee. The pie was cut, and Mr. and Mrs. Chapman came into the parlor to join the young people.

Mrs. Chapman sat in a straight chair near the fireplace, her husband next to her. She looked almost cheerful tonight, Lily thought, though her eyes gleamed a little too brightly. She had on makeup, which she seldom wore at home. Suzanne stoked the fire. Lily stared into the flames.

"We'll all be having quite the feast here soon," Mr. Chapman said and looked at Michael. "Do you have a crowd coming tomorrow?"

"I think so," he said. "I don't get too involved in the planning. There'll be aunts, uncles, cousins—that sort of thing. I'm more interested in after, when Lily and Abagail come over."

When he looked at Lily and smiled, she was afraid her mother would take offense, but she just continued to stare at them all, smiling. It would be such a relief tomorrow, she thought, at Michael's house when they could talk openly about the wedding. It was such a strain for her to constantly stifle her excitement.

They sat through the evening, as the candles burned down, enjoying apple pie and fresh cream while politely avoiding any talk that might upset Mrs. Chapman.

Chapter 26

THE COATING OF SNOW THAT FELL OVERNIGHT on Christmas Eve left the town of Stonebridge looking festive yet lonely in the early morning. With the shops closed and the streets deserted, only a few curs and feral cats wandered around corners, waiting for the scraps they might have gotten on a day when the butcher was open.

It was early when light, either candle or electric, illuminated windows, and inside, one could see the servants or the women of the house preparing feasts. Mrs. Cunningham was over at the Temples again. She had saved her best pies to bring to their Christmas feast.

• • •

SUZANNE WAS IN the kitchen earlier than most, doing last minute preparations for the Christmas dinner. The Chapmans always ate early on Christmas Day, which was fine with her because she already had the goose in the oven so she could serve when it was barely noontime; then, they would let her go to be with her own family.

It was good that Mrs. Chapman sat with her family last evening. It had been such a hard year for her, and, though she had heard that

Mrs. Chapman used to hold parties on Christmas Eve, she hadn't seen any of that since she'd been working here.

One bothersome incident *had* occurred last evening. As she was cleaning the dishes, a flicker of light went by the window, and Suzanne had rushed over and pushed aside the curtain to see carolers stepping through the yard. There was something curious though; one woman held her lantern low, peeking through the parlor window. She chided herself for having forgotten to close the drapes. Then, the doorbell rang.

"Carolers at the door," she shouted into the parlor. "Shall I let them in?"

"By all means," Mr. Chapman said.

They all got up and crowded around the doorway.

Suzanne put on her coat on and walked around the group. She saw Kathleen at the back and whispered, "Psst."

Kathleen put down her song book and came over. "Hello," she said. "Isn't it a lovely night?"

"What are you doing out here? I thought you were upstairs tonight giving Hillary the holiday off."

"I was invited to come caroling. Besides, my shift starts after this. I'll be with her overnight."

"And the reason for snooping?"

"I only wanted to see a happy family. I feel awful that their Nana is so sick at the holidays."

It was too dark to see her face, but Suzanne heard sadness in Kathleen's voice. She picked up her skirts and walked back, re-joining the other carolers.

She's only lonely, Suzanne thought. *It must be hard to be at the hotel with no family nearby to celebrate.*

"That's alright then," Suzanne called to her, "as long as you show up for shift on time to relieve Hillary."

• • •

THE NEXT DAY was a quiet meal at the Chapman's. Lily thought her mother looked overwrought from the late night they had. At least she had been there, sharing her time—even with Michael. She so missed her mother's optimism and hoped she would start up her literary nights again once the wedding was over. With all the talk of toys and children, Lily thought maybe it was just her mother finding it difficult to part with her daughters.

"Children do grow up," she had said last night before her mother went up to bed. "You knew we would grow up on you." Her mother had laughed, and they had embraced. Maybe she just wouldn't understand until she herself had children.

After they finished the Christmas pudding, Mrs. Chapman said she was going upstairs to rest for a while. Lily and Abigail sat with their father waiting for the Sawyer's carriage to arrive. Lily was restless and went to the kitchen to help Suzanne with the clean-up.

Suzanne tried to shoo her out. "You'll get you're dress all dirty."

"I'll put on an apron."

"Miss, Lily, really, I feel it is wrong for you to be doing my work, especially on Christmas."

"But I'm excited. I don't know what to do with myself."

"Waiting for Michael?"

"You know I can't stand waiting," Lily said.

Suzanne tossed her an apron. "I'll wash; you dry."

They stood by the sink together watching a light snow fall. "I bet you can't wait to get out of here, to be with your family?"

Suzanne smiled.

"How's your sister?"

"She's doing much better," Suzanne said.

"Did you know one of the carolers last night?" Lily asked. I noticed you were talking to someone."

"Yes, it was Kathleen."

"We should have invited her in."

"She was coming in soon enough. She's upstairs now covering the holiday so Rebecca can have a break."

"We should go up, bring her some dinner, and say Merry Christmas to Nanna. I'll fetch Abigail so we can see her before we leave."

"She'll probably be sleeping." Suzanne said scouring the large pots, seeming to put more concentration into it than the task required.

• • •

KATHLEEN WAS READING a book, and Miss Parker was resting quietly. Suddenly Kathleen looked up to see that the old woman's demeanor had changed and she was breathing rapidly. She looked to be in a kind of delirium.

"I need to help with the baby," she cried and lifted herself up.

Kathleen tried to calm her down and tucked her back in bed.

"No," Miss Parker insisted. "I'm needed for Mary's baby."

Kathleen's own heart beat faster. She must have been remembering helping at Mrs. Chapman's birthings. "It's alright, she said. "The baby is fine.

"The babies are born and grown now," Kathleen said. "They're fine, strong young women." This seemed to calm the old woman.

"That's right," Mrs. Parker said. "Fine, strong young women"

"Hush, now; it's okay. You're only remembering when Mrs. Chapman had her babies."

"Oh Yes," Miss Parker said. "It was wild around here the day you were born."

Kathleen did not contradict the old woman. What was the harm in her not realizing who she spoke with? She stroked the woman's arms to soothe her. "Did she have a hard time of it?" Kathleen asked.

"Indeed, she did." Miss Parker lay back down, calmer, just telling a story—no longer re-living it. She was still rambling, though. Kathleen could tell by her eyes that she still thought she was talking to one of the Chapman girls "The whole house was in an uproar with two women birthing here that day," she said.

"Two women?" She let go of Miss Parker's arm.

"There was a girl from one of the houses who'd gotten herself in trouble. Everyone said she was just sick, but we who lived here knew what was going on. I suppose they thought it was a good place to hide her away, what with your mother being with child as well."

"What house was she from?"

"It may have been the Sawyers. Everything was hush-hush, as you can imagine."

"What happened to her?"

"I think it was she who went into labor first; then everyone was called from her bedside when your mother started to have so much trouble."

"They left her alone?" Kathleen asked.

"No, some stayed to help her, but she didn't make it. So sad, she was a sweet thing. I tried to go in and help her, but they whisked me out the door. The baby died too, but it must have lived for a few minutes. I saw it wrapped in a blanket being rocked as I left the room."

Mrs. Parker sat up again, looking puzzled. Kathleen did not try to settle her this time.

"I went back to the room where you were being birthed and saw there was a special doctor who had been called—I think he was a friend of Mr. Winston. I wondered why they did not have Dr. Sands, but it was not my business to inquire, and it was a good thing because your mother was having difficulties. He had them walking her around, moving the flesh around her stomach, and even putting her in a tub of water, and she still screamed in pain. I thought his ways were peculiar, and there was really nothing that I could do at that point, so I left the room, but he must have known something because when I came back to see the missus, there you were, a healthy baby girl. It was a miracle you lived—*you* were a miracle baby. Miss. Parker closed her eyes. "But it was so sad about that other girl, so sad, but it was a long time ago, I suppose, nothing to fret about now."

Kathleen stared at the woman. She jumped up and dropped her book onto the floor as Lily and Abigail suddenly opened the door. She hurried out past them, saying she would be back soon.

Lily and Abigail assured her they would watch their Nana for a while and were glad to have the time alone with her. Kathleen sat at the bottom of the stairs trembling. When she heard the girls coming down, she passed them on the stairs quickly and whispered that she would keep watch for the rest of the night.

• • •

WHEN THE CARRIAGE finally came to take the girls visiting, Mrs. Chapman was back downstairs, so they left their parents to sherry and a cigarette and headed for the Sawyers' home.

"I have to warn you; we've got a houseful," Michael said.

"We want to be with a crowd. I'm sure it will be much cheerier than at our house. It'll get your mind off who's missing. You'll feel better around lots of people, too, won't you?" Lily took her sister's hand.

"Now I know how you felt when you two were separated this summer," Abagail said.

Michael looked at her. "I'm sure you'd rather be getting off a steamer than be in this contraption with us, but Abe and Gregory are at the house. They should keep you entertained." He looked at Lily. "I have to warn you. Mr. Winston is over too.

Lily's face reddened then paled. "Not that awful man from the gallery. He makes me so uncomfortable. Please tell me Louisa is not there, too."

Michael shook his head. "Thankfully she's back in Virginia. You know, for the life of me, I can't figure out why my father invited him. He seems to cause my father nothing but consternation, but still, he shows up at all our gatherings. It's like my father feels he owes him something."

"Does he have family of his own?" Abagail asked. "I mean besides his sister down south?"

"Don't know," Michael said, "but my father is not one to care about that."

The Sawyers' house looked so festive as they approached that Lily couldn't understand why she felt uncomfortable, even frightened. Was it the mention of Mr. Winston or was it seeing Nana so close to death?

Daisy took their coats as soon as they entered. People were everywhere, talking and laughing, even on the long staircase, where a garland of roses hung from each newel post. With arms entwined in Lily's, Michael began the introductions. Lily relaxed as all his cousins and friends congratulated them.

There were card games and even some dancing going on in the parlor. Everyone clapped as Lily and Michael entered. Abagail was introduced to everyone at once, and she shook her head saying she was bad with names and was afraid she would never remember.

Mrs. Sawyer came over and led them to a table set with pies and Christmas pudding. She poured them all champagne then took Lily by the hand to sit with her, saying she wanted the chance to get to know her soon-to-be daughter-in-law. Michael took Abagail's hand and asked her to dance.

Lily watched Michael walk away and felt an odd kind of longing that she'd also felt when entering the house. Though she was glad to have some time with Mrs. Sawyer. She hadn't been here for a long time; Michael mostly came to her house now, but she would have to get accustomed to her soon-to-be in-law's home. Mrs. Sawyer was a quiet woman, but you could see that most of it came from a lifetime of yielding to her husband. It had been hard for Lily to want to get close to her after she had seen her shopping with Louisa that day. She'd always wondered if Mrs. Sawyer also wanted that affair to work out, but she seemed truly sincere now as she took Lily's hand and told her how happy and excited she was about the wedding.

"My dress is here, already," she said. "Come upstairs and I 'll show you."

Lily hesitated but followed Mrs. Sawyer out of the room, stopping at the door and turning to stare at the game players and the dancers as if she were seeing a charade. Michael caught her eye, as his mother maneuvered her out of the door, and waved, his dark hair falling over one eye as he bounced merrily through the dance. She stood at the door for a few seconds; then, with reluctance, she crossed the threshold and walked with Mrs. Sawyer up the long stairs as the sounds of the parlor faded.

Mrs. Sawyer hurried her along the corridor upstairs as if she was being taken into some secret sanctuary. She wasn't sure if she was ready for the intimacy of being in an upstairs bedroom here, but, she supposed, they would soon be family. Once in the bedroom, Mrs. Sawyer went to the closet, took out a box, and handed it to Lily.

"It belonged to my mother," she said. "I always thought I would have a daughter. You can wear it at the wedding. It will be your something old."

Lily opened the box, and a neckless of gold and diamonds lay in folds of gathered silk. "Are you certain? Something handed down from your family?"

Mrs. Sawyer nodded. "I feel bad with all the hurt my husband has caused, all his interfering, and I want you to know that, though I can't well say it in front of him, I'm happy that you and Michael will be wed. This will be yours, the new Mrs. Sawyer."

Lily wasn't sure what to do, she wanted to embrace this woman who would soon be her family but was unsure of the decorum, which she knew was very important in this household; instead, she held the necklace to her heart. "Thank you," she said. "I will treasure it forever."

Mrs. Sawyer did not respond for several minutes. She stared out the darkened window, and turning back to Lily, she whispered, "I was always afraid that he would be so under his father's bidding, he might never marry."

"Afraid he'd never marry?" Lily echoed the strange words, put the necklace back into the box, and shot Mrs. Sawyer a puzzling look.

"Just a feeling I had, but I feel so much better now since you two are back together."

"Keep it here until the wedding," Lily said. "I'd be afraid carrying it around in the carriage tonight."

Mrs. Sawyer patted her arm. "You're right, dear. I'll send it over with Olive in the morning."

Lily took her arm as they walked back down the long dark corridor and down the candlelit stairway. She stiffened when she saw Mr. Sawyer coming out of his study with his brother-in-law and Winston. He rushed past them rudely, and at the door, he yelled back to his wife. "We're going out to the stables."

"Even on Christmas, he's got to think of business. He wants to build more stables." She shook her head. "I told him to wait until after the Holidays and after the wedding, but Mr. Winston showed up here trying to get the business for someone he knows."

When they were back in the parlor, Lily ran to Michael. "We must have a dance," she said.

Finally, he took her in his arms. She pushed his dark hair back from his eyes. *This is our best Christmas*, she thought, as he swept her around with the smell of pine and apple tarts.

"Ah, Lily," he said into her ear. "This is just the beginning."

When they went back in the carriage, it was snowing. At the Chapman's, Michael kissed Lily goodbye; then Lily and Abigail entered the quiet house and went to the kitchen to have tea before bed.

"In two weeks," Lily said, "I'll be a married woman."

They clinked the teacups together.

"What's it like upstairs in that house?" Abagail asked. "Mrs. Sawyer kept you up there for a while."

"Oh, I didn't tell you the best part. Mrs. Sawyer is so sweet. She gave me a diamond necklace that belonged to her mother. She wants me to wear it at the wedding."

"Wow. You're so lucky."

"Michael's friend Abe is sweet on you," Lily said.

"I know. I had fun today, but it only kept my mind off Neil."

"Maybe next year Neil and you will have a New England Christmas."

"Maybe," Abagail said.

Lily couldn't sleep once she was in bed. She tossed around straightening the pillow, and she finally sat up when she thought she heard noises in the attic room where her mother had been going up to in the afternoon. Mrs. Chapman had a chair and desk brought up there, and sometimes she wrote in a diary or sketched what she saw out the window.

Lily got up and went out to the hallway. The door to the attic was closed, but light came through beneath. She walked up the three stairs, opened the door, and saw her mother writing furiously in the journal, not even aware of another presence. The inkwell was spilled over on the floor, and a glass of sherry tottered on the edge of the desk.

Lily touched her mother's shoulder. "What are you doing here this time of night?"

Her mother jumped, turned around, covering her journal page with a nearby scarf. "I told you all; I come up here when I want to be *alone.*"

"But, Mother, it's the middle of the night."

"I couldn't sleep."

"Neither could I. Come with me down to the kitchen. I'll make us some tea." She picked up the spilled ink and tried to lead her mother down the stairs, but she slapped her hand away.

"I know you think you're grown up, but I am still your mother." She gave Lily a slight push and hurried back to the desk She was becoming hysterical. Lily would have to wake her father.

Chapter 27

MRS. TEMPLE OPENED THE BAKERY DOOR on an overcast December day, and Mrs. Cunningham smiled to see her friend again. Mrs. Temple had not opened the day after Christmas, and Mrs. Cunningham had some news. They sat at the usual table and saw that the streets were empty.

Mrs. Cunningham took a sip of coffee. "I, for one, am glad all the excitement is over for a few days. I'm worn out with all the baking and cleaning and what have you." She wiped her hands on her apron. She had just taken three tins of muffins from the oven. "Don't talk to me about baking. Thanksgiving is the only time of year I'm busier."

"I guess we shouldn't complain," Mrs. Temple said.

Mrs. Cunningham wiped crumbs from the side of her mouth. "It puts money in our pockets, I suppose." She looked at her friend. "You must have had a good season?"

"Oh, it was that," Mrs. Temple said. "It's sure to go downhill from here, though, for the winter."

"I imagine a lot bought clothes this year for the wedding."

"It's funny, whether they were going or not, everyone in town seems to have bought new clothes just to stand on the streets and watch the wedding party go by. I'm not complaining though."

"It will be a fine sight with the carriages."

"It's been a boon for me. I've sold more hats this winter than in the last ten years. I heard Sawyer is expanding his stables, as if they needed more horses and carriages there."

Mrs. Cunningham took another sip of coffee and moved closer to her friend. "Olive and Daisy were in yesterday, practically the only customers I had all day. They were talking about some ta-do over at the Chapman's on Christmas."

Mrs. Temple put her coffee down with a thud. "On Christmas Day?"

"Christmas night," Mrs. Cunningham said, nodding her head up and down. "Would you believe it?"

"Mary, again?" Mrs. Temple poured herself another cup, "Probably too much to drink along with Dr. Sands giving her all those tonics. They say she's come down with something that he can't treat."

"I heard that, too but he seems to keep trying. Anyway, there might be more to it. I overheard Olive and Daisy saying that Lily and Abagail went over to the Sawyers after Christmas Dinner. I don't imagine Mary was happy about that. They were in here all riled up, talking in whispers. I pretended to be dusting and made out bits and pieces."

"What did they say?"

Mrs. Cunningham moved her chair closer to Mrs. Temple. "At first, they just talked about the plans to enlarge the stables and a new employee that they hired. Daisy had seen him around town. You know that girl—she talked about how handsome he was."

"She'll be getting herself in trouble soon, that one."

Mrs. Cunningham nodded. "Well, then they talked of how Olive had been sent over to the Chapmans' early on the morning after Christmas to deliver a box to Lily. Then Kathleen came in and said she had been watching Miss Parker on Christmas night. She sat down and they hushed up."

"Did she know what happened?"

"All I heard was something about an attic room that Mrs. Chapman visits when she can't sleep at night. Mary had gotten agitated and gone up there and did not want to come down when Lily found her."

Mrs. Temple shook her head. "She should mind her business, keep to her place up in the servant's quarters with Miss. Parker."

"I think she just scrambled down for a moment to see what the fuss was about."

"She's worse than Daisy."

"Never mind that; they say she's compassionate in taking care of Miss Parker. As I was saying, they all hushed when Kathleen sat down, but Daisy apparently couldn't wait to find out what was in the box that Mrs. Sawyer was giving to Lily, so she asked Olive—with Kathleen sitting right there, and Olive gave her a look."

Mrs. Temple interrupted again. "What was in the box?"

"I'm getting to that. Anyway, Kathleen tells them that it's her cousin who was hired by Mr. Sawyer while the new stables are built, and right away, Daisy says how he's so handsome that she can't wait until he's in service at the Sawyers, and I can see that Kathleen stiffens and gives Daisy a guarded look. Then Olive goes on with her story about how Suzanne is all upset that she was not there when Mary had her episode, and I can see that Kathleen is listening very intently, although she is pretending not to and just staring and staring out the window."

"So, what was in the box?"

"A diamond necklace," Mrs. Cunningham said. "A beautiful diamond necklace. Suzanne told Olive that she had heard Lily telling Abagail that it belonged to Mrs. Sawyer's mother and she wanted to give it to Lily because she herself didn't have a daughter."

"Oh my, that couldn't have helped Mary's problems any. What with her background, I don't think she would have any family heirlooms to give her daughters."

"I'm sure it didn't improve her condition any, but you'd think she would be happy with her daughter marrying into a family of means."

"She's an odd duck," Mrs. Cunningham said as she brought the coffee back to the counter.

Mrs. Temple walked to the door and struggled to push it open, confronted with a cold, hard wind.

• • •

LILY AND MICHAEL walked hand and hand through the main street of Stonebridge. The week after Christmas had finally brought enough cold weather to make skating safe on the pond. The evening was getting on, so the children were off the ice and back home, and it was time for the young people of the town to have a skating party. Someone had strung lanterns around the trees, and already, a crowd twirled around the ice. Lily sat on a bench, and Michael helped her lace her skates.

His friend Abe skated by. "Watch yourself there," he said. "You're not married yet."

Michel laughed and helped Lily to her feet. When they were balanced, they took hands and skated out to the middle of the pond.

"This may be our last year to do something like this," Michael said. "Soon, we'll be a married couple with other things on our mind."

"Don't be so dour," Lily said. "The pond will still be here next year, and we will be just as likely to skate on it. In fact, I think this is what we should do every year on our anniversary. Come skating on the pond."

"Well then, why not just be wed here?" He picked her up and twirled her around and only then noticed that the others had formed a circle around them.

"Here's to the soon-to-be weds," Abe said, "who are not afraid to be seen among the riff-raff."

Gathered around them were many young people from town— from the mill workers, maids, and hired hands to the bank apprentices and hotel accountants.

"We'll soon begin a new century, my friends," Michael said. "Our lives will be different. We'll stick together, like in the unions."

There were shouts of hurrah and solidarity, and a few snowballs were lobbed. Soon, couples and singles were skating all around the pond, and the talk was of the new motorcars that would help everyone travel more freely and the new washing inventions that would give women more leisure time

"Just wait," one young man skating in the group said. "Within ten years, everyone will have a car"

"Pah, not for me," another said. "Horses are more reliable."

"Machines are cheaper in the long run; you don't have to feed them."

"Oh, it will take much more to feed your engine with gas, and that's not like grass and oats. You have to buy petrol from someone else."

"Then we should all go into oil. It will soon be much more lucrative."

"It will give more people jobs."

They all scattered and circled around the ice then met again in the middle. Someone asked Michael if there would be motorcars used in the wedding.

"I think that would be splendid," he said. "But my father would never allow it."

"Parents are always so old-fashioned," someone shouted, and they all nodded in agreement.

The skaters held hands then and formed a long line, moving from one end of the pond to another, talking of motor cars and other modern conveniences.

Kathleen was skating with her cousin Joseph just outside the group. Daisy and Suzanne broke the line and caught up with them. Joseph put his arm around Daisy then took her for a spin around the perimeter while Suzanne and Kathleen went toward the benches.

"It's fine for them to talk about motor cars," Kathleen said. "Not all of us will be getting them—or leisure time, either."

"It's just talk," Suzanne said. "I know most of the workers won't be able to afford them, but no harm in letting them dream."

Suzanne and Kathleen took off their skates. Joseph and Daisy came and joined them.

"When will you be starting at the stables?" Suzanne asked Joseph.

"Very soon," he said.

Daisy looked at him. "I can't wait. We'll see each other every day."

The four walked out onto the street together. Joseph was staying at the hotel where Kathleen worked. She had not been hired to watch Miss Parker since Christmas. They dropped off Suzanne, and the other three walked down the narrow lane towards the Sawyers' home. Kathleen asked Joseph to go on ahead.

When he was well in front of them, Kathleen turned to Daisy. "Joseph said you were out looking around with him at the stables on Christmas Day. He said you heard Mr. Sawyer and Mr. Winston making some kind of deal?"

"They were arguing."

"About money?" Kathleen asked.

"That, and the old man was yelling that Lily's mother was a whore and he didn't want to fork over any more money for one mistake he made when he was sowing his wild oats."

Kathleen stopped walking and grabbed Daisy by the elbow. "He said Lily's mother was a whore?"

"Yes. Then Mr. Winston said he would tell Mr. Chapman everything if he was not given more money because Michael was not going to be marrying his niece."

After that, they walked along in silence. Birth stories, death stories, it seemed to Kathleen that nothing in this town was what it seemed. She was glad now that Joseph had taken an interest in Daisy. Between the two of them, she'd find out what was going on.

• • •

LILY WATCHED from the window on the last day of the year. Everything seemed to be dragging by, though the wedding was barely a week away, and there was nothing left to do now but wait. Michael had come over earlier, and they had had a quiet celebration and a glass of champagne. She'd been a little disappointed when he asked if he could go out with his friends for the evening. Reluctantly, she had agreed to share him for this one last year, but she would expect a kiss from him at midnight on New Year's each year they were married. She didn't want to act like she was skulking around because her mother seemed to be looking at her with pity.

Abagail came in, interrupting her silence. "Some of the girls have rented a carriage," she said. "There's room for two more. Come. We're going into the city. It will be fun."

Lily shook her head. "I'm not really up for that. It'll be crazy on the streets tonight. They'll be a lot of ruffians out."

Abigail grabbed her hand. "Come on. We won't stay out long. It's your last chance to go out, as a single woman."

"What did Mother say?"

"She hates the idea."

"Well, maybe I'll go just for a while," Lily said.

When the carriage came, Mrs. Chapman insisted on speaking to the driver to make sure he was sober. They had decided to stay in town and go to the Stonebridge. It would be safer for women there, and if the driver did imbibe, they knew people there who could get them home.

The young women piled out of the carriage and up the stairs and were whisked by the desk to the spacious dining room. Most of the chairs and tables were set up against the wall for the evening, so there was room for dancing. They found a place in the corner and all sat on a long divan. It was like a cotillion, Lily thought, with the women all dressed up and waiting to be asked and led to the dance floor. She was glad she had already found her love, and soon, they would be dancing on this very floor, with their friends and family around her. She had taken off her gloves so her engagement ring could be seen and no one would ask her to dance.

She was surprised when Kathleen entered the room with a tray of drinks, although she supposed she shouldn't have been; chambermaids would sometimes be called on to be waitresses, especially on a night like this. It was probably just that Kathleen's presence reminded her of Nanna Parker. They should have gone up to see her before going out, but Hillary had said she barely opened her eyes anymore. Lily took up her glass of champagne and looked out the window. A few stars appeared in the dark sky.

Nana Parker had always told her such touching stories, and, whether it was of joy or heartbreak, Nana's stories had always made her feel better. She had once said that each person gathers and spreads information in their own way and tells it a little differently—and that each person has a different reason for speaking. "Some are curious, or should I say, nosy," she had said, chuckling, "and just like to spread gossip. "Some may wish to speak because they are dying and don't want a story to die with them. Some tell a story to comfort, some to wound, and others seek compassion. Some stories," she had said, "are for revenge, and some bring about forgiveness."

Lily closed her eyes and tried to block out all the noise for a few minutes until Abagail pushed her by the shoulder. "Wake up," she said. "Prince Charming is here."

And when she opened her eyes, Michael *was* there. He bowed and asked if he may have a dance. The men, it seems had had the hotel on their itinerary as well. They had even rented rooms to sleep it off at the end of the evening.

Lily couldn't believe it. She nearly fell from the chair getting up as Michael took her arm and led her to the dance floor. As they danced on the same floor that they would be dancing as a married couple in just over a week, Lily felt it might somehow be unlucky, and she held Michael tightly, afraid to let him go.

Chapter 28

THE SHOPS WERE CLOSED ON NEW YEAR'S DAY, and it was cold. No snow had fallen, so children ran through the cleared streets, pushing each other on toboggans, and the young people skated on the cleared pond. The next day, Mrs. Temple arrived early at the bakery with the new coating of snow.

"Here, come out of the chill," Mrs. Cunningham said, as she opened the door. She had been standing by the door arranging a table. Now she brought the coffee out from behind the counter.

"It's not so bad out there," Mrs. Temple said. "Not like a blizzard. There's been few of those around so far this season."

"Give it time," Mrs. Cunningham said. "There's plenty of winter yet."

Mrs. Temple stirred sugar into her coffee "Any news from the houses?"

"Nothing much for news this morning. I only heard a lot of the men never even made it home on New Year's—stayed at the hotel sleeping it off."

"That doesn't surprise me."

"Some even slept on the dance floor overnight, they said. Ones that hadn't thought ahead or hadn't the money for a room."

"They'll be busy now these next few days cleaning and getting it ready for the wedding."

"Oh, I'm sure it will be sparkling," Mrs. Cunningham said as she brought the coffee back around the counter. "And they'll be no talk around here except of a wedding."

• • •

AS DUSK FELL on the town, the streets and the ponds now abandoned, large flakes clustered on roofs, on the tops of buggies, wagons, and even on the hitching posts. It wasn't a heavy snow, just a steady flow of crystals caught in the light from the parlor as Lily opened the curtain to watch it fall.

It was not a cold snow, for as flakes hit the window, they melted and streamed down the glass. She touched the window, felt a chill in her fingertips, closed the curtain, turned around, and walked back to the fireplace. Suzanne was getting dinner ready in the kitchen. Mr. Chapman was in his study, and her mother and Abigail were upstairs. So much calm in the household, it made her feel uneasy. She would be married by this time next week and imagined it was just the waiting in these very last few days that made her feel so weary. Everything was ready, even her mother's dress. What else was there to worry about? She wished Michael were here though, felt almost despondent not having him by her side. Is this how all new brides felt days and hours before the wedding? Michael would have to work the next few days. His father had insisted, and with everything else going so well, he hadn't wanted to object, though Lily thought he should spend some time with her. It didn't matter, she told herself, because in less than a week now, they would always be together.

• • •

MICHAEL WAS GOING up to bed early, knowing he and his father would have to be up before dawn when his father called to him from the bottom of the stairs. He looked troubled, and Michael didn't feel up for an argument. Was he still so desperate about the wedding? He knew his father was afraid of the changes in their routine. Hadn't he tried to reassure him that they would still go to the stables together in the morning? He would come over and they would still care for the horses, he had told him.

They had argued earlier in the day because his father had hired the new stable boy to start tomorrow, and Michael thought he should not start till after the wedding. He felt it was a slap in the face that his father would have the young man start on their last uninterrupted mornings together. Michael walked slowly down and saw not anger but a kind of gruesome expression on his father's face, and he avoided Michael's eye.

"Father," he said. "I am just too tired to argue now."

"Please come," his father said. "We need to talk."

He led Michael into the study and closed the door firmly

The Sawyer house was eerily quiet as father spoke with son. The large snowflakes drifted onto the windows at just the time that Lily watched them drift by her parlor window.

It was no more than a half hour when Michael opened the door and rushed through the hall and up the stairs, covering his face so his father would not see his tears. He had barely made it to the top when the doorbell rang.

His father whisked his friend Abe into the entry. "I sent for Abe earlier," his father called to him up the stairs. "I thought you might need company."

Abe stayed upstairs with Michael for hours then ignored Olive's insistence that he take a bed overnight. It was snowing hard now, and travel would be difficult. Not heeding her, he left with his head down, saying he needed to be home for the horses in the morning. Daisy stood at the top of the stairs staring at Abe. She had listened at the door. She knew Kathleen would want to know about this, and it was also an excuse to seek out Joseph, who was spending his first night in the small hut that had been built for him by the stables. She hurried there and knocked on his door.

"Come in," he said, and she opened the door to a fire made up and Joseph taking his boots off. "What are you doing here, Daisy?"

She sat down next to him on the bed, a little put off by his lack of enthusiasm. She placed his hand on her knee. He shook her hand off.

"Daisy, tomorrow is my first day," he said. "I'll have to be up well before the sun."

She stood. "Well, I have news that might interest your cousin."

Daisy knew that he had taken this job partly because Kathleen would pay him to get information about the family. He was her lackey. Sometimes she felt jealous of her. She wanted to make him wait but couldn't keep anything in for long.

"Mr. Sawyer and his son were arguing again. Then his friend Abe came over, and I stood by the door in the room. Michael was sobbing, and you wouldn't believe what he said," she told him.

"Good. Maybe I'll make some money tonight."

"You're not thinking of going out to see her tonight in this blizzard?"

"Daisy, just tell me what he said."

"He said that his father told him Lily was his sister—and that Mrs. Chapman was not her mother at all," Daisy said.

Joseph began to put his boots back on. "She'll pay extra for this." He shook his head. "It doesn't look like they'll be a wedding after all." He was still shaking his head when he put on his coat.

"Wait," Daisy said. "I don't know if Michael believed him. It may not have been the truth. You can tell Kathleen tomorrow. I might have more information then." She tugged at his coat. "If you're going out in this blizzard, can we at least go together?"

"Daisy, honey, I am going to stay at the hotel tonight," he said. "I'll be back early. After I've groomed the horses and the men are off to work, come out here if you can get away, and we will be together."

They kissed, and Daisy reluctantly let him go, wondering if there was someone he was going to meet there—and wondering about him and his cousin.

• • •

IT WAS STILL dark the next morning when Michael and his father made their way silently out to the stables. Their new stable boy had not shown up, and Michael said nothing to his father as they brushed and fed the horses.

Mr. Sawyer at first seemed to be trying to appease his son, saying perhaps he had made a mistake hiring someone rashly. No one could be trusted these days; no one understood the meaning of work anymore. Still, Michael said nothing. Then his father told him to be a man and stop blubbering on about what could not be.

Michael shouted, "I won't let what you say ruin my life. I hardly believe you anyway."

"You can't change the past," Mr. Sawyer said.

Michael stood, looked at his father, and threw down the brush. "Well, it's a new century, so watch me. Why should I believe you?"

They heard a rustling, and Joseph came around the corner.

"Finally made it, did you?" Sawyer said to him. He looked at Michael. "I'm going in for breakfast. Are you coming?"

Michael followed his father into the house, but instead of going to the kitchen, he went into the study and closed the door. His father opened the door to the study and shouted, "Make sure you come in today, and don't spend the day moping." Then he slammed it again behind him.

. . .

LILY WAS HAVING trouble sleeping, so she tiptoed downstairs, afraid of waking her mother who was sleeping all night for a change. She went into the kitchen to make a cup of tea and then took a candle into the dining room. The room was dark, so she opened a curtain and noticed the snow had gotten thicker. Then she took her tea to the parlor where there was still a hint of burning wood in the fireplace. She sat on the couch with her feet up and covered them with a small comforter.

The room felt odd at this time in the early morning, and she must have fallen asleep, for in a waking dream, she put her feet down and saw Michael, sitting in a chair by the fireplace. She rubbed her eyes, and upon opening them again, he was gone. She'd heard of these illusions, tricks of light. Some people made a fortune out of trickery. She almost understood this, for in the first moment that she saw his face, she'd wanted to reach out her hand to the illusion.

It was little more than an hour later when everyone except her mother was in the kitchen having breakfast, that there was a knock at the door. Suzanne went to get it. Abe and the local constable came into the kitchen. Lily tried to read their faces. She tried to feel hopeful. Someone had perhaps gotten hurt, thrown by a horse? The teacup she had just sipped from was still raised, as if in a toast.

Her hand trembled, and Abe came to her side. *Don't speak*, she thought. She looked at him, pleading with him not to speak the words.

"There's been an accident," the constable said.

Lily looked up at Abe.

"It's Michael," Abe said, in a whisper.

Lily, still with the teacup poised, looked from the constable to Abe and back to the constable again. "Where is he? Please, I want to be with him. He needs me."

The constable shook his head.

"No," Lily said, and the teacup fell out of her hand. Warm liquid fell over the side of the table onto her nightdress. "No" she shouted "Take me to him, now. I have to see him."

Abe took one arm, Abagail took the other, and they led her into the parlor and sat beside her on the couch. She wouldn't listen at all to what they were saying, but her sense of hearing was acute, as she listened for just one hopeful word, one syllable that would lead to a fissure that would open Michael's sweet lips, his breath, his voice. She strained to hear the words that her father and the constable spoke in the doorway of the parlor. They spoke of a body—how it was found—where it was found, and she looked up and saw Michael again sitting in the chair by the fireplace.

Chapter 29

MRS. TEMPLE HAD CLOSED HER SHOP EARLY. She and Mrs. Cunningham sat in the bakery drinking coffee. As everyone else in town, they didn't quite know what to do. The streets were empty, and a heavy wind swept snow along Main Street like a phantom that no-one, even yesterday, could have imagined. Neither woman expected to see customers for the rest of the day.

Mrs. Cunningham heard the news early, and her shop had been crowded when Mrs. Temple showed up for their morning coffee. There'd been nowhere to sit. The millworkers, who rushed by every morning, had suddenly began to trickle back in pairs; then crowds of three or four began to retrace their morning steps.

Mrs. Cunningham, who saw them streaming past her door, hurried out asking what was going on. Had they been given another day off, another holiday, but faces looked solemn, and the groups gathered at her door said there had been a shooting at the Sawyer residence. No one would be working today.

She invited them all in for free coffee and pastries as the tables quickly filled, and others stood around stunned by the news, shaken by the sudden change in routine. Mrs. Temple entered and helped her friend pour tea and coffee. They handed out pastries and then stood behind the counter, trying to hear the conversations and distinguish between what was true and what was hear-say.

Olive came into the bakery after the crowds had dispersed. She had come to put in an order for a funeral. When she left, Mrs. Cunningham went over to her friend. "Olive just left me with an order of sandwiches and pastry for the wake and funeral."

"They're having a wake at the house?" Mrs. Temple asked.

Mrs. Cunningham nodded. "In two days."

Mrs. Temple trembled. "I wasn't sure if they would have a wake, what with the circumstances. Did Olive say anymore? Did she say he shot himself? It must have been an accident."

Mrs. Cunningham looked down into her coffee. "You know Olive. She doesn't say much, but she wanted to put a stop to all the rumors, so she did say she thinks it was an accident."

"Was he really shot in the head? How could that be an accident?"

"Olive said that something strange happened last night." Mrs. Cunningham moved in closer. "She said that they had a visitor late yesterday. It was Michael's friend Abe, and he was upstairs with Michael for hours. She tried to get Abe to stay overnight for his safety with the blizzard on, and she said he seemed rather disheveled, and his eyes were wild, but he insisted on leaving and mumbled something about help for Michael and scowled something about the Old Man."

"That is strange. Abe is generally such a polite young man."

"Anyways, she said it gave her an eerie feeling to see him like that, but then Michael came down a while later and went with his father to the stables early, before breakfast, as they usually do."

"I heard a new boy started there this morning."

"Yes, and Olive said she heard him tell the police that Michael and his father had been arguing."

"The police must all be over there today."

"Oh, yes. Olive told me they were questioning everyone, even her."

"She must be in a state."

"She was trembling as she spoke about it. She loved Michael like a son." Mrs. Cunningham shook her head. "And poor Lily."

Mrs. Temple knit her eyebrows. "Was that the last time anyone saw Michael, walking out of the house with his father?"

"It's the last time Olive saw him, but she did hear a commotion when they came back in. She heard shouting, and she sent Daisy down the pantry hall to see what was going on. Daisy came back saying they were arguing, and she was afraid to tell them about breakfast, so Olive was about to go down herself when Mr. Sawyer came into the kitchen alone for breakfast, looking more gruff and unhappy than usual. She was about go up the stairs and see if the missus needed help getting dressed when Sawyer said to bring Michael his breakfast in the study, so she sent Daisy off with a bowl for Michael."

Mrs. Temple sipped coffee hardly noticing it had gone cold.

Mrs. Cunningham continued. "She had hardly left the kitchen when they heard a of kind of bang and then a scream. She and Mr. Sawyer ran out to see if something had fallen or if maybe one of the new light bulbs they had just installed had popped. Then they saw Daisy slouched down against the wall just outside the study door and Olive was about to scold her for the making a mess of the breakfast scattered on the floor, but she could see that Daisy was very distraught. She'd just put her hand down to help Daisy up when they heard a loud shout and a low moaning sound coming from inside the study."

Mrs. Cunningham paused. She looked out the window then back again.

"It was like in a dream, she said. She stood by the door to the study only to see the old man cradling his son's head in his arms. Blood dripped from a wound near Michael's hairline, and as the old man rocked, it splattered onto his arms and shoulders. She said the old man wasn't crying tears but unearthly sounds like a wounded animal shook his body."

"When did the police come?"

"Olive sent Daisy to get Chief Simmons, and just at that moment, she saw the Missus coming down the stairs."

"That poor woman. Her only child"

"Olive said it was awful. She didn't want to be the one to tell her. She said it was like nothing she'd ever seen. Mrs. Sawyer could hear her husband keening and began to run, and all the time, Olive held her back because she didn't want her to see—didn't want her to know. And she said when Mrs. Sawyer first went into the study, she must have thought it was her husband who was injured because the blood was now trailing down his arms and into the rug. She ran in yelling to her husband. Then she saw that it was Michael he held in his arms, and she fell upon her husband, sobbing loudly."

Mrs. Temple shook her head and stared out the window. Dusk was overtaking the sky and covering the landscape of blowing snow. It would be dark soon. No one in this town would sleep tonight. "It must have been frightening for poor Olive to be questioned by the police."

"Oh, she said it was terrible. The police, the medical examiner— they were all there. She was trying to tell them as much as she could to keep them away from the grieving family. The doctor had come for Mrs. Sawyer. She said they had to practically pry her away from her son. She wanted to comfort Mrs. Sawyer, but they kept pulling her away to answer questions so she had Daisy bring her upstairs to bed, and she supposed the doctor gave her a sedative. She told Daisy not to leave her side, even if she was asleep."

Mrs. Temple was hardly listening now. She wanted to go home to a warm fire, put up her feet, and close her eyes. She looked at her friend and asked if she would be going home to get some rest.

"There's no chance of that. I have to start baking right now to make all they will need for the wake."

"Come walk home with me now. I promise I'll be in early in the morning to help. I won't be opening tomorrow. We'll bake together, and my daughters may be able to help for at least part of the day."

"That's sweet of you, but I don't know if I want to go home tonight. I don't know if I want to be alone."

"With all that's happened today, I don't blame you. Listen, come stay at my house. I have a guest room."

"I don't want to impose."

"You're not imposing. Really, finish up here. I probably won't sleep all night, so I would appreciate the company myself. My husband will be on the couch snoring by dinnertime."

"Are you sure?" Mrs. Cunningham asked as she got up and reached for her bag from behind the counter.

"I told you I need the company too," Mrs. Temple said as Mrs. Cunningham turned the lights out and locked the door.

We'll go to your house first," Mrs. Temple said, "and get what you need for a few days."

The two women lifted their coat collars high against the bully wind and stepped briskly.

• • •

THE MOURNERS overflowed into the parlor of the Sawyer house. The only sounds were a low murmur and Mrs. Sawyer's quiet sobbing. When Lily sat beside her, they held each other and began to keen loudly. Mr. Chapman looked at Dr. Sands, wondering what to do. Dr. Sands nodded, assuring him that everything was okay. Old man Sawyer sat silently beside his wife.

Relatives of the Sawyers who had already arrived at the hotel for the wedding helped the kitchen staff. Everyone spoke in guarded whispers. Besides all the food from the bakery, many people had brought dishes. Mrs. Sawyer's sister Rebecca did most of the organizing. She sent her daughter Josephine back home to stay with a neighbor. She brought a pot of coffee into the parlor and poured some for Abe who stood silently against the mantle, looking down at the floor. When he did look up, it was only to glare at Michael's father, who, in all his stalwart silence, seemed to quiver at the look. He crossed his arms, looked to the side, and his lips trembled. Abe's facial muscles twitched at this as he tried to suppress a sneer.

Rebecca sat down with a group of young people "That young man seems a bit more despondent than most," she whispered looking in the general direction of Abe.

"He was a very good friend to Michael," one said.

"Yes, and he was with him the night before . . . he died," another offered

"So, he's the one who last visited with Michael. Make sure you keep an eye on him. We don't want any more tragedies."

"Oh, we will ma'am, don't worry. We won't let him go off by himself."

"See that you don't," she said and got up heading back to the kitchen.

Abe seemed to be in a world of his own until Lily abruptly broke away from Mrs. Sawyer and began to walk toward the table. It was the sudden silence that had caught his wandering attention. Lily's father took her arm and led her to the couch. Everyone watched Lily without talking. Her father poured a coffee and put it in front of her.

"No thank you, Father," she said, not looking up. The tear stains were drying on her face.

"How about tea?"

She nodded.

Abe watched her closely. If he should pay his condolences anyone, it was her. He managed to break away from his sullen aloneness and went to sit next to her on the couch. Everyone else had left the area. People were starting to leave this room with the casket and move into the dining room. When Abe came over, Lily's father nodded at him and left them alone.

"I'm sorry, Lily," he said. "I wish I could do something to help you."

Lily looked straight into Abe's face. "I thought he loved me," she whispered loudly and looked over at the coffin, falling onto Abe. "He told me that he loved me." Her voice trembled.

"He *did* love you, Lily. He told me that he loved you too."

She cried hysterically. Dr. Sands came over, and Abe went into the study and closed the door. Mr. Sawyer, still sitting next to his son's coffin, started to get up. That was his study; no one had permission to go in there, but, then, he sat back down. A group of Michael's friends opened the door to the study, and Mr. Sawyer hit the arms of his chair, hard, but remained sitting. His wife, next to him, began keening again. Abe did not look up as his friends entered.

"You okay, old Pal?"

"Yes," Abe said. "Leave me alone. "Wait," he said, looking up. "Ask Lily to come in here. I want to talk to her."

Dr. Sands came to the door with Lily. She had stopped crying. They stood at the door looking at Abe.

"I want to talk to Lily . . . alone," Abe said. "Please."

"We'll keep the door open," Dr. Sands said.

"No, I'm alright now. Please. I want to talk to Abe too."

"Well, I will be right outside the door then." He looked suspiciously at Abe, hoping nothing would be said that would upset Lily more.

That's fine," Abe said and helped Lily into a chair. He sat down and leaned toward her, trying to choose the right words, trying to decide how much she needed to know. "I didn't want to tell you this, Lily. I really didn't, but you must understand that Michael loved you right up to the very end."

Abe's voice dropped off into a whisper, and Dr. Sands couldn't make out the words. He'd just had to wait and see what effect it would have on his patient. He wasn't optimistic.

Abe couldn't bear to tell her everything so he told her there was a lot of trouble at the factory—that Mr. Sawyer thought Michael was somehow involved with the unions. Then, he told her that he did not believe that Michael had taken his own life. He believed he had been murdered.

When Abe and Lily finally came back into the room, Dr. Sands was surprised to see that Lily wasn't crying or hysterical, although she did look pale and shaken, but actually a little stronger than before. She had more purpose in her eyes. Maybe Abe had been reassuring after all.

She went to where her father was sitting on the couch. "I want to go home now, Father."

"Right now? Mr. Chapman looked at Dr. Sands who nodded.

"Yes, I feel very tired."

"That's to be expected," Dr. Sands said.

Mr. Chapman and Dr. Sands stepped away while Lily stared into the coffin.

"You can stay here," Mr. Chapman said to the doctor. "They need you here."

Dr. Sands nodded. "I think she'll be okay. Give her these pills every six hours as needed. She'll probably sleep most of the day. I am somewhat concerned about Mary, however. Call for me if you need me for her. Make sure she takes her medicine and that someone is with her, even when she is sleeping."

Mr. Chapman took Lily's arm and sought out Olive in the kitchen. "Give my condolences to Mr. and Mrs. Sawyer again," he said. "We're leaving now. Lily is very tired."

"Of course, poor thing." She went over to Lily, who stood in the hallway right outside the kitchen door. She touched her shoulder. "I am so sorry," she said.

Lily went to her father, leaning on his shoulder. He took her arm and led her to the waiting carriage. When they got back, Lily went up to her room, and Mr. Chapman followed.

"I want to be alone father. Please leave me be," Lily said.

"I have some pills," he said. "Dr. Sands said they'll help you sleep."

She lay down on her bed and stared out the window. "I don't need them," she said. "Please close the door on the way out."

Mr. Chapman nodded, still very worried about her. He sat in a chair in the hallway and stared at the door until everything inside was quiet. Then he opened the door softly, and when he saw Lily resting on the bed, he tiptoed to the door and closed it carefully behind him.

Lily's eyes opened. She sat up in bed and listened to his footsteps receding down the hallway. She threw herself across the bed, buried her face in the pillow, and cried for a long time. *What did it mean? It couldn't be real.* She thought she heard a carriage pull up outside and ran to the window as, for one second, she thought it might be Michael. There was no carriage, no Michael. She collapsed into a chair by the window and watched as dusk fell. Then she listened to movement outside the door, footsteps up the stairs and down again.

They had let Suzanne go over to the Sawyers' because they had needed her help with the wake. She would have welcomed Suzanne's company now. The sunrise would only bring another day that she would have to live through without him. It was not real to her. She heard the door open downstairs and again thought for just a second it was Michael coming to take her for a picnic. She thought she heard his footfall on the stairs, his voice one more time. Nothing of it made sense. Abe had even said he didn't believe Michael would have put a gun to his own head.

There was a knock on the door, and Abagail entered. The sisters ran to each other, Lily collapsing into Abagail s arms.

"Whose here?" Lily managed to whisper.

"Suzanne is back."

"How is Mother?"

"She's coming along. It's difficult for all of us—especially you," she said, and they both began to cry again.

Lily wanted to say it shouldn't have been difficult for their mother at all. Hadn't she gotten what she wanted? Her body shook in anger. She would stay in her room all evening and all day tomorrow. She didn't want to see her mother.

Abagail led her to the bed, and they both sat silently. She took Lily's hands. "I don't know what to say to you." Lily moved next her sister, put her head on Abagail's shoulder.

"It's what happens when secrets are kept," Lily said.

"I guess we really never know. We think we know someone." Abagail squeezed Lily's shoulder and kissed her on the head.

'You don't understand," Lily said looking at Abagail. "I talked with Abe at the wake. Michael is not the one I couldn't trust. Michael was innocent himself. Abe doesn't believe Michael killed himself. He thinks he was murdered."

Abagail pulled away from her sister. "Murdered? Who would kill Michael?"

"I don't know, but Abe said he was with Michael the night before, and he said Michael was very angry with his father. He said his father had told him a pack of lies all his life, and he didn't know what to believe anymore. Abe said the last thing Michael told him is that he didn't know what to believe and that he was angry and . . ." Lily began to cry again and could barely talk above a whisper. "He was more determined than ever that we would be married."

Abigail held her sister on the bed, gently rocking her, as dusk turned into night.

"I'll stay here with you tonight," Abagail said. "We'll sleep in the same bed like when we were little girls."

Lily smiled then sighed. There was a knock on the door.

"I don't want to see anyone but you right now," Lily said quietly and moved to the window to draw the curtains.

Abagail opened the door half-way, shook her head, and brought in a supper tray that she set on the high bureau.

Chapter 30

IT HAD BEEN A LONG, SHOCKING DAY FOR THE whole town, and lights went out hesitantly as evening turned into night. Curiosity seekers and the press finally left the front yard of the Sawyers' house. Tomorrow would be another long day. The funeral procession would ride through town. There was talk behind doors about the events, and Mrs. Cunningham was still staying with Mrs. Temple and her family. They sat in the parlor having brandy in front of the fireplace.

"I thought a suicide couldn't be buried in the Christian Cemetery," Mrs. Temple said.

"You can be buried anywhere if you have the money," her husband answered.

Mrs. Cunningham sighed. "The poor family. The least they can do is let him have a Christian burial."

Everyone went to sleep, hoping they would wake from a long nightmare. Snow was falling by midnight, but in the dim kitchens of the next morning, more news was spreading. During the night, another strange death had occurred.

• • •

DAISY WHISPERED with Olive over the breakfast table. Olive had just told her that Michael's funeral had been postponed until tomorrow.

"How can you postpone a funeral?" Daisy asked, choking on her tea.

"Because there's been another death," Olive said. "Mrs. Chapman strangled herself."

"But how can that be?" Daisy asked. "She's a frail woman."

"Keep your voice down," Olive said to her. "I'm only telling you what I heard."

Daisy leaned toward her and whispered loudly, "Where did you hear it?"

"You know Dr. Sands stayed here last night in one of the extra bedrooms in case the missus needed help." Daisy nodded. "Well, someone came to fetch him in the middle of the night. I answered the door to the chief of police. He said they needed the doctor over at the Chapmans." Olive looked around, her voice barely audible as if afraid to say the words. "The old man came to the door behind me. I heard police tell him Mrs. Chapman had been found strangled in an upstairs room before I left to awaken Dr. Sands." She was quiet for a minute letting her own words sink in. "They said it was another suicide. She was very distraught. We all know, not a very well woman." Olive sighed. "I guess the tragedy of Michael's death just put her over the edge."

"But how could she kill herself?" Daisy asked.

"I told you she was found strangled or hung by some sort of cord or cloth"

"But why get Dr. Sands, if she was already dead?"

"Pipe down, for goodness sake. The medical examiner would want to know all the medicines she was on. They're doing an investigation."

"An investigation sounds more like they thought it was murder."

"Shh, don't even say that word in this house."

"Does the Mrs. Know what happened?" Daisy asked.

"The missus is out from a sedative, so don't you say anything. Not even a hint that something else is amiss. It will give her another day to rest before her son's funeral. I think they are hoping she will not even get up. I think they will tell her the weather was too harsh for the procession today."

• • •

THE POLICE CHIEF and the medical examiner tried to keep the news secret as long as they could, but by afternoon the crowds, press, and curiosity seekers were all now at the Chapmans' front door. The police force had a double task again of investigating, as well as keeping the family from undue harassment.

Mr. Chapman and his daughters sat in the parlor. The girls were both crying, but Mr. Chapman sat alone with his head down. When the officers came in to question him, they noticed his haggard look and bewildered, blank stare. The Chief of police stood next to him, as he would have to talk to them about what had happened last night. They would not approach Lily and Abagail at this time. They were too visibly shaken. It was Edward Chapman who had found the body.

The chief put his hand on Edward's shoulder. "Do you think you could come upstairs to the room where you found the body and answer a few questions?"

"Yes, I think I can do that."

Dr. Sands was watching Edward very carefully for signs of shock. The medical examiner joined them as they walked up the stairs and stood in front of the closed door.

"What time did you find the body?" the chief asked.

"About two-thirty, I think. I wasn't really watching the time."

"You were awake at that time?"

"I heard something, a thump maybe," Mr. Chapman said. "I turned over, and my wife was not beside me. I knew this was where she would come, if she'd awoken. Dr. Sands had given me sedatives to help her get through the night." The doctor nodded at the detective. "I didn't think she would wake up."

"You didn't go downstairs first? Check the stairway, in case she had fallen there?"

Mr. Chapman looked confused. "No, I rushed up here. I told you this is where she usually came to be alone."

"Seems funny that she'd want to be alone after all that had happened in the last few days."

Mr. Chapman's face contorted. Dr. Sands touched his shoulder and looked angrily at the detective. "Is this really necessary?"

Mr. Chapman looked at Dr. Sands. "It's alright," he said. "I knew she came up here, sometimes, when she couldn't sleep," Edward repeated "I was very worried. I even smelled her perfume as I walked up these stairs. She always wore perfume, even lately, when she had been so troubled." He began to sob.

"Are you alright?" the doctor asked.

Edward nodded. He stopped crying.

The investigator suddenly opened the door. "Is this how you found your wife, sir?"

Mr. Chapman almost collapsed and held on to the doorknob. "Yes, that is how I found her."

"She had already fallen down from the rafter and was sprawled over the desk when you got here?"

Mr. Chapman nodded.

"Is that your neckerchief?"

"Yes sir," Mr. Chapman said. "But she brought it up here sometimes to tie her hair back when she painted. It's an old one I don't use anymore."

The medical examiner and the detective exchanged glances.

Dr. Sands took Mr. Chapman's shoulder. He knew that they wouldn't move the body until the investigation was over, but why were they trying to needlessly shock him? Probably trying to surprise him into a confession, fancied they were like the police in New York with all the new forensic evidence and psychological profiling.

"She was a very troubled woman," Dr Sands said. "Is this really necessary? She was very ill."

"What was the nature of her illness?" the medical examiner asked.

"It was a nervous condition. She had been under my care for quite some time."

Mr. Chapman composed himself once again.

The medical examiner and the detective looked at each other.

"Do you have any idea what she did in this room?" the detective asked.

Mr. Chapman bowed his head. "She's been sick, as the doctor said. Troubled for some time now. For some reason, this room seemed to bring her peace. She used it as a kind of refuge. We had the desk brought up here. She liked to write. She had a diary."

"Where is the diary, now?" the detective asked.

Mr. Chapman looked up. "I think she kept it in the drawer."

The detective, wearing gloves, went over to the desk, careful not to disturb the body, and tried to open the side drawer, but it was locked.

"Didn't you ever look at the diary?" The detective looked back and forth between Mr. Chapman and Dr. Sands; then he pried open the drawer. There was nothing inside.

"That was where I thought she kept it," Mr. Chapman insisted. "Every time one of us came to check on her up here, she would quickly place it back in there. I did try to see it once," he admitted. "But, as you can see, she kept the drawer locked."

"Thank you, sir. You've been very helpful. Just one more question. Has anything else been removed from the room that you are aware of?"

Mr. Chapman looked around the room, his right hand trembling. "Not that I can see. Everything looks exactly the same."

"Very good, Mr. Chapman. We're done for now. My condolences to you and your daughters."

The trembling hand became a twitch up his arm, and Dr. Sands put his hands firmly on Edward's shoulder and led him down the stairs. "It's a suicide," Dr. Sands said. "Anyone can see that. It's her condition and the shock, from yesterday. It's not as unusual as you might think for one suicide to occur right after another. Don't worry about anything uglier coming out of this." He led Edward into the parlor and left him at the door. "I have to help with the investigation," he said. "Don't worry. I will let you know everything that is said."

Mr. Chapman nodded and joined his daughters in the parlor.

The day wore into night. It was overcast and getting colder. The people outside the Chapman household dispersed after nightfall. Up in the servant's quarters, Nana Parker still hung on, restlessly parsing out words and sounds to the few she thought were still around her. Kathleen was the only one who sat by her, as Hillary had been sent to the Sawyer's to help with the wake and funeral.

Chapter 31

THE SUN HAD BARELY BEGUN TO RISE when Mrs. Temple and Mrs. Cunningham rushed into the bakery to get out of the cold and whirling snow. Mrs. Cunningham started the coffee then sat for several minutes with Mrs. Temple.

They looked out at the storm and did not say a thing for several minutes until Mrs. Cunningham broke the silence. "They're not having people over after the burial today," she said.

"I heard that too. What with the storm and the poor Mrs. Chapman, who would want to gather?"

"I told them to come here after if they want, just the family. I told them I would close early if they wanted to come here and not be at home. There are too many on-lookers gathering now, just nosy people waiting to see what will happen."

Mrs. Temple nodded.

"I told them just to invite the few relatives and friends that would truly be a comfort, and I would close the bakery to the rest."

"I won't be opening today. I don't think anyone will be but you; I could help with the serving if they do come."

Mrs. Cunningham nodded. She watched the workers beginning

to come out, shoveling the streets. "They'll be at it for hours keeping ahead of this one. They're Sawyer's workers from the factory. It's closed today so they can work keeping the roads open."

"It's good to see so many rallying around the family," Mrs. Temple said. "I wonder what time they will be coming by?"

Mrs. Cunningham shook her head, and Mrs. Temple sighed. They sat in silence, watching the snow scooped in shovels and thrown to the side of the road.

They saw a woman with a long coat and a hood covering her face walk by—the only person they had seen on the road besides the workers. The two women got up and went to the window for a closer look, but it was impossible to see the face. She was walking briskly, despite the storm.

"It's not a coat I recognize," Mrs. Temple said. "Not one bought in this town."

A man followed behind her, as if trying to catch up. He was a young man, but they didn't recognize him either. He had nearly caught up to the woman when she disappeared down a side street, walking right into the high snow.

"Probably the press," Mrs. Cunningham said

"Why be out here in the storm?" Mrs. Temple arched her eyebrows. "I heard they had all moved over to the Chapmans' house."

The two women went back to the table.

"Poor Mary," Mrs. Temple said. "The shock was too much for her."

Mrs. Cunningham put down her coffee and touched her friend's arm. She spoke in a whisper. "Please don't tell a soul, but I opened late yesterday for a while in case the houses needed anything. The chief was in here late with the detective from Worcester, to get a coffee."

"They were discussing the deaths, in here?"

Mrs. Cunningham nodded. "After serving them, I stepped behind the counter and kneeled down on the floor, pretending to organize items in the lower cabinet. They might have thought I had gone to the back."

"What did they say?"

"They said," Mrs. Cunningham looked out at the flying snow, "that they don't know if Mary's death was a suicide."

Mrs. Temple leaned in close. "What do you mean?"

"They're looking into other possibilities . . ."

The snow did not let up for the procession to the cemetery, and the two women watched through the bakery window as the horses struggled for their footing. The family was protected inside the carriages, black curtains drawn, and the drivers sat stooped, holding onto the reins, their top hats and coats covering with snow and their gloved hands struggling to calm the bewildered horses. It wasn't the procession the town had expected only a week ago.

The struggles of the horses and the drivers seemed to mirror the desolation that had fallen over the town. Most people watched the dirge from their windows. A small crowd walked behind the last carriage, and the press stood in knee-deep snow, vying for the best pictures. Occasionally a reporter approached the crowds but was brushed off swiftly. One reporter even entered the bakery to get a story from the two women, but with the looks they gave him, he left very quickly.

The snow continued to fall heavily the day of Michael's funeral, and it didn't let up through the night. The next day was Mary Chapman's wake, but unlike the houseful at the Sawyers for Michael's wake, few people attended. It was as if the whole town was numb and didn't have the strength for another funeral so soon.

Mrs. Temple and Mrs. Cunningham trudged to the bakery early and began to make boxes of pastries to be delivered to the Chapmans.' They had intended to just drop them off, but Suzanne urged them to stay, anticipating the small turn out. Suzanne wearily went through the motions of greeting and serving refreshments to those who did come. Daisy was there to help, but Olive had stayed at the Sawyers,' keeping an eye on the missus, Daisy said.

Mrs. Cunningham and Mrs. Temple stayed for a while in the kitchen with Daisy. They were hoping to hear talk of the Sawyer place, wondering out loud if the Sawyers would come.

Daisy shook her head. "I don't expect them to leave the house today. The missus wasn't out of bed when I left."

"Just as well," Mrs. Temple said. "It would be hard for Lily to see Michael's family."

"I hope more people do come just to show their respect," Mrs. Cunningham said.

Daisy shook her head. "Don't expect many. I told Suzanne when I came. People in town are frightened."

Mrs. Temple gave her a look. "Frightened of what?"

"Just talk, you know. You know how things spread."

Mrs. Cunningham had stopped what she was doing and stood with one hand on her hip and one hand on the table. "What kind of things?"

Daisy whispered, "It's just, you know, two deaths happening so close like this, two suicides. I've heard people say things about secrets, about evil, about a curse."

"Don't be foolish," Mrs. Cunningham said. "Let's get out there and sit with the poor family."

Daisy moved closer to Mrs. Temple and Mrs. Cunningham. "People think there may be a spirit hovering over this town."

"Foolishness," Mrs. Cunningham said again as she followed Mrs. Temple through the pantry and into the dining room where they set down the tea, coffee, and pastries.

Mrs. Temple peeked into the parlor. Mr. Chapman and his daughters sat in strait-backed chairs right next to the coffin with a half a dozen mourners scattered around on the couch and high brocade chairs. No one spoke. The parlor doors were open to the dining room where the women set down the trays.

The doorbell rang, and Suzanne went to answer it while the women went into the parlor and looked into the coffin, crossing themselves.

Mr. Chapman rose. "Thank you for coming," he said.

Abagail looked up, and they motioned for her to remain sitting. Lily was staring out the window at the snow coming down, as if unaware that anyone was there.

Mrs. Cunningham crouched down between the chairs of the two young women. She took their hands in hers. "Bless you, girls. We all loved your mother," she said, wondering if she should add something about Michael to Lily, but she only held a bit more tightly to Lily's hand. "I am so sorry," she said. When she moved away, Mrs. Temple spoke with them, and Mrs. Cunningham busied herself with finding a comfortable place on the couch.

Suzanne came in with Michael's friends Abe and Christopher, and everyone looked over at Lily. She didn't seem to notice anyone in the room but sat stiffly, still watching the snow cascade and blow across the windows. Abe came over to her, and when he spoke, she seemed to awaken in grief, shuddering and sobbing loudly. She let Abe take her hand and lead her to the loveseat by the window.

Somehow this outburst had eased the heavy burden of grief in the room. People began to whisper quietly. Some went into the dining room for tea, coffee, and pastries. A few brought refreshments into the parlor. Lily was quiet after a while, wrapped in Abe's arms.

Mrs. Temple and Mrs. Cunningham soon were the only ones sitting on the couch on the other side of the room. The doorbell rang again. Kathleen came in taking off her coat.

"What's she doing in here?" Mrs. Temple whispered. "And why did she have to ring and make them answer the door? She should have come in quietly by the service entrance. I thought she was just here for serving or to watch over Miss Parker."

"Maybe she's just on her way to the kitchen to clear out some of the platters. Did you notice she didn't even kneel in front of the coffin?" Mrs. Cunningham asked. "She seems to be avoiding it. Did you notice she walked right past Edward, too? Didn't even console him?"

Mrs. Temple moved in closer. "She was the one rushing around in the snow yesterday. That's the coat, and I can tell you right now, she would never be able to afford a coat like that on her salary at the hotel."

"I don't know. Some of those houses in Worcester pay a good salary," Mrs. Cunningham said. "And Olive told me that's where she worked before she came to town."

"I suppose," Mrs. Temple said. "She may have had it for a long time. That material will last through many seasons. Still, if she's here as a server or helper for Miss Parker, whatever it is they are calling her, I think she should respect the family more at a time like this."

Kathleen had taken a chair next to Abe and Lily. Lily looked at her, startled. Abe held Lily closer. She touched Lily's hand. Mrs. Temple and Mrs. Cunningham looked at each other.

"Cheeky," they both whispered.

"Did you notice?" Mrs. Cunningham asked. "That the woman's hands are trembling."

"I don't believe she's much of a comfort to Lily," Mrs. Temple said.

"I wouldn't think so."

"Do you think we should say something? Tell her she's needed in the kitchen?" Mrs. Temple asked.

"Maybe we should talk to Suzanne. It would be better coming from her."

The two women went into the dining room and took Suzanne aside.

A burst of visitors began to arrive, and Suzanne, after answering the door and leading them to the parlor, had no problem explaining to Kathleen that she was needed for serving duties. Mrs. Temple and Mrs. Cunningham watched her get up and follow Suzanne, but she glanced back into the parlor at Lily and Abe.

Mrs. Temple and Mrs. Cunningham went back into the kitchen to see if they could be of any help and ran into another shock. Hillary had just rushed down from the servant's quarters. Nana Parker had just died, and she didn't want to burden the family with any more arrangements.

Suzanne said, as the hired help, they would take care of it all. Under the circumstances, with no family to come for the body, they would make arrangements for a quiet a burial in a few days.

• • •

MARY CHAPMAN'S funeral procession consisted of only a few carriages, and no one walked behind except for some reporters from the Worcester Telegram. It was snowing again, and people watched from the safety of their windows and warm fires as the workers continued to clear the roads for the small procession. Sawyer had not opened his mill today and had again offered work to anyone who wanted to clear the roads and the cemetery for Mary Chapman's funeral.

Sawyer re-opened the mill the next day. He had fired the new stable boy when he realized he was more interested in Daisy than caring for the horses, but now he had to take care of the morning chores alone. He groomed the horses silently, threw them feed, and leaned his bulk against the thick slats where the horses boarded. He had no appetite and scorned the thought of a hot breakfast. He arrived at the mill early and hurried around the factory, silently loading and unloading merchandise instead of starting the day in his office as usual. The workers watched but didn't say anything, only tipped their hats as he went by. They watched and stayed out of his way. He seemed to be doing their work for them, and they waited for him to bark his usual orders, but he was silent. He didn't go into the office at all until Abe showed up. Then he hurried Abe in, not even closing the door.

"We have a lot of work to do," Sawyer said in a weary voice, not noticing how Abe glared at him. "A lot of work. We're going to have to hire some new men. I'll need you more in the office."

"Oh, no—you'll have to hire someone besides me to fit right into Michael's position. I'll keep my own job in the warehouse or none at all." Abe knew how much Sawyer needed his help now. He wouldn't fire him, no matter how much he might want to. It didn't make good business sense. Above all, Sawyer was a businessman.

"You'll do what I tell you," Sawyer said, raising his voice, and the workers listened in silence.

Abe finally looked up. "I am not your son. You can't control me," he said, and he walked past Sawyer and went to work in the warehouse.

"Where are you going?" Sawyer yelled.

Abe shouted back, "To do my job."

Sawyer grunted. "Tomorrow, I'll need you to start in the office. Make sure you're here on time tomorrow."

"I'll raise myself from the dead if need be," Abe said, realizing too late how cruel his words were. "I'm sorry," he said quietly. "I'll be in on time tomorrow."

"I'll need you early. The books need to be done. I'll show you how after lunch."

Abe nodded and went back to work in the warehouse.

• • •

LILY, ABAGAIL, AND Mr. Chapman walked around the house silently. Days turned into a week, and Mr. Chapman could not bring himself to go back to work. He sat in his office at home, shuffling papers, occasionally making calls to the plant from a newly installed telephone. Abagail had not gone back to school. They seemed to all want to stay close to one another. In the evening, they would gather, and the girls would play music for their father, but they still did not speak.

They only drifted by one another and tried to take sustenance, but the coffee tasted bitter, and if the music could uplift them at one time, now it was all just a dirge. A dirge, however, they clung to as a family that somehow moved them along, through another day, and, at night, when they went to their separate rooms, it was like a promise they kept to each other that they would rise the next day and move about the house and not forsake one another in the gloom.

Lily stared through the window of her room into the dark sky, happy for the gloom of nightfall. It was as if, although her family did not speak, they silently assured each other by getting up every morning and moving from room to room, that no one else would disappear. She and her father and Abagail made sure to kiss each other goodnight now as if it were a pact to assure each other that though they needed this time alone, they would not kill themselves in the night because they knew how painful it was when someone you loved died like that.

How could her mother have taken her own life? It made her angry, as well as full of sorrow—and guilty too because when Michael died, she had, just for a moment, thought that maybe her mother had him killed.

She went to the bed and got under the covers still fully dressed, hugged her pillow, and stared at the ceiling. Above her was the room where her mother had gone, full of sorrow and secrets. She should have listened to her mother more. She should have listened carefully, and maybe her mother would have told her stories and she would have understood, as nanna said, that her mother had, at one time, had secrets and dreams. For now, she needed to know the stories, and secrets—the bad ones and the good ones—the ones that made you angry and the ones that helped you forgive.

And even Nana was gone. She needed Nanna now. She needed her mother, and she needed her nanna. She threw the pillow, kicked the covers off, and went to the window. She wanted to hit the pane, break the glass with her fist.

"Why?" she yelled to the dark sky. "Why has everyone left me?" The only answer was silence, and she fell to the floor trembling and sobbing. After a time, she sat up and thought about leaving her room and walking up the back stairs to the servants' quarters. She wanted to peek into Nanna's room, just to be in there and see her bed and smell her drawers that she always put caches of flowers into so her aprons always gave off a slight odor of violets beneath the onion and spicy smell of her hands. Then, she decided it would be better not to go so she could pretend for a while longer that Nana was still up there, resting away. Instead, she went to her own bureau and took a drop of the sleeping draught that Dr. Sands had prescribed for all of them.

Chapter 32

Mrs. Temple entered the bakery early the next morning. "Yoo-hoo," she called, and Mrs. Cunningham came out from the back with coffee.

They sat and watched the townspeople go by on foot or in carriages and were surprised when Abagail came in to pick up some pastry. They thought she had gone back to college and wondered why Suzanne hadn't come on the errand.

Mrs. Cunningham tied up a box for her. "How is Lily holding up, and your father?"

Abagail shrugged.

"Does Suzanne have the day off?"

"No, my father hired a new man for the house, Mickey. Suzanne is showing him around." Her voice trembled, and her eyes studied the floor. She took out several coins.

"No charge today," Mrs. Cunningham said putting her hand up.

"Are you sure?" Abagail asked.

Mrs. Cunningham nodded.

"Thank you," she said and left.

They were hardly seated again when the police chief, the detectives, and the medical examiner came into the bakery. Mrs. Temple stayed at their table and hoped that she was not too far away to hear. Mrs. Cunningham took their orders and went behind the counter. The best she could do was to pick up a few words here and there. After they were served, Mrs. Cunningham came back to the table. The women resumed a quiet conversation both with an ear to the other occupied table.

"Funny, that Mr. Chapman would hire a man for the house." Mrs. Temple said.

Mrs. Cunningham shrugged. "Maybe he wants a man around the house once he goes back to work. Maybe he thinks the girls will be safer."

They were quiet for a while, both trying to hear what was going on at the other table.

Mrs. Cunningham leaned in. "Last time they came, Dr. Sands was also with them," she whispered

"No need for him now, I suppose," Mrs. Temple said.

"But I should think he would want to be here. He's a very close friend to the Chapmans."

As they sat wondering, a boy came racing through the door. He ran to the table where the chief, the detectives, and the medical examiner were having their coffee.

"Come quick," he said. "There's been another death at the Chapmans."

• • •

LILY SAT ON the bench that had been cleared of snow in the back garden. She'd insisted she wasn't cold, but Suzanne had gone in, anyways, to get her a muffler and gloves. She wanted to be out of the house, no matter how cold it was.

Inside, they all just drifted. If she had been spoken to at all in the last several days, she had simply not heard, or perhaps had forgotten. She doubted any words had passed her lips. It hardly mattered, as she was having trouble keeping track of the days. The day was actually warm for January, and snow was beginning to melt. They had hired the services of a manservant, which they'd never done before, and he had shoveled the paths out back. It was odd having someone else around. She thought maybe Dr. Sands had suggested more help to Father, or with everything that had happened, perhaps he felt safe with another man around. Eventually, she supposed, he would be going back to work.

They had hired Kathleen as help. She seemed to be taking over some of Suzanne's duties because, though no one said so, she knew Suzanne's job was to keep an eye on her. She could feel her watching, even now from the window as she fetched the scarf. Unlike last spring, Suzanne did not try to engage her in talk or activities. She knew enough to leave her alone in her grief, and unlike last spring, it was a comfort to have Suzanne so close by. She was older now and knew the depth of pain that life could bring.

Abe would be coming over later. He was the only person she wanted to speak with since Michael's death. It wasn't only that she felt he had more understanding of what she had been through, but his anger was the only thing that could lift the numbness for a while. He insisted that Michael did not kill himself, and when he came to visit, she was comforted, but not for the reason everyone thought. Rather than seeking solace, they were conspiring together to prove that Michael did not die from his own hand. That was a fact both of them knew was untrue, and although she believed it, there was really no way they could prove it, but Abe's determination kept her steady.

He said he could get information—that there was more to the story. He said he only half believed what Old man Sawyer said, and since he was working in the office now, he had access to more information. He had told her it was the only reason he continued to work there. He was looking through logs and documents, going back over twenty years.

She was worried about her father and Abagail but was afraid to talk with them about her mother. The detectives and the police were still making reports. They were still treating her father badly, as if he were lying or keeping secrets. They had not let anyone go near the attic for several days, but she had been going there every night since. She walked quietly up the stairs, opening the heavy door in a certain way so it wouldn't creak. Suzanne slept in the room with her now on a day bed, but so far, she hadn't woken at Lily's night travels. She went up searching for clues, quietly riffling through drawers and papers. Sometimes she just sat for a while in the chair that her mother had sat in by the attic window and looked out at the sky, breathing in the cloying smell and the lingering odor of her mother's perfume. She never stayed long, not wanting to fall asleep and be caught out. Her time in the attic and Abe's visits were all she had for comfort.

The afternoon must be half over, and Abe would be coming right from work. At least it wasn't snowing today; the sun was warm. Maybe they could come out here to have privacy for a change. Abe had come the other day with an envelope tucked into his vest, and they had had to go from room to room for privacy. She didn't like so many strangers in the house—so many footsteps, so many voices. It was unnerving. That is why she clung to Abe when he came. He smelled like the outdoors, like the warehouse, the office. He brought that other world here to her—a world that she wasn't sure she could ever exist in again.

She was vaguely wondering what was taking Suzanne so long when she heard screaming from inside the house. She pushed herself out of the exhaustion of her grief and ran in through the back door. The door to the basement was open, and she ran toward the screams. Her father, standing at the top of the stairs kept her from going down.

Suzanne was at the bottom of the stairs crying. The new man servant appeared next to her, his face drawn. He looked at her father and shook his head. He helped Suzanne up the stairs and brought her to the parlor. Lily sat next to her.

"I've already sent a boy off," Lily heard the manservant tell her father as they disappeared back down the pantry hall.

She held Suzanne, who had so recently comforted her. Lily could feel the trembling letting up. Suzanne looked at her. "I'm so sorry," Suzanne said. "I am supposed to be comforting you."

"What is it?" Lily asked.

"It's Kathleen." Suzanne began to sob again, and Lily patted her shoulders.

"What happened?"

"I heard a thump and ran to the stairs. Mickey was already down there. He told me not to come down. He told me to get your father."

"Did they send the boy for the doctor?" Lily asked.

Suzanne shook her head. "I went down anyway, and there she was on the floor, blood everywhere. I wanted to go to her, but Mickey said we should not move her. I thought she must have fallen, trying to reach the top shelf. I tried to get closer, but Mickey wouldn't let me get near to her." She looked up at Lily, her voice getting louder. "I kept asking him why, why so much blood, but he just pushed me away, saying it was too late, so I pushed past him and saw then. The blood was coming from a wound in her throat."

Lily gasped.

"I wanted to pick her up. I went around the basement wildly looking for a sheet, a rag, anything to press onto her, anything to stop the bleeding, but Mickey said there was nothing we could do. It was too late. I don't want to go down there again. I'll never go down in that basement again."

They clung to each other and sobbed, Lily's head on Suzanne's shoulder.

Chapter 33

MRS. CUNNINGHAM AND MRS. TEMPLE WERE in the bakery until after sunset hoping to hear news of the latest death. They were also afraid, somehow afraid to leave the warmth of the bakery and walk the streets of town. They thought of what Daisy had said at the funeral. Everyone in town seemed to feel the same. All the shops had closed early, with everyone anxious to get back to the safety of their homes. They watched the millworkers who normally gathered here for coffee late in the day walk right by without looking up. They walked in groups, quietly, stunned as darkness fell, and word spread of another death.

Kathleen, the Chapman's new maid, had been found with her throat slit. It was being called another suicide.

"It doesn't make any sense," Mrs. Temple said. "I don't know how they can think anyone would believe all three deaths were suicides."

Mrs. Cunningham leaned in. "It's a cover up; anyone can see that now."

"But who? What would they be covering up?"

"I don't know, but Dr. Sands has a big influence on the medical examiner from Worcester, and he wouldn't want to get on the wrong side of either family; money talks."

"And the dead don't speak," Mrs. Temple added.

Though none of the locals came into the bakery that evening, the two women were rewarded with an outside perspective on what was going on for, just as Mrs. Cunningham was thinking of closing, a man and woman came into bakery asking the way to the hotel.

"I think it's closed now," Mrs. Cunningham said.

The couple looked at each other in distress, the woman about to cry.

"Please, sit and have some coffee," Mrs. Cunningham said. "We may be able to get you a bed for the night."

"Do you have any tea?" the woman asked in a small, strained voice.

"We have tea and some sandwiches left too if you're hungry."

"Just the tea, thank you," the woman said. The man nodded.

Mrs. Cunningham and Mrs. Temple went to the kitchen area and put on a pot of tea.

"They must be relatives," Mrs. Cunningham said. "There's no other explanation."

"So, who is she? Or, who was, she? The Chapmans should have looked into her more before hiring her."

"Well, you know, Daisy was so keen on her."

"But Daisy is so naïve," Mrs. Temple said.

"Olive recommended her too."

"Olive had her doubts though," Mrs. Cunningham said. "She ended up regretting having the girls involved in all the business in Worcester."

"Shush," Mrs. Temple said. "Let's not talk disrespectful of the dead."

When the kettle whistled, Mrs. Cunningham poured the boiling water into the pot, and said, "The two can stay at my house tonight since I didn't want to stay by myself anyway."

Mrs. Temple didn't like the idea of Mrs. Cunningham getting the story before her. "Why don't you stay at my place, give them the privacy of your house?"

"I think it best I stay with them. If they are family, they'll need comforting."

They brought the tea out together and some sandwiches in case they had changed their mind.

· · ·

AFTER A DARK, eerie night, the town was busy once more. Detectives came from Worcester, and officials were in and out of the police station and the hotel. The medical examiner and one detective were at the Chapman home, and only family was allowed inside.

Everyone in town was afraid they would be called and questioned about Kathleen. Unlike this death, there was no family in town to protect. The man who was detained for the longest at the police station was Mickey, another stranger in town who, along with Suzanne, had been the one to find the body. They wouldn't even let Abe in the house when he came in a carriage to comfort Lily until she became hysterical begging them to let her out of the house. She shouted, "There is something wrong here! The house is cursed, and the police chief reluctantly let her go. Abe assured Mr. Chapman he would look after Lily.

Abe helped her into the carriage. "Let's go to Worcester," he said. "Get you out of this town for a while."

Lily nodded. "I don't want to go back there," she said. "I never want to go back there again."

She sobbed and held onto the sleeve of Abe's overcoat. He let her cry and looked out the windows, having no idea what to say for comfort. After a while, she calmed down, and they stopped at a sandwich shop. It was not crowded, so they took a table in the corner where they could talk.

"I would have been married now," Lily said, her eyes watery with tears that refused to flow. Abe took her arm and moved close to her. She looked at him sideways. "I should be married."

"Shh," Abe said.

She looked around at the workers behind the counter. "They're staring at us," she said.

"They just think we're a couple," Abe said, "maybe having a spat." He wondered if he had taken her out too soon; maybe they should have found a quiet place in her home to talk.

"What happened at the service this morning?" she asked. "I heard the pastor talked about what happened."

"I never saw so many at church," Abe said.

Lily shook off her shawl and raised her chin. "I'm not surprised. Everyone wanted to see who was there and gossip. Were the Sawyers there?"

"Yes," Abe said. "Everyone gave them a wide berth."

She looked down. "I feel for them, especially Mrs. Sawyer. It's horrible going through this grief and having everyone watching."

"I feel bad for her, but not the old man. I'm only staying on at the mill to get information. You shouldn't be surprised if he killed his own son."

"Abe, don't say that. You gave me a shiver. Besides, he was with Olive, having breakfast. He couldn't have done it."

"He could have hired someone," Abe said. "He likes to hire people for his dirty work." He grimaced and looked away.

"But what about my mother and Kathleen? Do you think he killed them, too?"

He shrugged. "Had them killed, maybe."

"But he cooperated with the police."

"I suppose it is crazy to think he did it, but if the police suspected him, they wouldn't have done anything anyway. Even if they wanted, to they'd be afraid for their jobs."

"What did the preacher say, about Kathleen's death?"

"Nothing about her death just how people are saying there's a curse in the town. He told them to look to their neighbors for comfort. He said we shouldn't be afraid and not to listen to talk of evil spirits, that we mustn't lose faith and become desperate."

"Well, I am afraid," Lily said. "We both know Michael wasn't desperate. Even if it was true, what his father said to him about the business, he wasn't desperate when you left him, was he, Abe?"

"He was sullen, of course, but not enough to do something like that." He hesitated still to tell her the truth, wondered if she'd ever be able to handle it. Now that Mrs. Chapman was dead, perhaps she would never find out. "Who found Kathleen's' body?' he asked.

"The new manservant, Mickey. Oh God," she said. "Do you think he could have done it? He's supposed to be there to make us feel protected. Do you think he could have something to do with it? Now I'm afraid to go home."

"Was he alone when he found the body?"

"I'm not sure. I don't think so. He and Suzanne were both in the cellar when I heard the screaming and came into the house. Suzanne came into the parlor with me saying Mickey had told her to leave and not to touch the body. My father was standing at the top of the stairs, and I heard Mickey say to send someone for the police." She looked up. "I guess Suzanne would have known if he had done anything." She was silent for a minute. "But I'm afraid now, Abe. How is Mickey protecting us if another murder happened when he was right there in the house? I don't want to go back home, but I don't know where else to go."

"Don't get yourself get too worked up about Mickey. He was well checked by your father. I will stay the night on the couch in your parlor if your father approves. Would that make you feel better?"

Lily nodded.

Abe looked out the window at the carriages and horses and people walking. There were even a few motor cars honking their way downtown, *as if they own the road*, he thought. It was hard to be a friend sometimes not knowing what should be said and what shouldn't. He looked at Lily, wanting to tell her the truth but knowing she was still too fragile.

Instead, he whispered, "We should perhaps be wary of those we know rather than of strangers."

• • •

IT WAS OVER A week before Suzanne was allowed to move freely around the basement storage area, the crime scene. Her sister was better now, and she thought she would suggest to Mr. Chapman that he hire her because, now with Mrs. Parker gone, there was a hole that needed to be filled.

She walked around from stove to drawers, having trouble keeping her mind on her tasks. She had been wishing for this time when she could be alone without police and detectives and mourners crowding the hallways and rooms, but now, she felt queer. Now that all the people were gone, she felt the ghosts descend.

She knew the Chapmans were upstairs. Mr. Chapman and his two daughters were almost like ghosts themselves now. Seldom in the same room, they often took their meals at different times. It was so sad; she hardly ever heard them talking. Maybe they would move. She wouldn't blame Mr. Chapman if he wanted to sell the place, and she wondered how she would manage in a different household.

Until then, she would tend to her duties in silence, accompanied by the ghosts. She felt Miss Parker's spirit, which was soothing but also the troubled spirits of Michael and Mrs. Chapman. She felt the spirit of Kathleen who she'd always thought was very uneasy, even when alive. Maybe there was something to the séance they had attended; she'd have to discuss that again with Daisy.

After she kneaded the bread, she covered it with a cloth and put it aside to rise. Then she decided to do an inventory to see what might need to be ordered. She thought once more of Miss Parker as she did this, as it was a task she'd continued to do as she grew older. Now, Suzanne thought of the stories she'd heard from their Nanna of the girls when they were young—how they used to come down and help her prepare on Christmas Eve—how Mrs. Chapman actually let them do so. She described it as the highlight of her Christmas, the little ones all covered in flour, laughing, and calling her name, each one wanting to talk to her at once.

One thing about Mrs. Chapman—she never kept too much space

between the family and the help. She was a good woman, really. Though sometimes Lily thought she was unreasonable, it was only that she tried to protect her girls.

Suzanne opened each jar, making a notation of what was left. This was usually done earlier, and she could imagine Miss Parker scolding her because it had not been done on time. She checked on the canned goods, enough for the rest of the winter. She took some jars of peaches out, hoping to make a pie for later. There was plenty of flour, but the sugar was getting low. On the top shelf were jars that contained spices. She would need a stool to reach, but the only stool had been taken away because it had blood spatter on it, so she brought a chair over, making up her mind to stand on it to reach the top shelf. There was cinnamon up there that she would need to make the pie.

She stood upon the chair very carefully and reached for a large, metal container. It was the largest container because they used cinnamon more than anything besides flour and salt. As she took it down, she felt a presence, like a hand reaching to her and, as she grasped the container, she lost her balance and began to fall. Her heart beat fast as she grabbed onto the side of the shelf. The container fell to the floor, and the chair rocked back into place.

She quickly pulled herself down to the floor where the container had opened, and she saw a sealed envelope. It had Lily's name on it. Suzanne looked up as Lily rushed down the stairs.

"Are you alright?" Lily asked Suzanne.

"Just spice I spilled," she said. "No harm done."

She came over and embraced Suzanne. "With all that has happened here, you had me frightened out of my wits."

"There's an envelope here with your name on it."

Lily took it from her and smelled it. "It smells good being among the spices. I wonder what it is. It's probably been in there for years."

"No," Suzanne said. "It was right in the container, which I would have used to make pies at Christmas."

Lily sat on the chair, and Suzanne brought over another one. "Well, open it."

"I'm afraid to." Lily put her head on Suzanne's shoulder. "You open it, please, and read it to me."

"I'm afraid, also."

Lily turned toward Suzanne. They huddled together, the chairs and their shoulders touching.

"What if I ordered you to?" Lily asked.

Suzanne turned her head. "You've never given me an order before."

"I know," Lily said, "and I won't now."

They unsealed the envelope together.

Dear Lily,

None of this was supposed to happen.

They moved even closer, embraced each other, and read the letter silently as a shaft of sunlight found its way through the narrow window of the dusky basement.

Epilogue

Dear Lily,

None of this was supposed to happen. All I wanted in coming here was to find out what caused the death of my sister. What I found was secrets, betrayals, and evil, but I see now that evil only causes more evil, and I am distraught that the things I put into motion only ended up adding so much grief to your life. For this, I am truly sorry.

I made a plan. I knew it was not a good one, knew it would cause some heartbreak, for we always love the ones who mothered us. Babes always trust the first eyes they look upon. But you see, it was my sister who really birthed you before dying from lack of nursing, though I guess I cannot blame Mrs. Chapman either. It was that horrible man Sawyer who shamed and abandoned my sister.

It was he who was meant to be killed, not Michael. I should have done it myself and never have left it to Joseph, who just wanted the money and insisted afterwards that I had not told him which Mr. Sawyer, as if it was my fault, as if everything was my fault.

Oh, Lily, please forgive me. That bullet was not meant for Michael.

I am not telling you this to hurt you, but I feel you should know. Mrs. Chapman was not your mother. Mrs. Chapman's baby died, and my sister, who was in labor as well, died, but of course, no one rushed to her bedside.

She took you Lily. She stole my sister's baby and raised you as her own. When my sister's body was sent home to us in the coffin, it was closed. They said it was consumption. I was just a small girl at the time and will never forget how my parents grieved.

This is hard to admit to you. This I do regret now. It was not calculated but done in a fit of rage when everything went wrong.

I was so distraught that Michael had been shot instead of his father, I could not hold back my rage any longer. If I could have brought Michael back to life, I would have, but it was too late, and the only one to blame now was the woman you thought was your mother.

I went up to the attic room, and when I saw her—a broken woman, sitting pitifully alone, staring out the attic window, it made me furious, made me want to break that window and throw every tiny shard of glass into the throat of everyone who caused my sister and you such heartache.

She hardly made a sound. I pulled a neckerchief tight around her neck and hung her from the rafters above her desk.

I thought it would bring me peace to do this, but I still

cannot sleep. Though, as I write this, a strange calmness has taken hold.

Soon, it will be over, and I pray my spirit will find rest when I take up shards of glass and drag them across my throat. I will search for my sister in death, as I did in life. We will join hands in solidarity.

I hope you find love again in this twisted, broken world. Do not despair, but think of us, Lily. Part of us remains with you.

Remember our story as the world glides into another century.

Acknowledgements

I would like to thank two early readers of the story, Trisha Wooldridge and Terry Travers, for taking the time to read carefully and give me helpful ideas about content. I would especially like to thank my editor, Kimberly Coghlan, and all the people at TouchPoint Press for their dedication and belief in my book. Ron for bringing this story to my attention over thirty years ago.

Made in the USA
Columbia, SC
28 October 2021